TIME'S EDGE

Rysa Walker
TIME'S EDGE

BOOK 2
IN THE CHRONOS FILES

SKYSCAPE

SKYSCAPE

Published by Skyscape, New York

www.apub.com

Amazon, the Amazon logo, and Skyscape are trademarks of Amazon.com, Inc., or its affiliates.

ISBN-13: 9781477825822
ISBN-10: 1477825827

Book design by Cyanotype Book Architects

Library of Congress Control Number: 2014908348
Printed in the United States of America

*This book is dedicated to
Donna and Teri.
Thanks for giving me a push when I needed it.*

∞ 1 ∞

DALLAS, TEXAS
November 22, 1963, 12:05 p.m.

A pungent whiff of rotting fish hits my nostrils before my eyes open. I guess the stench explains the cats that wandered in and out of my field of vision each time I previewed this jump site over the past few days. Two of them, a scrawny orange tabby and a long-haired white cat with a torn left ear, hiss and watch me warily from the top of the large gray Dempster Dumpster directly behind me. A hand-lettered sign on the front reads "School Book Depository Use Only," but the fish bones and vegetable scraps around the bin suggest that at least one local restaurant owner either can't read or doesn't care.

The awful smell is undoubtedly why CHRONOS made this a stable point in the first place. No sane person would willingly venture within a hundred feet. A historian or two appearing out of nowhere would be noticed only by the cats.

I scan the faces in the photograph one last time and then tuck both the picture and my CHRONOS key under my sweater as I hurry down Houston Street. Turning at Elm, I head toward the

R. L. Thornton Freeway Keep Right sign. A crowd is starting to gather along the road. The motorcade is only about ten minutes away, which means this jump is cutting it much too close for comfort, but the minutes leading up to the shooting are the only time I can predict with anything close to certainty where my grandparents will be.

There are no fewer than seven stable points within a five-block radius, a testament to the enduring power of conspiracy theories surrounding Kennedy's assassination, even in the 2300s. I've tried three of those stable points already, and at this precise moment, three other versions of me are walking toward Dealey Plaza—one from Market Street, one from Main Street, and one from Record Street. The Kate on Main Street is even wearing this same sweater and blouse, with the silly Peter Pan collar, but about a minute from now, she'll get hemmed in by the crowd, and at twelve thirty, when the shots ring out in the plaza, she'll be a full block away. The other two Kates won't find Timothy and Evelyn Winslow either.

As I near the plaza, which is really just a small park with a white pergola perched on top of the hill, a young couple and two small boys stop in front of me. The older child, who is maybe four, has a tight grip on the skirt of his mother's red jumper. The littlest guy is sitting atop his dad's shoulders, both chubby hands grasping the collar of the man's plaid shirt. The boy leans his small blond head backward to view the world upside down and looks surprised when he sees me a few feet behind him.

His dad is nodding toward a triangular patch of grass in the median area across Elm Street.

"But . . . maybe we should just stay over on this side, Bill?" The woman appears to be in her early twenties, and her voice is squeaky-high, with a heavy southern drawl. "Over there, we got two streets to worry about them runnin' into traffic. If we stay here, they can play on the grass while we wait."

The dad swings the toddler from his shoulders in a smooth, practiced arc and sets him down on the infamous grassy knoll. He catches my eye as he stands up and gives me a shy grin, looking a bit like a shorter-haired version of the young Elvis Presley. A shiver runs down my spine. I'm not sure why, and then I realize these people are the Newmans, the family from the images and videos I've been studying online, who will soon have a front-row seat to the assassination. They'll be swarmed by the media after the shooting, dozens of reporters snapping photos as the parents lie on the grass, their bodies shielding the kids from the chaos.

I've apparently stared for a moment too long, because Newman and his wife exchange a confused look. I give them a nervous half smile and then push past, hurrying toward the concrete steps that lead up to the pergola.

A picket fence and some large trees camouflage the much less picturesque view of a packed-dirt parking lot behind the plaza. Most of the trees are still green, even in late November, but a few are beginning to shed their reddish-gold leaves. Three or four people are walking around near the fence. I keep reminding myself to just look for the powder-blue Ford Fairlane. Still, I can't help but notice a young guy with a thin mustache looking out over the grass embankment and staring intently toward the street, his left leg twitching slightly. He's leaning against the fence and smoking a cigarette. It's too warm for the jacket he's wearing—could that bulge in his pocket be a pistol? And that shaded space between the tree and the fence could definitely hide a rifle . . .

I shake my head, pulling my attention back to the more important issue, and finally locate the car that I glimpsed briefly from the sidewalk on my last jump, just before shots filled the air and ended any chance I had of getting close to the plaza. The Fairlane is parked about twenty-five yards away, behind a dirty red truck with a flat front tire.

There are many powder-blue 1959 Ford Fairlanes on the road in 1963, so this might be another dead end. I shift my path to the right, hoping to slip around the truck and a few other cars so that I can approach them unnoticed from the back of the lot. Assuming my grandparents are even in the car, and not hanging out over near Zapruder, photo-bombing his home movie. Or up on the sixth floor of the Depository, watching for Lee Harvey Oswald. We're putting a great deal of faith in Katherine's memory of a brief conversation with Evelyn nearly fifty years ago.

Connor oohed and aahed over the images of this "classic" car when we were researching the vehicle online, but I'm sorry—cars from this era are major eyesores. The tail fins alone have enough metal to make a Prius or two. Aesthetics aside, however, I'm currently kind of fond of the fins, because they provide a bit of extra coverage as I move around the car in full crouch mode.

There are two people in the car, but they're so entwined that I can hardly tell where one begins and the other ends, let alone be sure if they resemble the picture my dad gave me. If it *is* them, I know that this steamy embrace is mostly a cover. They're hoping the guy at the fence, or any other potential "second shooter," will ignore a young couple making out in the parking lot and they'll have front-row seats for history as it happens. They probably aren't even breathing heavy. But there's still something distasteful about sneaking up to introduce yourself to someone who may be your twenty-five-year-old grandmother when her shirt is half undone and your grandfather has just made it to second base.

I pull out my CHRONOS medallion. The picture and my phone are in my other hand. While I'd never be able to pick up a signal in 1963, the phone will still play the videos that Katherine and Dad recorded to support my story.

I debate for a moment whether to tap politely on the window. Her hair is the same dark copper as the woman in the Polaroid, however, so I decide to just go for it. With a quick tug on the chrome handle, the door of the Fairlane swings open. I'm in the backseat, holding up my CHRONOS key like a police badge before they realize what's happening.

Evelyn casts a furious glare at me in the rearview mirror and immediately starts buttoning up her sweater. Timothy looks back, and I have the odd sensation of seeing my father's "angry" face, fifteen years younger and maybe ten pounds heavier. Dad's really mellow, so I've only seen that face a few times—the occasion I remember most clearly was when I was maybe five years old and tried to see if the laser in a DVD player will heat up a Pop-Tart. (It won't.)

"We. Are. In the middle. Of research." He jerks his head angrily toward the guy at the fence. "That man might be James Files and—"

"And maybe he's the second shooter. Yeah, I know, and I'm sorry. One of you can keep watching if you want."

Evelyn slinks down in the seat so that she can keep her eyes pointed at the guy without being too obvious. "I've never seen you at CHRONOS," she says, "so I'm guessing you're from one of the earlier cohorts? Or later maybe?"

I hand the photograph to Timothy. It shows the two of them a few years older, laughing. He's holding a dark-haired little boy high over his head. A partial view of the passenger side of this powder-blue Ford is in the background.

"It depends on your perspective, I guess. I'm Kate. I'm your granddaughter. The little guy you're holding in that picture is my dad."

Most people never have to introduce themselves to their own parents or grandparents, but I seem to be making a career out of it. Three months ago, I sat across from my dad at a picnic table and tried to convince him that I was his daughter from another timeline. Then I chased two different versions of Katherine, my maternal grandmother, around the 1893 Chicago World's Fair. I gave the same introduction to her on both occasions in order to prevent her murder and my subsequent total lack of existence. If I ever meet my other grandfather, Saul Rand, I'll have a full set— but I really hope I never encounter him face-to-face. He's the reason I'm in this mess to begin with. And if his people find out I'm interfering, all hell is going to break loose.

Timothy glances from the picture to me, then back to the picture, before passing it over to his wife. She looks at me in the rearview mirror for a moment, then turns her gaze back to the guy at the fence. "She *has* got your eyes, Timo."

I can tell he's still annoyed, but his face softens a bit. "So, what's up, Kate? Unless CHRONOS rules change pretty dramatically in the next few decades, you're not supposed to be here. No interaction with family, right?"

Evelyn sighs. "Let's just go back to the stable point. We can check out this guy on the next jump. We should get back to CHRONOS, and so should she."

I'd like nothing more than to get out of this parking lot, since we've got only a few minutes before someone here, at the School Book Depository, or both will fire at the black Lincoln Continental convertible carrying JFK and Jackie. But I feel a bit guilty. They've been working on this puzzle for months.

"If you really want to know whether that's James Files, you need to keep watching. You won't be able to make another jump. CHRONOS is gone."

They both turn and stare at me for a moment, then Timothy cranks the ignition and shoves the gearshift into reverse. "If that's true, we need to get out of here while we still can. We've got bigger problems than figuring out which thug killed Kennedy."

∞

The first route he tries is cordoned off for the parade, but two blocks over, the congestion clears up pretty fast. None of us talk until the car crosses a bridge a few blocks away. Evelyn keeps glancing across the backseat at me, her face conflicted. The light sprinkling of freckles across her nose looks a bit like my own, but otherwise, I look much more like my mom's side of the family. Aside from the green eyes, which were clearly passed down to Dad from the man in the driver's seat, and a fading scar on my neck just below the right jawline, which is a recent acquisition, I'm pretty much a dead ringer for my aunt Prudence. That complicates my life considerably, given that she's playing for the other team.

"What happened?" Evelyn asks. "We knew there was something going on when that guy dragged Shaila into the jump room. I told Timo the jump felt wrong. I twisted my ankle when we landed at the stable point on Wednesday and that just never happens."

The car turns off the road into a small parking lot. A dark orange rectangular sign—*A&W Ice Cold Root Beer*—juts out from the top of a low building.

Evelyn's eyes narrow. "And *why* are we stopping here?"

Timothy pulls the car up beneath the orange-and-white-striped awning, near a cluster of picnic tables arranged in the center. "I'm hungry and thirsty, and I suspect this is going to be a long talk. From what Kate's saying, we can't wait and eat when we get home, can we? What do you ladies want?"

She rolls her eyes. "Not hungry, Timothy."

I just shake my head. Timothy shrugs, then gets out of the car and walks over to the building, where a middle-aged man in a white paper hat slides open the window to take his order.

"If we're stuck here long, he's going to gain forty pounds," Evelyn says. "He's gone up two belt notches since we started researching Kennedy. I don't know how people live past fifty on this diet."

I give her a weak smile but say nothing. It won't matter how many chili dogs he eats. Keeping his cholesterol low won't stop the log truck from hitting their station wagon in 1974. Neither of them will survive, and Dad will wake up in the hospital two days later, a five-year-old without a family. And I can't say anything that might change that path, since it's the one that produces me, and, as Katherine is fond of saying, I'm the new last best hope for Earth. Or at least for the majority of its population.

"So, how long *are* we—" she begins, and then holds up her hands. "Never mind. Wait until he's back, or you'll just have to say everything twice."

We sit there for a few moments, and while we wait I hit the "Video" button on my phone and start to record. I get a few seconds of Evelyn watching Timothy with an affectionate but still totally exasperated look on her face. Then he walks back to the car, holding a metal tray with three tall frosted mugs and a couple of chili dogs piled high with cheese and onions. He taps on Evelyn's window with his knuckle. She turns the window crank. "You're the one eating these things, so why don't you put them on your side? They stink."

He ignores her, attaches the tray to her window, and then heads back around the car to the driver's side. Evelyn waits until he's seated and then hands him the chili dogs, her nose wrinkled in disgust.

"Ev is vegan," Timothy says. "I am, too, usually, but hey—when in Rome, right? I just treat these trips as a vacation from vegan." He takes a big bite out of the first dog as Evelyn passes a root beer back to me. I kind of agree with her about the chili dogs, but the root beer—I don't know if it's the frosted mug, the crushed ice, or the lack of high-fructose corn syrup, but it tastes a lot better than the stuff I'm used to drinking.

I raise my eyebrows in silent question, and Evelyn nods. "Go ahead and start, Kate. I *think* we'll be able to hear you over his chomping."

"Actually, it might be easier to let Katherine tell you." I navigate to the video that we made at Katherine's house, turning the screen toward Timothy and Evelyn. I've seen it at least a dozen times, and I know it by heart. We spent a full week trying to figure out how much we could say without endangering the timeline.

"Evelyn, Timothy," Katherine begins. "It's been a long time."

Evelyn draws in a sharp breath through her nose. When they saw her a few days ago, Katherine was around their age, midtwenties, with long blond hair. The woman on the screen is in her sixties, and her gray hair, although a bit longer than when I met her, is still very short due to last year's chemo treatments. She's sitting in the library, at a desk near the window.

"I don't know if you've tried to pull up headquarters, but you won't be able to reach anyone. It's just a black void. My jump took me about six years ahead of you.

"I know you'll want to try your keys, if you haven't already, and I don't blame you. I wouldn't take this on faith, either. But they won't get you back to HQ. It's been more than forty years, and I still get nothing but black with a bit of static mixed in.

"So . . . the emergency protocol is in place. I'm sure you know better than I do where the closest CHRONOS safe-deposit box is. Once you get your new identities—"

Evelyn holds up one hand. "Switch that off. Now."

I pause the video.

"She's saying that we're stuck here, Timo. Just like I was afraid of when my diary vanished. When I couldn't pull up HQ." Her face is pale. Timothy reaches for her hand.

"But if the keys don't work, if CHRONOS is gone, how did you get here?" he asks me.

I glance down at the video. "Maybe we should let Katherine finish? She can tell this better than I can."

I push "Play," and Katherine's voice continues. "—you'll need to get on with your new lives. In case you're wondering, it was Saul in the burqa with the knife to Shaila's throat. He caused the explosion. And . . . a few hours before that, he killed Angelo."

Tears well up in Evelyn's eyes as Katherine continues. "Richard and I had just found Angelo's body and asked the jump coordinator to call security when Saul burst in, dragging Shaila in front of him, and told them not to cancel the jump. He took Shaila's spot—based on what we know now, I'm pretty sure he's landed sometime after 2020.

"Saul's hope was that destroying CHRONOS would allow him to jump from one point in time to the next, without being forced to return to HQ after each jump. But he miscalculated. He can't use the CHRONOS keys any more than we can, but he's learned the same thing I did. The CHRONOS gene passes on to our children and our grandchildren. I was pregnant with twins when I arrived in 1969. One of the girls, Prudence, had an accident with the key when she was fourteen. She's been with Saul ever since. The other daughter, Deborah—well, I introduced her to this guy."

Dad moves into the picture, with me at his side. Katherine and I argued for hours over whether this was a good idea. She said no, absolutely not, and initially Connor sided with her, but I won him over to my point of view. Timothy and Evelyn would probably believe me either way, but would they be willing to turn over their

CHRONOS keys? I thought *that* plea would be much more effective coming from their son.

"Mom. Dad. If I could use the CHRONOS key, I'd have come myself." Dad choked up a tiny bit when we recorded that part, and we had to restart the video a few minutes later. He barely remembers either of them, and he would love nothing more than to have taken my place. "It kind of glows when I touch it, but I can't operate it."

He puts his arm around me and gives my shoulders a squeeze. "So anyway, I'm sending Kate, in my—"

Evelyn reaches out for the phone and touches the screen to pause it, as she'd seen me do a moment ago. "Timo and I—we're not around whenever this is, are we?"

"You know I can't tell you that . . ."

"You don't have to. It's written all over his face."

Damn it. Katherine was right. And as much as I love Katherine, I really don't like it when she's right.

"And," she continues, "if we were around, you'd be showing a recording of the two of us explaining all of this, not Katherine."

That's true as well, and it makes me feel better about pulling Dad into the video. They would probably have figured it out either way. I push "Play" again, and Dad continues. "—place. Things are kind of crazy now. This Saul guy has set some things into motion that I don't fully understand, but Kate says he's planning to wipe out a good chunk of the population. So we're trying to do an end run around his people and collect these keys before they can."

Katherine leans back in. "I think Kate can answer any other questions you might have. The reality is simple—you can't use the keys, and if you keep them, Saul's people will try to take them. I'm really sorry—I wish I was able to give you better news, to tell you that this was just a temporary glitch and CHRONOS would have everything patched up shortly, but you'd find out soon enough anyway.

"You're going to hear from a much younger version of me in a few years. It would be best if you don't mention Kate's visit to her . . . mention it to *me*, that is. It could . . . complicate things even more than they already are. Take care, okay?"

The video stops there. We had recorded a few minutes more, but Katherine thought that Dad saying goodbye might tip them off about future events, so she had Connor cut that section.

Evelyn grabs the phone from me and pokes the screen a few times, but nothing happens. "How do you reverse this stupid thing?"

"Should I go to the beginning?"

"No. Just back to—" Her look is raw and vulnerable. "What's his *name*, Kate? What is my son's name?"

"I can't. You know I can't tell you—"

"Oh come on, Ev. Give her a break. You know his name. He's Alphonse, after your dad. We've discussed this half a dozen times. And if he'd been a girl—wait, he *is* named Alphonse, right, Kate?"

"You *know* I can't tell you that." I begin rewinding to where Dad starts talking, trying to keep my face neutral, so that nothing I do influences their decision. But it's hard to keep from grinning at how close Harry Keller came to being named *Alphonse*.

I find the spot on the video and push "Play" again as I hand it to Evelyn. She pauses it before Dad can start talking. She doesn't say anything, just stares at the screen.

After a moment, her expression shifts to a tight, almost angry look, and my heart sinks into my stomach. If this doesn't go well, Katherine won't exactly rub my face in it, but she will almost certainly find a subtle way to remind me that she was against Dad being in the video. This jump was supposed to be a sure thing. Before Saul, Prudence, and their Cyrist underlings managed to reset the timeline, these two keys were in our possession. Kiernan said they were relatively easy to get, but he doesn't know the specifics because that other version of me, *his* Kate, Other-Kate, Kate-Past, whatever you want to call her, handled that jump before they met. And I have no clue what *that* Kate did, because in every sense that matters, she's not me.

"I'm not sure if Katherine knows," Timothy says, "but this was supposed to be a five-day trip. Everything around Dealey Plaza is going to be locked down and cordoned off, so we can't get back to the stable point until around noon tomorrow at the very earliest. I'm not saying I don't believe you. We've known something was wrong since Ev's diary disappeared. She tried to send a question to HQ, and instead of getting an answer, it just . . . kind of . . . evaporated."

"Katherine said that happened to her, as well."

"But," he continues, "even though I do believe you, Katherine was right. I don't think we should give up these keys until we know for certain there's no return trip. I hope you can understand that?"

I nod. We'd kind of expected this.

"You're not going to be able to get out until then, either, Kate. I mean, unless you came in from a stable point outside of Dallas, you're stuck—"

"I can actually leave from right here," I say. "I have to arrive at a stable point, but I can jump to another point from any location. It's what Saul was trying to set up for himself, but it didn't work."

Evelyn is still staring at the frozen image of Dad with his arm around me, tears streaming down her face. I'm not sure if she's even listening.

"What does he want, Kate?" Timothy asks. "Why did Saul do this?"

A few months back, I asked the same question of Katherine and Connor. The only answer they had for me then was that Saul wanted power, all the power he could get. And while we have more information now, that's still the gist of it.

I shrug. "He wants to play God. To decide who lives and who dies. To create his version of paradise, where only those who see things his way get to stick around."

We're all silent for a moment, and then I ask, "Where should I meet you tomorrow? And when?"

Evelyn turns toward me halfway through the last question, like she's just remembered I'm in the car, and hands me back the phone. She pulls her CHRONOS key from underneath her sweater and blouse and yanks the chain over her head, almost throwing it at me.

"Just give her your damn key, Timothy! We've tried to reach HQ five times already. There's no reason to think we'll get a signal tomorrow." Her voice softens a bit as she looks at me. "You don't need to come back, Kate."

"Thank you, Evelyn." As I'm stashing her key in the pocket of my sweater, something occurs to me. "Um—if I should happen to show up again and start asking questions, double-check my eye color, okay? And look for this." I pull back my hair a bit and turn my right cheek toward her, revealing the relatively new and, thankfully, fading pink scar on my neck. Aunt Prudence might be smart enough to wear green contacts, but she doesn't know about my encounter with H. H. Holmes in Chicago. "If you don't see the scar, it's not me, and you can't tell her anything. She's with Saul."

Timothy pulls the CHRONOS key from his pocket as he unfastens the little clip that attaches it to his belt loop. He holds the glowing blue circle level in the palm of his hand and stares at the hourglass in the center, watching as the sands flow back and forth.

"What color is it for you, Kate?" he asks.

This seems to be the CHRONOS equivalent of chatting about the weather. Everyone sees the light at the center of the medallion differently. "It's blue," I reply. "Like an impossibly bright sky."

A sad smile touches his lips. "Really? Me, too. It's pink for Ev."

I smile back at him and then glance over at Evelyn. "Dad can only pick up the light occasionally, but when he does, he says it looks pink to him. So, I guess he gets that from you."

Her bottom lip quivers a bit. She reaches over and places her hand on the side of my grandfather's face, a face so much like that of the son they'll never see grow up.

"Timo, that life is over. Just give her your key so she can get back home. And get rid of that stinking chili dog. We're not on vacation anymore."

∞2∞

"Got them!" I tug the medallions out of my pocket and wave them in front of me.

"Was there ever any doubt?"

Kiernan is sitting cross-legged on a wooden crate, exactly where I left him, a smile still on his face. For him, only a minute has passed since I left for Dallas on this most recent attempt to get the keys from Timothy and Evelyn.

This storeroom is listed as an official CHRONOS stable point—that is, one of the locations that historians can jump to—between the years of 1898–1932. The first time that I traveled to 1905 Boston, I came in the middle of the night, slipping out of the storeroom into the darkness of the main store. I left an envelope just inside the door with Kiernan's name on the front and nothing inside but a slip of paper with today's date and the time, 7 a.m. For me, that was three weeks ago, and I've popped in twice since then to get Kiernan's feedback on our plans for collecting these two medallions.

"It may have been a foregone conclusion for you," I counter. "But things looked shaky for a while. Evelyn picked up on the fact that they were probably dead."

He shrugs, his dark hair brushing his shoulders. "I think that happened last time, too. You told me then that Katherine was against your dad getting involved, but you insisted. Timothy and Evelyn were still an easy grab. Who could deny a request like that from their own granddaughter?"

"Uh . . . Saul Rand, maybe? Otherwise, I would just waltz up to him and say 'Pretty please, Grandpa*pa*, abandon your evil plan for world domination. For me?'"

"You have a point," Kiernan concedes with a chuckle. "I should have clarified that any human being with half a soul would not deny that request. But perhaps you should find Saul and ask. He might be a sucker for pretty green eyes."

I can feel the blush rising to my face, so I turn away and pretend to be interested in the containers of tobacco on the shelves behind me. I lift a lid and breathe in deeply. The pipe tobacco has a rich, earthy aroma—nothing like the secondhand cigarette smoke I'm forced to breathe in along the DC sidewalks. I used to enjoy the scent of a fire on a winter's night, but since my recent encounter with H. H. Holmes at the World's Fair, the slightest whiff of smoke makes my body tense up. If Kiernan hadn't come back to rescue me that night, I'd have been one of the many skeletons found in that hotel.

"So, who's next?" I ask him. "I mean, last time, which medallions did *she* go after?"

She is the other Kate, the one that I know Kiernan wishes were here in my place, the Kate-Past who doesn't exist anymore, thanks to Saul rejiggering the timeline.

"I have the information that we were working from back in my room." His emphasis on the word *we* is faint, but I know he's trying to remind me that Other-Kate is just the flip side of me, even if I can't remember her. Kiernan reaches his hand out toward me. "It's a short walk away. Shall we?"

"I should get back home. Katherine's waiting."

"Oh. I assumed you'd gone home before coming here." There's a hint of question in his voice. I know he's wondering why I'd share good news with him before telling my grandmother, Dad, and Connor.

I'm kind of wondering that myself. I pulled up Boston 1905 without even thinking. As I look down at my shoes, however, I realize that I can't stay, even if I wanted to. The knee-length skirt, sweater, and brown saddle shoes were appropriately demure for 1963 Dallas, but they'll draw far too much attention here. "I'll come back later. I'm not exactly dressed for—"

"Don't be silly," he says, walking toward a tall cabinet in the back of the storeroom. "We both know that you can arrive back at Katherine's at the exact same time you left, so they'll never know you were delayed. And I've got a solution to your fashion dilemma."

Kiernan opens the cabinet door and holds up a dress on a padded hanger. The dress is one piece that's meant to look like two. The white blouse has a high Gibson-girl neckline, and the dark skirt is narrow and looks like it will hit me about midankle. He takes it off the hanger and turns the dress around, revealing a long row of pearl buttons. There is a slight ripping noise as he pulls the sides apart, and I think at first that he's torn the fabric. Then I see the white strip of Velcro running up the back.

"That is *so* not CHRONOS approved," I say, stifling a laugh as I shake my head. Katherine nearly blew a gasket when she caught me with a pink toothbrush in 1893, so I know there's no way that she gave this the thumbs-up.

"We're not CHRONOS. And dozens of pearl buttons don't exactly make a dress easy to get in and out of, do they?"

There's a touch of sadness behind Kiernan's smile. It probably should have occurred to me immediately, but it's only now that I realize Other-Kate brought the Velcro back to 1905. This was *her* dress. I decide not to think about the reasons she might have had for wanting to get out of her clothing quickly.

The dress seems large enough to fit over the slim skirt and shell I'm wearing, so I just slip off the cardigan and hang it on a hook in the cabinet. Then I step into the dress Kiernan is holding open and turn around to let him fasten the Velcro. He pulls the dress together around my body and then slowly runs his palm down my spine from neck to waist to seal the seam. His hand is warm through the fabric, and a little shiver runs through me.

Bad girl, Kate. He's not Trey, and you are not his Kate, I remind myself. *This is only about stopping Saul and the Cyrists.* I plaster on what I hope is a get-down-to-business look before turning back around to face him.

He hands me a pair of brown, low-heeled shoes, with a sensible strap and absolutely no need for a buttonhook. I smile and slip the saddle shoes off my feet. I'm about to stash them back in the cabinet, but Kiernan pulls out a small drawstring bag and tucks the shoes and sweater inside.

It's still not the jeans, T-shirt, and Skechers I prefer, but it's oh-so-much better than the 1893 getup I had to wear the last time Kiernan and I ventured out together. Of course, *that* time he was eight years old and I had to look down to meet his eyes, rather than up.

After fastening the last buckle on my shoe, I stand. As I do, Kiernan pushes my hair a bit to the side. "Do I need to pull it up to avoid the wrath of the propriety police?" I ask, but my voice trails off as I realize he's looking at the scar on my neck.

"No," he says. His tone is harsher now. "Leave it down."

"Kiernan, it's okay. Really. It doesn't hurt at all, and it's barely noticeable with a bit of makeup." He probably knows I rarely wear makeup, unless Other-Kate had entirely different fashion sense. But I have to say something, because I don't like seeing the wounded look on his face. "You did the best you could. I would have been dead, but I'm still here, right? Perfect health? Ready to save the world as we know it?"

His lips twitch up the tiniest bit on one side, and then he leans over and presses them against the scar, very gently, very briefly. I feel myself stiffen slightly and step back. His voice is softer as he repeats, "Leave it. I like it down. And I don't care what the stuffy old maids of Boston think."

Kiernan flicks up the little metal hook that locks the thin sheet of wood serving as a makeshift door between the tobacco store and this storage area.

"Wait," I say. "You said Jess is a friend, but what does he know? I mean, does he know I'm here from the future?"

He shakes his head.

"Then how does he think I'm getting in here?"

"I have a key to the store." He pulls it from his pocket and bounces it once in the palm of his hand before stashing it away again. "I worked here for a while. In fact, I slept in this storage room for a few months. If I'm meeting you here, I always come in when he's closed or when he's stepped out for a few minutes."

"What exactly does he think we're doing in here?"

Kiernan's grin is back. "Like I said, he's a friend. And a gentleman doesn't ask questions. He likes you, Katie. Just flash him a smile and say thank you."

"Thank you for wh—" I begin, but he's already pressing the door open with his shoulder, so I paste on a smile and step out behind him.

Kiernan said Jess was his friend, so I expect someone in his teens or early twenties, or at least younger than my parents. I definitely expect someone younger than Katherine or Connor. This guy looks like he's in his eighties. He has a grayish-white beard reaching halfway down his chest, and he's slightly hunched over as he stocks a glass jar with pipe cleaners from a small wooden box. I'm surprised to see that pipe cleaners in 1905 are much the same as pipe cleaners today, except these are all white, not bright neon like the ones we used in kindergarten crafts.

The old guy looks up at the sound of the closing door. He squints a bit, then a big smile lights up his weathered face.

"Miss Kate! I am mighty glad to see you again! You gave me a bad turn, taking off like that." He moves toward us slowly and gives me a tight hug. I stiffen a bit initially, but he smells warm and familiar, a lot like the tobacco in his storeroom. After a moment, I return his hug, shooting Kiernan a quizzical look. *Who is this guy?*

"I told you she'd be back, Jess. She's just been away . . . in New York, then down in Washington. With her grandmother."

Jess's face looks skeptical for a moment, and then he laughs. "More likely you've just been a greedy boy, keeping her all to yourself. Like I told you before, Kate, when you get tired of his shenanigans, you just let me know, and I'll tell my Amelia to pack her bags."

"You will not, you horny old goat," Kiernan says. "This store would close tomorrow if Amelia didn't keep you in line, and you know it."

I raise an eyebrow at Kiernan's language—so much for the idea that younger people respected their elders in the "good old days." But Jess just cackles and tosses a small wooden box at Kiernan, who catches it easily with one hand.

"Put that in the back room, boy. Be sure you get it on the right shelf, or these old eyes won't find it. And I'll fetch what Miss Kate is wanting from the icebox."

Jess shuffles off, and Kiernan leans in toward me. "It's ginger ale," he whispers before heading back to the storeroom.

It is indeed ginger ale, pale brown in a tall, clear bottle, etched with the words "Clicquot Club." Jess pries the top off with the bottle opener attached to the side of the counter, sticks in a paper straw, and hands it to me.

"Thanks."

"No thanks necessary."

I take a long draw of the soda, and I'm instantly hit by a coughing attack. The effect is like snorting raw ginger, spicy-sweet and so potent that it takes my breath away.

"You okay?" Jess laughs. "You should know better by now. You need to sip that stuff."

Kiernan is back by the time I catch my breath. He's laughing, too.

I shoot him an annoyed look and then smile at Jess. "Yes, I'm okay. Just went down the wrong way, I guess. How much do I owe you?"

As the words leave my mouth, it occurs to me that what money I have is in the pocket of my sweater in the storeroom—and none of it has a date earlier than 1950. So I'm relieved when Jess says, "Not a penny and you know it, young lady. Just thank your uncle again for me."

Kiernan puts an arm around me and pulls me toward the door, grabbing two dark brown candy sticks from a little jar near the edge of the counter as we go. "You still have plenty of the pills, Jess?"

The old man nods and smiles again. "Should last to the end of the year, unless it flares up." He shifts his glance over to me. "If your uncle ever decides to sell those little beauties in Boston, you let me know. I'll clear out a whole shelf."

I try to hide my confusion and give Jess a little wave as Kiernan steers me onto the sidewalk. "What was that about?" I ask as soon as we are out of earshot.

Kiernan moves to the outer edge of the narrow sidewalk, which is raised slightly above the muddy roadway. He takes my arm, leading me toward an intersection with a larger, paved road a few storefronts ahead. A dozen or so horse-drawn carts, a few bicycles, and a lone car move cautiously along the brick road in front of us, going only slightly faster than we're walking.

"The story Jess has," Kiernan replies, "is that your uncle is a druggist in New York with this proprietary blend for arthritis. You packed some generic Advil in an old tin box, and Jess has been feeling a lot better since then."

"Wow. Katherine would totally flip."

"Katherine doesn't need to know. Or at least that's what you said before . . ."

Kiernan trails off, probably in response to my expression. I'm growing a little weary of being lumped with Other-Kate. I just met Jess, so I've clearly never said anything about any of this before. But I doubt it will do much good to remind Kiernan again that I'm not *her*, that she doesn't even exist in this timeline. He knows that better than anyone.

"Wait—" I pull him to a stop. "How does Jess remember the other . . . *me*? He doesn't have a CHRONOS key."

"Uh, no. But I was at his place when the timeline changed. The one that . . . took you. The temporal shifts make me kind of dizzy, you know?"

I nod. Even thinking about the three times I've felt those shifts is disorienting. When the last one hit, I collapsed to the floor as trig class morphed around me into a brand-new reality.

"Well," Kiernan continues, "Jess saw the look on my face and grabbed my shoulder when I stumbled. And the poor guy has been balancing two sets of memories ever since—one where there were few Cyrists and one where his middle daughter is a member. There's a grandkid he remembers that no one else does. His family thinks he's had a stroke or he's going senile, even though in all other ways he's sharp as a tack."

"That's sad." I take another tentative sip from the ginger ale and glance back over my shoulder at the storefront—*John Jessup, Fine Tobaccos and Sundries*—and wonder how many other people have accidentally come in contact with a medallion or someone wearing one. And how many of them are in mental institutions? "I hate that he was drawn into all of this. But he seems to be handling it pretty well, all things considered."

Kiernan flashes me a grin. "He's convinced they're the crazy ones." He bites off a chunk of the candy stick, and a strange, sickly sweet smell fills the air.

I wrinkle my nose. "What *is* that stuff?"

"Hoarhound candy," he says, crunching off another bite. "Want some?" He waves the other stick under my nose.

"No." I push it away. "It smells awful. I don't like it."

A teasing smile, just this side of a smirk, crosses his face. "Of course not, love. You never have."

∞

His place is actually a bit farther away than I'd imagined, although I guess the phrase "short walk" might have a different meaning in 1905. Kiernan deftly steers me away from the edges of the buildings, where puddles of waste decay in the summer sun. I know the tenants have little choice, given the general lack of plumbing, but it still makes for an unpleasant walk.

When we reach his building, a group of thin, dirty children crouch in the entryway, playing jacks, and a few others sit in the stairwells as we climb to the fifth floor. Kiernan stops on the last landing to chat with a blond tyke who is maybe six. "Manners quiz, Gabe. I have an extra stick of candy. Would you like it, or should I offer it to the lady first?"

"You should offer it to her," the boy says, appraising me with big blue eyes. "But I'll take it if she don' want it."

I smile at the boy and give Kiernan's shoulder a nudge. "Stop picking on him. You know I don't want that nasty thing."

Kiernan grins and pulls the candy stick from his pocket. There's a bit of lint stuck to it, but the kid doesn't bother to inspect it.

"And what do you say, Gabe?" Kiernan asks. The boy responds with something that could be *thank you*, but it's impossible to tell with his mouth full of candy.

We cross the hallway, and Kiernan unlocks a door with "#411" scrawled on the wall next to it. His room is neat, small, and hot. A white powder of some sort is on the floor in front of the door, which makes me suspect the ceiling is crumbling. A twin bed with a worn quilt is squeezed into the right rear corner, next to an old tobacco crate that serves as a nightstand, and a rope is tacked to the walls, with a piece of red fabric strung up to form a curtain blocking the opposite corner from view. Books are stacked everywhere.

The ceiling slopes downward to the only window, which faces an alley. At first, I think that's why the room reminds me of my own space at Mom's townhouse. I've cracked my head more than once on my low ceiling, and I'm only a few inches above five feet, so this has to be a bit of a squeeze for someone as tall as Kiernan.

Then I see the other reason it looks familiar. Kiernan's ceiling is covered with glow-in-the-dark stars, just like the ones in my room.

Kiernan closes the door behind us, tosses the bag with my shoes and sweater onto the bed, and opens the window. He sits cross-legged on the floor, moving a large book beneath the bed frame. "Have a seat. There's no chair, so it's the bed or the floor I'm afraid." His expression is a bit strained, and he seems to be avoiding my eyes as he hunts for something.

I sit down on the edge of the small bed and look around the room again. I don't want to ask, but I blurt it out anyway.

"Is this where you lived . . . before? I mean, when . . . ?"

"Yes."

I feel a blush creeping to my cheeks. From everything Kiernan has said, another version of my body—a few years older, but my body, nevertheless—spent many hours here with him. In this bed. I bite my lip and shift a bit closer to the footboard.

"I thought about moving somewhere else, maybe closer to work, out near Newton," he says, still not looking at me, "but I want to stay close to Jess for a bit longer. He needs to talk to someone who doesn't think he's lost his marbles. And this is close to the train, so . . ."

"You aren't still working for Jess?"

He shakes his head. "I still help him out occasionally, but he can't really afford to keep me on full-time. And I have something else going. Something we were . . . something *I* was working on, from before." Kiernan takes a penknife from the nightstand, flips open the thin blade, and starts to pry at one of the floorboards. "This stupid board is stuck again," he says. "The heat always makes the floorboards swell up."

"So . . . where do you work now?"

"I guess you'd call it an amusement park." He looks up for a moment and flashes me that grin. "Come back on Saturday, and you can watch me in action."

He doesn't wait for an answer. He just yanks on the board, pulling it loose and also banging his knuckles on the underside of the bed. I expect him to hand me an actual list, written on paper, but it's a CHRONOS diary.

"Didn't know you had one of these."

"I do," he says, examining his skinned knuckle. "But this isn't mine. This one is y—"

He pauses and takes a deep breath before he continues. "*Hers. It was Kate's.* You can take it. You'll need it more than I will."

I open the slim book, which is probably best described as a twenty-fourth-century version of an iPad stuck inside an old book cover. It has pages, only they're more like touch screens. Aside from the cover, I don't think this device would have fooled anyone who inspected it carefully in the eighteenth century or whenever Other-Kate happened to be traveling, but it was probably a better option than flipping open a high-tech gadget right under their noses.

My grandmother's name is handwritten inside the cover, just as it was in the diary she gave me when she first broke the news that I'd inherited the ability to activate these devices. I drag my finger along the first page. The words, written in a flowery script that is clearly not my writing, begin to scroll upward.

"Katherine's research is stored in the first few pages," Kiernan says, "but if you flip ahead, there are newer entries, with some pretty detailed background on the jumps you made—what went right, what went wrong, and so forth."

"Oh, wow. This could save us a lot of time. Katherine will—"

"Umm . . . yeah. You might want to preview these before you show them to anyone else. Some are full-fledged rants, mostly about Katherine. You might want to pick and choose what you share. And you didn't—" He shakes his head and then goes on. "Kate didn't have much patience for writing things down. All of her notes are video, so you should probably wait until you get back home."

No question about that. I don't even like watching myself on normal home movies, so it will be hard enough to view diary entries from this me-who-isn't-me without doing it in front of Kiernan, who probably still finds it painful to hear her voice—which is, of course, the same as my voice, so I just sit there silently for a moment.

I feel a soft touch on my ankle. "Something wrong, Kate?"

I shake my head, and he just lifts his eyebrows. He knows I'm hiding something. But I'm not sure how to put any of the things I'm feeling into words.

"Everything okay in the twenty-first century?"

I nod. "Katherine and Connor are back from their trip. She's gained a few pounds, so I think she's doing a bit better. Dad and I have moved our stuff out of the cottage on campus, so I'm at Katherine's half of the week and spend the other half with Mom. And I'm back in karate, more or less—I have private lessons with the improbably named Sensei Barbie twice a week."

He gives me an odd look, and I realize he doesn't get the same visual image I did when I first heard the name—a tall, leggy blonde with a ponytail and disproportionate boobs. She's actually only an inch or so over my five foot three, nearly double my weight, and runs my butt ragged for an hour each Monday and Wednesday without ever breaking a sweat herself. Kiernan probably doesn't even know what a sensei is, for that matter, so I just continue.

"I also celebrated my seventeenth birthday—again. So it's the same old routine, pretty much. Aside from the occasional journey through space and time, that is."

And the dreams, but I don't mention those or the fact that the past few months have been really strange. I tried to keep up with my classwork when I lived in the other timeline this past spring, even though I couldn't attend school for the simple reason that there was no record of my existence. As a result, the schoolwork in the last few weeks of my junior year was relatively easy, except for the occasions where I stumbled across something different in this reality—a different president or some famous author, scientist, or inventor I'd never heard of.

It was also odd experiencing events at Briar Hill that I'd only heard about secondhand from Trey in the previous timeline, especially since Trey won't even be at Briar Hill until the fall in this reality. The sign for the prom that went up in May is a good example. Before, I'd have walked right past that sign and never have considered going. In the previous timeline, Trey said he'd never have gone without me—but we both would have been happy to go together. I guess I could have asked him to go this time, but we're not really at the prom-date stage yet.

So yeah, it's been weird. And I can't even gripe about all of this weirdness to my best friend, Charlayne, because she doesn't know me. In this reality, she's probably hanging out with her Cyrist pals, totally unaware that we were ever friends.

Kiernan's dark eyes are soft as he watches me. His arm is resting on the frame of the bed, and his hand cups my ankle, causing me to pull in a shaky breath.

"And Trey? Are you seeing him much?"

"Yes."

He raises his eyebrows like he doesn't believe me.

"Really, everything is great. He's coming by this evening, in fact."

That last bit is the truth. But the part about seeing him much isn't. Trey has barely been in DC since I gave him the DVD with video conversations between the two of us and a clip of himself, or I guess I should say his alternate self, attempting to explain our relationship. We went to the movies that first weekend after I gave him the DVD, and it was wonderful to see him, but it was awkward to say the least. I kept wanting to say (and do) things that I would normally never dream of on a first date, and I'd have to pull back and remind myself that he wasn't really my Trey, at least not yet. I could tell he felt uncomfortable, too. He was going to come for dinner later that week, but then his dad surprised him with a three-week trip to Peru to visit friends he'd made when they lived in Lima. We texted a couple of times, and Trey posted a few scenic pictures on Facebook, but he spent most of his time at the beach.

He's back now, and the dinner is tonight. And while I'm really, really looking forward to seeing him, I'm simultaneously dreading it. Every time I'm with Trey and it's not the same as before, a little piece of me withers.

I have no idea why I didn't just tell Kiernan the truth. That I've barely seen Trey. That everything is far from great. I opened my mouth, and the lie rushed out, and now I feel a little guilty.

Apparently, it wasn't even a convincing lie, because he's giving me this sad, sympathetic smile. "But, it's not the same as before. Is it?"

It's definitely *not* the same, not yet, but I'm nowhere near the point of giving up. And it seems cruel to give Kiernan false hope, so I just shrug and say, "Rome wasn't rebuilt in a day, right?"

"No. I don't suppose it was." He gives my ankle a quick squeeze and then lets go. I'm relieved but also a bit flustered to realize that I miss his touch.

I flip to the back of the diary and see there's a page of sequential numbers. They're underlined, like the videos I'm accustomed to seeing in the diaries, but only a couple have dates or titles after the numbers. The link at the bottom of the page is 28, but when I tap the margin with my fingernail, the page starts to scroll upward. It scrolls for about thirty seconds, and the final link is 415. This is going to take forever.

"There's so much here. Do you think you could give me a CliffsNotes version?"

Kiernan just looks puzzled.

"That means the *short* version." I laugh. "A cheat sheet?"

He shakes his head. "I haven't watched most of them," he says. "I skimmed through the last twenty or thirty when I thought they might give me some clue as to where she'd gone, but then once I saw you on the Metro that day, I knew it was no use. If this version of you exists, then that one doesn't. And later, when I was missing her, I watched a few entries I remembered her recording when she was here, but . . ." He shakes his head.

"Are you sure you don't want to keep it?"

"It's okay, Kate. Take it."

"Maybe I could make you a copy or something?"

"No. Most of this was her private diary. I wouldn't have watched them when she was . . . when she was here with me. I don't feel right watching them now. And they don't bring her back."

The hours I've spent watching the DVD of my conversations with Trey spring to mind as he says this. Watching them over the past few months has been somewhat bittersweet for me, and there's still a chance that Trey and I will be together at some point. Would I keep those videos if I knew there was no hope? I'm not sure.

I give him a weak smile. "Any advice on these jumps? Is there one that's really easy?"

"Port Darwin, if you want to get an easy one out of the way. I'd definitely suggest waiting on the 1938 jump. The one to Georgia. It was the last one we tried, and . . . it didn't go well. If you want to tackle them in the same order that she did, you should start brushing up your Russian."

"But . . . I don't speak Russian."

He nods. "I know. But you're going to need to learn at least a few phrases to find the historian who's there to gauge Soviet reactions to . . . I can't remember the name. Some satellite thing. Mid-1950s?"

"*Sputnik?*" I throw my hands up. "Are you serious? What kind of crazy people decide to observe events in a dictatorship? One wrong move and I could end up in a freaking prison somewhere in Siberia."

"I'm sure there's a long rant on that very subject in the diary you're holding," he teases. "If that's any help. We never found that key, actually, so hopefully you'll see something new in the evidence."

My expression must show my doubt on that front, because he laughs.

"I don't suppose *you* speak Russian?" I ask.

He shakes his head. "If the jump was to Ireland and you needed some Gaelic, I might be able to dredge up a few handy phrases. But my Russian doesn't extend beyond *borscht, da,* and *nyet.* And *dosvedanya.*"

"Well, you're still four words ahead of me. I suppose I should get back and order a copy of Rosetta Stone. It sounds like there's a lot of work ahead."

"Yes. I know you're up to the challenge." He gives me a smile that I'm sure is meant to be encouraging. Unfortunately, it has the opposite effect. Maybe Other-Kate was up to the challenge, but she wasn't thrust onto the fast track.

"I'm not so sure." I protest. "It's hard to get enthused about the jumps that are ahead. What if something I do just screws everything up again?"

His smile fades. "How could you possibly make it worse than what Saul is planning?"

"If they're really putting this Culling thing into action, then no, but . . ." I pause for a moment and then continue, measuring my words carefully. "Don't get me wrong, okay? I don't think you're lying about any of this. But how *certain* are you? I mean, a lot of religions talk about end times and how only the faithful will be saved. Maybe Saul was just looking for a way to get a lot of money and a lot of power, and he and Prudence will just . . ." I shrug, looking down. My mental image is the two of them rolling around in piles of cash, laughing maniacally, but that's too silly to say out loud.

"I'm certain, Kate," he says quietly. "And so were you."

"No!" I snap my head up and stare directly into his eyes. "Maybe *she* was certain. Not me. I'm not certain about anything except the fact that I don't know what I'm doing. And even if you *are* certain, this Culling might be scheduled for a hundred years in my future, two hundred years for you. Maybe the wisest course of action would be to wait until—"

"Until what?" he asks, his voice rising. "Until the Cyrists are even more powerful than they are today?"

"Until I know what the hell I'm doing! Like you said a few minutes ago, this jump was easy. I had a video of their son. Dad and I both have Timothy's green eyes. I knew pretty much where to find them. They were speaking English, for God's sake! The others won't be as simple, and the next time someone tries to kill me, I might not get off with just a scar."

He doesn't respond, and I wish I could take back those last words. I didn't mean them as a rebuke—I really do think I was lucky to escape with only this small reminder, but I can tell from Kiernan's expression that he took it personally.

I soften my voice. "I'm sorry. I don't want to argue with you, Kiernan, and I'm definitely not saying I'm backing off. But I also don't want to get in over my head. I want to plan these next steps carefully."

He stares down at his hands for a moment. "As well you should. Speaking from past experience, I don't think Katherine will like me being in on the planning stages, but I want to help. Just tell me what you need."

I nod and give him a tentative, peacemaking smile, then lean forward to unbuckle my shoes. I take my sweater and the other pair of shoes from the drawstring bag, and my fingers brush against the edges of something rectangular at the bottom. It's another diary. Giving Kiernan a quizzical look, I hand him both the diary and the bag.

"That was my grandfather's," he says. "It's mostly in Gaelic, and as I said, my Gaelic is pretty rusty. I just use it for the CHRONOS field. Even with those booster cells sewn into the hem, that dress would have vanished at Jess's store if it wasn't within range of a diary or a key."

Once my shoes are swapped out, I stand to unfasten the Velcro at the back of the dress, but Kiernan is already there. The fabric slides to the floor, leaving me in the sleeveless shell and skirt I wore to Dallas. He rests his hands on my bare shoulders for just a moment and then helps me into my sweater.

"You'll get the dress and shoes back to the storeroom?" I ask.

"I *could*," he says. "But it might make more sense to leave them here and set this room as a stable point. That way you can just pull up the location and check to see if I'm home. And you won't have to sneak in and leave notes for Jess."

It does make more sense, but I'm hesitant. "I don't want to intrude on your privacy."

That brings his grin back, although it's a bit subdued. "What if I promise to dress and undress behind the curtain?"

I hadn't even thought about that particular aspect of privacy, but suddenly it's difficult to think of much else. "Wouldn't having the dress here just be a reminder of when . . . she was always around?"

"It doesn't matter, Kate. I'm never really alone in this room." He follows my glance upward and smiles. "And it's not just the glow stars you . . . *she* pasted on my ceiling. Little things hit me at the oddest moments. Your dress and shoes under my bed won't make the slightest difference."

I glance up at the stars again. For some reason, their presence nags at my brain, like a mystery that needs to be solved, but I can't find the clues. Maybe it's just the intrinsic weirdness of seeing something you'd buy at Spencer's in this tiny apartment that lacks a toilet, electricity, or running water.

I take the CHRONOS key out of my sweater and run my hand across the center to activate it, punching in the few keystrokes needed to set this room as a jump location. Then I start to pull up Katherine's house so that I can leave, but Kiernan places a hand on my arm.

"Will you come on Saturday? I really want you to see Norumbega Park. If you're here by ten, we'll have time to see the sights before I start."

"Before you start what?"

He shakes his head. "Not telling. You have to come and see."

There's a mischievous light in his eyes, and in that moment he looks so very much like his eight-year-old self, waiting for my decision to hire him as a guide at the Expo. Who could say no to those big, dark puppy-dog eyes?

I laugh. "Okay, okay. You win."

And even though I don't want to give him false hope, I can tell from his smile that I have.

∞ 3 ∞

There's a definite drawback to scheduling a time jump in the morning, especially when it takes four tries to get it right and you decide to add in a two-hour side trip. I walked the better part of a mile on each of the four jumps to Dallas and nearly that far in the heat of Boston in July. While you're there, the adrenaline surge that comes from being out of your time and place keeps you going, but the aftereffect is a bit like jet lag. And it doesn't help that I'm already wiped out from lousy sleep. I don't think I've had more than two or three nightmare-free nights since I returned from the Expo.

So while my internal clock would swear it's nearly midnight when I arrive back at Katherine's, the microwave clock begs to differ. It's 10:32 a.m., exactly one minute after I left for that last jump to Dallas. Katherine, Connor, and Dad are still at the kitchen table, drinking coffee. Daphne is still chasing a squirrel in the backyard, happy to have a door and a few hundred feet between her and an activated CHRONOS key.

"So?" Katherine is the first to speak, but all three of them are leaning forward.

I pull the two medallions out of my pocket and toss them on the table along with the diary. "Two down. That makes fourteen if we count the two that Kiernan has, so ten to go, right?"

She nods and then pulls the diary toward her. "I haven't been collecting the diaries, but that's a good idea." She flips it open and then looks back at me, an eyebrow raised. "This isn't from Evelyn and Timothy. It's one of mine."

I hadn't thought about that when I tossed the diary on the table. "Um . . . yeah. I stopped in Boston to get the information Kiernan said that they had gathered. In the other timeline." I point toward the diary. "Her notes are in there."

"So you stopped in Boston and kept us waiting?" Connor says.

"You were waiting a sum total of sixty seconds, regardless of whether I stopped in Boston. And now we can start planning our next moves. I'm still worried that we're going to trigger some change to the timeline that will alert Saul and Prudence to what we're doing before we finish. And I'm even more worried now, because Kiernan says the next jump is to Russia—or at least that was the next one we attempted last time."

Katherine is about to say something else, but Dad cuts in. "They were okay with all of this? What did they say?" He takes a sip of his coffee and tries to look nonchalant, but I know what he's thinking. I just saw his parents, the ones he can't even remember. He'll want to know every word they said, every expression, every gesture.

"Oh, Dad. I'm sorry. I wasn't even thinking." I sit down with him at the breakfast nook, giving him a big hug. "I don't know if this is CHRONOS protocol," I say, glancing over at Katherine and Connor, "but I brought back a few minutes of video. Before you watch it, though, I need to make sure I didn't mess anything up. You were still adopted by John and Theresa Keller, right?"

He nods, and I continue. "You still teach math?"

Another nod.

"And your name is still Alphonse?"

Picking on my dad at such a vulnerable moment is probably kind of evil, and if there's really a karma police, I'm sure it will earn me a demerit or two. But the look on his face is truly priceless.

"I'm joking, Dad. But it was a pretty close call, apparently. You were very nearly named after your grandfather. I'm not sure why they decided to switch."

"Please tell me it's because you stood up for your helpless, unborn father and insisted that they reconsider," Dad says.

"Nope. I don't owe you anything on that front, since you stood by and let Mom name me after Prudence."

Dad grins. "Touché. Although I really think Alphonse is worse."

"I don't know." I hand him the phone with the video and head for the coffeepot. "I could see you as an Alphie. Or you could have been the prototype for the Fonz."

"I wasn't alive in the fifties," he says. "And if I'd walked around in a leather jacket saying 'Aaay' in the eighties, I'd have gotten my band-geek ass kicked on a daily basis."

When I turn back to the table, Katherine is holding the diary and has clicked to activate one of the video links. A holographic image that looks a lot like me appears above the diary and starts talking.

"Katherine! What are you doing?" I cross the kitchen in two steps, sloshing a bit of coffee on my saddle shoes. I snatch the diary from her hands and turn off the video. "That's private!"

"I don't see why," Katherine counters. "It's my diary, after all, and there may be some things in those entries that I need to know." She glances around the table. "Although, maybe we should watch it upstairs. It's a bit rude to do it down here, since Connor and Harry won't be able to see and hear what—"

I press the diary closer to my chest. "No. I haven't even seen the videos yet. *I* will watch them upstairs, and if there's anything you need to know, I'll tell you. It will also take twice as long if you're doing it."

Katherine can see and hear the videos in the diaries and even preview some of the jump sites in the *Log of Stable Points,* but the CHRONOS gene seems to mutate and degrade over time, or maybe it's due to the tumor and the medicines. Holding the signal for very long is difficult for her. In the past, she's joked about it being like going through a tunnel while talking on a cell phone, but her eyes narrow a bit when I mention it, so she's apparently not in the mood to joke about it today.

"What if you don't realize that something is important?" Katherine asks. "I'm far more familiar with what we're doing here than you are. Something could easily slip through the cracks. And may I remind you that you viewed mine—at least the ones that were relevant to your jump to 1893."

Okay, that part is true. I watched Katherine's private entries in preparation for the trip to the World's Fair. But she knew what was in those diaries when she handed them to me. Furthermore, the Katherine I viewed in those entries was part of her distant past.

I, on the other hand, have absolutely no clue what I'll find in these videos, aside from Kiernan's caution that there might be some things I don't want to share. Even though the Kate in this video isn't exactly me, the idea of sharing her diary bothers me. This Kate isn't part of my past but part of some alternate present and future. I'm not even sure *I* want to watch these clips, and I'm completely and totally positive I'm not watching them in the same room as my grandmother, especially when Kiernan said it's full of rants about her.

I match Katherine's stubborn expression with one of my own. "This is not negotiable, Katherine. When I've determined which of these entries are relevant to our work, you'll be welcome to view them. While you're waiting, maybe you should order me a Russian language course. Kiernan said Moscow is next if we follow the same order as last time, although I'm inclined to skip ahead to Australia. He said that one was pretty easy."

Katherine grimaces. "Adrienne . . . I can't imagine she'll be cooperative, although *easy* sounds about right."

I have no idea what she means by that, but she doesn't respond to my questioning look.

"And I already have a language course," she continues. "I'm well aware that Wallace's Moscow trip is on the agenda."

The criticism in her voice sets me on edge. "There's an agenda? Maybe you could print me out a copy of that? It might come in handy since I'm the designated traveler."

Katherine glares at me and pushes away from the table, then storms out of the kitchen. Connor shoots me a reproachful look and follows her.

Dad's expression is pretty much the same as Connor's. "You should go a bit easier on Katherine, you know."

"I'm sorry, Dad. But . . . it's like she wants to control each little thing. She doesn't give me the information I need, and then ten minutes later, she expects me to know every detail. I'm not a mind reader. And this diary is private." I grab a blueberry muffin and napkin from the table and then lean over and give him a quick kiss on the cheek.

"What was that for?" he asks.

"Apology for the Alphonse joke. And just because. Aren't you heading out soon to pick up Sara?"

"Yeah, I need to get a move on. Sure you don't want to come with?"

I shake my head. "You know I like Sara, and you know I like art museums. But I do not like Sara and art museums together." His girlfriend teaches art history, and while she's a lot of fun anywhere else, she goes into docent mode when there are paintings or statues around.

"We could make up fake histories like we did last time," he offers.

"Sara didn't find that nearly as funny as we did. And anyway," I say, holding up the diary, "I have a date with my other self. You'll be back early, right? Trey's supposed to be here—"

"Yes, I know. At seven thirty." He laughs. "Don't worry. The lasagna just needs to go in the oven. The salad is made. I'm bringing back dessert and fresh bread. Everything will be perfect."

I give him a goodbye hug and head upstairs. Even if everything *is* perfect, I'll probably be too nervous to eat. Part of me thinks that having dinner here was a bad idea, because it's too much pressure on Trey. But this is also where we spent most of our time together in the other timeline, so maybe there's a vibe here that we're missing.

Once I'm upstairs, I change out of the less than comfy 1960s clothing and curl up on the sofa. I pick up the diary and stare at it for a moment, still not entirely sure I'm ready for this. For all of Kiernan's insistence that this Kate is really me, just with a different set of experiences, I can't help but view her as an imposter—a fake Kate who was off using my identity and my body and apparently having a pretty good time with them before she vanished. It's not logical, but I resent this Other-Kate thoroughly, and there's this huge part of me that really doesn't want to know anything more about her.

But if I don't watch the videos, Katherine most certainly will. One of us has to—it would be beyond stupid not to learn from the mistakes we made in this alternate past. So I open the diary, flip to the pages at the back where Other-Kate saved her videos, and click on the first link.

My face pops up in the holographic display, so close at first that I can see every eyelash. After a moment Other-Kate moves a little farther away. She seems nervous, and I can't help but remember the time Charlayne and I made this silly video to post on her Facebook page. But there's no Charlayne in this video, just someone who looks exactly like me, minus the faint scar on my neck and jawline.

The first entry, entitled simply 1, is really short. Other-Kate says:

> Okay, I'm not sure this is working. I'm going to turn it off and check, then I'll be right back.

The next entry, again with no descriptive title, begins with Other-Kate looking much more relaxed. She's sitting in a room that seems a bit smaller than this one, and the skyline in the window behind her doesn't look like DC. Other-Kate folds her legs into a half-lotus position and takes a deep breath:

> Okay, this is my first diary entry, and I'm not really comfortable with this thing yet, but Katherine says it's a good idea to keep a record of everything we're doing, and this is a lot faster than writing it all down each day. I'd rather do it on my computer, but I guess this will help me get used to the equipment. It has been an insanely crazy month in more ways than one, and, I don't know, maybe this will do me good. So much change in just a few weeks can really mess with your head. Maybe if I vent here, I can avoid seeing a shrink. Although I still have moments when I think all of this is some sort of psychotic episode and that I should be seeing a shrink. I suspect Mom would agree if she were here.

Where is Mom in this timeline? Is she okay? Unfortunately, I don't have a psychic link to this Other-Kate, and she barrels onward with her monologue:

Where to start? Okay, this week I've been learning about stable points. What they are, how to set them, why they're important. Katherine has this big book of them, some of which are also in my CHRONOS key. And I can create new ones, too—or at least I'll be able to create new ones in a few weeks when Katherine thinks I'm ready.

Mostly it's just history right now, an all-day-every-day history class. Either I'm getting a future history lesson on this CHRONOS place or a past history lesson on the areas and times when the historians were stranded. We've been at this for nearly a month, and it's getting really boring.

Although my CHRONOS initiation was the condensed version, I remember well having to stare at the *Log of Stable Points* for hours on end while trying to figure out exactly when and where Katherine had been killed. I raise my coffee mug in a sympathetic salute. "I hear you, sister. Been there, done that."

And that's when it occurs to me that this is how I need to think of this other me on the screen—like a long-lost, identical twin sister. Not me. The same cellular makeup, yes, but a different consciousness. Some shared experiences, but also some different experiences. Not the enemy, but still not me.

∞

I wake up on the couch, unsure why I'm there. Then I notice the diary on the floor. I close my eyes again, still a little sleepy. Other than learning that Mom took some sort of fellowship for the year at a college in Italy, I haven't picked up much information from the other timeline. My alter-self is bored, Katherine and Connor occasionally get on her nerves, and she's nervous about starting a new school in the fall. I'm increasingly sure she's not in Bethesda or anywhere in the DC area—she mentioned going to some mall called Water Tower Place.

Then I remember that Trey will be here in a little over an hour, and that brings a short burst of energy. Unfortunately, it's the nervous variety. I'm simultaneously really looking forward to seeing him and totally dreading it. I just know I'll say something stupid and Trey will decide this isn't going to work out. I never felt like that the first time around, and I doubt he ever worries that he'll do something to screw things up. When the relationship starts with the girl saying she's in love within the first five minutes, the guy's work is pretty much done, right?

I get into the shower, taking deep, calming breaths as I wash my hair. I've had dinner with Trey, here in this house, at least a dozen times. Nothing to freak out over.

I'm still kind of freaking, however. And for the first time since I handed him the envelope with the DVD inside, I wonder if I did the right thing. I mean, I promised Trey that I would find him as soon as I got back, but this thing is still far from over. Even if the pieces of our relationship magically fall into place and we become *us* again, how long will it last? How long before another time shift steals those memories?

I resolutely push those thoughts back into the corner of my mind. The fact that Trey is coming here tonight and I'll see him in a little less than an hour should be making me happy, not sad.

I rinse away the shampoo, and a small leaf that must have been caught in my hair slides down my leg toward the drain. It's red, dappled with gold, and I realize that I must have carried it back from Dealey Plaza.

I watch this leaf that was in the air the day that Kennedy died, decades before I was born, as it dances around the bathtub with the shampoo bubbles, rushing toward the drain. I'm suddenly seized by the urge to save it, but before my fingers can latch on, the leaf is sucked away.

∞

"Katherine, can I get something different for you? There's chicken salad left from last night."

The rest of us have been finished for several minutes now. Katherine, on the other hand, has only picked around her plate, taking a few bites of the limp noodles in the middle and pushing aside mushrooms and anything even slightly crispy.

"Oh, no," she says. "I'm just not very hungry, Harry. The lasagna is fine, even with having to be held warm for so long."

Trey was only twenty minutes late, which really isn't bad around here, given that traffic can be unpredictable. He called to let us know he was running behind and apologized profusely, so it's really rude for Katherine to bring it up again, even indirectly.

I'd chalk it up to her unpredictable moods, but I'm pretty sure this is intentional. She thought it was foolish of me to give Trey the DVD, and she wasn't too happy when I told her I was inviting him for dinner. Any second I'm not spending with my nose in a diary or off tracking down the CHRONOS keys is apparently time wasted. Still, she could at least be polite.

I might have restricted my response to a dirty look, but I catch Trey's face—embarrassed, a little hurt—and can't hold my tongue. "The lasagna is perfect, Katherine. It's lasagna, for God's sake. It's supposed to be crispy around the edges."

And then I realize I sound shrill and mean, which isn't really the picture I want to paint for this Trey who barely knows me. So I give her a smile, hoping to pass it off as a joke.

She doesn't smile back, just slides her chair from the table and says, "Trey, it was a pleasure to meet you . . . again. I think I'm going to skip the rest of the evening, since I'm feeling tired and I suspect Kate will just have to introduce you to us all over again at some point. And please, try not to keep Kate up too late—she has a lot of work to do tomorrow."

Trey, as always, is super polite. "My pleasure, Mrs. Shaw. I promised my dad that I'd be in by ten, so I'll have to clear out within the hour anyway."

That seems a bit odd. We usually wrapped things up by midnight . . . before. If Trey had a curfew, he never mentioned it, and ten o'clock? Yikes. That was my curfew in middle school.

I help Dad serve the cheesecake. Connor takes his and exits, probably checking on Katherine. Dad, Trey, and I chat briefly about Briar Hill, whether Trey liked his school down in Peru, and something about a sport-fishing trip Dad took to Costa Rica a few years back.

I watch Trey as he tells Dad about fishing down in Peru. His hair is a little longer and blonder than I've seen it, and his skin is a few shades darker. His nose is a little pink in places, like it suffered a bit of a sunburn a few days back. I guess this is his summer look. We never made it to summer last time. I want to just sit there and drink him in with my eyes, but I make myself look away to avoid giving off a stalker vibe.

I put the dishes in the sink, and Dad makes some excuse about course planning, which leaves me alone with Trey. Well, except for Daphne, but I'm kind of glad she's still here, because I'm suddenly feeling awkward and petting her gives me something to do with my hands.

"I'm sorry about Katherine," I say. "Earlier."

Of course, *earlier*, since she's not in the room now. He must think I'm an idiot.

"It was rude of me to be so late, and she called me on it. Not your fault."

"Not really yours, either."

Trey shrugs. "No, it *was* my fault. I should have left earlier. There were just a bunch of things that Dad wanted me to get done today, and it took a lot longer than I thought." Then he reaches down to pet Daphne, too, and I'm reminded that this is at least as odd for him as it is for me.

This awkwardness feels a lot like our last date. We watched the movie, which was okay, but it was the sort of generic date-night flick that neither of us really likes. In retrospect, I should have taken him up on the offer to pick the film, since I have a better idea of what we'd both like. We held hands in the theater, which was nice, and he kissed me good night, a kiss very similar to the one he gave me on the porch that first night in the other timeline—brief, tentative, a little shy.

"You want to go outside?" I say. "It's kind of dark, but there should be enough light from the patio for the Frisbee."

He looks surprised. "You want to play Frisbee?"

I laugh. "Well, not especially, but Daphne will be all over it. You used to . . . I mean, I . . ."

I sigh, understanding a little better now why Kiernan has such a difficult time finding the correct pronouns when he talks to me.

"Sure," Trey says. "Sounds like fun."

And it is fun. It's hard not to have a good time when Daphne is so enthusiastic. Trey tends to overthrow it, because he's not used to her range, so she keeps bringing it back to me, giving him these disappointed side glances. And I have to wonder—does she remember him? She's been under the CHRONOS field, too. Is she juggling two sets of memories—one where she's just meeting Trey and another where he should already know exactly where she likes her ears scratched and how far to fling the Frisbee?

Trey overthrows it again, and this time it lands near the garage, skidding under the base of this rusty, swinging bench left behind by the previous owners. The Frisbee is wedged in pretty tight, and Daphne is a little spooked by the fact that the swing moves each time she tries to grab it.

I run over to help her, and Trey follows. He holds the swing back as I dislodge the disc, and then, after I toss it to Daphne, he pulls me down onto the bench.

This kiss is much closer to right. And Daphne doesn't even pretend to play chaperone this time, so maybe she does remember Trey.

"Were you serious about needing to be home by ten?" I ask when the kiss ends. "Because we could watch a movie or—"

"No," he says. "I really do have to go. Dad actually wanted me to cancel because . . . well, we're flying out to see my mom really early tomorrow morning. She's on assignment in Haiti, and she wants to be with me for my birthday, so . . ."

"Oh. I didn't know."

"Neither did I. Dad just told me yesterday—he's suddenly all about surprises." Trey's voice takes on a slightly snarky tone, and I'm about to ask why, but he continues. "Anyway, it was very last minute, so the only flight he could get leaves at five thirty in the morning. I'll need to be up by around three."

"Ouch. How long will you be gone?" I try to keep the tone light, because I don't want to be that kind of girlfriend, the one who clings too tight, especially since I'm not really even his girlfriend at this point.

"Should be back the Friday before school starts."

"What will you do in Haiti?"

"Well, we won't actually be in Haiti. Mom wants a break—this is her vacation time—so we're going to meet her at Punta Cana, over in the Dominican Republic. It looks nice, but to be honest, I'm a little beached out. I'd rather stay in DC. Unfortunately, that's not an option."

"I completely understand about family members dictating travel plans. I have a few trips coming up that I'd much rather skip, believe me."

"So . . . you really went to Dallas 1963 today? Did you bring back any souvenirs?"

I might be imagining it, but there's a tiny hint of doubt in his voice, and I suspect that when he said *souvenirs* what he really meant was proof. I'm not surprised, but I make a mental note to give him an actual demo at some point in the near future.

"No souvenirs," I say, although my mind flashes briefly to that leaf tumbling down the drain earlier today. "It really wasn't a sightseeing trip. I met my grandparents, although it's really hard to think of them as grandparents when they're maybe six or seven years older. I got their medallions. And I stood on the infamous grassy knoll. I may have even seen the so-called second shooter, but we had to leave the area before there was any evidence one way or the other."

"Incredible. Just wow." He shakes his head. "Where to next?"

I shrug. "We're still debating. It's looking like World War II Australia. At some point, I'm probably heading into Soviet Russia. And 1938 Georgia, but that one is apparently complicated, so I'm saving it until the end."

"You mean you can go anywhere, to any time you want?"

"If a stable point has been set, then yes, I could. There are stable points going back to early civilizations and going forward to just before CHRONOS was established in the late 2100s. But I'm not sure I want to know that much about the future—I'd like to live a normal life when this is all over—and when I go back in time, there's always the risk of changing something that affects the present."

He laughs. "'I wish, I wish I hadn't killed that fish.'"

I give him a blank look.

"Homer with the toaster? The dinosaurs? Ned Flanders as Big Brother? You've got to be kidding me—you've never seen that one?"

"Not ringing any bells, so I must have missed it."

"Oh, wow, we will most definitely have to fix that right now. You *do* watch *The Simpsons*, don't you?"

"Yes. Mostly the old ones that come on around dinnertime." To be honest, I haven't actually watched anything lately, because Katherine doesn't have a TV and Dad has our old set in his room. But I used to catch the reruns most evenings while eating dinner at Dad's and sometimes at Mom's, if we didn't watch *Wheel of Fortune* instead.

Trey lets out an exaggerated sigh of relief. "Thank God. You had me worried that my alternate self had fallen for someone who wouldn't get a lot of my jokes."

"So unfair. I miss one little episode and you doubt me. Tsk, tsk."

"Hey, it's not just any episode. It's a *Treehouse of Horror*. Must fix."

He pulls out his phone and types something in. "Just a sec. Trying to find the right one." Another pause and then a muted curse. "They only have clips online . . ."

After a few seconds, he says, "Okay, this is it. It's not the whole thing but may be enough to patch that gaping hole in your cultural education."

I dig my elbow into his ribs, and he laughs, putting his arm around me. We watch the video, laughing at the same bits, and I realize that it's this kind of thing, just being together, doing little or nothing, that I've missed the most. The earlier chats on the phone and our date at the movies and even dinner tonight all seemed staged, like we were playing roles. This is the first conversation we've had where Trey feels like my Trey. It's the first time that it feels *easy*.

The video is almost finished when his phone rings.

"It's my dad," Trey says, a bit unnecessarily, given that we're both looking at his screen and the word *Dad* just popped up in big, bold letters. He gets up from the swing and walks a few steps toward the house.

"Yeah, Dad. What's up? . . . Yes. Estella told me. I'll stop by the drugstore on the way back . . . Yeah, Dad. Five minutes . . . Yes." His voice is a bit sharp. "Everything's ready . . . I said I would, didn't I?"

He listens for a moment and then says, "Fine," and hangs up, shaking his head.

Something's wrong with this picture. Trey's dad was so relaxed when I met him, and I didn't get the feeling he was the type to set many boundaries. I think back to all of the nights—many of them school nights for Trey—when we were on the computer for an hour or more, often well after he should have been in bed.

"Everything okay?" I ask.

"Yeah," he says, but he doesn't really sound like it's true. "Dad's just jumping my case about everything lately. But, he's right—I probably do need to get going."

He trusts my judgment. I remember Trey saying that about his dad on more than one occasion, and I can't help but wonder what happened.

We walk around to the front of the house where his car is parked.

"Is there a stable point on that key of yours for Punta Cana?"

I laugh. "Unless some historical battle or something happened nearby, I seriously doubt it."

"Too bad," he says. "I'll try to give you a call in a couple of days. Maybe we can do something when I get back?"

I nod. "I'd like that."

He gives Daphne a quick pat on the head and me an equally quick peck on the cheek and then takes off down the sidewalk.

As he gets into the car, I have the strange sensation that we're being watched. I glance around and realize it's probably because I'm standing almost exactly where I was when Simon tried to snatch my medallion. I'm outside the protective zone, inches away from the spot where Trey whacked Simon over the head with a tire iron. Inches away from the spot where Katherine disappeared.

I quickly retreat four or five steps toward the front porch and give Trey a final wave as he flips on his headlights and pulls away from the curb. And then a second set of headlights flips on about half a block down the road, and a dark blue van drives off after him.

Just the neighbors going out for a gallon of milk or something.

Probably.

Except I don't really remember seeing that van around before. And the feeling that I'm being watched disappears along with the van.

∞4∞

I spend the entire next day with Dear Diary, and the only real accomplishment is that I manage to pinpoint Other-Kate's location—Chicago. That seems weird, because I've never been to modern Chicago, just the one in 1893. It's hard to imagine that the skyline I see outside her window is the same place I visited a few months back.

Eventually, the diary becomes more interesting, probably because Other-Kate began to skip a day, then several days, and sometimes even a week between entries. So instead of page after page about her training and other daily minutiae, she occasionally had something to say when she finally sat down to log a report.

I'm just about to click on the next entry when my phone rings. There are only four possibilities in my newly truncated social life: Mom, Dad, Trey, or Sorry, Wrong Number. I'm really hoping for Option Number Three.

It's Option Number One. "Hi, Mom. What's up?"

"Why does anything have to be up? Isn't it possible that I just want to talk to my darling daughter?"

"It's possible, but what's up?"

She laughs. "Okay, I confess. It's both. Are you free for dinner at O'Malley's?"

I start to say no, that it's been a long day, and I'm tired, but it's only a few minutes after four. Since Mom knows nothing about my time traveling second life, she'll be hurt if I say no. And O'Malley's means onion rings. Big, fat, juicy, really, really bad for you onion rings, with just the right amount of spice.

I can tell I've hesitated too long, because she says in a flat voice, "But if you already have plans . . ."

"Actually, O'Malley's sounds great, Mom. Should I meet you there or at the townhouse?"

"No, no. I'll pick you up."

"On what, your bicycle? It's going to be a long ride to O'Malley's with me on the back."

"I'm outside that Zipcar place across from campus, and that cute little blue Mini Cooper convertible is there. Do you remember the one?"

"Yes . . ."

"Well, it's taunting me again. I think I'm going to have to rent it for a few hours."

"Ohhh-kay," I say, letting just a hint of suspicion creep into my voice. This isn't Mom behavior. Not only is she renting a car, something she's done maybe five times since we moved to DC, but she is driving here, to Katherine's house. That's her personal equivalent of waltzing into the lion's den. Now I *know* something is up.

"Let me guess. You've met the man of your dreams, and you're running away to live au naturel on a secluded island in the South Pacific."

She laughs again. "Yes. I also won the lottery. Does five thirty work for you?"

∞

My Cobb salad is finished, and there are two onion rings left in the basket next to my plate. I raise my fork and stab it down onto the red-and-white-checked paper lining, a fraction of an inch from my mother's pinky finger.

She knows better.

"Deborah Pierce," I say in my best Judge Judy voice, "you are centimeters away from violating paragraph three, section two of the Onion Ring Accords. Keep your fingers on your side of the table, lady."

Mom and I have an agreement about O'Malley's. We don't share our onion rings. If one of us is a pig and can't make the onion rings last as long as the entrée, she must do without.

Unfortunately, looking at those last two rings on my plate reminds me of Trey surprising me with O'Malley's on my first test jump to the Lincoln Memorial and on our last day together before the jump to the Expo. That, of course, reminds me of everything else going on in my life that I can't really talk to my mother about.

Mom, being a mom, naturally notices my change of expression. "Hey, I wasn't really going to swipe an onion ring. Although I'm pretty sure they gave you more in your order than they gave me. Your flirting with the waiter must have paid off."

I raise an eyebrow. "I did *not* flirt with the waiter!"

She grins. "Nope, you didn't even notice him. And he's kind of cute, too. Are things so serious with this boy you're dating that you don't even glance at a hot guy now?"

I really don't want to talk about Trey right now. I've given her a plausible half-truth concerning our relationship, saying that I met him at a Briar Hill meet and greet for incoming students and that we've gone out a few times. All of that is more or less true, and since I have to leave out the parts about alternate timelines, the fact that the meet and greet was on his doorstep, and that I had to pretty much stalk him in order to arrange the meeting and greeting, there's not much else to tell.

So I stab the larger of the two remaining onion rings and toss it onto Mom's plate. It's partly meant as a distraction and partly because they really don't look as tempting as they did before my thoughts turned to Trey.

"Who are you, and what have you done with my daughter?" Mom gives me a fake evil glare, and for a fleeting moment, I see a resemblance to Saul. For some reason, I'd thought of him as Prudence's father and even as my grandfather, but I'd never really lingered on the fact that he's her biological father, too. I shouldn't be surprised that there's some resemblance, but I have to admit that it creeps me out a teensy bit.

I give her a tentative smile. "The Accords do say that either party can voluntarily grant control of an onion ring to the other party."

"True, but that's never happened."

"Maybe I'm just growing up and have decided that it's nice to share?"

"Hmph. As long as you don't expect me to reciprocate."

"The treaty remains in full force. And I actually do have an ulterior motive. I want to finish eating so that you'll finally tell me this big news."

She's been playing coy since she picked me up. And I was wrong about her venturing into the lion's den. She called at 5:40 p.m., ten minutes after she was supposed to arrive at Katherine's, to say that she was running late and I should meet her outside or we'd lose our table. On a Thursday night . . . at a place where reservations aren't recommended, let alone required. Yeah, right, Mom. You retain your crown as the Queen of Avoidance.

I finish off my last onion ring and wipe my fingers on the napkin in my lap. "Okay, we have now eaten every bite. So spill."

"You don't want dessert?"

"No! Stop stalling."

"Fine," she says with a nervous little hand gesture that really isn't typical for her. "I'm just very excited about this, and a little . . . well, hesitant. I don't know whether you'll be all right with it."

"Um, okay." I give her a quizzical look. "I'm going to repeat back to you a question you've asked me many, many times. 'Exactly who is the mother and who is the daughter here?' Last time we discussed this, the answer was that you were the mother, so unless something has changed, why would you need my permission?"

"I don't *need* your permission, but I don't want you to feel abandoned. It's—I've been offered this incredible opportunity, a research sabbatical with some minor teaching duties. But it's in Italy. For a year."

My expression must shift a bit, because she immediately says, "But I don't have to take it, Kate. I'm sure there will be other opportunities—"

"No, no." I can't tell her that the expression was due to déjà vu because I just heard something very similar in the diary entries by Other-Kate. "Really, Mom. Tell me more."

She looks skeptical. "It's just a research grant. I could probably delay it for a few years, until you're in college," she says, although I can tell from her voice that she doesn't really believe it.

"Um . . . I said tell me more, not tell me why you shouldn't go. Where in Italy? What would you be doing? When would you need to leave?"

"It's near Genoa, but I'd be traveling to five or six different cities in Europe and also in Africa. There's a private donor who is funding oral histories of women survivors of the genocides in Rwanda and Bosnia. It would be a comparative study, and I'd pull in my research on women survivors of the Holocaust and maybe even have a chance to interview the few still alive in Europe. Someone else must have backed out at the last minute—I've never heard of anything moving this quickly in academia. The grant would cover my salary, plus my traveling expenses, and even compensates my department for having to cover my classes at the last minute. They want me there a few weeks before their fall semester starts, which gives me a whopping six days to get things in order. That's counting today, so five really."

Her eyes are wide and excited throughout that long speech, which might strike someone who didn't know her as odd, given that she's talking about the prospect of an entire year filled with some pretty grisly and emotional stories. It's not like she revels in the suffering of others. This is just the one subject she's passionate about. She wants to be sure these women's stories are told and remembered.

"I think you should take it, Mom. I mean, I'll miss you, but I could come over on vacation, right? Or you could fly back here?"

She doesn't say anything for a few seconds. "Are you sure, Kate? A year is a long time, especially at your age."

"True. It would be a shame for you to miss my first step."

She rolls her eyes. "You know what I mean."

"I do. But I'll have Dad document every homework assignment and report back to you if I grow an inch or my shoe size changes. You should *do* this, Mom."

I try to make my expression as sincere as possible, both to counteract her earlier assumptions and to hide the fact that part of me really and truly doesn't want her to go. It's not just that I'll miss her. I was also looking forward to having a part-time refuge from CHRONOS and Katherine. A few days a week at Mom's house, being a normal teenager, going to school, sleeping in my tiny, cluttered room, curling up on our battered, old sofa with her to watch a movie—all of that would have given me a break from the current insanity.

I'm also pretty certain Katherine is behind this grant, although I've no idea why I think that. With few exceptions, this timeline seems much like the one in which Other-Kate existed, so maybe this opportunity came Mom's way based on her professional reputation. There's just something about the phrase "private donor" and the fact that the university is in Italy, where Katherine lived for a number of years. And the timing . . . this just came out of the blue.

The bottom line is I know Mom needs this. Dad has his teaching and me and also Sara. He has Grandma and Grandpa Keller, who raised him from the time he was five. He loves teaching, but if he had to switch jobs tomorrow, I doubt it would change him. Given the breach between Mom and Katherine, she has her work and me, and I'm at Dad's half the time. Sometimes she looks at me with this odd, sad expression, and I'm pretty sure she's imagining what it will be like in a few years, when I'm on my own and all she has is her work.

I haven't seen her eyes light up like this about anything in years—maybe not since she and Dad split up—so there's no way I'm going to let on that I'm suspicious. If Mom thought Katherine was involved, her interest would evaporate instantly. And it would be so selfish for me to keep her here just because I want an escape from round-the-clock Saving the Universe duty.

"You should *do* this," I repeat.

"Nothing is decided yet. I'll need to be sure it's okay with Harry . . . and your grandmother, I guess. But I wanted to discuss it with you first, because if you don't want me to go, I'll tell them no deal."

"It will be fine, Mom. This will be a busy year for me. I'll have Dad, Katherine, and Connor around if I need them—and you and I can video chat, email, text. It's not like you're going to Mars. And this opportunity was tailor-made for you." All of that, especially the last part, is totally honest, so I don't have to struggle to look like I'm telling the truth.

She holds my gaze for a long time before responding. "And you're not saying this because you know that I really want to do it? Like I said, I can probably get a deferral."

"Mom, go! Live a little. Embrace your academic destiny."

That earns me a laugh, and I can tell she's relieved but also still conflicted. Which guarantees that she'll be asking me these same questions up until, and possibly well after, she arrives in Italy, so I need to keep my game face on.

∞

It's nearly ten when we get back to Katherine's. Mom decided we should celebrate with a bit of shopping. So there's a new pair of leggings and a gorgeous red sundress in the bag I'm carrying as I swing my feet out of the little rental car. Mom even bought a few dresses for herself, and she's normally as much of a jeans-and-T-shirts sort of girl as I am.

"You're sure you don't want to come in? Everyone is still awake. Connor's actually a nice guy. You could tell them about the research trip, and you could meet Daphne . . ."

"Maybe next time. It's late."

"Katherine doesn't bite, you know, or at least not often. You're just afraid you might actually like your mother if you gave her a chance. So . . . I'm pretty sure I'm going to have to call chicken."

"Ahem. Thin ice, Kate. And I really do need to get the car back before I owe for an extra hour."

I shake my head. "Just be sure to clear all of the feathers out of the car, or else they'll charge you extra."

She snorts. "You are so like your father. Get in the house before I run you over."

"Threatening to run someone over with a Cooper really isn't a credible threat, Mom. You should rent a Hummer next time. Love you!"

I had mixed feelings about her coming in tonight anyway. Trey called while I was in the dressing room. I didn't answer but sent him a quick text saying I'd call him as soon as I got back to the house. That was over an hour ago, and my stomach has been doing little flip-flops ever since.

I kick my shoes off and stack them in the closet in the foyer. The living room is empty, so I'm guessing Dad is either asleep or out with Sara, and Katherine and Connor are probably in their rooms. Hopefully, I can slip upstairs unnoticed. Katherine was moderately grumpy about me going out when we had work to do, and I suspect I'm still on her list for the smart remark when Trey was here.

No such luck. I'm halfway to my room when Katherine sticks her head out of the library on the second floor. "Kate, I'm glad you're home, dear. Did you have a good time with Deborah?"

"I did. She said to tell you hello." Which isn't true, but I'm going to pretend that Mom just forgot to say it. "I'm just—I'm going to sleep now."

"Okay. I was just wondering whether you learned anything from the diary?"

I shake my head. "Not really. It was just starting to get interesting when Mom called. I do know that I was in Chicago with you and Connor—not sure about Dad. Mom's off on some sort of research trip."

I watch Katherine's expression to see if it changes when I mention Mom going on a trip, but she just smiles. "Chicago. I'm not too surprised. It's a wonderful city if you know which years to avoid. Well, get some sleep so that you can get back at it bright and early, okay?"

After saying good night to Katherine, I hang up the new dress and stash the leggings in a drawer. Then I change into a nightshirt and curl up on the couch to call Trey.

No answer. I start to leave a message, but then I notice that he left a voice mail for me earlier, and I decide I should listen to that first.

"Hey, Kate. Just a quick call to say we arrived . . . and I . . . uh . . . are you going to this barbecue thing the Saturday before school starts? I'm guessing not, because it says new students—Briar Hill and Carrington Day. Anyway, it says RSVP and number of guests, which probably means they expect parents, but neither of mine can make it, and I kind of need to go. It's also a farewell party for this guy who taught both Dad and Granddad, and I promised them I'd stop in and say hello, or goodbye, I guess. I'm sure it'll be hideously boring, but it would be a lot more fun if you were there. So . . . um . . . just let me know, okay?"

I suspect he's right about the hideously boring part, but he could invite me over to help clean out his refrigerator—a chore I truly detest—and I'd still agree in a heartbeat.

So I call again. When he still doesn't answer, I leave a message saying, yes, I'd love to go.

As I get up to plug my phone into the charger, a glint of light outside the window catches my eye. At first, I think it's a CHRONOS key, because the light has a bluish tint, but it's not the right shade. It's just the street lamps, their light already kind of blue, reflecting off the top of that blue van, which is parked in the same spot it was yesterday.

The view from my window is just treetops—a big expanse of green. It's the thing I like best about this room. I like seeing the trees when I wake up, and seeing the moon and stars at night reminds me of the skylight in my room at the townhouse, so I've always left the curtains open.

But now as I stare out at the van, I have that same creepy feeling of being watched . . . which is stupid. Seeing the van parked in the same place could just as easily confirm that it belongs to the neighbors. It doesn't mean we're being watched.

I close the curtains anyway.

∞5∞

The smoke stings my nose and throat as I run through the hallway, panicked, the fingers of one hand trailing against the wall to keep from losing my way in the pitch-black maze. I glance behind me, and the man with the lantern is still coming, and he's moving a lot faster than I am. It's like I'm running through Jell-O.

In my other hand, the CHRONOS key is activated, but it's speeding through dozens of stable points so quickly that I can't lock on to anything. As Holmes gets closer, I see the gun in his hand, and then there's this burst of flames, red and gold, barreling straight toward me. Just as they reach me, they morph into a cascade of autumn leaves, falling around my face.

I bolt upright and look around for a minute, disoriented, then fall back onto my pillow, rubbing my eyes. The dreams have been coming a little less often in the past few weeks, and although my heart is still pounding, at least it's not the same blind panic I felt the first few times sleep dragged me back to the World's Fair Hotel. And the whole flames-turning-into-leaves thing is a strange, new addition.

This is the first time I've had two nightmares in a single night, however. The first dream woke me up around two fifteen. I was so wired after that one that I went upstairs and beat the hell out of the punching bag, until I was so exhausted that I assumed I'd get nice, peaceful dream-free sleep. But apparently I was wrong.

A gentle rain is falling outside, and I watch the drops trickle down the window as I focus on pulling in slow, steady breaths until my pulse returns to normal. I have almost half an hour before my alarm is set to go off, and I'm tempted to yank the quilt back over my head, but I know I won't be able to fall asleep. It's partly the dream but also because I smell bacon. And, if I'm not mistaken, blueberry pancakes.

Dad is in the kitchen when I come down. He has his earbuds in, and he doesn't hear me at first. If we were back in our cottage at Briar Hill, he'd have been blasting his music while he cooked—I've been awakened many, many times by the Ramones' "I Wanna Be Sedated"—so he must be worried that his musical tastes would not appeal to Katherine and Connor. I'm not sure what they listen to, if anything. My first thought is that Katherine would be a Peter, Paul, and Mary fan or something like that, but she probably prefers music similar to whatever she listened to back in the 2300s—and I haven't the slightest clue what that would be. Punk music from the 1980s might sound like something from the baroque era to her.

I reach around Dad to snag a strip of bacon from the plate on the back of the stove, and he swats at my hand with the spatula. "You're getting slow, old man," I say, shoving the bacon into my mouth. "What's the occasion? Pancakes are usually weekend fare."

He pulls the earbuds down around his neck. "No occasion. The blueberries were just at the tipping point, so I decided we should finish them off. And since I only have a few days left until school starts back up, at least for us poor, downtrodden teachers, I'm treating each one like vacation."

We eat in silence for a couple of minutes, and then he says, "What were they like? I mean, I watched the video—thanks for that, by the way—but what were they *like*?"

It takes a few seconds for me to realize he's talking about Evelyn and Timothy. I finish the bite in my mouth and then answer. "Your father is so much like you. He even makes the same expressions when he's grumpy. He's a little bit heavier than you, though." In that regard, he reminds me a bit more of Dad from the previous timeline, who was a little thicker around the middle, too, and I push away the thought that my dad might be one of those people who tend to be chubby when they're happy.

"Your dad likes food that's bad for him," I continue, "even though he said they were usually vegan. Your mom is the more no-nonsense of the two . . ."

I spend the next ten minutes or so answering his questions.

"I'm sorry, Dad," I say after I've exhausted all of the details that I can remember. "I should have told you all of this the other day when I got back. I know you're curious about them."

He smiles. "That's okay. If you'd done that, I'd have been late picking up Sara. And this is the first time since then that it's been just you and me. That's the one thing I kind of miss since we moved from the cottage."

"Me, too. But now you have this ginormous kitchen. And I don't know about your bed, but mine is a major upgrade from the pullout sofa." I slide the last bite of pancake around the plate to pick up the remaining syrup. It isn't up to the task, since I usually dump way too much syrup on my pancakes, and I give in to the urge to run my finger around the plate to get the rest.

Dad looks at me for a minute, and I think he's going to remind me that what I'm doing is kind of gross, but he just says, "Even with the bed upgrade, you don't look like you slept very well . . ."

"I slept okay, I guess."

He raises an eyebrow. "You were up in the middle of the night again, weren't you? My room is right below the attic. I was going to come up and check on you, but then the thumping stopped."

"Oh, crap. I didn't think about that. Sorry I woke you."

One side of the attic has been converted into a mini dojo and gym combo. Thick mats cover most of the floor space. A weight machine and rower take up a small corner, but the rest is devoted to a standing kick bag, a Muay Thai banana bag, some kettlebells, and other assorted equipment that Sensei Barbie suggested.

"You didn't wake me for long," he says. "Couldn't fall asleep?"

"Couldn't fall *back* asleep. Stupid dreams."

"Are they getting worse?"

"Not really, but it's usually not a double feature. This last one was where I'm running from Holmes. Except this time the fire shooting out of the gun turned into leaves, like the ones that I saw in Dallas the other day. It was kind of weird."

"Hey, leaves are safer than flames, right? Maybe you're starting to control the dream, rather than it controlling you. Have the other dreams changed too?"

"Nope. Pretty much the same." There's fire in those dreams, too, but instead of trying to save myself, I'm trying to save other people—sometimes people I know and love, sometimes people I've never seen before. In a few of the dreams, I hear someone crying and I dig through all this rubble, but just as I'm getting close, the person vanishes. In others, I'm pushing people out this big window to save them, but we're high above the ground, so they just hit the sidewalk below, popping apart like they're made of Lego blocks. (Apparently my dream censorship committee isn't a fan of blood and gore, something for which I'm eternally grateful.) In the dream, I know the people will hit the ground, and I know they'll die, but it's like I have no choice. Out the window they go, like it or not.

"These dreams have been going on for a while now, Katie. Do you think you need to see someone? I mean, a professional?"

"And tell them what? If I told them the truth, they'd lock me up."

"True, but maybe you could get something to help you sleep? To relax? We could say you have test anxiety or something."

"If it gets worse, maybe."

He looks like he's going to say something more but then changes the subject. "You missed a fun day of Exploring Art," he says.

"Did you go to the National Gallery again?"

"No. We visited a few of the smaller galleries over on R Street. I'd planned to stick my head in and say good night when I got back home, but you were talking to someone, so I didn't interrupt. Was it Trey or your mom?"

"It must have been when I was leaving a message for Trey. He asked me to some get-acquainted thing at school next weekend. Are you going?"

"No. I heard about it, but it's a private party, not an official function. It's at the house of one of the incoming students. I think it's just the administrators and a few of the more senior faculty at Briar Hill. Probably to help smooth over the merger. You want more coffee?"

"No, thanks. What merger?"

Dad looks surprised. "You don't remember all of those meetings I complained about?"

I shake my head, and he gives me a puzzled look before continuing. "Carrington Day, the private school over near Silver Spring that purchased Briar Hill?"

"What? No. Although I think Trey said something about Carrington Day in his message. When were these meetings?"

"The worst of them were right after I started in January, but they dragged on for several months. It was so crazy I was about ready to quit. Briar Hill parents were raising hell about their middle school kids now having to go all the way over to Carrington." He stops. "Oh, wait. Timeline change?"

"Must be. I don't remember any of this."

Every few days I stumble upon some other little change in the timeline. Sometimes it's easy to see how it's related to the Cyrist surge in numbers—there are dozens of towns scattered around the world that are named Cyrus City or whatever. Southern Florida is almost entirely Cyrist, and I'm pretty sure that wasn't the case before. Other differences just seem to be odd ripple effects. Like the *Iron Man* series. I'd swear on my life that Gwyneth Paltrow played Pepper Potts in those movies. I've seen them, and I know this for an absolute fact. But I watched a trailer online the other day, and someone named Cassie Mortimer was playing Pepper. According to IMDb, she's always played Pepper. Gwyneth is still an actress, and she's done very well, but that particular role went to this Cassie person. And she isn't nearly as good.

Every time I notice some new point of disconnect, I can't help but wonder what other changes I'm going to discover, especially once school starts back up.

"Kate. Earth to Kate."

"Oh. Sorry. I'm just beginning to worry about school. I mean, I did okay the last few weeks of school last year, but how much of the history that I remember is history? Or literature, for that matter? Did Shakespeare even write *Romeo and Juliet*? Did Picasso—"

"Did who write what?"

I just stare at him, and he stares back at me, all wide-eyed and innocent, but he doesn't even last a full second before cracking a grin.

"So not funny, Dad."

"Hey, I owed you one for the Alphonse joke."

"Fine, but I'm being serious here." I grab the plates and carry them to the dishwasher.

"I can see that," he says as he clears the rest of the table. "But, Kate—it's not like there are huge, gaping differences. You'll be okay. You just might have to study a bit more than usual."

I roll my eyes and jam one of the plates into the bottom rack. "Yeah. Because I have nothing else to do this year, right?"

Dad takes the last plate out of my hand and puts it into the dishwasher, then comes around to give me a long hug. I sink my head into his chest.

"Kate, I will do everything I can to help you. Both with the school stuff and anything else you need. You know that, right?"

I nod and feel myself relaxing the tiniest bit.

"But," he adds, "I know you don't want to hear this, and it pains me as a teacher to even suggest it—but maybe Katherine's right? Maybe you shouldn't be worrying about school at all right now? Or anything else. Maybe that would decrease the stress factor?"

And I tense right back up. I give him one last squeeze and pull away, pacing toward the windows. We've been over this before.

"Maybe," I say, my hands clenched at my sides. "Or maybe it would just increase the stress factor. Has anyone thought about that? It's like she expects me to be some sort of machine that just zips around and collects these damned medallions. And I know it has to be done—especially if billions of lives really are at stake here. I mean, I'm not a monster."

Dad doesn't say anything, just watches me pace.

"Did you know—" I pull in a long breath. "Did you know I spent a couple of hours researching Maryland's handgun laws this week? I was going to sign up for firearms training. But you'd have to buy the gun, since I'm not eighteen yet."

"You hate guns."

"Yes. I do hate guns. Especially handguns. The idea of touching one completely creeps me out. But being chased by someone who had a gun when I didn't also creeped me out."

I wipe away a tear, but there's another one right behind it, so I just say screw it, and let them flow. "And who knows what's coming next, Dad? Do I go into Russia unarmed? And what if I go in with a gun and have to shoot someone, assuming I even *could* shoot someone, only then I get back and discover that some butterfly effect means World War Three happened in 1960 and none of you were ever born? What about all of the people who never exist because of something that's my fault?"

I think back to the video clip Trey played the other night and hear Homer saying, "I wish, I wish I hadn't killed that fish," and I start laughing. But even to my own ears, the laugh sounds hysterical, and apparently Dad agrees, because he crosses over and wraps his arms around me. He walks me over to the window seat and rocks me back and forth, back and forth, while I cry and laugh at the same time.

A minute or so later, he says, "No, not now," to someone, his voice sharp. I don't know if it was to Katherine or Connor. Daphne was with whoever it was, and she ignores the command or maybe just realizes it couldn't possibly have been meant for her. If someone's crying, Daphne has to check it out. It's probably good intuition on her part, because it's hard to stay quite as upset when she's nosing at your hand to see what she can do to make you feel better.

I eventually get my act together and sniff back the tears. "Sorry, Dad. I sort of fell apart there."

"No, I'm sorry," he says, pulling me close again. "I'm sorry I can't fix this. No seventeen-year-old should have to deal with this kind of pressure. I'm not sure how you've held up as well as you have. And I'm sorry I wasn't here the first time you were going through all of this."

"Well, that really wasn't your fault. You had other obligations, and, even so, you still wanted to help." He knows the entire story of how I met his other self, happily married and teaching at a school in Delaware. I didn't mention that he was carrying ten extra pounds or so of happily married chub, but I told him everything I remembered about the two little boys John and Robbie. I don't know if that was doing him a favor or not, but it was one little thing I could do toward pulling them out of nonexistence.

"Do you ever think about that other life, Dad? I just wish I'd taken the time to find out her last name."

"What? Whose name?"

"Your Emily in the other timeline. I mean, maybe she's not married, and maybe—"

"Hey, hey—no. No, Kate. I have Sara in this timeline, and I'm perfectly happy with that." He gives my shoulder a squeeze. "And I have *you* in this timeline, and I'm even more happy with that."

We're both silent for a minute, and then he says, "To be honest, Kate, I haven't thought about it much. I mean, what if I told you some story about how you'd decided to stick with the piano lessons when you were nine—"

"That wouldn't happen in any timeline, Dad."

"—and you became this seventeen-year-old virtuoso, playing at Carnegie Hall? Would you spend time obsessing over that lost future?"

I don't even have to think about it. "No, but I wouldn't want that future. I hated practicing, and I hated recitals, so no. But it's not the same thing. You seemed really happy."

"And I've been really happy in this timeline, too. I'm not exactly doing the happy dance right now, because my kid is carrying the weight of the world—and I mean that very close to literally—on her shoulders, and I can't do much to help. But I'm holding out hope that I'll be really happy again at some point. So no, Kate. I'm not going to sleep at night thinking about that alternate future. If that's one of the things weighing you down right now, it shouldn't be."

I turn around so that I can look him square in the eyes, and I'm pretty sure he's telling me the truth. "Okay. But to get back to what started this whole meltdown, the thing that got me through the jump to 1893 was knowing that it was the only way to get my life back—or at least to get you, Mom, and Katherine back."

There's a pause, and then he says, a bit hesitantly, "And Trey, too?"

"Yeah." I was thinking exactly that but opted to sidestep the whole talking-with-Dad-about-my-love-life thing. "Three out of four's not bad. And I'm not giving up on making it four out of four."

He pulls me forward and plants a kiss on my forehead. "Give it time, Katie."

"That's sort of the problem. I want to give it time. I want to spend time with him. I want to see him at school and hang out with him, because there *is* a connection there. I can feel it just below the surface . . ."

I sigh. It's hard enough to wrap my head around this, let alone put it in words. "I guess . . . last time, I didn't have a choice. I had to set the timeline straight in order to get my life back, and there was at least a small chance of getting Trey back as well. And I had a concrete, specific task—save Katherine at the Fair. Not exactly a piece of cake, as it turned out, but at least I could . . . conceptualize it, you know?"

He nods, and I continue. "This time, however, I'm kind of okay with the timeline I see right here and now. Trey and I aren't where we were, where I want us to be, but I think it could happen eventually. Whatever Saul and the Cyrists are planning is this big, amorphous evil that I can't pin down. I don't even know where these other medallions are, and even after we find them, we still have to take on Saul, Prudence, and probably Simon to get their keys. Prudence has warned me not to interfere again, and any little step I take seems like I'm poking the bear, you know? Asking for trouble.

Part of me just wants to lay low for a while, live my life, and hope maybe she'll let her guard down."

"But . . . ?" he asks.

"The other part says I'll never get a decent night's sleep until every single medallion is crushed into smithereens so that no one, not even me, can tamper with whatever timeline we end up with. The only thing that both parts of me agree on is that uncertainty drives me crazy."

"Okay, what I said earlier about talking to someone—" He holds up his hand as I start to speak. "No, wait, hear me out. You're right—if we took you to see a professional, they'd lock you up or have you on so many antipsychotic drugs you wouldn't be able to see the medallion, let alone use it. But. Maybe you need both parents in this? Your mom would take a little while to adj—"

"No, Dad. No. Yesterday, I might have agreed with you, but . . ." I might as well tell him. "Okay, she's planning to call today, and I'd rather you didn't let her know I told you first, but she's got this really incredible work opportunity. I'll let her give you the details, but it means a lot of travel, and she's leaving middle of next week. I don't think she'll go if we tell her about this. And even though I think Katherine . . ."

I'm about to mention my suspicion that Katherine is behind Mom's research opportunity. But I don't have any logical reason to suspect Katherine had anything to do with it, and she didn't look at all guilty when I mentioned it, so I don't say anything.

"You think Katherine what?"

"It's just . . . they'd argue about all of this. You know they would. Katherine doesn't need the extra stress, and neither do I."

He nods, but his green eyes are wary.

"I know what you're thinking, Dad. I promise I'll take the blame if Mom finds out. I'll say you absolutely begged me to tell her before she left on this trip, but I said no."

"That might pull my ass out of the fire but not yours. I don't want her angry at you, either." His eyes flit up toward the library.

"That won't happen. Mom and I will not end up like Mom and Katherine. Pinky promise."

"Double pinky promise?"

I link our fingers on both hands. "Done and done."

He smiles and squeezes my pinkies with his. Then he glances down at the knuckles on my index fingers, both of which I've gnawed to an angry shade of pink, and the smile fades. "I'm going to have a chat with Katherine. You take this at whatever speed feels best to you, okay? You need time off, you take time off. In fact," he says, looking down at his watch, "you are under parental orders to not even think about any of this for the next twenty-four hours. Get dressed, and pick out a movie. I'm thinking something animated, but it's your choice, as long as it's a comedy. Then, dinner someplace that isn't here. After which you will sleep a minimum of ten hours, with no freaky dreams."

I roll my eyes, but I'm also smiling. "Yeah, right."

"Don't argue with your father. You're not to go anywhere near that diary until tomorrow. And if Katherine can't handle that, she can find another time traveler to run her errands."

∞

Pixar and popcorn rock as a distraction combo. Then we go to Dave and Buster's, and I kick Dad's butt at *Fruit Ninja*. (And he kicks mine at Skee-Ball.) My mind slips back into worry mode a few times, but this afternoon is the closest I've been to stress-free in months.

We get back, and I work out for a little while, but I'm a bit sore from my marathon session last night. When I finish, I run a hot bath, toss in some lavender-scented flakes, and enjoy a long, luxurious soak. It's still only a little after eight when I get out of the tub. I pull on pajamas anyway and curl up on my couch, debating whether to download a new novel or watch a movie.

I'm movied out, so I opt for the book, but a half hour later, it isn't holding my interest. I keep glancing at the diary, which seems more tempting now, possibly because I'm under parental orders to ignore it.

I pick it up and click on link <u>34</u>, recorded shortly after the Dallas trip in this earlier version of the timeline. Other-Kate is eating baby carrots dipped in something green that I can't identify, so I get to listen to her crunch and talk at the same time. I'm both kind of disgusted and kind of thinking the carrots look good, especially if that dip has wasabi in it.

She starts out talking about training, but then the word "*Sputnik*" catches my attention, so I scan back to the beginning of the sentence:

> Anyway, Katherine thinks Moehler's there to observe a press conference about *Sputnik*, but this is based on her recollection of a weekly meeting where the historians went around the table and reported on what they were doing. There were thirty-six altogether, and when she was in that meeting, she had no way of knowing that it would be the last one. Also, that was over forty years ago, so who knows how much she really remembers?
>
> Apparently no one in the U.S.S.R. thought the launch was a big deal, until they realized the American press was in a frenzy. What started out as a one-paragraph blurb on an interior page of *Pravda* on October 4th balloons into a multipage, patriotic frenzy in the next day's edition. So, the conference could be on either of those two days.

She stops to crunch another carrot before continuing:

But Connor doesn't think the Russians bothered with press conferences at all. Why hold a press conference when you have state-owned media? You'd just give *Pravda* what you wanted in the paper. He thinks Katherine is barking up the wrong tree, and I agree. Since Connor rarely argues with Katherine to her face, however, I had to challenge her on it.

The bigger question for me is what kind of idiots send observers to Russia in the middle of the Cold War? I mean, sure, they probably trained for years, and they probably could blend in with the locals a lot better th—

I hit "Pause." Anytime this Kate strays away from talking about events that happened and ventures into the land of opinion, it's a bit like watching myself in a mirror. It's both freaky and boring, because she says what I've been thinking, using the same phrases and the same hand gestures. There's a good seven minutes of this remaining, and I'm pretty sure she's just venting and isn't going to say anything I haven't thought of already, so I fast-forward a few minutes and click "Play."

—putting together an early 1900s outfit. I can't say I'm wild about that, but going to Florida sounds good. There's a stable point at Fort Myers, beginning 1895, labeled "Edison/Ford/Koreshans." Thomas Edison and Henry Ford had summer homes there, and after a little digging, I found out that the Koreshans were an obscure cult who moved about ten miles outside of Fort Myers in 1895 to start their own little utopia. Here's the thing that caught my interest—*Koresh* is the Hebrew word for Cyrus.

I stop and replay the last part to be sure I heard correctly and then rush down the hallway and into the library, eager to share my find. Katherine is at one of the three computers. I slide the diary in front of her and click to play that section again.

"It's not Saul," Katherine says before the clip even finishes, turning again to face the computer screen.

"How do you know? That would have to be a pretty major coincidence, right? Did you catch the last part?" I start to rewind the video, trying to hit the sweet spot after Other-Kate finishes complaining about Katherine and before she starts talking about Florida.

"I caught it. I've checked this before. Koresh is not Saul." She opens a browser window and pulls up a picture of Cyrus Reed Teed, a.k.a. Koresh. He's a middle-aged man with deep-set eyes and a square face, and he doesn't look anything like Saul.

"I'm not saying there's no connection or that Saul didn't know about him," Katherine continues. "He was a religious historian, and he studied a lot of these fringe groups. But they were definitely around before he started tweaking the timeline. They're an obscure group, but you'll find several mentions of them in the library." She inclines her head toward the shelves behind her, where hundreds or, more likely, thousands of books fill the walls from top to bottom on three sides of the room.

The books in this library were all written before Saul made the changes that created Cyrist International. They've been under the constant protection of a CHRONOS field, thanks to the gizmo Connor rigged up that makes this house a safe zone. It also makes the library look bizarre, at least to anyone with the CHRONOS gene who can detect the brightly colored tubes that stretch from floor to ceiling and meet in the center of the room in a large X.

"The Koreshans are, as you put it before, 'real history,' not something Saul manufactured, and Cyrus Teed is certainly not Saul."

I sigh. "Fine. I'll get back to it, then."

"Wait. Could we talk for a minute?"

I nod, even though I can tell from her expression and clipped tone of voice that this is likely to be an uncomfortable conversation.

"First, your mother called while you were out. She said she's already discussed this Italian trip with you and you're fine with it, but she wanted to be sure that it was okay for you to be here full-time while she's away. And I told her of course it's okay."

I hesitate for a moment and then decide to ask straight out. "So you didn't know about the trip until she called?"

Katherine looks confused. "No. Why would I?"

"Well, you worked at a university in Italy, and . . ."

She laughs. "There's more than one university in Italy, Kate. You make it sound like Italy is a tiny village. I can assure you Deborah didn't get this opportunity because I pulled strings."

Katherine seems sincere, but I don't entirely believe her. She's a skilled actress, and it's less the location that makes me suspicious than the timing. This opportunity landed in Mom's lap just when it became convenient for Katherine to have her out of the way for a while. But I'm not sure it really matters either way, since I wouldn't tell Mom even if Katherine confessed she instigated the whole thing.

"Second, I had a long talk with your father this morning. I'm . . ." She stops and takes a deep breath. "I'm *sorry* if I've been pushing you too hard. That's the last thing I want to do, Kate."

I shrug. "It's okay—"

"No," she says, taking my hands in hers. "It's not okay. It may be somewhat unavoidable, but that still doesn't make it okay. I love you, and I would give anything for you to be able to return to your regularly scheduled life. If I'm pushing too hard, it's because I'm frustrated I can't do this for you."

I give her credit for not stating the most obvious source of her frustration—the tumor that is the eight-hundred-pound gorilla in the room, even though it probably only weighs an ounce or so. Absent that, Katherine wouldn't feel like her clock was running out, like she might never know if we stop Saul. And even though she doesn't say it, the fact that she's dying, that she may only have a few months left, hangs in the air like something tangible.

I give her a sad smile and reach over to take the diary from the desk. "Well, if it's not Saul, I should get back to it. You said you had a Russian language program of some sort?"

"On the shared drive. You'll also find a file labeled *Agenda*, although it's really more my detailed recollections of who was going where the day of that final CHRONOS jump. Take a look at it, and then let us know what you're willing to do and when you're willing to do it."

Her apology a moment ago sounded sincere, but I can't help feeling that this last statement is a bit of a dig at me, as though I'm acting like a prima donna or something. "Katherine, I'm not trying to call all of the shots here. I just . . ."

She presses her lips into a thin line and holds my gaze for a moment. When she speaks again, her voice is strained. "You're the one making the jumps, so you'll be the one setting the pace and deciding what happens when. Harry made that quite clear this afternoon. I'm working now on getting together the costumes, but otherwise, the only thing Connor and I are good for is background research. So, like I said, just let us know."

With that, Katherine turns back to the computer screen, a clear signal that I'm dismissed. I return to my room, feeling that I'm being childish and unreasonable but also resenting the fact that she's made me feel that way. She has an uncanny ability to make an apology feel like a scolding.

I open the diary again and click on the next entry. This is one of the rare clips that's actually named instead of just numbered: <u>Fort Myers 040302</u>. When Other-Kate pops up on the screen, I see that she's on location in this video. Maybe that's why it gets a name?

Her hair is pulled back in a bun, with a few wilted strands sticking to her neck and forehead. The bed behind her is wrapped in some sort of thin cloth, and she's seated in a high-backed wooden chair, wearing a white camisole that's plastered to her body, the glow of the CHRONOS key showing through the fabric. A long-sleeved, white blouse-and-skirt combo hangs from one of the bedposts. It's similar to the one that I wore in Boston, except the blouse buttons up the front.

She doesn't look happy and speaks in a low whisper:

> Remember when I said that going to Florida sounded good? Well, it's not. This is a godforsaken jungle with mosquitoes as big as hummingbirds. I found a fat green lizard sitting smack-dab in the middle of that bed, like he owned the place. I couldn't catch him, so he's still around here somewhere. Very glad I'm not actually sleeping in this room. I've set it as a stable point, however, so I can come and go from here, and I'm waiting now for my luggage to be delivered from the boat—the story is that I'm a reporter doing a feature on Koreshan Unity for a newspaper up north. And the room will give me some place that I can retreat to so that I don't pass out from wearing multiple

layers of clothes in this insane heat. This is April, but it feels more like August.

Anyway, tomorrow is Sunday—

Her body tenses for a second, and then she raises her right hand and slaps her left shoulder. She wrinkles her nose in distaste as she stares down at her palm and then holds it up to the camera. A large black-and-red smear decorates the inside of her hand.

> See? They are huge, bloodthirsty monsters, but at least I got one of them.

Part of the mosquito still clings to her skin. I reflexively wipe at my own shoulder, which is, of course, free of mosquito splatter. It's hard to concentrate on what she's saying with that reddish-black streak staring at me, and I wish I could reach into the holographic display and wipe it off my—her—shoulder.

> Okay . . . what was I—oh, yeah, Sunday is when the Koreshans have musical concerts. There's an open invitation to people in the surrounding area—they have several flyers up here in Fort Myers, and a boat will be at the docks to take people to the settlement at 1 p.m.
>
> I know Katherine is right, and this place was around before the Cyrists were formed, but several things bother me. The fact that Koresh means Cyrus. The fact that they were in Chicago for several years around the time of the World's Fair, when Katherine and Saul made dozens of jumps to that city. Finally, a few of the dates don't match up. According to what Katherine has in the CHRONOS-protected files, Estero was founded in 1904, but when Connor started digging around, he discovered the group

incorporated three years earlier in this timeline and seems to have a larger following. The date could be a typo, but we agreed it was worth checking out—

So do I. Curious to see if the dates have also changed in this timeline, I close the diary, grab my tablet, and open a Wikipedia search for *Koreshan Unity*. I'm instantly redirected to a different page. I stare at the words at the top of the entry for a minute, then jump up and rush down the long, curved hallway to the library.

"Katherine! I thought you said—"

But Katherine is no longer there.

Connor holds up his hand. "Downstairs. But I'm pretty sure she's napping, so it'll have to wait. What's up?"

I drop into an office chair, roll toward him so that we can both see the screen, and point to the little link under the words *Cyrist International*. It reads "Redirected from Koreshan Unity."

Connor nods. "Yeah. That's one of the groups the Cyrists gobbled up. It was perfect for Saul, since Koresh is another word for Cyrus."

"But Katherine said, just a few minutes ago, that they weren't connected. That Saul might have known about them but nothing more. And, yeah—I mean, he's definitely not Saul, based on the picture she showed me, but if Wikipedia redirects . . ."

"Because Wikipedia is infallible?" he laughs, setting the iPad down on the desk.

"No. But why did Katherine tell me they aren't connected when they clearly are?"

He leans back in his chair. His elbows are on the armrests, and he rubs his temples, his mouth forming a grim line. It's probably just that I've seen Kiernan do the temple-rubbing gesture several times, but this is the first time Connor has ever reminded me the slightest bit of his great-grandfather.

"What?" I ask.

Connor still doesn't say anything for a few seconds and then tilts his head back and looks at the ceiling. "She's *sick*, Kate. You know that. She's always saying she's fine, but this isn't the first time she's forgotten some difference between the two timelines. And the mood swings—she gets annoyed a lot more easily, especially at you. Minor personality changes can be 'roid rage from the steroids, or maybe the tumor is growing faster again. Either way, she won't take time out to go back into the hospital when there's really nothing they can do. Hell, she won't even let me hire a nurse to help keep track of her medications, because she's worried it would be too difficult to hide this CHRONOS insanity from someone coming in and out of the house on a daily basis. You remember the fit she pitched about the whole karate thing, and that was only two hours a week."

I definitely remember. I was in my room, going through some diary entries last Monday. When I glanced up at the clock, I realized it was nearly four thirty, which meant I'd completely missed my three o'clock karate lesson with Sensei Barbie. Katherine was downstairs when she rang the bell and turned Barbie away at the door. She canceled the lesson, saying there'd been a change of plans. The only reason I found out is that Barbie called my cell and left a message, noting that Katherine not only didn't pay her but didn't even apologize for making her drive all the way over. I called back to apologize and promised she'd be reimbursed for her trouble but only got her answering service. I'm guessing Katherine was incredibly rude, because Barbie still hasn't called back. Katherine's response? She decided I was too busy with research to take time off for a lesson. I told her not to cancel my plans without asking and chalked it up to the fact that she'd been lukewarm about lessons all along. Now I wonder whether it was another of these mood shifts.

"So you think she's getting worse?" I ask.

"She's terminal, Kate. That means she will *only* get worse. Based on what the doctor said the last time, I think she still has several months left, but there are no guarantees, especially when she isn't resting like she should. I mean, the whole drama over the diary when you got back from Dallas . . ."

"Yeah?"

"I don't blame you, but it wouldn't have mattered. She can barely use the equipment at all now. I don't know if it's the tumor or the medications, but I saw her hurl one of the diaries across the room the other day, because she couldn't get it to scroll." He leans forward and says in a lower tone, "If you mention this to Katherine, I will totally deny I said it. I'll flat out lie, because she needs to feel someone is in her corner right now. But I don't think we can count on her to make decisions at this point."

I cross my arms and look down at the floor. "Okay. Understood. I'll just get back to—"

"Kate, wait a minute, okay? I saw you this morning in the kitchen, and I was here when Harry talked to Katherine today. I *get* it. I do. This is just a god-awful situation for everyone and—"

"And I'm the only one who can do anything about it."

He nods. "It sucks, but yeah. That pretty much sums it up. No pressure, right?"

I give him a halfhearted smile. "So, since Katherine isn't a reliable resource right now, what can you tell me about these Koreshan guys? Do you know why the dates are different?"

"Well, Saul isn't Koresh, and he isn't the half dozen or so other cult leaders whose followers he, um . . . appropriated? But we do know he sank a lot of resources into those groups to lure them into the fold. The dates are probably just different because they had more followers and more money at that point. But I'll do some research."

"Thanks. I'm going to be at Mom's for the next few days—we don't have long until she leaves, and I need to spend some time with her. But I'll put together a tentative list of the order in which I think we need to tackle these jumps while I'm there and talk it over with you, Dad, and Katherine when I get back. Does that work for you?"

"It does, but I'm wondering why you're leaving out of the equation the one person who actually has the ability to help you."

I don't follow him at first, and then I realize he means Kiernan. He's right. Kiernan's abilities with the key may be somewhat limited, but he's the only other person who can use it—at least, the only one who's on our side. And he knows more about what we've tried in the past than anyone else, except for Other-Kate, who isn't exactly available for a question-and-answer session.

I pause a little too long, I guess, because Connor continues. "You think he's still loyal to the Cyrists?"

"No. Absolutely not." I think back to Kiernan's expression at the cabin on the Wooded Island, after he saved me from the hotel, when I asked if he was still in this fight. "He hates them as much as anyone. It's just—it's hard for him to jump very far out of his timeline. He said it drains him and . . ."

"Hard, but not impossible for a short time." Connor gives me a long, searching look. "That's what you said before, right? Is there some other reason you're keeping him at a distance?"

I sigh and pull my knees into the chair. "Kiernan wants to help. But . . . it feels like I'm rubbing salt in a wound. I don't want to make it worse or to . . . encourage him, I guess? He's been hurt enough. When he looks at me—"

"He's an adult, Kate. If he hates Saul and the Cyrists as much as you say, shouldn't you let him make that decision?"

"I don't want to hurt him. I already feel like I owe him so much, and I have nothing to give back. I'm just a reminder of what he's lost."

Connor shakes his head. "The only valid reason to keep him at a distance on this is if, deep down, you really don't trust him."

"It's not a question of trust, Connor."

Unless, says this teeny-tiny voice in the back of my head, *you don't entirely trust yourself?*

∞6∞

BOSTON
July 25, 1905, 11:35 a.m.

Kiernan sleeps with his head on one arm, his body curled around a pillow. I watch him for a moment, and then a shiver runs through me as I imagine how I'd feel if I discovered someone was, without my knowledge, watching me while I slept. But why is he still asleep at ten in the morning? I thought people were all early to bed, early to rise in 1905. Apparently not Kiernan.

It also occurs to me that I have no clue what he sleeps in. Or doesn't sleep in. And he could throw those covers off at any second. So I jump ahead to noon, only to discover an empty room. I work my way backward in five-minute increments and finally hit the jackpot at 11:35. He's awake and sitting on the bed, in black pants and a long-sleeved white shirt, buttoned up to the neck. A thin black strip of cloth—a tie of some sort, maybe?—hangs down around his collar on both sides.

He got a haircut, and it really looks better long. Not that it's any of my business, of course. I take a deep breath and then blink to lock in the destination.

As always, his face lights up when he sees me. "Kate! It's Thursday. I thought you were coming on Saturday?"

"Oh. No. I mean, yes, I am." I'd actually kind of forgotten about Saturday, which I suspect would hurt his feelings. Hopefully, if I just barrel ahead, I'll outrun his uncanny knack for reading every expression that crosses my face. "This is something else. I was going to ask for your advice about a couple of jumps, but I can see you have plans. I'll just come back later."

"I'm heading out to work, yes. But I can just as easily go tomorrow. What's up?"

"No, that's okay. I'd hate to make you miss a day of work."

He laughs. "I don't plan to miss a day of work. I'll go to today's work tomorrow. Or the day after."

I glare at him, because he's clearly enjoying messing with my head. I really should be getting a handle on this whole temporal-relativity thing, however, after the past few days. The cancer may limit the time Katherine has left, but as long as I don't screw with my memories by having two versions of myself in the same place at the same time, there's nothing to stop me from doubling and tripling up if needed. All told, I've put in about a hundred hours of research and an additional thirty hours spending time with Mom, running errands for her and so forth in preparation for her trip to Italy.

"Okay," I say, sitting on the side of his bed. "I've spent the last . . . I don't know, but it feels like a century . . . watching the diary entries and going through Katherine's notes. We're going to have a meeting about it tomorrow, and I think it would help if you were there."

"So, it's been what . . . a week since you were here?"

"The calendar says six days, but I did most of those hours two or three times."

"What happened to your decision to take things slow? To wait until you—as you put it—know the hell what you're doing?"

"Partly Katherine. But mostly me realizing I'll probably never know the hell what I'm doing." It was intended as a joke. A lame one, admittedly, but Kiernan either doesn't get it or doesn't think it's funny, because his eyes are somber, still locked on my face.

"Can you tell me what you remember about two trips discussed in the diary?" I ask. "The first is to 1902. You've talked about the Cyrist Farm on a number of occasions, but where was it?"

"There's more than one. I was at a farm in Illinois just before you and I met at the Expo, back when that place was the head-quarters. That farm still exists, but most of us had moved down to Estero by 1902—"

"That's in Florida, right? And that's where you met Other-Kate?"

"Yeah. She was nosing around Nuevo Reino—well, that's not what it was called back then, but it's what they call it later. Cyrist International is still officially headquartered in DC, but Saul has been in the Miami area since shortly after he landed in 2024. Only a few people know exactly where, because he moves around, but he has a house there."

I make a mental note to let Katherine and Connor know the actual year Saul landed and then get to the main point. "So, here's the thing. Katherine says the Koreshans aren't the same as the Cyrists. That they were around before Saul. But everything I'm seeing—"

"Katherine's sort of right and sort of wrong. The Koreshans definitely existed. They were an odd little group that thought the universe was a hollow sphere, with Earth in the center, based on some visions that Cyrus Teed had after getting the bloody hell shocked out of him during a scientific experiment in his basement. He said this beautiful woman came to him and told him he would lead his followers to salvation and eternal life by building this new community. He renamed himself Koresh and developed plans for a place he called New Jerusalem that would one day hold ten million people, or so he claimed. He was pretty forward thinking on some things—believed women should have the vote, for example, and that God was both male and female. That's probably one reason that he attracted a lot of followers, especially women, and they were happy to turn over their money to help him build this new paradise.

"When Teed died in 1908, he said he'd be reincarnated or resurrected. It was all built up around this idea of communal purity. If men and women lived together in pure—that is, sex-free—harmony, they'd become immortal. Cyrus died three days before Christmas, so they all thought he'd rise up on Christmas Day. His followers just put him in a bathtub and waited. In the pre-Saul timeline, I think the county eventually came in and made them bury him."

"Yeah," I say. "I read about that in an old religious history text in Katherine's library. The group gradually died out after realizing Koresh wasn't coming back."

He nods. "Which is how most of these groups end. In this case, they decided if God didn't resurrect Koresh himself, the very foundation of their faith, what hope did his lowly followers have?"

"But the records show Cyrist International was founded back in the 1400s, right? So . . . why take over this group in the early 1900s?"

"Sometimes it's easier to just change the historical record, rather than changing history itself. The date you'll usually see for Cyrist International—I should know this—1470 something . . ."

"It's 1478."

"Yeah, well the only thing that happened in 1478 is that Prudence, or maybe it was Simon, went back and paid this guy William Caxton, who was the first person in England with a printing press, to print up some copies of the *Book of Cyrus*. A few years later, they do the same for the *Book of Prophecy*. Then, they make sure those books end up in a few archives. The *B of P* included accounts of so-called miracles Cyrus would perform later—in a couple of cases, it even gives a rough idea of the dates. And there's lots of predictions in there too, things that shouldn't've been known when the book was printed. As those dates roll past and predictions come true, folks start thinking maybe this Cyrus guy was the real deal."

"So the miracles—are those the cures that Katherine mentioned? Things Saul did before he blew up CHRONOS headquarters?"

"Yeah. And the prophecies start attracting believers kind of like that Nostradamus guy, except the *B of P* doesn't leave as much room for interpretation. So, with the Koreshans and a handful of other groups, all Saul did is cash in on an opportunity. He invested enough money in Cyrus Teed's little commune to push the plans for the move to Estero forward by about six years. And he had Prudence orchestrate several so-called visions, convincing Teed to give up this silly Hollow Earth idea and some other views Saul thought were bunk. And in these visions, Prudence tells Teed that she's his future female incarnation, which he probably thought was a pretty sweet upgrade. She even shows up as a vision to a few of the other Koreshan leaders. Then, Teed dies."

"Only it's now in 1901 instead of 1908, right?"

"Yeah. I suspect his death wasn't entirely accidental in either timeline, but Saul pushed it forward seven years. Then, the true believers pile him into the tub, and—"

"Did these people actually think Teed was going to rise up out of that tub after being dead for several days? How could any-one possibly take those claims seriously? Especially when he was spouting all of that Hollow Earth nonsense."

Kiernan starts to say something and then stops, just staring at me for a minute, like he's weighing something pro and con. Finally, he says, "We need to go on a field trip."

"What? No!"

"Some things you have to see, love. Me telling you is a poor substitute." He gets up and goes behind the red curtain tacked up in the opposite corner.

"No," I say and start to follow him. Then I remember what he said about dressing and undressing behind the curtain and sit back down. "This is a very bad idea, Kiernan. I'm not going anywhere, so you might as well leave on your waiter or maître d' uniform or whatever it is."

"Not a waiter. Not a maître d'. If you want to know what I do out at Norumbega, you'll just have to come see on Saturday."

"I already said I would, and I will. But I'm not going to this Nuevo . . . whatever you called it."

He comes out from behind the curtain, tucking the ends of a tan shirt into a pair of brown pants. He gives my clothes a quick scan and shakes his head, apparently dissatisfied with my shorts and tank top. "I'd say to just go in that, since no one will see you, but you'll freeze."

"Kiernan, I'm serious. I'm not going."

"Safe, Kate. It's totally safe." He crouches on the floor in front of me and starts to pry up the loose board under his bed.

"You can't know that. What if someone sees us?"

He pulls out the cloth bag that contains my dress and shoes and puts it in my lap.

"I lived on that farm, Kate. I worked in that stable most days. I know every nook and cranny, every hiding place, because I put all of them to good use. And . . ." He lets out a breath. "We were there in the other timeline. We watched from the loft. No one saw us then; no one will see us now."

"But that means we'll run into *you*, so—"

He shakes his head. "It doesn't matter that I remember being there with my Kate—although I do remember it vividly. New timeline means if you're not there, I wasn't either. You and I will be the only two souls in that loft."

"Ri-i-ght. But . . ."

He gives me a sly smile. "Isn't there any way you trust me? I swear on the soul of my father, Durango Montoya—"

"Stop it." I glare at him. "First, it's *Domingo* Montoya. And second . . ."

"Second?" he asks when I don't finish the sentence.

Second, you're not the person I want quoting "The Princess Bride" to me. But it would hurt him for me to say that, and I don't want to hurt him. It's perfectly natural that Other-Kate shared the things she loved with Kiernan. Just as I did with Trey. And it isn't fair to hold that against him.

"I don't need a second reason," I say, forcing a smile. "The first is enough to count twice."

He's giving me that searching look again, like he's reading my face for hidden clues. He gives up after a few seconds and just stares down at the floor. "Do you honestly think I would ever put you in danger, Kate?"

"No. I know you wouldn't. If you didn't believe it was relatively safe, you wouldn't suggest it. But even if there's only a teeny, tiny, infinitesimal risk, is it worth it just for a bit of amusement?"

His eyebrows shoot upward. "You think this is for pleasure? Oh, God—no. You're not going to enjoy this one bit. Neither will I." He takes my hand and looks up at me. "Can you please just trust me on this one? You need to *see* this. You need to see firsthand the type of resistance we will face."

∞

ESTERO, FLORIDA
December 24, 1901, 11:50 p.m.

News flash: the Sunshine State can be freaking cold on a windy December night. The 1905 dress covers almost every inch of skin above the ankle, but it's thin, and I immediately feel the wind cutting through the fabric. Kiernan told me to crouch low prior to the jump, so the first things I see when I open my eyes are the wooden slats of the floor beneath my feet. Pale yellow light seeps through the spaces between the boards, diffused by a thin layer of straw. Several yards away I see the dimly lit walls of the stable below us. Someone is playing a violin. After a few notes, I recognize the song—"O Holy Night."

I quickly drop the CHRONOS key into a leather pouch Kiernan gave me and pull the drawstring to close it, tucking the bundle down the front of my shirt. Kiernan is crouched a few feet to my right. He looks at the hay bales on both sides of us, and then he motions for me to follow. I creep toward him, and we inch forward about three yards to the right, squeezing through an opening between the bales of hay. I crawl into the far corner, and Kiernan sits with his back against the hay so that he can watch the ladder.

There's a window in front of me, and a tiny sliver of moon hangs in the sky, nearly obscured by the clouds. I'm quickly discovering why people say "drafty as a barn," because the wind whistles around us, and the chill cuts clear to the bone. I pull my arms around my legs and tuck the edges of my skirt underneath me. Kiernan reaches behind the closest bale of hay and pulls out a blanket, which he unfolds and wraps around us. It is a bit musty but wonderfully thick. This seems an odd place for a blanket, however, and how did he know it was there? I give him a little nudge with my elbow, and when he looks at me, I flick my eyes down to the blanket, then back up to him, one eyebrow raised in question.

"It's . . . I've spent some time up here, okay?" he whispers, seeming embarrassed. "The view is a little clearer over to the left of the ladder, but I knew you'd need the blanket."

I decide not to press the point and definitely not to think about who else might have been under this blanket. It's bad enough to visualize Kiernan with my other self. I most certainly don't want a mental image of him up here with Prudence.

The stable below us appears fairly ordinary, but this is based entirely on secondhand experience from stables I've seen in movies or on TV. There's a line of stalls along one wall and a large, open space in the middle, punctuated every twenty feet or so by a vertical support beam. It looks like there might be stalls on this side of the building as well, but I can't tell from where we're sitting. Farm implements and horse gear—saddles, bridles, and such—hang from one wall, along with a shelf that holds tongs and some odd-looking tools. Straw covers the ground, and most of the stable is at least partially hidden in the shadows.

Directly beneath us is a brightly lit circle, where a cluster of people are gathered around a white claw-foot tub. A sheet of something—glass, maybe, since it reflects the light from the lanterns—rests on top of the tub, with flowers decorating one end. I can't see what's under the glass, and I'm perfectly okay with that.

Seven chairs, draped with white cloth, are arranged in a row just to the left of the tub and are occupied by women of varying ages, similarly dressed, with their hair pulled back into a knot. Beyond the seven chairs, dozens of people, maybe even a hundred or more, extend to the back of the stable. About two-thirds are women and children, and almost everyone is dressed in white. Most are standing, some leaning against support beams, some sitting on hay bales. A few adventurous kids straddle the tops of the low walls separating the stalls.

"The women in front?" Kiernan whispers. "They're the Seven Sisters of the Planetary Court."

I nod. I vaguely remember reading something about them in the historical account but can't recall exactly what their role was in the commune.

When the violinist finishes "O Holy Night," he launches immediately into "Silent Night," and several voices join him. A bearded man with reddish-blond hair pulls out a pocket watch and says something to the matronly woman sitting closest to the tub. She stops singing for a moment, then nods as she closes her eyes and continues with the second verse.

The scene below us would be almost pastoral if I didn't know there was a moldering corpse in that tub.

The blond guy glances at his watch again, then taps the woman's shoulder. She stands and raises her arms high above her head. She's nearly as tall as the man, and her dark hair is streaked with gray. The music stops abruptly, and the other six women rise to join her. They all begin to sway, their eyes closed and faces raised to the rafters.

They move back and forth for about thirty seconds, and then the first woman pulls her arms down abruptly. There's a domino effect as each woman down the line stops swaying, and I choke back a laugh, because they look a lot like fans doing the wave at the Washington Nationals game Dad took me to last summer.

The tall woman's eyes snap open, and she cries out, "Koresh! Our beloved Koresh! We do not mourn your passing."

The crowd murmurs in agreement, and Kiernan moves close to my ear, whispering, "Annie Ordway, but they call her Victoria Gratia. It means 'victory by grace' or something. Koresh's second in command, at least for now."

"For," the woman says, "as the sixth messiah, Jesus, rose on the third day, so shall the seventh messiah rise this Christmas Day. We await your second coming, our prophet, to build our New Jerusalem, our heaven here inside the Earth."

Kiernan gives a silent, little chuckle. "Annie is one of the remaining Hollow Earthers."

"What?"

"Later. Shh . . ." He holds up his hand and leans forward. "Just watch the tub. In three, two, one . . ."

There's a flash of bright blue behind the tub, and a small young woman appears. She's also dressed in white, but it's more like a toga, cinched at the waist and shoulder, with a gold chain reflecting the blue beams from her CHRONOS key. Her arms are stretched out to her sides, her head thrown back, with all-too-familiar dark curls cascading over her shoulders.

Prudence. And she's glowing. It's not just the medallion. Her skin and clothes are literally glowing, like polished metal.

A girl near the horse stalls quietly faints, but no one notices. They're all facing forward, most of them smiling, all of them mesmerized by the vision behind the corpse-laden tub.

Annie Ordway doesn't seem happy, however. She looks stunned and a bit confused, as do two of the other Sisters. The confusion only lasts for a few seconds, and then Ordway goes to her knees. As if on cue, the remaining Sisters drop as well, followed by everyone else in the stable.

"It's paint," Kiernan whispers with a hint of disdain, and I flash back to 1893 and his eight-year-old self looking down at my crimson toenails and telling me his mum said only whores wear paint. "Phosphorescent paint. See the beam over her head and how it looks kind of purple?"

I nod.

"Portable black light, set with a timer for midnight."

The crowd below was silent at first, but a few cries of "Praise God!" and "Praise Koresh!" begin to circulate. Gradually, the exclamations build to a crescendo.

Prudence holds her hands out to the people kneeling before her. I can't see her face at first, until she tips her head back again. She's younger than when I saw her at the Expo. And she's either a killer actress or she's convinced herself, because her face, which is eerily like my own, is illuminated not only by the phosphorescent paint but also by a smile of ethereal joy.

"Rise, children of Cyrus! Rise, rejoice, and follow me in The Way!"

The crowd stumbles to its feet, and Ordway steps forward. Her arms are open. "Welcome, Sister in Koresh! I am Victoria Gratia, and I welcome you into our Unity."

The smile fades from Prudence's face, replaced by an air of stern compassion. "I know you well, Sister Annie. You shall have my grace and my patience as you work to overcome your sins."

Ordway's smile collapses. "My . . . sins?"

"Yes. You and . . . these others," Prudence says, picking out two of the other Sisters with her eyes and a nod of her head, "are guilty of the sin of lust. You placed temptation in the path of Brother Cyrus, but I stand here as proof that his soul remained pure. He has escaped the bonds of mortality and sin."

It's hard for me to view any of the three women as temptresses. The youngest is at least fifty, and all three are covered from neck to ankle. There are gasps, and then a muffled hum fills the stable as one neighbor whispers to another.

Two Sisters at the end farthest from the coffin-tub take a step back from the others. They wear wreaths in their hair, the shorter woman's made of red rosebuds and the other's made of pink. At first, they seem to be arguing, then Pink Rosebuds steps forward and embraces the shorter woman. They just stand there with their heads together for a moment, forehead to forehead, grasping each other's shoulders.

My eyes are drawn back to the center of the barn when one of the women Prudence just outed as a sinner falls to her knees, head bent, and begins to sob. The second woman looks around at the others in the barn, pulls in a deep breath, and joins her on the straw-covered ground.

Ordway stares at the two as she feels behind her for the chair. She sinks into it, looking as though she might vomit.

Prudence smiles at the prostrate women, her face both falsely and genuinely radiant. "Do not grovel, Sisters. There is always hope for those who show remorse."

Her eyes flit briefly to Annie Ordway, still seated, with her chin tilted defiantly. Then Prudence looks back to the two on their knees. "You still have time for your souls to reach perfection. Death cannot claim the pure of heart."

"If Koresh is risen, then why is his body still here?" Ordway challenges.

Prudence tilts her head, giving Ordway a patronizing smirk before smiling back toward the crowd. "What lies before you here is a useless shell, an empty husk. I stand before you as Brother Cyrus, Sister Prudence, Koresh—call me what you will. We are all one in Cyrus. And those who follow me in The Way will find the same reward."

I feel Kiernan's body tense up next to mine. I glance at him, but he shakes his head, directing my attention back to the scene below. He grabs my hand, however, and holds it tightly as the two women who were huddled together in the shadows break apart. Pink Rosebuds walks quickly toward the back wall and grabs something off a shelf near the bridles, while the other one moves into the center of the light, directly facing Ordway and Prudence.

Red Rosebuds points a pale finger at Annie Ordway, but her eyes are on Prudence. "Eloise and I—we never stopped believing, Koresh. After we saw you last week, down at Bamboo Landing, we told the others, including Annie—"

There's a soft gasp from the others, and Red Rosebuds turns to them and says, "I will no longer call her Victoria Gratia, for she is impure. She is not of the Unity." She turns back to Prudence and says, "I told Annie and the others that you would soon die but that you told us not to despair, because your purity would be rewarded with a new, immortal form, just as you've always said. Annie laughed and said we were naive."

Pink Rosebuds, who I assume is actually named Eloise, steps forward at this point. "Not so naive, Annie. We saw how you watched Koresh, how you touched him not as a Sister but as a temptress. But we never wavered, and we, the truly pure, will follow him now."

She turns to Red Rosebuds. "Are you ready, Sister Mary?"

Red Rosebuds nods and Eloise leans across and kisses her on both cheeks. "Go with Koresh, Sister."

There's a flash of something metallic as she steps back. Kiernan's grip on my hand tightens, and then I stare, shocked, at the red line on Mary's throat, just above the collar of her dress. Blood seeps through the lace, but she still smiles at Prudence as she slumps to the ground.

Someone screams, but before anyone can move forward, Eloise turns and says, "I go with Koresh! If you are pure of flesh and spirit, then follow!" She pulls the knife swiftly from left to right across her own throat and slumps down, her blood spattering the coffin-tub in front of her as she falls next to Mary.

Her legs are twitching under the long skirt, as are Mary's, so they're still alive. A small group of people rushes forward, including an elderly man. He bends down, and it looks like he's feeling for Eloise's pulse. Then I realize he's taking the knife from her hand.

Prudence's eyes are huge, and her mouth just sort of hangs there. It's clear that she didn't anticipate this. I want to scream at her to say something, to speak out, because she's the only one who has the power to stop this.

But I'm silent as Kiernan's arms encircle me, and his fingers fly over the interface of my CHRONOS key to bring up the stable point in his room. "Kate, we have to go. There's nothing we can do here."

The old man raises the knife to his throat. I'm pretty sure that my nightmares aren't going to be PG-13 tonight, and I definitely don't want to push them up to NC-17 by watching another suicide. I snatch the medallion from Kiernan, look down at the stable point, and blink.

∞

BOSTON
July 25, 1905, 12:05 p.m.

I arrive in Kiernan's room and sit there, shaking, wondering where the hell he is. Then it hits me that I'm blocking the stable point, so I slide toward the bed.

When he appears, I fly at him, hitting his chest with both fists. "Why did you take me there? Why didn't you warn me?"

"Kate, I'm sorry." He grabs my wrists and moves toward me, trying to put his arms around me, but I push him away. "I'm sorry, but you needed to see that."

"You don't get to decide what I need to see! Just because you showed her—"

"Damn it, Kate—no. No, no, no. That's not it at all." He's still holding my wrists, and he moves closer, his deep brown eyes imploring me to listen. "She took *me*. That's how I knew you needed to see it. I've seen that look of doubt before, not in your—" He sighs. "I didn't see it in *her* eyes. I saw it in my own, in the mirror."

He lets go of my wrists and slumps back against the side of the bed. "Kate made me go back to Estero and see it again. Reminded me just how seriously they take their beliefs and how far they might go to protect them. Reminded me that any group that would stand by and encourage or even allow that type of fanaticism must be opposed. I'm sorry you had to see that. But I still think it was the right thing to do."

A little of the anger drains away, but my eyes are still stinging as I blink back tears. "What happened to the rest of them, Kiernan? The others in the stable? How many died?"

"Only three died in the stable. Then Pru snapped out of it and told them to stop—said that even the purest of soul and body couldn't be resurrected if they resorted to suicide. Told them they had to trust God and the Prophets to know when their time was right, instead of taking it into their own hands. But two more still took their lives before it died down."

"So five people?"

He nods. "The community wanted all five of them put in tubs like Koresh had been. Of course, none of them were resurrected, and that's where the old timeline and the new merge a bit—the county health inspector showed up and made them bury the bodies after about a week. Annie Ordway was more than happy to comply, of course—she was suspicious of Pru from the beginning—but she sacrificed her last bit of credibility with the group when she ordered the burials. They pushed her out. And, yeah, they voted her out in the other timeline, too, but it took a lot longer. Once she's gone, Pru became the leader, although really she was more of a figurehead, since she was gone most of the time."

I'm silent for a moment, thinking through everything he's just told me. "Wait . . . you said Kate made you go back? You were there when it happened?"

He stares at the floor, clearly uncomfortable. "I didn't see anything other than Pru all lit up. I was at the rear of the stable, with Simon. I helped him set up the lighting."

"So you knew what had happened? That those people cut . . ."

"Yes, but it wasn't like that was part of the plan, Kate. You saw Pru's face. She was shocked. I don't know if Saul had any clue that something like that might happen, but she didn't. She was really upset about it. We all were."

My mouth tightens. "Not too upset, or one of you would have gone back and changed it."

He shakes his head. "Pru thought about it, or at least she said she did. But Saul was set against it, and he convinced her those deaths would serve as a warning to others not to assume they were pure enough to be . . . resurrected. Or reincarnated, whatever you want to call it. *Rebooted* was Simon's word for it. Anyway, Saul's argument was that those deaths would deter others and make the community easier to control. It was for the greater good."

"And everyone just said, 'Okay, Saul, whatever you say, Saul'? You, too? No one questioned him at all?"

There's a defensive note in his voice when he responds. "I was barely sixteen, Kate. And tell me, why didn't you yell out that Prudence was a fraud just now? Why didn't you scream when you saw that first woman fall?"

My eyes narrow. "I very nearly did, but we both know that's not the same thing, Kiernan! I was observing something that has already happened. If I screamed, what might have changed? Another timeline where I don't exist? Prudence deciding this little truce we have is off? I couldn't risk that. And it all happened so fast—"

"Exactly. It all happened so fast," he says. "Step back for a minute, and think about what you're saying. Try to see it from my perspective back then. I'm not making excuses for anything, Kate. I was a Cyrist. You know that. I didn't fully trust them, but Mum did."

"But why? You told her about your suspicions. Why would she trust them?"

"Yeah, back when I was *eight*." He laughs, but it's bitter. "Did your mum listen to you about anything even slightly important when you were eight? Mum was unskilled, widowed, and she had a kid to feed. And I *was* still a kid, no matter how grown-up I tried to act. The Cyrists offered her food and shelter for the both of us, and she took it, gratefully. That's true of many, many people who've followed them over the years, Kate. I lived there among them for eight years. Longer than Da was around. You start seeing things different after a while."

He leans back, his elbows on the bed, his face pointed toward the ceiling, still covered with those improbable stars, and lets out a slow breath. "I think trusting them was the only thing that kept my mother sane after my dad died. Because she's the reason he took that job at the Expo when Pru brought it up. She talked him into trusting Prudence. If she hadn't, he'd never have been at the Ice House the day it caught fire and he was killed. So if she was wrong about trusting Pru and the Cyrists . . . well, then maybe she's the reason he died, you know?"

He closes his eyes and is silent for a moment. "I never blamed her. But I knew she blamed herself, so I bit back my suspicions, and we returned to the Farm after the Expo closed down. When they merged with the Koreshans and moved to Estero, we followed.

"Three months before that night in the stable, Simon took me around on a little time tour, to locations selected by Saul. Or maybe older Pru chose them. I don't know for sure. Ever seen videos of concentration camps? Genocide? Nuclear or chemical weapons? One stop was in Africa—a place called Chad—in the early 2020s. A famine in the region, made worse by climate change. Add in refugees and groups who turned on each other when the food and water got scarce. The stack of bodies was taller than I was, and there were dozens of those stacks, Kate. In just that one town. And the rest of the world did nothing until it was too late. That famine was only one of the many places he showed me. Let's just say that 2070 isn't a pleasant decade between the bioweapons and—" He opens his eyes and shifts them in my direction. "I'm guessing you don't want the gory details?"

I shake my head. Leaving aside the fact that I really don't want to know history that won't happen until I'm old and gray, I've seen enough gory details for one day.

"Most of the people I saw died slow, nasty deaths. Saul and Prudence said it just went downhill after 2070. Said they were working for a future that'd change all that, which sounded like a pretty good idea to me at the time. They didn't give me specifics, not then. Not a word about a Culling to wipe out half of mankind. So, yes, I was still a Cyrist when we met at Estero. It took you—she—damn it, I mean *her*." He pounds his fists on his thighs. "It took Kate dragging me back to look directly at that fiasco to make me accept that I'd been part of something evil. Small in scale, maybe, compared to what was coming down the pike, but still capital-*E* Evil."

"What about your mom? Is she still . . . with them?"

"My mom died about eighteen months ago. A little after I left Estero."

I put my hand on his arm. "I'm sorry."

"Yeah, well—she'd been sick for a while," he says, not looking at me. "So it wasn't really a surprise." He claps his hands once and turns to me with a crisp, businesslike smile, clearly intent on changing the subject. "You said you needed to ask me about two jumps. Earlier, when you arrived?"

"Um . . . yeah. 1938?"

"Thought so."

"It's just . . ." I pause, then start over. "I think I have a handle on the other two, pretty much. I mean, we haven't found the guy in Russia yet, and I'm not saying that either of them is straightforward, but I don't get the sense that those jumps are—I don't know, destined to go wrong?"

"We never got the Russian key."

"Okay, but still, knowing what I know about the other timeline, it's pretty hard not to see the 1938 jump to Georgia as a sort of Waterloo, since it's right after that when . . . your Kate disappears."

He nods, but doesn't respond.

"Anyway, I think the Cyrists must currently hold at least one of those keys. Probably all three. She barely enters anything in the diary by that point, and when she does, it's all cryptic. Something about London, and then she's talking about Georgia again, something about the Federal Writers' Project. And then she goes off on a rant about racial injustice, and I'm not clear how all that connects."

"Kate was driving herself pretty hard by the end," Kiernan says. "I mean—don't take this the wrong way, okay? I loved her more than you can ever know, but there were moments she reminded me a bit of Pru that last night we were together. There was a death in 1938. One of the historians was murdered. And she felt responsible. Not like she caused it, but more like she could have stopped it. Should have stopped it. And I'm pretty sure she would have gone back and stopped it if she'd gotten the chance."

"Did she get their keys?"

"Yeah, she did." Kiernan leans forward, staring down at the floor with his elbows on his knees and his hands clasped behind his head. "I was there for that part. They didn't give them over voluntarily. I was along as muscle, in case she needed it, but the knockout drug Katherine gave her worked just fine on the three of them. Then Kate found out later that Katherine . . . she knew all along one of them was gonna die a few days later. And she didn't tell Kate."

"Ouch. Not that I'm exactly surprised, but . . ."

"Kate was so . . . I've never seen her that angry. I convinced her to wait here until I got back from the audition for this job so I could go with her. She needed to calm down before confronting Katherine." He tilts his head to the side and looks at me. "That's the one thing, maybe the only thing, that seems a bit different to me. Between the two of you. She had a harder time reining in her temper."

"Hmph. Well, she'd been with Katherine, what—a little over two years? My own temper is probably on a shorter fuse now than it was a few months ago. I mean, it's partly dealing with Katherine, but I'm guessing the other Kate probably had trouble sleeping, too—"

"Dreams," he says, nodding. "It was rare she slept the full night through. Are they bothering you, too?"

"Yes," I say, and he looks guilty. That look always tugs at my heart, but I have to admit it doesn't tug quite as hard this time, given that what he's just shown me will almost certainly make the nightmares worse. Maybe a little bit of guilt will discourage him from dragging me off on another grisly field trip.

But, deep down, I know he was right to take me. As much as I would like to unsee what happened in Estero, it's one thing to know that there are people out there who believe so strongly in something that they are willing to die for it. It's another thing entirely to know you're up against people who will slit their own throats from ear to ear and continue to smile as their lives drain away, confident that the sacrifice was worth it.

∞ 7 ∞

I've just printed out five copies of a tentative schedule when the doorbell rings, triggering not only the chimes but also a round of Daphne barks from the backyard. I head down the hallway to grab the copies from the printer in the library, assuming someone is downstairs to open the door, until the bell rings again.

I peek out over the railing and through the living room window, where I see two cars parked at the curb. One is the blue van, again, and I get the creepy feeling, *again,* even though I can see there's no one inside—well, at least not in the front.

The other car is a red sedan with a Valenzia's Pizza sign on top. I make it downstairs to open the door just as the deliveryman is reaching out to ring for a third time.

"Someone here definitely ordered that," I say with an apologetic smile, "but he didn't tell me. Hold on, and I'll find some cash."

"No, no, no," the guy says in an accent that is Indian or maybe Pakistani. "He already pay it. Just sign slip." He taps the square of paper and shoves a pen in my direction.

I glance at the receipt and see it's in Connor's name, so I scrawl something that might pass for his signature, add a four-dollar tip, and take the boxes and the bag, which I'm really hoping contains their Greek salad.

Connor comes down the stairs and takes the boxes from me. It's possible that he's just being a gentleman, but I suspect it's more an issue of staking his claim on the pizzas.

"Sorry. Had the headphones on, so I didn't hear the doorbell. I thought we'd order out and give Harry the night off, since he's back at work now." He holds out a small stack of papers. "I'm guessing these are yours?"

I take the papers and put them on the kitchen island. "Not a bad idea. Meetings always go better with pizza."

I let Daphne in from the backyard, and I'm sitting down at the kitchen island, glancing back through the papers for that one typo or omitted word you never find until you're reading a print copy, when it occurs to me that Connor is acting a bit odd. For one thing, he's in the same room as pizza, but the box is still closed. He's usually on his second slice by now. Instead, he's putting away a few pots and pans that were drying on the rack, something I've never seen Connor do. In fact, it might be more accurate to say he's *trying* to put them away, because he's on his third cabinet door before he finally finds the right place for the large pasta bowl.

"You feeling all right, Connor?"

"Yeah, sure. Why?"

"No particular reason. You're just acting a little strange . . ."

He tosses the dish towel down and leans back against the counter before pacing back over to the cabinet to pull out some plates. "Well, this whole situation is strange. I didn't really think about it until a few hours ago, but I'm about to meet my great-grandfather. I've spent the past several years blaming him for the role he played in screwing up my life, cursing him on a daily basis I might add, and then it turns out he might not be quite the bastard I thought. And then to add to the weirdness, the two of you were—" He shudders.

I give him an annoyed look. "No. We were not. That was the other Kate. I can't be held responsible for her actions, you know. And you were the one who said I should pull Kiernan into this—"

"And it was still the right thing to do," he says. "I just hadn't thought through the details. I mean, how do you react to a twenty-year-old great-grandfather?"

"Welcome to my world. At least you don't have to worry about interrupting him while he's making out with your great-grandmother in a parking lot."

"I guess that's some consolation," he says.

Connor goes off to tell Katherine and Dad the pizza has arrived. I'm tossing the contents of the three Styrofoam containers into a big wooden salad bowl, when Daphne lets out a little yelp and cowers under the table.

"What's wrong, girl?"

When I turn around, Kiernan is standing a few steps away from the "Katherine's Kitchen" stable point that I transferred to his key the last time I saw him. He's wearing a plain white shirt and a pair of jeans. If you ignore the CHRONOS key around his neck, he could pass for a typical twenty-first-century guy.

He gives me a smile when my eyes work their way up to his. "Levi Strauss, best friend of time travelers since 1876. Or maybe earlier, I don't know for sure. 1876 is when I got these."

"Lucky you. But I'm pretty sure that Katherine would say it's inappropriate for a female time traveler to wear jeans to any time before the 1960s."

I slip down to the floor and reach under the table to give Daphne a hug. "It's okay, Daph. I'm sorry. I forgot Kiernan would be coming in with the key. You want to go back outside? I'll save you my pizza crusts."

Her tail starts wagging, and she heads to the door, giving Kiernan a wide berth.

"Daphne usually loves visitors," I say as I close the door behind her. "But she's not a big fan of the medallions."

"I've yet to meet a dog that is. Cats just stare at you when you use the key. Some of them will even come over to check it out. Dogs want nothing to do with the bloody things, which makes them the wiser of the two creatures, in my view." He glances around, his nostrils flaring just a bit as he sniffs.

"Are you hungry?"

He sniffs again. "Pizza? Pepperoni, if I'm not mistaken."

"Pepperoni and bacon, to be precise. Your great-grandson's pizza of choice."

"I'm glad to hear that the little tyke has good taste."

We grab a few slices, and I convince him to try some of the salad, which he eyes with suspicion. "What's all the white stuff?"

"The white stuff," I say, grabbing two sodas out of the fridge, "is feta. Greek cheese. The black stuff is olives. Those are also Greek. And that green stuff—"

"You're very funny, Kate," he says as we squeeze into the breakfast nook. "I lived on a farm most of my life, you know, and believe it or not, we grew that green stuff."

We both look up as Katherine, Connor, and Dad enter the kitchen. Kiernan tries to be polite and stand, but I'm on the outside of the bench, and the table has him wedged in, so the most he can manage is a half crouch, which looks terribly uncomfortable.

I grab the back of his shirt and tug him back down to the bench. "Dad, Connor, this is Kiernan. Katherine, you've already met."

"He's changed quite a bit in the past thirteen years, however," she says. "And I suspect that I've changed even more in the past five decades."

Kiernan returns her smile. "It's good to see you again."

Dad steps forward and shakes Kiernan's hand. "It's a pleasure to meet you."

"My privilege, Mr. Keller."

"It's Harry, please. You saved my daughter's life, so I think we can dispense with the formalities."

I've rarely seen Kiernan blush, but he does now, and then he nods. "Harry, then. Pleased to make your acquaintance."

Connor follows Dad's lead and steps forward to take Kiernan's hand. "I'm Connor Dunne. And you can call me Mr. Dunne."

There's a slight twinkle in Connor's eye, so I think he's joking. But whether he meant it that way or not, Kiernan laughs.

"The hell I will, sonny boy. You need to show your elders the proper respect, or I'll take you behind the barn and give you a good strapping."

Connor snorts. "No barn, and I'd love to see you try."

I just shake my head at the two of them and take a few more bites of my pizza and salad while Katherine, Connor, and Dad get their food.

When the chomping dies down a bit, I pass the handouts around. "Take a couple of minutes to look things over while you finish eating, and then we'll discuss, okay?"

The paper is basically a three-page summary of everything I've managed to glean from Other-Kate's diary, Katherine's recollections of the CHRONOS historians' itineraries, and several additional, torturous hours of observing jump locations in the *Log of Stable Points*. At least with the diary entries, someone's talking. The stable points are like silent movies—if silent movies also carried the risk that you'd jump into the middle of them if you accidentally blinked too hard. If I start getting any sensory input other than the visual when I'm watching those, I have to look away really fast. During training, there were several occasions where I was so close to *there* that Katherine said I seemed to fade, like I was half-in and half-out of the location.

Katherine looks up first. "You really think you're ready for the Australia jump now?"

I nod. "I'd like a day to look back over everything and get ready, but Adrienne didn't put up any resistance according to the diary. I'll just need you to record a video explaining things to her. Maybe toss in something that only you would know, so she'll believe you're you?"

Her mouth twists. "I think I can come up with something."

I wait a second to see if she's going to fill us in on that, but apparently she's not.

Dad says, "Don't you have that"—his eyes shift for a split second over to Kiernan, like he's not sure how much to say in front of him—"barbecue thing for school that day?"

"Yes, but it's in the evening." At least, I assume Trey and I are still on for that. Other than a brief text message two days ago, I haven't spoken to him. I finally called him last night but had to leave a message—again. And, of course, I'm now imagining him on the beach with two girls rubbing suntan oil onto his back.

"And we have everything you need for Australia?" Connor asks.

"We have the 1940s' swimsuit. I can't think of anything else. Although I'd feel much better if I could disremember that crocodile."

"Crocodile?" Kiernan's eyes are wide. Everyone else was around to hear my views on the wicked-looking creature that strolls past the stable point around dawn on the morning I'll be going.

Dad nods. "Big one. But that's hours before she arrives. They usually stay away from the beach later in the day, at least from what we were reading." He sounds like he's trying to reassure himself as much as Kiernan and me.

"Yeah," I say. "I'm just hoping Mr. Croc reads the same articles we do. Anyway, counting Timothy and Evelyn's keys, and also the two that Kiernan has, we now have fourteen, correct?"

Connor and Katherine nod, and I continue. "Then that means there are ten more out there. Three of those are in the possession of Saul, Prudence, and Simon, and I think we'd all agree those should be the last ones we attempt to retrieve, both because it will tip them off to what we're doing, assuming always that they don't already know, and also because it's probably going to require force, maybe even lethal force. That's not a discussion we necessarily need to have right now, but at some point I . . ."

I take a sip of my soda, partly to disguise how rattled I am at even having to contemplate killing anyone, but I also want to gauge their reactions. I doubt anyone at the table has qualms about killing Saul. Connor would do it with his bare hands if we had a way to push him far enough into the future that he could confront Saul one-on-one. The consensus on Simon is pretty much the same, although I wonder about Kiernan—from what he's told me, they were once friends. I'm probably the one who's the least okay with the idea of killing either of them, but then I'm almost certainly the one who'll get stuck doing it. Some things sound a lot easier in the abstract.

Prudence is a different matter. She's Katherine's daughter, Mom's sister, my aunt. I don't even like to think about the possibility that the only way to end all of this is to end her, and I suspect Kiernan has similar views.

And that's only stating the three most obvious people who might have to be killed in order to stop the Cyrists. How many others might we have to go through to get to them if or, more likely, *when* our cover is blown? From what Kiernan showed me at Estero, we could face quite a few who are willing to risk their lives for their beliefs. I take a deep breath, trying to forestall an anxiety spiral.

Katherine is at the opposite side of the table, her mouth pressed in a tight line. "As you said, we can cross that particular bridge when we come to it. Saul, Simon, and Prudence will be the final keys."

Kiernan's hand is beneath the table, and he gives my knee a brief squeeze before he speaks. "And when we do reach that bridge, you *will not* be on your own." He looks over at Katherine. "I don't know how much Kate's told you about my relationship with your daughter. All I can say is Prudence was a very troubled young girl when I knew her, and that's only gotten worse now that she's older. Despite the role she played in all of this, it's hard for me to wish her ill. She's battling her own set of demons. Some of her own making, and others Saul created for her. But Kate knows—and I want to be certain all of you know—where my loyalties lie. Leaving aside everything they've taken from me, I don't want the future they're planning."

Katherine nods and then says, "It's good to know we now have two people who can use the keys on our side. Even as historians, when we were simply out there to observe, CHRONOS generally advised us to travel in pairs for the first few years. I've never liked the idea of Kate traveling without backup, no matter how capable she claims to be."

I'm not sure if there was a subtle emphasis on the word *claims* or if I just imagined it. I flash Katherine a tight smile and look back down at the list. "So that leaves seven keys we need to find first."

"Six," Katherine says. "Marcus—the one who was studying the Nazis? He destroyed his key."

"And you're sure that he actually destroyed it?" Dad asks. "For that matter, how *do* you destroy the things? What are they even made of?"

"They're made of something called trinium," Connor says. "A superstrong alloy that hasn't been invented yet."

Dad raises an eyebrow. "Did you say *trinium*? Why does that ring a bell?"

Connor rolls his eyes. "Because it was a geek test. Trinium is a case where the sci-fi name became a self-fulfilling prophecy. So, right now, it's sci-fi, but by Katherine's time, some geeks gave the name to something they created that's stronger than titanium."

"Okay," I say. "Let's pretend that makes sense so that we can get back to Dad's first two questions—do we know for certain this Marcus guy destroyed his key? And second, *how* do we destroy them?"

"I'll add a third," Kiernan says. "Shouldn't you go ahead and destroy most of the ones you already have? Keeping them around seems like it's asking for trouble."

Connor nods. "All good points. I'll take the second question. Short answer: you can't physically destroy it. At least, you can't destroy it with anything I've found. But you can turn it into a relatively worthless hunk of metal. The trinium casing is just the shell, inside which the time travel guts are housed." He nods toward the medallion on Kiernan's chest. "That thing is actually two pieces of trinium fused together. While I can't create a high enough temperature to melt the metal, I can separate the two pieces just enough that the seam along the edge is permeable. Not easy, but it's doable. And while the microscopic pieces inside the shell may be waterproof, they're no match for sulfuric acid."

"Waterproof?" Kiernan says to me out of the side of his mouth. "Knowing that would have made showering a lot easier."

I smile, and then I feel a blush rising to my cheeks. Because now I'm visualizing Kiernan in the shower. And it's clear from the smirk on his face that he's guessed what I'm thinking, which, of course, makes me blush harder.

Katherine's voice yanks me back to the here and now. "So it would actually be more correct to say that we have thirteen working keys and one useless trinket. And that is exactly what Marcus showed me when I caught up with him in Vienna a few years back. I couldn't see the light at all, and the hourglass on the front was perfectly still. It was the only time I'd ever seen how the medallions appear to everyone else. Deborah has a point when she says it's an eyesore."

"But"—Connor looks around the table—"to answer Kiernan's question, I'm not sure there's any point in destroying them until we have them all. I know it seems like we're tempting fate, keeping them here when Saul could probably arrange for the National Guard to take them if he really wanted to. But if someone shows up with a CHRONOS key, planning to steal our stash, and finds them deactivated, what's he or she going to do next?"

There's a moment of silence, and then Dad says, "Figure out when you deactivated them and storm the house just before."

Kiernan shakes his head. "With all due respect, I disagree. Destroy them. Why make it easy? Yeah, they'll backtrack if they don't find them, but that may buy us a day or an hour. And we may need that day or hour. Maybe they're *waiting* for us to collect them all, so they can come steal our stash."

"Hmm . . . Grandpa has a point," Connor admits, a bit reluctantly. "I'll narrow it down to the minimum we need to keep the house and all of us safe, and maybe keep a spare, just in case. The rest get the acid bath."

I grab a pen from the counter behind us. "So we mark the Nazi historian off the list, and we're down to six. We have five that we can pin down with some degree of certainty—one in Russia in 1957, one in Port Darwin in 1942, and three in Athens, Georgia, in 1938. That leaves one."

"Or maybe two. Saul might have traveled with two keys," Katherine says. "I think Shaila's was destroyed along with the others at CHRONOS headquarters, but I can't be sure. Saul might have grabbed it."

"Okay," I say. "Leaving Shaila's aside, you're certain that other key is in the past and not ahead of our time?"

"Yes. The three cohorts were roughly divided by era, so that we had our research days to prepare for the various trips at the same time. That way, we could share expertise with others looking at the same general historical period. As I noted before, only two cohorts were in the field at a time, so that meant that the modern history group wasn't on the jump schedule. Shaila's was the most recent—sometime around 2020."

"It was 2024," Kiernan says. "That's when Saul landed."

"Nice to be able to pinpoint that after five decades of wondering," Katherine says as she jots it down on the sheet in front of her. "As for that remaining key, I have nothing beyond what I put in the document I gave Kate. Esther was studying a matrilineal society in Africa sometime between 1100 and 1300. I'm pretty sure it was the Akan, which would put her location at the one and only jump site in Ghana at that time. But, that was seven hundred to nine hundred years ago. I suspect that one is buried somewhere, most likely with Esther, and will never be found. Think how long it took you to observe the various sites in Dallas, Kate. Can you imagine trying to do that over a two-hundred-year span?"

I shake my head. "I've had no luck with finding the guy in Moscow during a two-day window. Two centuries would be impossible. I guess we'll simply have to assume that key can't be found."

"Well, maybe not," Kiernan says. "I don't know if Kate mentioned it in her diary, but I'm still working on something that we started together before she . . . before she disappeared. We're pretty sure we've located a key in 1905."

"Is that what she was talking about in London? She mentioned something about getting some flyers printed, which made zero sense to me, but there was nothing specific about a key. And it was all mixed up with the stuff about Georgia in 1938. She seemed kind of flustered those last few entries." I glance at Katherine, but she's looking down at her plate. She pushes her salad around with her fork until she finds an olive, which she spears and drops onto Connor's plate.

"Yeah, well, 1938 wasn't going so well," Kiernan replies. "But to get back to 1905, I haven't seen the evidence yet, but Kate was certain. She saw Houdini with it twice, once in London and once in New Y—"

"Houdini?" Connor's eyes are wide. "You're telling me Houdini had a CHRONOS key?"

Kiernan nods. "That's what Kate, my Kate, told me. She was positive enough that she and Katherine—by which I mean the Katherine in the other timeline—put a good deal of effort into setting up . . . well, Kate called it a *sting*. And I now know exactly how much effort they put into it, because I've had to re-create all of their steps. I was back to square one after the timeline reset, but I think I have all of the puzzle pieces in place once again, and I'm back to working undercover."

"Undercover as what?" I ask.

"Nice try," he replies with a grin. "You're still coming, right? Norumbega Park?"

"I promised, didn't I?" I glance around the table. Dad and Connor are pointedly looking elsewhere, and Katherine still has her eyes on her plate, although they seem a bit unfocused. "Let's go ahead and pencil that in for tomorrow morning. But maybe you could give us an overview now, for the sake of the others?"

"Nope," he says, still grinning. "You can report back to them when you get home."

I look over at Katherine, hoping she'll chime in and say that she doesn't want to wait, but she still doesn't look up, so I'm on my own.

"I think we have a dress that will work for 1905, if we make a few alterations," Connor says.

Kiernan shakes his head. "No need. There's a dress at my place . . ."

At that point everyone, including Katherine, looks up at him, and even though there's no reason for either one of us to blush, we both do.

"It's sort of a hand-me-down," Kiernan says. "From . . . before."

I flip through the pages I'm holding to pull their attention back to the business at hand. "So, back to the list? The jump to 1938 makes me nervous."

Truthfully, even mentioning the 1938 jump to Athens, Georgia, makes me nervous, because I'm certain Katherine knows more than the smattering of information she included. There's not a word about anyone dying in her overview. It's bare bones, with just the names of the two historians she remembers—Abel Waters and Delia Morrell—the fact that they were married, and a note that they were trainers.

"Can you tell us anything more about that jump, Katherine?" I ask.

"I'd suggest that we focus on getting Adrienne's key and Wallace Moehler's key first. If we manage to do that without Saul's people bashing in the door and ending this entire enterprise, *then* we can talk about 1938."

I'm reluctant to let this go without more information, but perhaps this isn't the time or place. "Fine, Katherine. Let's move on to the Russia trip. They never got that key in the previous timeline."

We debate the various possibilities for a few minutes, and Connor asks Katherine the same question that Other-Kate said he'd raised in the previous timeline—why would the Russians even have press conferences in a country with a state-controlled media?

He has to repeat the question, but Katherine finally says, "I don't know. That's a good point, Connor. But that's definitely where Moehler said he was going."

"Well, what if we look at this another way?" Dad asks. "Where else might they have held a press conference on this issue? Maybe the jump wasn't to Russia after all."

Katherine spins her head around and blasts Dad with a look that is pure venom. "I. Was. *There!*" she screams, leaning forward, her thin body rigid as both hands grip the edge of the table. "I know what I heard, Harry. I think the much more likely scenario is that your daughter did a half-assed job watching the stable points. She was probably online flirting with Trey or thinking about going to some damned park with this guy."

Kiernan's jaw clenches, but he doesn't say anything. Dad looks kind of stunned, and I suspect my face wears the same expression. Katherine gets snippy; Katherine even gets a little bitchy, but I've only heard her raise her voice a few times. This is not Katherine.

She shifts her eyes over to me and then takes the handout and rips it in half, tossing the pieces on top of her plate. Her voice goes even higher than before. "If you took this at *all* seriously, Kate, we'd already be—"

"Katherine!" Connor says, his voice sharp as he grabs her hand. She yanks away from him and sits back, her face slowly draining of expression, her shoulders slumping downward. After a minute, Connor puts his arm around her, and she leans into him. "It's okay," he says, and his voice reminds me a bit of when I was comforting Daphne. "Just family here. Want me to walk you back to your room?"

"No," she says in a small voice that worries me even more than the shrieking. "I need to stay." She takes the torn pages and puts them under her plate and then says, almost in a whisper. "I'm sorry, Kate. And Harry."

I give her a smile, which I doubt she sees, because her eyes are glued to the table. "It's okay, Katherine."

"Sure," Dad says. "Not a problem."

Connor looks around at the three of us and gives us a grateful nod. "Okay," he says, his voice all back to business. "I don't think it's very likely that Kate missed Moehler. There were four new Diet Dr. Pepper cans in the library when I went in this morning, and nobody else here drinks that nasty stuff. I'm guessing she's put a week's worth of effort into this over the past four days, in between getting Deborah off for Italy. Am I in the ballpark, Kate?"

"Closer to two weeks' work, if we're sticking to the standard labor laws."

"Then Harry's right," he says. "We need to look for alternatives to Moscow. Ideas?"

"Well," Kiernan says, "if you can pinpoint his location at any point prior to his death, Kate or I could go ask him."

Katherine's head snaps up, and she gives Kiernan an odd look, a bit sad and a bit confused. "An excellent point, Kiernan. I don't know why I didn't think of it."

She's just echoed my own thoughts pretty much verbatim. The idea hadn't even occurred to me until Kiernan said it. I guess I still haven't fully wrapped my head around the concept of time as a two-way street. Kiernan has been dealing with this a lot longer than I have.

Not longer than Katherine has, however, and I'm pretty sure that's exactly what's running through her head right now. She looks over at Connor and says, "I think I will go back to my room—I'm tired. You can fill me in later."

And as they leave the kitchen, Connor holding on to her arm, it suddenly hits me that they're together. Like, *together* together—a couple. I don't know if this is something new or if I've been incredibly naive or if they've just kept it well hidden. But if they have been hiding it, why? It's not like I'm a little kid who would be shocked— although I have to admit I *am* a little shocked that I haven't noticed it before.

After they're out of the room, Dad slides over on the bench a bit so that he's facing me and Kiernan. "I don't know how well you knew the other Katherine," he says to Kiernan, "but that's really not her." He looks at me. "Has Connor said anything more to you about her health?"

"Just that it's not going to improve. He said he's seen several of these outbursts, and he thinks it might be the steroids. Apparently they mess with your mood."

"Katherine didn't even have cancer in the other timeline," Kiernan says. "Maybe we could go forward, get some better drugs." His eyes shift down to my jawline for a split second, and I know he's thinking about the hydrogel he used after I was splashed with the acid in Hotel Hell. I don't even want to think about how badly I would be scarred if he hadn't.

"Maybe," I say. "Katherine and I talked about it before, but she said it was something they have to catch early. I don't know if it would just be a matter of pills at this stage of the game, but they might have something that would buy her some time. I'm not sure how I'd convince some future doctor to help. How did you get the hydrogel?"

"Swiped it from the medical center at Nuevo Reino."

"So . . . do you think you could get in there and snag an anti-cancer drug from . . ." I stop and think for a minute. "Katherine said around 2070, I think?"

"Nope." Connor's back in the kitchen. He walks over to the fridge and pulls out a beer. "Harry? Kiernan?" They both nod, and he brings the bottles to the table.

"What do you mean *nope*?" I ask after he sits down.

"It's not going to happen, Kate. You cure her, and you risk screwing up any progress we've made thus far. Katherine and I have discussed this many times, and I can't budge her on this one. It could change too many variables. So, nope."

He reads my expression and says, "I don't like it either, Kate. But we both know she's right. I can't shake the feeling that we're skating on ether each time you grab a key. It's like that Kerplunk game—eventually you'll pull out a straw that brings all the marbles tumbling down."

I doubt Kiernan even knows what Kerplunk is, but he nods and takes a sip of his beer. "Last time the final straw was 1938. I don't know why. Maybe one or more of those keys ends up with people in the inner core—I'm not sure where Simon's key or Patrick Conwell's key comes from, or any of the other regional temple leaders."

I turn toward Connor. "So how much do you know about the 1938 jump? I've got the information Katherine gave me and a little from Kiernan, but there's not much in Other-Kate's diary."

"I know there were three historians stranded there, all embedded with the FWP—the Federal Writers' Project. That location was used frequently by CHRONOS, because it was a sweet setup. The project hired thousands of unemployed people to record the life stories of average people. In places where jobs were scarce, if you could write a coherent sentence, they'd put you to work."

Connor takes a swig of beer and then goes on. "Any place where the FWP was active was a great place for CHRONOS to hide, and it made an excellent training ground for new agents. Given all of the New Deal publicity about the FWP, people weren't the least bit surprised if someone they didn't know, maybe even from another town or up North, showed up on their doorstep, asking them to tell their experiences under slavery or whatever—"

"Slavery?" I ask. "It's 1938."

"So? Someone born in 1855 would be in his mideighties in '38, likely to have some pretty solid childhood memories about living under slavery."

"And," Dad adds, "they'd have even better stories about the Reconstruction era. Your mom used FWP interviews in one of the classes she taught."

"Yeah," Connor says. "There are transcripts online, even a few audio recordings. But to get back to CHRONOS, the publicity around the program meant they could slip in and ask some questions of their own, especially in places like Athens, Georgia, where there was a lot of FWP activity. Anyone whose research dealt with the late eighteenth or early nineteenth century did an FWP jump at least once. Katherine was at the Athens site in February of '38, trying to get information on popular arguments against allowing women on juries, something Georgia resisted until the early 1950s. She thinks Saul was there once in '37, possibly a few other times. Abel Waters and Delia Morrell spent a lot of time at the two CHRONOS FWP sites in the South, so it's not too surprising that's where they got stranded. They were there with a trainee—Katherine can't remember his name."

"I think it was Grant," Kiernan says. "Although I don't know if that's a first name or a last name."

"Well, this jump worries me," I say. "We save it for last. But I want to do at least one trip ahead of time to get my bearings. I can observe Delia's crew from a distance, maybe, but mostly I just want to get a feel for the time and place."

"Okay," Connor says, penciling something onto the paper in front of him. "So, first Australia, then Russia, or wherever Moehler is—and we work on Georgia as we go along?"

"Yes." There's one last question on the list, so I turn to Kiernan. "Do you have any idea how many medallions the Cyrists have in total?"

"No. Simon and Prudence always have one. And I've never seen Saul without his, although that's clearly a power thing, since he can't use it. I thought that each of the regional leaders had a medallion, but if they do, then the numbers you mentioned earlier don't add up."

Kiernan stares at his bottle for a minute. "If I'd had to guess before I heard Connor say how many keys you have here, I'd have said they had twelve keys, because that's how many people they have with a reasonably decent ability to use them, at least to the best of my knowledge. But if you have fourteen, some of them can't have a key."

"Have you ever been in a group of them?" Dad asks. "A meeting, maybe?"

"Yeah." He tallies something up on his fingers and then says, "Six. I think. Counting mine. That's the most I've seen in one place. So, even if we don't count the Houdini key, it means at least one of the five keys we're going after on these three jumps is one currently in their possession. One they're gonna miss. We take that key and . . ."

"All the marbles come tumbling down," I say. "Kerplunk."

∞8∞

My 1905 dress is on top of the faded quilt that covers Kiernan's bed. I don't see him at first, and then there is a slight movement in the periphery as he walks into view and crosses over to a small mirror on the wall next to the red curtain. He's wearing the white shirt and black pants again, although I don't see the tie.

He catches sight of me in the mirror a few seconds after I blink in. I expect his usual grin, but this time his face is troubled.

"What's wrong?"

He runs his tongue across his teeth and shakes his head. "I've just . . . I've decided this isn't a good idea."

Okay, if someone had told me yesterday that Kiernan was willing to call off this trip, I'd have been relieved. My experience with his field trips hasn't exactly been positive. I guess I'm just contrary, however, because now I don't like that he's canceling it, especially since he didn't bother to ask my opinion on the matter.

But mostly, I know that Kiernan was looking forward to this. I glance around this room, this bubble he lives in where he can still imagine that his Kate exists. I don't know if it's because this project was something he shared with Other-Kate or because it's something concrete that he's doing on his own to fight the Cyrists, but when he talks about it, that tiny, fluttering spark of hope in his eyes flares into a flame. And though I really shouldn't let myself care about that, I do.

"What about getting Houdini's key?"

"He won't be there today. I don't know when or even if he'll take the bait and . . ." He sits on the edge of the bed. "I've been thinking about what you said before. About how if there's even a tiny risk, it's not worth it."

"So, when Houdini does show up, are you going to need my help?"

He narrows his eyes, clearly suspicious that I'm walking him into a trap. "Probably."

"And are our odds better if I know what we're doing? And a little about where and when we're doing it?"

"Probably," he repeats.

"You mean yes. We both know I'll learn more about how to get around in 1905 with a few hours in the field than I'll ever learn by you talking me through it."

Kiernan is silent, but he doesn't look convinced. I wait a moment and then sit next to him. "What if I promise to jump straight to Katherine's if we encounter anything out of the ordinary? And since you're the 1905 expert, I'll leave that call entirely up to you. No questions asked."

He snorts, and a smile lifts one corner of his mouth. "No questions? Is that possible for you?" He looks at me for a long moment and then sighs. "If we're going to do this, you'd better get dressed, or we'll miss the train."

"So what exactly is it that you're doing out at Norumbega?" I ask.

"How about I tell you once we're on the train that we're going to miss if we don't *hurry*?"

He helps me into the dress, and then I take off my Skechers and slide them under the bed.

"How far is it?" I ask.

"To the train station? Maybe a mile." Kiernan grabs a black drawstring bag, slings it over his shoulder, and then opens the door to the hallway. "After you."

I step out, and Kiernan looks around to be sure that no one is watching. Then he reaches into the bag and pulls out a red-and-white tin of Johnson's Baby Powder, crouching down to sprinkle a thin coating just inside the door. Next he takes out a piece of newspaper and tears off a small strip. He licks it thoroughly and plasters the wet ribbon of paper across the seam between the door and the wall before locking the door and dropping the key into his bag.

"So you want to tell me what that was all about?"

"Security system of sorts. If someone's been in the room when I'm not here, I'll know."

"And you do that entire routine every time you leave the room?"

"Only way to be sure."

"Yeah, but if it's Prudence or one of her crew, would they go in through the door?"

"Probably not. But Pru had one stable point set, and it's behind that red curtain. She agreed to erase it, but even if she kept her word, I'm guessing Simon has it, too. At any rate, that stable point is booby-trapped, too. I can't stop them from coming in, but if they do, I'll know they've been there. And so far, so good. I can't guarantee they aren't using that stable point to watch the room, but if they are, they're only seeing the red drape. And now, on occasion, they're seeing me naked."

"Better them than me," I say, and he laughs.

I can't shake the feeling, however, that his precautions are pointless. Prudence or Simon could set a stable point in this hallway. They could be watching us right now. That thought makes my skin crawl, and I glance back over my shoulder. I suspect I'm being paranoid, but then again, how would we know? I look back one more time and then shake my head, following Kiernan down the hall.

The stairwell is kid-free this time, so we manage to escape without pleas for candy. We step out, and the sky is clear, with a few clusters of clouds. The first half mile or so is a mix of apartment buildings and small stores similar to those we saw on the way from Jess's tobacco shop. I manage to avoid outright gawking, but there's still something that catches my eye on each block, whether it's a poster advertising something I recognize, like Schlitz beer or Fig Newtons, or the fact that cars already have license plates. That makes sense, I guess, but it hadn't even occurred to me.

We turn onto Harrison Avenue, and Kiernan nods to a cluster of newer buildings across the street. Through the gaps between two of the buildings, I see some toddlers playing in a small, fenced garden.

"That's the headquarters of the local settlement house, South End. A few years back, kids that age would have been on the street all day, while their parents worked in the factories, but now they get breakfast, lunch, and someone to make sure they don't tumble into the river. Of course, they could take in even more kids if Cyrist House hadn't lured away some of their donors."

"Cyrist House?"

"Yeah, it's in the West End. Their original plan was to co-opt this house, but the leaders resisted, like Hull House did in Chicago. Jane Addams was willing to make a lot of compromises to keep Hull House up and running, but she drew the line at serving up a helping of 'Praise Cyrus' with the stew each night."

Okay, I know Jane Addams was, by all accounts, a wonderful person. Unfortunately, I can't help but shudder, because every time I hear her name, I automatically think about H. H. Holmes. Not that she was anything like Holmes, in fact, she was pretty much the direct opposite. It's just that Trey and I watched a documentary about her work at Hull House when I was trying to clear my mind of the really creepy DVD we'd just seen about Holmes and the World's Fair Hotel. Trey made a quip about preferring "Hull House" over "Hell House," and now the two are forever linked in my mind.

"Did you know Jane Addams when you were in Chicago?" I ask.

"Not really. I held the door open for her once after a meeting with Prudence—Older Pru, maybe ten years older than when you met her at the Fair. Pru was offering a big chunk of money to buy out Hull House. Even though they agreed on a lot of issues, Addams politely told Pru to go to hell. Addams wanted to help people regardless of their religious views, and it was clear that there were pretty thick Cyrist strings attached to the deal."

"And the same thing happened here at South End?"

Kiernan starts to answer, but we have to maneuver around a horse cart and a trolley. Once we're back on the sidewalk, he says, "I'm not entirely sure what happened at South End. It was before I moved to Boston, so I wasn't in on the negotiations. Simon helped set up the West End Cyrist House, recruiting a bunch of college students to run it."

"Simon?" The name sets my teeth on edge. I have a hard time picturing him negotiating business deals, except, of course, with monsters like H. H. Holmes.

"Yeah, well, Simon does whatever he's told. He wants to lead Cyrist International when Saul is gone, so when Saul says jump, Simon says how high."

"So—do they know you're back here? In Boston?"

He shrugs. "Pru knows. I've no clue what she shares with the others these days. But she believes I've lost most of my ability to operate the key. And I think I've done a pretty solid job of convincing her that I don't remember the other timeline. Pru's got a bunch of Cyrist toadies at her beck and call, and she's got her pride, too. She'd take me back into that circle if I asked, but she's not gonna beg me."

"So why does she think you warned me on the Metro? That day when Simon grabbed my backpack? You said they knew what you'd done."

Kiernan looks back down at the sidewalk and presses his lips together. "This isn't anything I can prove, Kate. It could have been entirely accidental that I found out what they were planning. But Pru was the one who delayed me in the hallway and led me in that direction. If she hadn't, I'd never have overheard Simon."

"I don't get it. She tells me to stay away from you at the Expo, and then she—"

"From her point of view, once I warned you on the Metro, I'd done what she needed me to do. And to be honest, I don't know if Older Pru remembers any of it."

"Okay, that doesn't make any sense at all."

"Maybe not, but it's the key to understanding your aunt. What if you had the chance to go back and tell yourself not to make the mistakes you made? A chance to change everything you think went wrong in your life?"

"Well, I sort of do. But . . . it's dangerous, right? Katherine says it messes with your head, and I'd like to have as many marbles left as possible, if we make it out of this alive."

"Katherine's right. But either Pru didn't know that or at some point she moved past caring. She runs her younger self pretty ragged, tasking her with errands that she won't entrust to anyone else. I guess, from her perspective, it's no different from what

Saul had her doing when he'd order her to show up in visions or at church events—he didn't like it when she started to show signs of age, so he'd have someone go back to the middle of the night when she was under twenty, wake her up, make her up, and pack her off to wherever he needed a message delivered."

"So twenty is old to him?"

"I don't know. It's think it's more that the Cyrists have pitched Pru as ageless. She's a big part of the whole eternal-life myth for the Koreshan Cyrists, and a lot of Cyrists still believe that. I guess you could say she's sort of a living trademark."

"That's insane. How many times has she . . ."

"No clue. A general rule of thumb I follow is the older the Prudence, the more likely she's bat-shit crazy. You'll get flashes of sanity, but they're rare as she gets older, because so many bits of memory have been overwritten. Do you know about VHS?"

The question is such a total non sequitur that it literally stops me in my tracks, and then I have to hustle to catch up. "What? You mean, like video tapes? A little, I guess. We've used DVDs as long as I can remember. What does that have to do with—"

"When you get back, ask your dad what happens when you record over them. I don't understand the technology, but it helped Kate get a handle on it before. Something about afterimages. Anyway, the more I've thought about it, the more certain I am that Pru wanted me to know what they were planning with you. I don't know if she was put up to it by her older self or if she just happened to learn something accidentally, but she led me to that doorway and then disappeared. That's when I heard Simon running his mouth to someone, probably one of the trainees, about going after you to get the diary and the whole plot to erase Katherine in 1893."

We're approaching a crowd of about twenty men, a few with kids in tow, lined up outside a café. Once we're past the group, Kiernan holds up a finger for me to wait and then steps over to whisper something to a thin man near the end of the line. A boy of five or six, with long blond hair falling down over tired eyes, clutches the man's pant leg, staring up at Kiernan as they talk.

The guy listens to Kiernan for a moment, then shakes his head and waves him off. He looks back, however, as though he's reconsidering what he was told, as we're walking away.

"What was that about?" I ask.

"They're lined up for the bookie. Told him the smart money's on the Browns, 'cause Cy isn't pitching, which actually isn't true, but they lose anyway. Don't think I convinced him. Must be a diehard Americans fan."

"Is this baseball? I thought the Browns were football, and I've never even heard of the Americans."

He covers his heart in mock pain. "Of course, it's baseball. The Americans become the Red Sox. The Browns are Saint Louis. Don't know what they become. You know Cy Young, right?"

"I've heard of the award. A pitcher, right?"

"Not just a pitcher. The best pitcher ever, who, even in your day, holds the record for consecutive hitless innings. That game you and I watched on the 4th, my God, he pitched twenty innings, thirteen without giving up a single run."

"But baseball's only nine innings." I'm pretty sure on this point, based on the three or four games I've seen.

"Yes, but there were eleven extra innings. Then Cy gave up two runs at the end. Even though we lost, that was one incredible game."

I can't help but smile, because he sounds as animated as when he was a kid back at the Expo. "You said we went to the game. Was Other-Kate into baseball?"

"Um, not really," he admits with a little frown. "It was an early birthday present for me. She slept through about half the game."

The Nationals game I saw with Dad didn't go into extra innings, and I was still ready to snooze after an hour, so she has my sympathy. I don't mention it, though, since Kiernan would clearly consider it blasphemy.

"The games are a lot of fun, though," he continues. "The Americans are at home next week. I could get tickets—"

"I don't think so."

He grins, and I'm pretty sure he's making Other-Kate comparisons, but it isn't worth sitting through a game to prove him wrong, especially when I'd probably end up dozing off and proving him right.

We stroll along in silence for a few minutes. Or rather we're silent, though I can't say the same for the city. From what I can tell, there isn't any order at all to the traffic. Trolley cars, horse-drawn buggies, and the occasional car—all painted black—share the road, but they are sharing only in the loosest sense of the word. It's more accurate to say that it's every vehicle for itself. Every few seconds you hear a loud clang from one or both ends of a trolley trying to avoid braking for one of the many carriages, bicycles, or pedestrians wandering on and off the tracks.

Another bell rings out behind us, and I turn toward Kiernan. "Is it always this crazy? I wouldn't have thought there'd be so much traffic on Saturday."

"This isn't busy. You should see this area before the subway is built."

As I glance away from the traffic and look again at the buildings, I realize that at some point we crossed an invisible culture line. Most people two or three blocks back looked European, but the residents here are almost entirely Asian, and most of the signs appear to be written in Chinese.

Kiernan notices my expression and says, "Yeah, we're in Chinatown. But don't worry. It's safe."

"Why would you assume that I'd think it wasn't safe?" I ask.

He looks puzzled. "Well, I don't know. Because it's different?"

I raise an eyebrow, but then I realize he isn't being intentionally racist. It's like this experiment we did in sociology class last year. Things that are different, things that don't fit into our own typical surroundings, do tend to set off some sort of subliminal trigger in most people. Your pulse beats faster, you become more aware of your environment, more in touch with your fight-or-flight response. So I just give him a smile and say, "I've been to Chinatown before. In DC. This can't be much different."

"Maybe not," he says, sniffing the air. "Do they have *bao* in DC's Chinatown?"

"They do. I've seen them at dim sum." I take a deep breath and catch hints of bread, garlic, and sesame. Looking across the street, I locate the source of the aroma—*Lock Sen Low Chinese Restaurant*.

"I don't know dim sum," he says. "But I do know bao. They were breakfast for me and Da most mornings at the Expo. And since I haven't had breakfast . . ." Without warning, he grabs my arm and executes one of those suicidal maneuvers I've seen several other people try in the past few minutes. Rather than cross at the corner like a civilized person, he yanks us into traffic, just before a trolley comes barreling around the bend. So now we're the reason the conductor is clanging the bell and shouting as the trolley misses us by mere inches.

As soon as we're on the other side, I yank my arm away. "Have you lost your mind?"

"What?" He looks like he hasn't the slightest idea what I mean, until I shoot a pointed glance toward the street.

"Waiting politely won't get you across the street in Boston," he informs me, "at least not in 1905. There aren't any of those blinking idiot signs that show a hand and count down the seconds for you."

"I like the idiot signs," I mutter. "Your method seems more likely to get me killed."

Lock Sen Low is apparently on the second floor, but there's a cart just inside the stairwell. A young Chinese guy opens the lid of the large bamboo steam tray, and Kiernan points to a plain white bun and then to one scattered with black sesame seeds.

Kiernan hands the sesame bun to me. It's huge. "I thought these were for you. I'm really not that hungry." While I'd have sworn that was true, my tummy picks that precise moment to contradict me with a growl, possibly because the bao really does smell delicious.

I would also have sworn the street was far too noisy for Kiernan to have heard that small noise, but either he's got excellent hearing or my glance downward at my traitorous stomach tipped him off.

"Sorry, but I think you've been outvoted," he says, taking a big chomp out of his bun, which smells like barbecue pork. "Just take a bite. I'll finish what you don't want."

It tastes even better than it smells. We walk as we eat, thankfully avoiding any more near collisions. Kiernan polishes off the pork bao while I still have a good half-dozen bites left, and I hand him the rest of mine, even though I could definitely have finished it. Maybe a bit of deprivation will teach my stomach who's boss.

Boston Commons is only a few blocks over, and we catch the train just this side of the park. Once we're on board, I clear my throat, giving Kiernan an impatient look.

"What?"

"We're now on the train," I say. "You owe me information."

He nods and begins to rummage around in his canvas bag, pulling out a crumpled piece of paper. I smooth it out as best I can and see that it is a flyer. *See the Amazing Boudini, Now Disappearing Nightly at the Great Steel Theater.* The words are in the foreground in green, printed over the black silhouette of a top hat.

"The poster is nice—" I begin.

"Thank you. I thought it turned out rather well myself."

"But Boudini? You can't be serious?"

"The name wasn't my idea." He lowers his voice and leans in so that we're not overheard. I follow his lead, although I doubt anyone could make heads or tails of this conversation if they did catch a few snippets. "That part is historical. Apparently some other guy pulled this same stunt or, rather, will pull it this coming September, calling himself Boudini. Houdini finds out and gets all pissed off. Or we think he does. It might have been a publicity stunt Houdini was in on from the beginning. Either way, he challenges the guy to an underwater competition, which Houdini, of course, wins. The other guy nearly drowned, or at least that's what the newspaper says."

"What's this other fake Houdini going to think about you stealing his plan?"

He shrugs. "Don't care. Kate tried to get past Houdini's bodyguards in London to ask about the key, but she failed. This was Plan B—get Houdini angry enough to come here and challenge me. Then we confront him, and he hands over his key."

"Which he's going to do willingly?"

"Maybe. He's supposed to be a nice enough guy. He's not a fan of people who try to manipulate others through bogus claims about the spirit world, so maybe we can convince him. But willingly or not, we'll have to get his key."

He's right, although I have the feeling this isn't going to be as easy as he thinks. "So . . . where did you learn to do magic?"

"I picked up the basics watching street magicians that year at the Expo. You watch long enough and you can tell what they're doing. And a guy over on Cairo Street taught me a few tricks. I'm not really good with the showman side, but I can still do enough to prime the audience for the main event."

"I'm guessing that's an escape trick?"

"Yep. The assistants put cuffs on me, and I hop into the container. When they open it up a few minutes later, I'm uncuffed and unchained. Ta-da. As long as I can reach the CHRONOS key, it's easy as pie."

"So who unlocks the cuffs?"

He looks down at the floor. "Um, Jess did, the first few times. But I don't like pulling him into this. I've just been doing it myself, back at the apartment."

"That's . . . not a good idea, is it? I mean, from what you've told me . . . from what Katherine's told me—"

"It's not ideal, but I can handle it. I don't say anything to myself, and I schedule all the jumps for the week on my day off, at a time when I'm half-asleep." He shrugs. "It takes a little longer to get the cuffs off when I'm groggy, but it's not bad if I go right back to sleep. Kind of like it was a dream."

"No. I'll do it. What time did we leave your place this morning? A little after ten?"

"Sounds about right."

"When you do the trick today, set the coordinates for your place at 10:15 a.m., and I'll be there. Then do it for 10:16 for the next jump, and a minute or so later for each of the others. We'll get a week out of the way before I go. It will only take a little of my time, and it would be nice if you came out of this with your marbles intact, too."

His expression is a combination of reluctance and relief, so it must be a bigger deal than he's letting on.

We switch trains at Lake Street, boarding an open trolley that Kiernan says will take us out into the suburbs. I spend most of the ride looking at the scenery and thumbing through a day-old *Boston Globe* that someone stuffed between the benches.

Kiernan reads over my shoulder, and when I flip the paper around to the back, he points to an advertisement for Keith's Vaudeville House.

"Lambert and Pierce. They'll start at Norumbega next week."

"Two Men in Black?" For me that pulls up a visual of Will Smith and that other guy in dark sunglasses fighting intergalactic troublemakers.

"Yeah, Kate got a kick out of that, too. It's a minstrel show— they should call it *Two Men in Blackface.* Like a lot of acts, they run a circuit of vaudeville houses within a few hundred miles. Some headliners travel the entire country, even around the world."

"So is that your goal, O Great Boudini? Bump Houdini out of the limelight and take it for yourself?"

"Dear God, no. Not my goal and not even a remote possibility. Houdini actually has some escape-artist skills, and he's a master showman. It's not just the CHRONOS key. I'm lucky to keep them awake until I do the vanish."

"Do you think there's any chance he'll be here today?"

"Houdini? No. I'm pretty sure I'll get a letter from his attorneys before the great man himself comes all the way to Boston. Like I said, this is just prep, so we could have ski—"

"No. We couldn't have. I could've read for weeks and never have gotten as much information about 1905 as I have in the past hour."

He chuckles. "Careful, love. You're starting to sound like a true CHRONOS historian."

I shake my head. "Not CHRONOS. Just the cleanup crew."

∞

Kiernan's description of Norumbega as a poor man's World's Fair is dead-on. There's a huge fountain near the center of the park that looks like the electric fountains at the Expo, scaled down and heavily speckled with bird droppings. A carousel sits near the center of the park, and Kiernan says they're planning to add a Ferris wheel and other rides. The Charles River is a much smaller stand-in for the shores of Lake Michigan.

The main attraction at Norumbega seems to be canoeing. There are so many canoes on the river that I can barely see the water.

"Is it always this crowded? The boats can barely move."

Kiernan laughs. "The passengers aren't in it for exercise. They'll gradually work their way a quarter mile or so downriver. The police have increased their arrests, but the couples keep on coming."

"Arrests? For what?"

"Necking in the canoes. Canoedling, some of them call it."

I give him a skeptical look. "Why make out in a canoe? There are people all around them. It's not very private."

"People in the other boats are doing the same thing, so they aren't gonna pay you any mind. In a few years, when there are autos everywhere, the backseat will put these canoe vendors out of business, but right now, those boats are the most privacy you can buy for a dime."

We wander around for a while, and then a light rain begins to fall, so we trudge up the hill toward the building at the top. The sign out front reads *Great Steel Theater*, and that's a pretty accurate description of the massive gray structure.

Kiernan groans, then digs in his pocket and pulls out a couple of nickels. "If Josephine was working, you wouldn't need a ticket," he says in a low voice. "But Agatha is hard-nosed. I'm pretty sure she resells some of the tickets and pockets the difference. She's gonna get caught if she's not careful. Easley may be stupid, but his wife isn't."

He slides the coins across the wooden ledge. "Hi, Agatha. I brought a guest today. We'll go backstage first, but she'll be watching the show afterward."

A heavy-set, older woman glances up briefly from her book and does a double take at my face, like she's trying to figure out where she's seen me before. Sure enough, there's the fading ghost of a lotus flower on her hand. I don't hold her attention for long, however. The book—a tattered paperback entitled *Mischievous Maid Faynie*—is clearly more interesting than a girl who bears a passing resemblance to a picture at the temple.

We wait for a moment, and then Kiernan says, "Her ticket, please? Just in case Tito checks."

Agatha gives him a foul look and then tears off a ticket, shoving it toward us.

The show doesn't start for twenty minutes, but there are already a few people who've come in early to snag a spot near the front. The auditorium is partly enclosed, but the large steel curtains on the sides are open, letting in a bit of a breeze. Kiernan leads me toward a door near the stage, and we walk into a dim room crowded with stage props. There's a trail of sorts between the junk, and Kiernan seems to know where he's going.

A few yards in, we pass a wooden coffin on a raised platform, and he knocks on the top. "This was the trick I auditioned with. But I've upped the ante since then."

At the back of the room, a small flight of wooden steps goes up to stage level. A curvy blonde in her midtwenties turns as we approach, a welcoming smile on her face.

"Somebody pinch me. Are you Kate? I'm Eliza Easley. It's nice to see you actually exist." She slides her hand up Kiernan's arm and winks at me. "You have no idea how many girls ask me to introduce them to this guy, but he keeps saying he's taken."

Kiernan shoots me an apologetic glance and squeezes my hand. I wouldn't blow his cover either way, but I wish I could believe that he's been saying that simply to ward off her matchmaking attempts rather than because he's still convinced that we belong together.

"Hi, Eliza. Nice to meet you."

"I'm gonna show her the setup," Kiernan says, "then take her out front. I'll be back about five minutes before I go on."

She shakes her head. "Sorry, kid. Perry up and quit. I'm going to need some extra muscle moving the sets between acts."

He makes a face. "That's okay. I'll get her settled and come right back. Why'd Perry quit?"

"Same reason you'll quit, and same reason I'll quit eventually. My jackass of a husband." She grins, but I get the feeling she's not exactly joking.

Kiernan nods, then leads me to the other side of the stage, toward a black rectangular box about the width and maybe two-thirds the height of a telephone booth. It's sitting on a wheeled platform a few inches above the floor. He pulls the curtain that surrounds the box to reveal a glass case, filled with water. Another cart a few feet away holds an assortment of metal cuffs and chains.

"You're kidding me."

"Nope," he says. "We pull someone from the audience and cuff him, just to show everyone these aren't trick cuffs. Then I jump in the bath, they pull the curtain to hide me and parade around—and when they slide the curtain open, I'm out of the cuffs."

"What about your tux?"

He taps his chest. "Bathing suit. Underneath."

"Oh, please tell me it's not one of those one-piece things that come down to the knees?"

"Yes. And I look very handsome in it," he deadpans.

"I'm sure you do," I say, fighting back a laugh.

The auditorium is filling up rapidly when Kiernan walks me out. The light rain has turned into a downpour, and most of the people coming through the doors are shaking water out of their hair.

A tall, thin man with a mustache, wearing a deep red jacket, is on the far side of the auditorium, trying to lower a heavy metal curtain to keep the rain from gusting in. He's already fastened the one on the wall closest to us, but it looks like the other curtain is stuck. He jerks the crank back and forth to jar it loose, but it doesn't seem to be working.

"It's gonna be a full house. Ticket sales always go up when it storms. I was hoping you'd get a better seat. Do you want to go backstage and jump back a few minutes so we can get you closer?"

I shake my head and take a seat in the center aisle, a few rows from the back. "That's okay. I can come another day and get a closer look if I need to."

"As much as I enjoy your company, I think we should avoid that. Listen, I'm gonna help Tito with that storm curtain, and then I've got to get backstage. See you after."

He pushes through the crowd, and I watch as the two of them give the crank an extra hard shove and the barrier begins to roll down. When it reaches the bottom, Kiernan pats Tito on the back and says something to him, nodding in my direction. Then Kiernan hustles down the aisle, turning to flash me a quick smile before he disappears through the stage door.

I start to feel a little uneasy as soon as he's out of sight. I tug at the ruffled neck of my blouse until I locate the cord attached to my CHRONOS key. I rub the cord between my fingers nervously while I look around at the audience. Some are eating popcorn from soggy cartons, while others try to read the program in the dim light.

After a couple of minutes, a small orchestra begins to warm up. A violinist takes his bow for a practice run across the strings, making an eerie screech at exactly the same moment I feel a tap on my shoulder.

I jump, but it's just the guy Kiernan called Tito. He's older than he looked from a distance. When I look up at him, I see a flash of recognition in his eyes.

Dear God, do they only hire Cyrists at this park?

But then he breaks into a grin that deepens the wrinkles in his face. "You are Kate?"

I return his smile, still a bit wary.

"The magician boy, Boudini, he ask me to give you this." His accent sounds Italian, or maybe Portuguese. He hands me a program and leans in a little closer. "So it finally work, eh? You make him notice you?"

I look at him, puzzled, and shake my head.

"Ah, no need to be shy. Tito will keep your secret. I no forget a pretty face, such pretty eyes. And is nice to see you smile for a change. Every show I see you watch him, you and the other man." He nods toward the other side of the theater. "Then you sneak away before the next act, never stay to see the whole show. You stay today, okay? Is good show!"

The smile is frozen on my face, as I glance around the auditorium to see if I spot Prudence or the blue glow from her medallion.

Tito obviously mistakes my expression for embarrassment, because he pats my hand and says, "No, no, don' worry. The magician boy likes you. I can tell these things. And he seems a lot nicer than your other *namorado*. That one, he no make you smile, so is good you get rid of him."

"Thank you, Tito," I say and give him the biggest smile I can muster, hoping that he'll leave if he thinks I'm happy. It works—he pats my hand again for good measure and then heads down the aisle to the orchestra pit.

I wait until his attention is elsewhere and then move toward the exit, keeping my head down. From the corner of my eye, I'm almost certain I see the blue flash of a medallion off to my left, at the very back. I tell myself not to look in that direction, but when I reach the rear of the theater, I do. Everyone is moving forward, folding umbrellas, shaking water from their hair and clothes, and craning their necks to find a cluster of seats where they can sit together.

All but two of them, that is.

The couple near the back isn't wet at all. Their backs are pressed against the rear wall of the theater. The guy is a little above average height, kind of chunky, and I recognize Simon's pale, pudgy profile scowling out at the people pushing in front of him. He has a tight grip on the upper arm of the girl standing next to him, who wears a high-waisted dress. Prudence is about my age, my height, pretty much my everything, but it's her face that draws my attention. It's slack, almost vacant. She's staring at the door that Kiernan entered a few minutes ago, her mouth slightly open, her eyes empty.

Whirling around, I shove my way through the stragglers still filing into the theater and run out into the rain. I tug the medallion out of my blouse as I look for a place with a bit of cover. The rain is coming down so hard that I decide it's probably a lost cause, and I just press myself against the side of the building, pull up Kiernan's room at 10:15 a.m., and blink.

I take a deep breath and then slide away from the stable point, leaving a trail of water behind me on the wooden floor. A few seconds later, Kiernan appears, dripping wet, with three sets of cuffs on his arms and two on his ankles, the CHRONOS key clutched in his hands.

The black one-piece suit does in fact look good on him.

It takes a second for him to register that I'm as soaked as he is. "What happened?"

"You're being watched, Kiernan. Every day. Every show."

∞9∞

I open my eyes in the library. Rain drips down the windows, and I can't help but feel that dreary weather is chasing me through space and time—first in Boston with Kiernan, then in Port Darwin, Australia, and now here.

Katherine and Connor are right where they were when I jumped to Port Darwin. All things considered, Adrienne took the news that she's stranded in 1942 fairly well. She was nice. I hope she makes it out before the bombs hit.

I toss the key in Connor's lap. "One more for the trash heap."

He smiles. "No problems, then? No crocodile?"

"I think someone may have killed him, actually. Either that or he found something rather large to eat, because there was a big pool of blood on the beach."

"I still don't understand why you were determined to go alone," Katherine says.

"Like I said before, Kiernan's being watched. Prudence knows he's up to something, and it's not going to help either of us if she connects the dots. And this was a snap once Adrienne realized she was stranded. The only shaky point was when she asked whether she survives the bombing, but she didn't push when I told her I couldn't say. I do want to see what happened to her, though—"

"Why?" Katherine interjects. "What's the point, Kate? You'll just feel bad if you discover she was caught in the attack."

Katherine's right, at least on the surface. There's no concrete purpose served in tracking Adrienne down, other than satisfying my curiosity and the fact that she asked me to. I liked her, and I'll be tempted to go back and warn her if I find out that there's a nurse's assistant on the casualty list now who wasn't there before. I don't know if I'd actually *do* it, but I'd be tempted.

I consider dropping the point, because I'll run that search later on, whether I admit it to Katherine or not. Either way, I want to know. But this is as good a time as any to raise the issue of the death in 1938. If Other-Katherine knew someone was going to die, I'm pretty sure this Katherine does too. And we might as well thrash it out now.

"So is it Delia, Abel, or this Grant guy who gets killed in 1938?"

She arches an eyebrow at me and looks back at her computer screen. "It's irrelevant. He died before Saul started changing the timeline."

He died. Okay, she didn't answer the question, but at least she narrowed it down to Abel or Grant.

"No, Katherine, he didn't. Saul started changing the timeline when he stranded the three of them in 1938. If not for that, the man would have made it back to his own time, right?"

Katherine shrugs, still looking at the screen. "Probably. But as I noted earlier, we can't worry about that timeline. Our priority is to restore this reality, the one in which you exist to *stop* Saul. Anything else is a luxury, and we cannot afford to experiment."

We've gone over this before, and yes, I know she's partially right. We have no way of telling how many people are dead in this timeline who weren't in some other reality or who don't exist here but did exist there. My mind strays back to Dad's two kids in the other timeline, and while it's not exactly the same, never-existed and dead are functional equivalents.

But once again, Katherine's made herself the sole arbiter of right and wrong and the one who defines what I need to know. I'm not down with that. Based on what Kiernan told me, neither was Other-Kate, and she had the advantage of a Katherine whose brain was fully operational and not hampered by steroids and who knows what else. Even though Katherine thinks the issue should be closed, I know it can't be.

"For argument's sake," I say, "let's pretend I agree on that point, even though we both know I don't. I still need to know every single thing you can tell me about those three historians, what they were doing in Georgia and why you think they wouldn't give up their keys. This is almost certainly the jump that brought everything down around our ears in the last timeline. That Kate no longer exists. And before she disappeared, that Kate was so angry at you that Kiernan thought she needed a chaperone before confronting you. I think it's a reasonable assumption that if I repeat what she did last time, I won't exist either, and there's an excellent chance I'll discover the same thing that made her want to punch you. So, maybe we should try something different this time?"

That seems to get her attention. Connor's, too, although he shifts his eyes back down to the book he's pretending to read.

At first, it seems Katherine's going to argue the point, but then she says, "I don't really remember Grant. He was a trainee. This would have been his first or second jump. It's Abel who dies. I found out when I tracked Delia down, after Prudence began changing things. Delia was alive until about six years ago—taught for most of her life at a women's college up in Maine. She remarried, and judging from the number of offspring, I'd say she intentionally flaunted CHRONOS protocol about minimizing changes to the timeline."

"Well, that was before birth control, wasn't it? It was probably hard to—"

Katherine sniffs. "Before the pill, yes. But there were reasonably effective methods available long before 1938, if you knew where to look. Delia would have known. Seven children, twenty-five grandchildren—that's bound to ripple the timeline a bit. But, to get back to my point, she told me Abel was killed right after that last jump."

"Killed how?"

"Murdered," Connor says, flipping his book shut. "I don't know if it was the KKK or some other group, but he was lynched."

Katherine narrows her eyes at him. "We only have Delia's word on that. There's no record of a lynching in Athens after 1921."

"*Lynched?* Why was he lynched?" I ask.

Connor shrugs. "A man of color involved with a white woman in the 1930s. In Georgia. If I had to guess, I'd say someone saw them together and took offense. And Katherine's right—there's no record of a lynching in Athens in the 1930s. But you've got a little county just to the south, only seven miles or so down the road, that split off during Reconstruction. A major lynching there in 1905. Another nearby in 1946. And plenty of lynchings were never recorded."

"What about the third person who was there, Grant? Maybe he could—"

"I was never able to locate him," Katherine says. "Delia told me she didn't know where he was, hadn't seen him since she left Athens, right after Abel died. And then she said she'd see me in hell before she'd give me those keys." Her blue eyes are troubled. "I understand her being upset, obviously. But it's not like I had anything to do with his death."

"Did you tell her it was Saul who sabotaged the jump?"

Katherine nods. "But I made it clear that I knew nothing about what he was going to do. I combed through all of my diaries, Kate, over and over—looking for clues as to why he did this, when he started planning it. And I can't find anything. There were a few odd events, yes. I think you watched the entry where I was complaining about his taking unapproved medicines on a jump."

I nod, and she goes on. "And there were a few times he was evasive or secretive, but that was just his nature. He hated anyone knowing about anything that could be perceived as a weakness—never reported sick, even refused to go to CHRONOS Med one time when he burned his arm on a jump. It would never have left a scar if he hadn't been such a . . ."

She trails off and then adds, "It's not like I could have stopped him, Kate."

I don't say anything. *Could* she have stopped him? I don't know. Even if she didn't know what Saul was planning, she did know he was breaking CHRONOS rules, maybe a lot of them. And she knew he was involved with some questionable people, but she waited to turn him in until it was too late. No, she didn't know for certain, but she had more to go on than anyone else at CHRONOS.

Katherine is either thinking the same thing herself or else she reads my thoughts from my expression, because her face tightens. I brace, afraid she's about to lose it again, like she did the other night at our meeting, but then I see tears in her eyes.

"You blame me, too, don't you?"

I glance back over at Connor, who has very conveniently decided to go back to his book, and try to figure out how to tell her the truth without being too harsh.

"No, Katherine. I don't *blame* you. I think you made some mistakes, but you were young. People sometimes do stupid things when they're in love. Although—" I'm about to say I can't understand why she was in love with Saul. Nothing I've seen or heard makes him seem remotely appealing. And even though I catch myself before the words actually come out, she guesses what I'm thinking.

"You didn't know him then, Kate. He was handsome, suave, smart, and, believe it or not, he could be very nice when he wanted to be. I don't know how much of that was an act, but I was far from the only one who fell for it."

"I do have the benefit of hindsight," I acknowledge, deciding not to mention that Adrienne, the historian I met in Port Darwin, *did* know Saul, and she found him repulsive, too. "But to get back to the original point, I'm going into Athens with an open mind. I'm not going to assume this guy's death is unavoidable. For all we know, that assumption is what caused us to fail last time."

"Because you know best, obviously, based on your many years of experience." Her voice is dripping with sarcasm, and I'm opening my mouth to snap back when I hear muffled music. It takes me a second to realize it's a ringtone, coming from inside my swimsuit. It's the Clash, "Should I Stay or Should I Go?" I downloaded that one just before Mom left, when she was having the inevitable second thoughts about leaving her baby girl.

I'm not about to fish it out of my swimsuit in here, so I turn to leave the library. "It's Mom," I say as I head down the hall. "We'll finish this later."

∞

Mom hasn't really met anyone to talk to in Italy, since most of her new colleagues speak English as a second language. That means phone calls with her are a bit on the lengthy side, because she has to talk to someone. She's enjoying Genoa, however—the weather is nice, the food is great, and she's looking forward to getting started on the research.

And she thinks I should definitely wear the new red sundress to the party. I suspect it's too dressy for anything billed as a barbecue, but Trey did say that this is more likely to be the grilled-scallops and brisket-on-brioche type of barbecue than burgers and baked beans.

The sundress does seem much more likely to take Trey's breath away than the denim skirt and silk tee I'd planned to wear, and I really do want to take his breath away tonight. The rain from earlier in the day has cleared up, so it should be warm enough. I finally give in to temptation and take the dress off the hanger, then search around for some shoes that match.

Unfortunately, the sundress doesn't offer a hiding place for the medallion, and there are far too many Cyrists around who might recognize it for me to wear it openly. I finally pop it into the leather pouch Kiernan gave me and tape it to my abdomen with an oversized bandage, like the one that I wore on my leg after my encounter with the Cyrist Dobermans. And I snag two of the smaller Band-Aids for my knuckles, which I really need to stop chewing when I'm nervous.

I apply a touch of lip gloss, slip into the sandals, and grab my clutch bag and the bandages so that I can return them to the cabinet where Katherine keeps her large supply of medicines, herbals, and mystery teas. I check the hallway and peer over the banister before going downstairs. I've managed to avoid Katherine since our argument in the library, and bumping into her right now would spoil my party mood.

Connor is making coffee when I walk in, and I'm surprised to see he's using the coffee grinder and beans that Dad bought. Maybe there's hope for him. He turns when I close the cabinet door. A smile spreads across his face. "Wow. There's a girly-girl inside you after all."

I blush but return the smile. "I let her out to play every now and then. *If* she behaves."

"Oh my God, poor Trey."

"What do you mean?"

"He's going to walk up to that door in a few minutes thinking he has some degree of control over this evening, only to have that illusion completely shattered the second he lays eyes on you in that dress."

I glance down. It *is* a little lower cut than what I usually wear, but I hadn't really thought I was entering jezebel territory. "It's too revealing, isn't it? Maybe I still have time to change."

"No, no, no." Connor reaches out and grabs my elbow. "It's not even close to indecent. I just meant that you look beautiful. Trey won't be able to take his eyes off of you, and he'll probably have to fight to defend his turf from the other guys. Well played, Kate, well played."

I raise an eyebrow, partly because I'm unsure how I feel about being referred to as *turf* and partly because he's turned a simple clothing decision into something that sounds very Machiavellian. I mean, I did pick it because I thought Trey would like it, but . . .

"Trust me, Kate. You should definitely wear the dress. And I'm speaking from experience, both as a former teenage boy and as a father."

"So," I ask, "you'd have let Andi wear it?"

Andi is his daughter. Or rather, was. Connor didn't use to talk about his kids, but lately he'll bring up some little thing he remembers or mention an anniversary or birthday. Andi would have graduated college this year, if she existed in this timeline. His youngest, Christopher, is gone as well, just like Connor will be if he's ever caught outside of a CHRONOS field.

Connor nods, but his smile turns a little sad. "Yes, I would've let Andi wear it. But I'd also have been at the door to make sure that her date remembered she was still my little girl. And on that note, I'm going to go give Harry a heads-up that he needs to get ready to answer the door."

∞

Dad's overbearing-father act needs serious work. It doesn't help that he's a good four inches shorter than Trey, but the biggest issue is that it's just not his personality type. He does manage one lame, half-joking comment about getting me home by midnight, but it's clear from Connor's expression, as he watches from inside the kitchen doorway, that he is totally unimpressed with Dad's performance. I'm pretty sure lessons on how to intimidate your daughter's boyfriend will commence as soon as we're out of earshot.

Trey's car is parked out front, half-hidden by the hedge that wraps around the front and sides of Katherine's yard. Once we're past the line of parental sight, he turns toward me and takes my hand, pulling me in closer. He's looking incredibly handsome in navy pants and the same blue shirt he wore when we had breakfast at his house on my birthday, just before our misadventure at the Cyrist temple.

Even if I were the type to fault him for a first-date wardrobe repeat, which I'm most definitely not, I can't hold Trey accountable for what he can't remember. I'm much more interested in the other thing that's the same—the very familiar light in his eyes when I smile up at him.

"Listen," he says, "I know your Dad and Connor might prefer that the kiss come at the end of the evening, when I've returned you safely to your doorstep, but it has been ten entire days. And you look—whoa." He shakes his head and gives me *that* grin, the one that just melts me, and then follows up with a long, lingering kiss.

"I missed you," he says into my hair when we come up for air.

I lean into his chest, breathing him in. "I missed you, too."

After a moment, Trey reaches over to open the car door for me. Once I'm in, he crouches down and runs his forefinger along the underside of my bottom lip. "Now I see why tradition holds that the kiss comes at the end of the date. How much lipstick am I wearing?"

I laugh and rub his lips with my fingertip, which removes the gloss but not the color. "Hmm," I say as he gets behind the wheel. "Maybe we should find you a Kleenex or something before you meet the rest of Briar Hill?" I open the glove compartment, and there's a small stack of fast-food napkins—I'm pretty sure they're the same ones that Trey gave me in the other timeline, when I was in tears after my meeting with Other-Dad.

I hand him the napkins, and he scrubs his mouth, but it's still a little pink.

He flips the mirror back up and smiles as he starts the engine. "Oh, well. I guess I could just kiss you again when we walk in the door so that they have no questions about where the lipstick came from. Or who you're with."

Connor's *turf* comment echoes briefly in my mind, and I shake my head, laughing. "That would make an interesting first impression. So . . . where is this place?"

"Just off of Falls Road." He nods toward the holder on the dash, where his phone is displaying a GPS app. I zoom in close to the destination and see huge blocks of green.

"Good thing we didn't opt for casual dress," I say. "We're definitely headed into Estate Territory."

"Yeah, I noticed. I hate this type of thing," he says as he merges onto Rockville Pike. "It's always a game of one-upmanship—who has the fastest car, the biggest house, the most obscure and expensive artwork. There will be at least one truly awful sculpture or painting in an alcove that's carefully lit to ensure you simply can't miss it. I think it is written into the contract when you buy a house with more than eight thousand square feet."

I don't say anything, mostly because I have zero experience on that front. Katherine's house is easily the largest I've been in, but she decorates with books and Connor's odd contraptions, designed to boost the CHRONOS field. Trey's house is probably the second largest, but it felt like a home, not a museum.

"I'm sorry," he says, squeezing my hand. "I don't mean to be negative. It's just that I saw so much of this at the school in Peru. I'd finally managed to find a group of friends who were laid-back, but then we moved. I only agreed to finish up at Briar Hill because Dad said it wasn't as snooty. But now with this Carrington Day merger, I'm beginning to wonder."

"Yeah. But at least they aren't switching our classes up. I mean, the schedule I have is the one I signed up for last year."

We spend a few minutes comparing our schedules and are happy to discover we have two classes and lunch at the same time. It might actually be three classes, because Trey can't remember whether he has calculus second period or fourth.

He turns onto Falls Road, and after a mile or so, the houses begin to drift farther apart, separated by wooded areas. Oversized homes are pretty standard in the DC area, but the ones in this neighborhood flaunt the true indicator of wealth—actual land surrounding the house. These aren't your typical McMansions, squeezed onto a lot the size of a postage stamp, but sprawling residences with multilevel decks, at least one pool, and a tennis court.

We turn onto a smaller side road and drive past an iron-fenced estate, with an enormous brick house in the distance and a pond closer to the road, where two horses have stopped for a drink. The scene is very picturesque but also a bit intimidating.

Trey follows my gaze and, apparently, my thoughts as well. "Unless you have objections," he says, "I'll locate Dr. Tilson, tell him Dad's sorry he couldn't attend, and then we'll find an excuse to clear out."

"Yes, please." I'm not a fan of parties in the first place, and if Trey is worried about feeling out of his element, I'm going to be a fish totally out of water. "Maybe you could just say we have to attend this soiree to christen your dad's new yacht and they'll let us take our burger to go?"

He laughs. "Hey, this might actually be fun, if we make a game out of it. Now we need to come up with a pretentious hobby for you—maybe dressage?"

"You've apparently forgotten that you're arriving with the math teacher's daughter. At least a few people will remember I lived in one of those tiny little cottages on campus, and believe me, there's no place to hide a dancing horse."

"Okay, no dressage. We'll use your real hobby. I doubt any of them have a time machine."

"Probably not. Unfortunately, I can't bring that shiny toy out for show-and-tell."

He's about to suggest something else when we see the marker ahead for 10804 Lochmere. The drive is gated, of course, but the gate is open, and a bouquet of helium balloons is tied to each post. The lane winds through the buffer of overhanging trees and ivy hiding the house from the road and then opens to a carefully manicured lawn surrounding a massive white colonial that looks as though it could easily house half the student body of Briar Hill. A dozen or so cars line the sides of the drive. I'm beginning to wish I'd worn my ballet flats rather than these heeled sandals, since it looks like we're going to have a bit of a hike and the ground is still squishy from the morning rain.

But Trey doesn't pull in behind the last car as I'd expected. Instead, he continues toward the drive that curves around the ornate fountain in front of the entranceway. Two men stand at attention beside the middle columns, their dark blue uniforms a vivid contrast against the pristine white of the house. Trey brings the car to a halt, and the attendant on the right steps forward to open my door as the other moves around the front of the vehicle to take the keys.

As we walk to the door, I lean in and whisper, "Valet parking for a high school barbecue? Oh. My. God."

Trey laughs and puts his hand around my waist, pulling me toward him. "And the judges award ten snoot points to Carrington Day."

The valet who assisted me darts up the steps ahead of us to open the front door. A woman with a guest book stands at a little podium in the foyer. Trey steps forward, pulling the invitation from his pocket. She glances at it and then at me, an uncomfortable look on her face.

"I'm Trey Coleman," he says. "This is my guest, Kate Pierce-Keller."

"Oh, yes. Hello, Trey. Welcome to Briar Hill! I was just a bit surprised, because all of the other guests have been parents . . ."

"Mine are out of town, unfortunately, and Kate was kind enough to accompany me."

"I'm sure it's not a problem."

She fumbles around on the podium shelf and locates Trey's printed name badge, along with a blue Sharpie and a blank *Hello My Name Is_____* sticker for me. I'm sorely tempted to write *Inigo Montoya* in the blank, just to see if anyone here will get the lame joke, but I resist temptation and print *Kate Pierce-Keller*.

Then I realize there's no place to put the stupid thing. I try to stick it to the bodice of my dress, but between the lack of sleeves and the lower neckline, the only swatch of fabric big enough for the sticker is right on top of my breast, which makes it stick out funny and means that everyone will have to stare at my boobs to find my name. The gathers at the waist keep it from sticking there, and it would look silly anyway. I finally just slap it on my little black bag.

Trey is leaning against the doorway when I look up, clearly amused at my dilemma. "Clever solution."

"Well, it was either that or paste it to my forehead."

I return the marker, and the woman nods toward the center entrance. "The hosts are greeting everyone out on the patio. Just walk through there, and you'll see the doors off to the left."

There are tall windows on two sides of the room, one facing the front lawn and the other, on the left, opening to the patio. A large crowd is milling about, most of them on the flagstone patio. Fewer than half seem to be around our age, so clearly the woman was correct that most of the guests were parents. Beyond the patio, out on the lawn, are two white party tents, covering the buffet tables. Another tent, off to the side, has smaller tables laden with silver serving trays and about a dozen uniformed attendants behind them.

I glance around the living room for Trey, a task complicated by the room's immensity. It reminds me more of a hotel lobby than any living room I've been inside. There is a grand piano in the right-hand corner, near the entryway. A few chairs are scattered along the walls, and on the far side of the room, opposite the piano, is a cavernous stone fireplace, along with a collection of sofas and chairs, all of which look more decorative than functional.

Small art niches are positioned around the walls, about three yards apart, each as carefully lit as Trey had predicted. What catches my eye, however, is the larger niche centered above the windows overlooking the front lawn, which displays an enormous Cyrist symbol. It resembles a cross in some ways but has a loop at the top, like an Egyptian ankh. The arms of the cross are looped as well, sort of like an infinity symbol, and there is a large lotus flower in the center, where everything overlaps. The Cyrist symbols on top of the temples are usually white, but this one is chrome and crystal, about fifteen feet high.

I turn back toward the patio windows and see Trey, who is also staring up at the thing with a stunned expression. I walk toward him, but he turns and crosses quickly to the center of the room to intercept me. "Maybe we should go," he says. "Dad will just have to . . ."

It's not like I thought I'd be able to avoid Cyrists entirely. That's kind of hard to do, now that they're about a quarter of the population. On the other hand, I had most definitely planned to avoid strolling into one of their lairs, since that didn't really work out so well the last time I tried it. My eyes dart around for Dobermans, but the house and yard seem to be hound-free. And even though part of me is screaming that we should really get out of here, I also don't want Trey to have to disappoint his dad because of me.

"Hello?" We both turn around as one of the large doors leading to the patio slides open. A friendly-looking woman, about Katherine's age, but with a good deal more padding, waves in our direction. "The party is out here," she says. "I'm Angela Meyer, Eve's grandmother. Please, come and join us."

Eve. It's not that uncommon of a name. There have to be dozens of Cyrist girls in the DC area named Eve, right?

I pull Trey close so that I can speak without the woman overhearing. "It's okay, Trey. Really. We won't stay long. It may not even be the same Eve, and even if it is, I doubt she'll remember anything."

"Eve?"

He looks puzzled, and I realize he probably didn't understand all of our video chats. For that matter, I'm not even sure how much we said about that disastrous trip to the Sixteenth Street Temple. Between Trey feeling bad about me getting bitten and me feeling bad about dragging him there in the first place, we were both pretty eager to forget it.

I start to explain, but Mrs. Meyer is looking at us expectantly, so I just pull him toward the door. "Find Tilson and say hello for your dad. Then I'll pretend I've gotten an emergency call."

He still looks doubtful but follows me to the patio. Mrs. Meyer steps forward and takes my hand in both of hers. She reminds me of the woman on the Grandma's Oatmeal Raisin cookie box—curly silver hair, glasses, a sweet smile, and a twinkle in her eye—except she's wearing a stylish dress in a pale coral instead of a flour-dusted apron and she smells like Estée Lauder rather than cinnamon and sugar.

"I'm so delighted you could make it . . ." She glances downward, searching for the name tag.

"Kate Pierce-Keller," I say, holding up my bag. "The name tag wouldn't fit."

"They really don't make those badges for us girls, do they?" She stops midlaugh and tilts her head to the side, her eyes squinting as she looks at me. "But I know you, don't I? Are you a friend of Evie's from the temple?"

Her eyes slide down to my hand, clearly looking for a lotus tattoo. "Oh, I guess not," she says.

Trey steps forward. "I suspect she gets that all the time, Mrs. Meyer. She looks a lot like one of the girls on a Disney Channel show. I'm Trey Coleman, a new student at Briar Hill this year."

I have no idea what show he's talking about, but I'm thankful for the save.

She lets go of my hand in order to take Trey's. "So nice to meet you. Please, both of you, come in—or, I guess I should say, come out!"

Mrs. Meyer leads us across the light gray stones toward a table with rows of tall, stemmed glasses. She glances around, head shaking in dismay. "Everyone is all jammed together on the patio. I'd so hoped we could spread out a bit, but the rain left the lawn all mushy. Those of us in heels are going to have to tiptoe to avoid sinking in." She hands a glass to each of us, then grabs a third for herself.

"It's just sparkling cider for you young folks. And for the hostess as well. I'll have my champagne when all of this craziness is over." She winks at me and then stands on tiptoe in order to look around the crowd. "I was going to find Evie and her friends so that I could introduce you, but I don't see her. Oh dear, there are more guests at the door now. I'm going to have to leave you on your own, sweetie . . ."

She hurries back to her station at the edge of the patio, and I turn to Trey, who is scanning the crowd.

"Well, she seems nice," I say. "Too bad it didn't filter down to her granddaughter."

"How do you know her granddaughter?"

"I'm pretty sure she's Eve Conwell—both of us met her in the other timeline. That's what I was trying to tell you inside. I don't know if she'll remember it. Probably not, unless she was at the temple when the time shift occurred. But she might still recognize me—"

"Great," he says, his voice a bit harsh. I can't quite read his expression, which strikes me as odd, because Trey's face is usually easy to decipher. Then he says, in a softer tone, "After we leave here, we need to go somewhere and talk this whole thing through, okay? I have some questions. My dad does, too."

"Your dad? How much did you tell him?"

He shakes his head. "Later, okay? Let's just find Tilson." He grabs my hand, and we move away from the drink station. I accidentally bump my shoulder into a tall, auburn-haired woman who is trying to eat from one of those little appetizer plates and balance her drink at the same time. A chunk of something orange, cantaloupe or maybe mango, slides from her plate, splattering her shoe. She tosses an angry look my way, but the expression quickly morphs into something else as she stares at my face. She looks almost shocked when I apologize.

"No, no. Entirely my fault."

I open my mouth to say it really *wasn't* her fault, but Trey is pulling me forward, so I just give her a little smile.

Trey stops a few yards later, his neck craning up to look over the crowd. "I don't see him."

"Do you have a description?"

"Nothing beyond really, really old."

We make our way around the pool, which is covered with dozens of floating lotus flowers. They seem real at first glance, but then I realize the centers change color very slowly, so they must be some sort of pool lights. I see a few faces I remember from school; otherwise, it's all people I don't know. And aside from Eve's grandmother, still at her post by the glass door, everyone seems to be under sixty, so I don't think any of them could have taught Trey's grandfather.

It's mostly parents and teens, and the parents seem to be having a better time, possibly because their glasses contain something other than sparkling cider. A tall black man, who's facing the guesthouse, claps another man who just arrived on the shoulder. The laugh sounds familiar, and when he turns in my direction, I recognize Mr. Singleton, Charlayne's dad. I scan the people nearby and finally catch a glimpse of her when one of the guys in the teen cluster shifts a bit to one side.

She's looking out across the lawn, wearing an expression I remember well from our days at Roosevelt High—Charlayne is bored, bored, bored. One of the other girls leans forward to tell her something, and she smiles politely and nods, brushing at the skirt of her dress, navy and white, with cap sleeves and an angled hem that falls just a bit above the knee. It's still too prim and proper for the Charlayne I knew, but the white edging is nice against her dark skin, and the dress is definitely an improvement over the drab getup she wore when I last saw her at the temple—a meeting that she, fortunately, won't remember.

Charlayne must feel my gaze, because she turns toward me. Her eyes travel down to my hand, still linked with Trey's. She frowns, but I can't tell if it's disapproval or just annoyance that I was staring.

"Hey, I think I see him," Trey says.

"What? Where?"

Trey starts across the lawn to the tent closest to us, where the Briar Hill principal and a few others are gathered. I follow, but as soon as I'm off the flagstones, I realize Mrs. Meyer was right about the soggy turf.

Trey stops and glances down at my sandals. "Why don't you wait here? I'll only be a minute."

I nod and step back onto the patio. Someone touches my elbow, and I jump, sloshing a bit of cider onto the flagstones.

"Oh, I'm sorry! I didn't mean to startle you. I'm Charlayne. Charlayne Singleton. I was just telling Leann—that's her over there in the pink—anyway, I was telling her I'm pretty sure we're supposed to be mingling with new students from Briar Hill. But it looks like we've separated into enemy camps or something, you know? And since your friend seems to have wandered off, I thought I'd just say hi . . . and introduce myself?"

The question at the end reminds me that I haven't introduced myself yet. "Oh, hi—I'm Kate Pierce-Keller. I'm not exactly new to Briar Hill, since I started last year. I'm just here with Trey."

"So, you've known Trey for a while?" Her eyes shift almost imperceptibly down to my hand, then back to my face. It hadn't even occurred to me that Trey holding my hand was a flagrant example of PDA to any Cyrists in attendance. Charlayne's brother dated his girlfriend for six months before they were allowed to hold hands. Cyrist rules about dating and sex are strict: no sexual activity until age twenty or marriage, all dates are chaperoned, and all marriages must be approved by the Council of Elders.

"Oh, yes. We've been together for the better part of a year." It's not *exactly* a lie. The time I spent with Trey was definitely the better part of my year.

I look over at the tent, where Trey is standing near someone who must be Tilson and the rest of the Briar Hill contingent. The old guy is waving his hands, apparently distraught, and Trey looks like he's trying to find a good time to interrupt the conversation.

"He's really cute," Charlayne says, shooting me a little smile. It's a timid shadow of the wicked grin that used to accompany her assessment of anything male and remotely hot, but I'll take it.

I return her smile, remembering us having pretty much this same conversation about the various boys who caught her eye in the cafeteria at Roosevelt last year, before I transferred to Briar Hill. "He *is* cute, isn't he?"

"Well," she says, "I'll be sure to let the Evelettes over there know that he's taken."

"Evelettes?"

She nods her head toward three girls sitting on a bench near the guesthouse. "Those three are like Eve's backup singers. Everything she says, they echo it twice and toss in a few oohs and aahs for emphasis."

I laugh. "So . . . Eve's not your friend?"

Charlayne wrinkles her nose and then gushes loudly, "You mean you haven't met Eve? She is an absolute *angel*. You couldn't ask for a better friend."

Then she continues in a much lower voice. "But off the record, let's just say no one crosses her. Anyone with half a brain keeps her distance—which tells you a little something about the three twits over there on the bench. Eve has been the Queen Bee of Carrington Day from the beginning, and she's not exactly happy about switching to a new school her senior year. This little shindig is supposed to ensure that everyone at Briar Hill understands that she's the new boss." Her eyes slide over to the patio door. "I'm guessing she'll make her dramatic entrance in about five minutes."

"Thanks for the warning." I look around for Trey. Hopefully he'll finish up with Dr. Tilson and we can get out of here before Eve arrives.

Charlayne asks what classes I'm in, and we've just finished comparing schedules when I feel Trey's hand on my shoulder.

"Did you talk to Tilson?"

He nods and glances over at Charlayne.

"Oh, you haven't met, have you? Trey Coleman, this is my friend Charlayne." I hesitate at the end, realizing that from her perspective, we've only known each other for a few minutes, so the word *friend* might sound weird. But she either doesn't notice or doesn't care.

"Charlayne Singleton. Pleased to meet you," she says, sticking out her hand.

He shakes her hand, his eyes grazing briefly over the pink tattoo. I wonder if Cyrist girls find the tattoo useful sometimes? I can see how it might be easier to just put "not gonna happen" out front when talking to some guys.

Charlayne turns her smile back toward me. "Nice meeting you, too, Kate. I'll see you in AP History—but for now I'd better get back into position before the curtain goes up." She wags her eyebrows at me before scooting back over near the Evelettes.

"What was all that about?" Trey asks. "Isn't she with Carrington Day?"

I nod, still a little baffled at this turn of events. When we met in the other timeline, Charlayne seemed to be under Eve's thumb, but now I'm wondering if that was a misperception on my part. Or maybe it's just because she was at the temple. Maybe my Charlayne is somewhere in there, dying to break out of her Cyrist shackles.

"We should go." I put my empty glass on one of the small tables. "I'll fill you in when we get to the car."

"I totally agree. I think this party could get . . . interesting . . . once the Carrington Day folks encounter Tilson. That is, if the rest of the Briar Hill faculty *lets* them encounter Tilson."

I give him a curious look, but he doesn't respond, so I glance across the crowded patio, looking for the clearest path to the door. Mrs. Meyer is no longer at her post greeting newcomers, so hopefully we won't have to make any sort of excuse for leaving early. We maneuver around a few groups of people and are nearly home free when I come face-to-face with the reason why Mrs. Meyer is not by the door.

Eve stands next to her father, grandmother, and an older man I haven't met. I turn on my heel quickly and bump into Trey's chest. He catches the hint and shifts us a few steps back, apparently hoping we can take cover behind the two rather large men who are a few feet to the left. One of them is Charlayne's dad, who carries an extra forty pounds or so in this timeline.

But the movement catches Mrs. Meyer's eye. "There you are! I found Evie—"

"I'm sorry, Mrs. Meyer, but we have to leave," Trey says. "Kate just received a call from her father, and her grandmother has taken a turn for the worse."

It's a good effort, but I feel eyes on me and reflexively glance up. Sure enough, it's Eve. She's wearing a wicked, little smile that tells me, beyond any doubt, that she remembers every little detail of our last encounter.

"Oh my." Mrs. Meyer pats my arm. "I'm so sorry to hear that. I'll have Patrick put her on the prayer list."

I return her smile. Then Eve slides between us, and her grandmother says, "This is my granddaughter, Eve Conwell. Evie, this is"—she looks at Trey's name tag—"Trey Coleman and Kate . . . Oh, I've forgotten your last name, sweetie."

"Pierce-Keller."

Eve's blue eyes widen. "But we've met already, Gram. I never forget a face." She pauses like she's trying to remember. "I believe . . . we met at your aunt's place. Yes, that's it. But I could have sworn your name was Kelly."

I flash her a tight-lipped smile. "No. It's Kate."

"That's wonderful that you know each other!" Mrs. Meyer says absently, her eyes straying over toward the food tent. "I've got to go see why the hot appetizers aren't circulating. Kate, I wish your grandmother a speedy recovery." And then she's off, flagging down one of the servers.

I take another step toward the door, with Trey following closely, but Eve steps in and grabs my left forearm with her right hand. "Just a quick word before you go, Kate?" Her pale pink nails are pressing ever so slightly into my skin, and her voice is light, almost chirpy. "I'm so glad that we'll be together at Briar Hill. I know how concerned your aunt is that you stay focused on your education, rather than—um, extracurricular activities?" On the last two words, the smile widens and she digs her nails in hard.

I wince for a second, but then paste on a fake smile to match Eve's, as several pairs of eyes are now watching us. Trey clearly realizes what she's doing, because he exhales sharply from just behind me.

I decide to try out one of the pressure-point tricks that Sensei Barbie and I were working on. I reach over like I'm going to clasp Eve's hand in both of mine and place my thumb inside the pressure point on her radial nerve, just above the wrist, where a nurse might take a pulse. Then I push downward with a rubbing motion. Eve is gripping my arm very tightly, and it works like a charm—her hand pops open, and she lets out a surprised yelp as she stumbles forward.

I'm pretty sure she would have fallen, just as I did when Barbie demonstrated that trigger point to me a few weeks back. It's not one of the potentially lethal grips—she showed me a few of those as well—but it definitely hurts, even when you're expecting it and have been warned to keep a light grip.

Eve doesn't fall, however. Trey's inner gentleman kicks in, and he catches her, propping her back up on her high heels.

"Oops," he says in a low voice. "You should be more careful, Eve."

She flashes him a smile that doesn't go anywhere near her eyes as she rubs her injured arm. "Indeed I should," she says. Then she leans toward him and whispers, "You should be careful, too. Kate's aunt says she likes to keep a little something going on the side. You might want to ask her about that."

I step forward, jaw clinched, but Trey slides his arm around my shoulders and steers me toward the door. "That was a neat trick. What exactly did you do to her?" he asks.

"Ninja secret. I'll show you later."

Patrick Conwell's ice-blue eyes follow us as Trey opens the sliding glass door and we slip inside. The afternoon sun is now lower on the horizon, casting the cavernous living room into shadow and making the brightly lit art alcoves stand out even more starkly. My eyes drift over the artwork in the niches as we hurry toward the foyer, until the painting in the third alcove stops me dead in my tracks.

The canvas is about three feet wide and maybe five feet high, so it takes up most of the niche. Several recessed spotlights illuminate the painting—a bizarre cross between the Virgin Mary and a fertility goddess. Prudence sits on the grass, legs crossed in the half-lotus position, her face tilted toward the sky, eyes closed. A loosely draped white dress conceals her very pregnant body. Her hands rest on her bare abdomen, and long dark hair cascades over her shoulders. I suspect Sara would classify the work as hyperrealist, because every leaf, every curve, every curl is finely detailed, the colors seeming to pop off the canvas, like a photograph on steroids.

No wonder Mrs. Meyer thought I looked familiar. If you ignore the extended belly—something I'm having a very difficult time doing—the fertility goddess in her living room looks exactly like me.

∞10∞

We're on a bench, waiting for the valet to bring Trey's car, when the front door swings open. Mrs. Denning, the Briar Hill principal, leans out to say something to the second valet, who holds the door open as she backs through, pulling a wheelchair. When she turns the chair around, we see the passenger: a very old, very dignified, and very angry man in a light gray pin-striped suit, his hair and mustache a shade darker than his jacket. A pair of wire-rimmed glasses sits atop a nose that is just a little too large for his face, and his eyes stare straight out at the lawn.

Mrs. Denning spots us on the bench. "You're Kate, right? Harry Keller's daughter?"

"Hi, Mrs. Denning."

She kneels down so that she can look Dr. Tilson in the eye, but he's still staring straight ahead. "Harvey, I'm going to leave you here with Miss Keller and . . ." She's clearly trying to remember Trey's name and then decides not to bother. "And the young man you spoke with earlier. I'll find Tony and have him take you home. He can come back for me later. I'm sorry you weren't made aware of the location, but you just can't say those things in public. We would have made other arrangements for your retirement party if I'd had any idea your . . . *prejudice* . . . against Cyrists was so strong."

Tilson whips his head toward her, pinning her with a steely glare. "A prejudice is an irrational opinion based on faulty or incomplete information, Carol Ann. My views are fully rational, based upon an extensive, decades-long study of these charlatans." He turns his gaze back toward the lawn, dismissing her.

With a shake of her head, Mrs. Denning looks at me and says in a semiwhisper, "You don't mind, do you, Kate? I shouldn't be but a few minutes."

"Oh, no. Not at all. We're just waiting on the car anyway."

Mrs. Denning pushes the wheelchair over and parks Tilson next to me, giving the old guy one more indignant look before scurrying off, her low heels clicking on the stone.

Once the door has closed behind her, Tilson glances briefly at Trey, then at me, lingering on my face. His eyes narrow and then dart down to my hands, which are mostly covered by the full red skirt. "Are you one of them, young lady?"

I start to answer, but Trey leans forward. "Dr. Tilson, this is Kate Pierce-Keller. Her dad teaches at Briar Hill? Harry Keller?"

"Don't know him. And she hasn't answered my question."

I lift my hands up and turn them around so that he can see the backs. "No, sir. Not a Cyrist. Not a fan, either," I add in a lower voice.

"Anyone ever told you that you resemble their female demigod?"

Demigod?

I give him a pained smile. "Yes, sir. That fact has complicated my life more than once."

His expression thaws slightly. "Well, you're a pretty girl, nonetheless, and more importantly, a smart one, if you want nothing to do with those frauds. I just wish you and Mr. Coleman had the privilege of graduating from Briar Hill before it sold its soul to the goddamn devil." He nods toward Trey. "As his father and grand-father can attest, it was once a fine school."

"It was still a fine school last year," I say.

"So your father teaches there now. Did he support this merger?"

"I don't think he had much say. He only started last January, a few months after we moved here from Iowa." I glance around and then continue in a lower voice. "But he didn't know Carrington Day was Cyrist, or he'd have told me. We're—well, I guess you could say we agree with you on that topic."

"And how about you, Coleman?"

Trey also looks around before he speaks. "I'd have said I was agnostic on the Cyrists a few months ago, but I've . . ." He gives me a quick smile and then looks back at Tilson. "Let's just say recent events have opened my eyes a bit."

Tilson nods vigorously. "Ah, the election."

I'm pretty sure that's not what Trey meant at all, but the old man continues. "I've never trusted them and never understood how anyone could fall for their bill of sale, but between the last campaign and some of the laws they've passed in the last few months, you'd think more eyes would be opened. Whatever happened to the First Amendment? Freedom of religion? Of speech? I'd like to think those laws will be overturned, but the Supreme Court is as useless as tits on a bull these days."

Trey and I just nod. It seems the safest response. I make a mental note to ask Connor for an update of recent events, because I've been paying too much attention to the past to focus on the here and now.

"But most people are fools," Tilson continues. "They see exactly what they want to see and nothing more. It's like Niemöller said, if you ignore it when they're taking rights from everyone else, pretty soon they'll come after yours, and there's no one left to protest."

Just then a stout man in his late fifties huffs through the door. "Dr. Tilson, Carol Ann tells me you're not feeling well. How about I take you back home?"

Tilson gives the two of us a conspiratorial glance. "Carol Ann is mistaken, Anthony. I've never felt better. I was just enjoying a pleasant conversation with two students whose futures your wife and the rest of the board have sold down the river. But, yes, all in all, I do think it's time to go home."

The man doesn't reply; he just glances around for the valets. They're both off fetching cars, so he turns the wheelchair around and begins lowering it, rather clumsily, down the stairs.

Trey jumps up. "Wait, I'll help."

Between the two of them, the wheels reach the pavement safely just as the cars arrive, Trey's blue Lexus following behind a tan SUV that must belong to Denning.

Tilson gives me a quick smile as they wheel him around to help him into the car. "Au revoir, Miss Keller."

I wave goodbye as I get into Trey's car. He joins me a minute or so later, shaking his head. "Well, now that we've ruled out barbecue for dinner, how do you feel about Mexican? There's a good place over on Wisconsin."

"Mexican is fine with me."

Trey calls ahead for a reservation. As we pull away from the house, I cast a parting look at the wide, green, soggy front lawn. The sky is beginning to cloud over again. Mrs. Meyer's party probably isn't going as well as she'd hoped, given the mushy grass and Tilson's unceremonious exit. Her comment about having Patrick put Katherine on the Cyrist prayer list gives me a shiver, especially since she seemed so sincere about it. Either she's a good actress or she really is oblivious to what's going on under her nose. I suspect it's the latter, since she seems oblivious to the fact that her granddaughter is a total bitch. I rub the inside of my arm, now decorated by four angry, blood-filled crescents.

Once we're out on the main road, I say, "Tilson is . . . interesting."

Trey laughs. "Yeah, that's one way of putting it. Someone should really have told him where his retirement party was being held. Even I knew he had strong views on the Cyrists, based on one of Dad's stories about his classes. When I introduced myself, he said I should tell my dad and granddad to be thankful they were students at Briar Hill when it was a real school and not the propaganda wing for a bunch of lotus-wearing parasites."

I laugh. "He actually said that?"

"Yeah. One of the teachers coming to Briar Hill from Carrington was within earshot, too, and you should have seen Principal Denning's face. Beet red. So . . . this demigod he was talking about?"

"Prudence—the aunt I mentioned who's working with Saul? Although I can't say I've ever heard her referred to as a demigod." I hesitate and then ask, "Did you see the painting in their living room?"

"Which one?"

I shudder. "If you have to ask which one, you didn't see it. Let's just say it would have to be entitled *Mother Prudence* rather than *Sister Prudence*. I thought you must have seen it, since you stepped in with that Disney Channel comment when Mrs. Meyer was trying to place my face."

He looks surprised. "No, I just hate when people spend five minutes trying to figure out who you look like, then decide it's their cousin Ed when he was your age, or whatever. And you do look like one of those girls. I can't remember the show, but she's cute, kind of short, with long, dark hair."

"Well, I look much more like Prudence, unfortunately." I decide to hit Google Images when I get home so that I can inoculate myself against the Cyrist notion of religious art. I don't want to be caught off guard the next time I'm walking along the National Mall in downtown DC and find a sidewalk vendor hawking statues of the Madonna Prudence next to the black-velvet paintings of Elvis.

"Who was the girl you were talking to?"

"Charlayne Singleton. My best friend before the Cyrist takeover, or whatever you want to call it. In that timeline, her brother, Joseph, was dating a Cyrist, but her mom and dad had mixed feelings. With this latest shift, Joseph is already married, and Charlayne's parents have been members of the Temple since before she was born. You actually met Charlayne in the other timeline. And Eve."

"I take it you and Eve have a history?"

"You could say that. I hit her over the head with a chair. And sort of kicked her dog."

A smile lifts the side of his mouth. "I'm going to guess they both had it coming?"

"Eve was planning to turn us over to Cyrist temple security. I apparently didn't hit her hard enough, because she released the hounds before we could get out of there. And yeah, the pup definitely asked for it." I lift the hem of my dress about two inches. Trey glances away from the road to see the two thin pink lines on my thigh from when I was bitten.

"Ouch." His expression shifts a bit, like he's thought of something he didn't particularly want to remember. He can't be remembering our close call at the temple, since that's simply not possible.

"It could have been much worse, believe me."

"Oh, I do," he says.

I don't really know what he means by that, so I just look out the window as the big estates give way to smaller lots and then, after we cross the Beltway, to a mélange of strip malls and apartment buildings. A gray sky forms the backdrop, with a few patches of orange-and-purple twilight peeking through.

Trey puts on some music—I think it's The Shins—and we ride along for a while in silence. Not the companionable kind of silence. More the I-have-no-idea-what-to-say-next kind of silence, and it's miserable.

Apparently Trey feels the same way, because after a few minutes, he blurts out, "God, Kate. What are you in the middle of? Do you have any idea how much power those people have? The *president* is Cyrist! Tilson is an old man in a wheelchair, so everyone thinks he's just a grumpy old jerk who wants kids to get the hell off his lawn. But you're talking about overthrowing them. Do you think they'll just sit still for that?"

I'm stunned by his outburst, and it's a moment before I'm able to respond. "No, Trey. I'm not *talking* about overthrowing them, at least not to anyone other than you. The only thing I told Tilson is that I'm not a fan of the Cyrists, and that could just as easily be me not wanting to further upset an already angry old man. You said the same thing. And if I'd known it was Eve freaking Conwell's house, I would never have agreed to go."

His brow creases further, but he doesn't say anything. After a minute, I remember the other thing I wanted to ask him. "You said your dad has some questions. How much have you told him?"

He shoots me an incredulous look. "Um . . . everything? I mean, I didn't let him watch the videos that I recorded of the two of us in the other timeline. That was . . . private. Between us. But the one I made for myself . . . yeah, he watched that. I don't know if he's showed it to Mom or not, but I can tell she's worried about me, and I don't think it's just that I'm starting a new school. I've done that every couple of years since kindergarten."

"But . . . why, Trey?" It hadn't even occurred to me that he might talk to his parents about this, probably because he hadn't in the other timeline.

"You really need to ask that? If a guy you'd never met showed up on your doorstep with something like that, are you telling me you wouldn't have talked to your parents or someone?"

Okay, he's got a point. I'm silent for a few seconds and then say, "You're right. I would have. It's just . . . you didn't tell them last time, so I guess I thought . . ."

We drive past the restaurant, which has a big neon cactus in the window. There's no parking near the front, so Trey goes down a few blocks and pulls into a garage.

I don't say anything until he switches off the car, and then I turn toward him. "So, your dad, does he believe any of this?"

"I'm not sure, Kate. I think the fact that the DVD included a file of his he's never shared with anyone, not even me, may have convinced him. But he won't admit it. The one thing I can tell you is he doesn't want me involved in any of this. In fact, he's made me promise that I *won't* get involved in it. I've had to hide or face an argument with him each time I've called you. He says the Cyrists have friends in very high places—"

"Yeah, he said that last time. Before we went to the temple. You told him we were just checking on Charlayne. That's when he mentioned the spreadsheet he was keeping. The one you put on the DVD. He was . . . nice. So was Estella."

I can hear the note of regret in my voice. I'm guessing neither of them will be so eager to meet me in this timeline. My eyes start to water, so I look down to detach my seat belt and start to get out.

I'm about to close the door when I remember to grab my clutch from the floorboard. It still has the stupid *Hello* sticker on the front. I yank it off a little too forcefully and fling the sticker back on the seat.

Trey is behind me, and he grabs my hand as I turn around. "Kate . . ."

I don't bother to hide the hurt in my eyes. "What, Trey?"

He just whispers my name again. And then his arm is around my waist, and there isn't even a fraction of an inch between our bodies, and I can barely breathe, but who cares? He wraps his other hand in my hair and pulls my lips toward his, the kiss hungry, with an undertone of despair.

It feels like a very specific kiss, one I've thought of every day since I went back in time to save Katherine.

I don't know how long we stand there. I just know that I don't want the kiss to end. Ever. Because when it does, we're going to walk into the restaurant and he's going to tell me that we need to step back and keep things light or maybe end it altogether. And that conversation isn't us. This is us. This is my Trey, right here, right now.

But eventually he pulls away and rests his hands against the side of the car. He stares at me for a long time before finally smiling. It's a little bit haunted, however, and it doesn't light up his face in the usual way. "We should get inside before they give our table away."

He reaches down for my hand, but I pull it back. "Trey, maybe you should just take me home. I think I know where this is going, and I don't want to have that conversation in a restaurant."

"*What* conversation?"

"The one where you tell me all the reasons this isn't going to work."

He looks confused. "Um . . . Kate? Was I the only person here a minute ago? Because I'm pretty sure you were here with me."

"No," I say, fighting down the urge to just grab him and kiss him again. "I was definitely here. But . . . that kiss . . . it felt like our very last kiss that day at Katherine's, before I left you behind. It felt like goodbye."

My voice breaks on the last word, and he pulls me to his chest. After a minute, he tilts my face upward until our eyes meet. "I can't remember that other kiss, so I'll have to take your word on whether they were the same. But I *have* watched the DVD I made, Kate. Quite a few times. And I can promise you that other kiss wasn't me telling you goodbye. It was me saying that we have to find some way to make this work, because I don't want to lose you."

∞

The restaurant is noisy and crowded, but given that it's Saturday night, we're probably lucky to have a table. Mexican movie posters line the walls near the entrance, and the waitress leads us to a small table near the emergency exit, just beneath a tall, colorful painting of a cowboy, his hat pulled down low to hide his face. Trey and I make several attempts to talk over the music, the party of twelve next to us, and the couple behind us with two grouchy toddlers, but we finally give up on conversation and just settle for entwining our feet under the little table while we eat our fajitas.

The rain slacks off a bit by the time we finish, and Trey suggests we find someplace quieter to talk. We seem to have landed on one of the few blocks in the DC area without a Starbucks in sight, so we duck into a little café and order coffee and cobbler à la mode, supposedly to share. I think the dessert is going to be all Trey, because I just pigged out on fajitas. But it's blackberry, and it smells really good when the waiter slides it in front of us, so I give in and try a bite.

When the cobbler is history and the waiter has topped off our mugs, Trey grabs my hand across the table, lacing our fingers together. "Okay, what I said back there in the garage? I meant it. We have to find some way to make this work. And I think doing that is going to require complete honesty and openness on both sides. Shall I start?"

I nod, and he continues. "When you gave me the DVD, I watched it a few times, and then I called Dad in. I knew it was me—I mean, the thing about knowing what I did that Saturday—"

I grin. "Yes. I've been meaning to ask you about that."

He gives me a grimace, then he says, "Okay, first revision of the ground rules. Complete honesty and openness about anything we've done after age fourteen."

I laugh. "Hmm. I'll have to consider that one."

"Anyway, I knew it was me. But, Kate, I'm pretty sure you've watched that video more than once, too. What did you see?"

Confused, I raise an eyebrow. "I saw . . . you, recording a message for the two of us."

"Yeah, but . . ." He shakes his head. "That guy in the video was me, but he looked kind of rough. I don't think he'd slept in days. He certainly hadn't shaved."

"You look good with a little scruff."

"I'll keep that in mind. But my expression . . . I mean, I looked hopeful, but underneath that, I looked kind of manic. Terrified. Like this was a last-ditch effort and if I didn't get you back . . ." He shakes his head. "Anyway, look at the DVD when you get home tonight, and try to put yourself into my dad's shoes. Or your parents' shoes, if you were the one in that video. What advice do you think they'd have given you—even leaving the political and time travel aspects out of the equation?"

I think for a minute. Mom would have overreacted. She'd have been terrified and would probably have gotten a restraining order to keep Trey as far away as possible. And I would have known that's what she'd do, so I wouldn't have told her. But Dad? I'm pretty sure I'd have confided in him, and . . .

"Dad would have told me to be very, very careful. To think everything through and be sure I knew what I was getting into."

He nods. "That was pretty much my dad's response. He said I needed to be sure I was thinking with my brain instead of . . ."

"Your heart?"

"Sort of," he says, with a wry grin.

"Oh. Got it."

"Yeah, well—let's come back to that point in just a minute. To get back to Dad, he was debating having me finish up down in Peru, at my old school. That says a lot about how worried he was, since that would have meant disappointing his own dad on the whole three-generations-at-Briar-Hill thing. And I said no, even though six weeks ago that was what I wanted—I mean, who really wants to switch schools your last year, you know? But I knew he was suggesting it only because he wanted to put some distance between me and you."

I've only met his dad once, but that stings. I feel like a disease he's trying to protect his son from, and as much as I hate to admit it, he has a point. I try to hide my reaction, but Trey can tell.

"Hey." He raises our joined hands up to his lips and kisses my fingers. "He doesn't know you, Kate. He will, eventually, and once all of this craziness is over, he's going to see why I think you're worth fighting for."

I shake my head. "I won't come between you and your parents, Trey. I don't know what I was thinking, pulling you back into this. Your dad is right, I was selfish and—"

I try to pull my hand away and get up from the table, but Trey just grips it tighter. "What? Don't I get a say in this? Sit down, Kate. Let me finish. Please?"

I slide back into the chair and stare at the empty dessert plate. He doesn't say anything for a minute, just rubs the crease between my thumb and forefinger until I finally look up at him.

"As I was saying," he continues, "I put my foot down on the whole Peru thing. Eventually, we reached a compromise. He's been acting overprotective, but deep down, he trusts my judgment. I told him I'm not going to stop seeing you, but I will do my best to keep clear of this whole Cyrist thing. From what you've told me, there's not much I can do to help anyway. I mean, I want to know what you're doing—hell, I'm going to worry either way, but I think it's better knowing than not knowing. But . . . I need to ask you a couple of questions, okay? First, about the whole timelines thing."

"Okay . . ."

He bites the side of his lip. "I'm not quite sure how to put this, but that other version of me? Do you think he still exists somewhere? I mean, I've heard about this multiple universes theory where different realities sort of coexist. Do you think that's what happened—you spun off a different reality when you went back and saved Katherine?"

I shrug one shoulder. "I don't know. Katherine said they weren't even sure about that in her era. I do know what your opinion of that theory was in the other timeline, however."

"And?"

I squeeze his hand. "You said it was total BS. That the other timeline would end and we'd get a fresh start."

He looks a bit skeptical but smiles and says, "Okay, I'll defer to the wisdom of the other me. Now, the second question . . ." He stares down at the table for a second, and I realize he's blushing. "Were we . . . have we . . . um . . ." He glances up to my face and raises his eyebrows.

"Oh," I say as I realize what he's getting at. "No. We haven't. Close but not quite." I give him a little grin. "I wanted to, but you were playing hard to get."

"Really?" He laughs. "Based on every bit of evidence to date, I find that hard to believe."

My expression grows serious. "It's true, and as much as I hate to say it, you were right. You said we both needed to be able to remember our first time, and you wouldn't have. And . . . again, as much as I hate to say it, that situation hasn't changed. I can't promise this timeline is stable, although I am working on that about seventy-two hours a day."

"Literally or figuratively?"

"Literally. I should probably warn you that if this keeps up much longer, you're going to be involved with an older woman."

He grins like he's imagining the possibilities. "I think I could deal with that."

I nudge his shoe with mine. "Back to the present, Mr. Coleman. Any other questions?"

"Probably, but I can't think of them right now. My mind is still back on the whole close-but-not-quite comment."

"Well, your mind needs to catch up, because I need to tell it a few things."

And I do need to tell him a few things, because he's right about total honesty and open communication. I have to tell him about Kiernan. I would probably have done it anyway, but after Eve's snide comment, I don't want to leave any doubts in his mind.

"Okay, this is kind of hard for me," I begin. "I still have a difficult time wrapping my own head around it. But just as there was another you in that other timeline that you can't remember, there was also another me in an entirely different timeline. At some point when there was one of these shifts that Kate wasn't under the protection of a medallion. When the Cyrists changed that reality, she just—poof. She was gone."

"So how do you know about her? I mean, I can't remember this other Trey, and you said that the only reason you can remember him is that you were wearing the medallion, right?"

"Right. I don't remember that Kate. But . . . someone else remembers that timeline. He's not supposed to. The Cyrists or, more specifically, my aunt Prudence thought she'd taken care of that by swiping his CHRONOS key. But he had another one, a key that I gave him when he was a kid back at the Expo. He kept that one hidden from her."

"Why would she want to wipe this kid's memory?"

"That's where it gets confusing. Kiernan wasn't a kid anymore when she did that. He was twenty, and he'd been a member of the Cyrist inner circle before he . . . fell in love with that other Kate."

I spend the next half hour trying to unravel my rather complicated, multilevel past with Kiernan. And, as I expected, Trey's eyes grow more and more wary.

"That's what Eve was talking about, then?"

I nod. "Prudence told me to stay away from Kiernan. But that's hard to do, since he's the only other person on our side who can use the medallions. And he has information on what we tried before in the other timeline, and—"

"Okay, he was in love with that other Kate. Is he in love with you?"

I'm not sure how to answer that. Is he in love with me? Or with a ghost who looks like me?

"I don't know, Trey. He's definitely still in love with *her*. He wishes I was *his* Kate, that she was still here. And I'm pretty sure he thinks if things were different, I could *become* that other Kate, but . . ."

"Could you?"

I shake my head. "I'll admit I care about Kiernan. It's hard not to. He saved my life. I guess I saved his as well, although he'd never have been caught in Holmes's hotel as a kid if he hadn't been helping me. I can definitely see how that other Kate fell in love with him in different circumstances. But in order for me to be that Kate, I'd have to give up everything. I don't want to live in 1905. I don't want to give up my family."

"I can understand that."

"But aside from all of those issues," I say, looking deep into his eyes, "there's one other major impediment, Trey. I'm already in love with you."

He doesn't say anything for a really long time, and when he finally speaks, his face is troubled. "I don't like it. I don't like that this guy is going to be hanging around. And I *really* don't like that he can help you when I can't." He squeezes my hand. "But, that said, if I could help you, it would blow my compromise with Dad and . . . while I suspect you can generally take care of yourself, the fact that there's someone watching your back, someone who would risk his life to save yours? It makes me breathe a little easier. Does that make sense? Jealous as hell but also a little grateful?"

"Yes. If this were reversed, I'd feel the same way. But you said before that you want to know what I'm doing, and I'm wondering— would it be easier if I didn't mention things involving Kiernan? I don't want to make you feel jealous. I wouldn't like thinking about you with some girl who . . . feels about you the way that Kiernan does about me."

He shakes his head. "Open and honest, even when it hurts. That's the only way this can work, Kate."

I pull in a deep breath and then let it out slowly. "Then I guess I need to tell you that I'll be seeing him tomorrow. We have to go to Depression-era Georgia."

"Well," Trey says, "at least he makes it easy for me to take you places that are more fun."

"I think I'd prefer 1938 Georgia to another barbecue at Eve's house." He laughs, and I add, "And this isn't a date. It's work."

"Okay," he says. "When?"

"Two o'clock."

"Here's the deal, then. You do what you have to do, but after you get back from this . . . assignment . . . or any other time you're going to be working with this guy, you call me, so I can come right over. Or better yet, call me before you go."

It will take some creativity. Katherine would have a fit if Trey came by during a jump, and I don't want to upset her. But it's definitely doable. "Okay," I tell him. "But . . . why?"

"Because I don't want him on your mind for too long. That seems a little dangerous to me. I know you said you're not *his* Kate, but I want equal time to make sure you remember you're *my* Kate."

∞11∞

The alarm went off fifteen minutes ago, but I'm still in bed, trying to organize my brain. Thoughts of the party and the clash with Eve compete with much more tempting memories of the final part of the evening with Trey. He delivered me to the doorstep a few minutes before twelve, as promised, and gave me the final, chaste kiss he seemed to feel was appropriate, just in case anyone was peeking out the windows. The act might have fooled a casual observer, but we were both still breathing a bit heavy from a long interlude in a secluded parking area overlooking Cabin John Creek.

Aside from Dad, who was dutifully parked on the couch with a book when I walked in, the rest of the house was quiet. I gave him the brief answer to his "Did you have a good time?" (*Yes, wonderful!* along with a kiss on the cheek) and then floated up the stairs.

But it is now morning, and I need to report back to the team on the elements that weren't so wonderful.

First, however, I run a Google Image search on "Prudence" and "Cyrist." There are no photographs, but there are dozens of drawings and paintings, all very similar, including quite a few of her in the late stages of pregnancy. Even in the clip art, the face is clearly defined, the hair long and curly, and the entire package disturbingly like me. Not identical, however. Most of the paintings show a face that's a little wider than mine, especially across the brow. Her nose is a bit shorter, the shape of her lips slightly different. Her breasts are definitely larger, but then she's pregnant in most of the paintings and being depicted as a fertility goddess in others, and I've never seen a fertility goddess with normal-sized boobs.

Out of curiosity, I run a similar search for other religions. There seems to be a bias against redheaded Marys, but you have blond Marys and brunette Marys and Marys of almost every ethnicity. Depictions of the various Hindu goddesses don't have the same range, but their appearance varies at least somewhat from one picture to the next. I have a feeling no one's plagued by constantly being told she looks like Mary or Lakshmi or any other religion's demigod or patron saint.

I take the iPad down to the kitchen, still in my pj's. Daphne's at attention at the far end of the counter. She's too well trained to snatch anything, but it looks like she's trying to will a slice, or maybe even the entire platter, to jump off the counter and onto the floor. So far, it isn't working.

Dad, who's chopping vegetables by the sink, has put Connor to work mixing the eggs. But Connor is stirring them instead of whisking them, which means we're going to end up with rubbery omelets. I set my tablet down on the other side of the bar and hold out my hands for the large silver bowl. "I believe that's *my* brunch assignment. But you can make yourself useful and pour the sous chef some coffee."

"With pleasure." Connor gives me the bowl and grabs a mug from the cabinet. "Did you and Trey have a good time?"

"We had a very good time, but . . . also a rather complicated time. Is Katherine eating with us?"

"Not sure. She was still asleep when I . . . checked on her."

"I *know*, Connor," I say with a sympathetic smile. "It's okay. I'm not a little kid. You guys don't have to hide it anymore."

"Yeah, well, you'll have to clear that with your grandmother. And I suspect you don't want to have that conversation with her, right?" He gives me a tight little grin as he hands me the coffee.

I respond with a point-taken look.

"So, why were you wondering about Katherine?" Connor asks.

"Just debating whether to wait and fill everyone in when she's here, too."

"Her sleep is off due to the change in her medications, so I'll just give her the highlights later." The upside of Katherine's outburst at our pizza summit the other night is that it finally convinced her to see the doctor to adjust her meds.

"Okay." I grab the milk from the fridge and pour a bit into my coffee, then add a larger splash to the eggs and start whisking again, putting a bit more muscle into it this time so that the omelets will be nice and fluffy. "So, Dad, did you know that Carrington Day was Cyrist?"

He looks over his shoulder from the stove. "Uh, no. That's something I'd definitely have mentioned."

"That's what I thought."

"Who is Carrington Day?" Connor asks.

"The correct question would be what is Carrington Day."

"Okay, *what* is Carrington Day?"

"Carrington Day School is merging with Briar Hill," Dad says. "It was decided back in January, right after I started teaching. In this timeline, at any rate. Kate didn't remember it."

"As I discovered last night, Carrington Day is a Cyrist school. I don't know if it's officially owned by the Cyrists, but the party was held at the home of Eve Conwell. Her grandparents have this larger-than-life painting of Prudence in their living room, with her pregnant belly sticking out. It was like looking in a weird funhouse mirror."

"So I take it you didn't stay long," Dad says.

"Correct. Trey needed to speak with this teacher who's retiring from Briar Hill, but we left just after."

"Harvey Tilson, right? He's been out on sick leave since I started teaching."

"Yes. Whoever decided to hold his retirement party and the Carrington Day welcome at the same time clearly didn't ask for his input. He was livid. Said he'd spent decades researching those charlatans, and let's just say he thinks the merger is a bad idea. That it'll turn Briar Hill into a propaganda tool."

"That probably *is* a risk for science, although I'd think it's a bigger issue for social sciences. But I doubt it will affect my department. How would you politicize math?"

Connor snorts. "There are always the word problems, Harry. 'You have ten apples. You give one apple to Cyrus. How many do you have now?' And the correct answer will be, 'It depends. If you only have nine, Cyrus does not find you worthy.'"

We toss around a few more word problem possibilities. None of them are particularly funny, and Connor's quip about subtracting the unfaithful from the global population is gallows humor, pure and simple.

"Well," Connor says finally, "this definitely means you won't be going to school."

"No, it doesn't. Eve's memory wasn't wiped—she remembered our encounter at the temple. And Prudence seems to be using her as a messenger. They're *watching* me, and I don't think Pru's exactly happy with what she's seeing. I don't know if this has to do with me working with Kiernan or what, but Eve said my aunt was very concerned that I focus on my studies, instead of what she called 'extracurricular activities.' Which reminds me, have you noticed the blue van outside? The one that's always parked at the curb?"

"You mean the one that belongs to the guy next door?" Connor asks.

"I guess. You're sure about that? I've gotten a weird feeling . . ."

"Yes. I've talked to the guy. Kate, you know as well as I do that the Cyrists don't need a surveillance van to see who's coming and going. All they have to do is set up a stable point and have someone with the CHRONOS gene monitor it for activity."

"Yes. But you can't hear them. For that, you'd need the type of equipment that you might be able to hide in a van. But whether they're watching from a van or a stable point doesn't matter— either way, they'll know if I'm not going to school. We're in a state of truce right now. If they see me stepping out of line, things are going to heat up really, really fast."

"All the more reason to hunker down and get this over with," Connor says.

Dad gives me a meaningful glance over his shoulder. *Your call, don't let him bully you.*

"Maybe," I say. "But school starts on Tuesday, which leaves today and Labor Day. I'm still researching the other two jumps, and there are only so many times I can repeat the same day. I pulled several seventy-two-hour days last week, and unless I start sleeping in the past or sleeping less than eight hours, it's going to be hard to cram much more than three days into one twenty-four-hour slot. And that's doubly true if I'm going to avoid bumping into myself. Since Katherine said that's a bad idea and Kiernan's pretty certain it's a key reason Prudence is now several fries short of a Happy Meal, I'd kind of like to avoid it."

"So you think it's a good idea for you and Harry to just stroll into Briar Hill every day? Like nothing has happened?"

"I'm not sure we have a choice, Connor," Dad says as he pours the last of the eggs into the pan. "As Kate just noted, she can't wrap all of this up before school starts, even if she repeats the next two days over and over. Prudence might suspect Kate's working against them, but she's going to be even more suspicious if Kate disappears. If I had my way, I'd pack her into the car and we'd go back to Iowa—"

"Ick."

"Or *somewhere* remote, and hope and pray they don't find us," he continues, giving me an annoyed look for the interruption. "But since we can't pick up the apparatus you have protecting this house and take it on the road, I'd prefer to have Kate, and myself for that matter, sleeping under a stable CHRONOS field until this is over."

Connor huffs. "Which was kind of my point, Harry. When the two of you are at school, you aren't under a stable CHRONOS field."

"Connor," I say, "we can go round and round about this, but the reality is that we need to stall Prudence for at least a week or so. Dad's right. She has eyes and ears at Briar Hill. If I'm not in class, she'll know something is up, and I don't think anything we have here is going to protect us from a full Cyrist onslaught if Prudence decides the truce is off. She was adamant about two things when we clashed at the Expo: stay out of her way, and stay away from Kiern—"

As I'm finishing the sentence, I realize there was a third thing. *Be nice to your mother.*

"It wasn't Katherine," I say softly.

Connor pauses midbite. "What wasn't Katherine?"

"Mom's trip. I thought—"

"Why would you think Katherine was connected to that?" Connor says.

"And," Dad adds, "if you thought that, why didn't you say something earlier?"

"Well, Mom wouldn't have gone if she thought it had anything to do with Katherine, and she was so happy about the grant. And I didn't have any proof . . ."

"You definitely didn't," Connor says, "because Katherine didn't have anything to do with it. But what made you figure that out now?"

"Something Prudence said at the Expo. I think maybe Prudence arranged the trip to be sure Mom is far away from here."

Dad looks alarmed. "Then we need to let Deborah know. She could be in danger."

I shake my head. It's more of a gut feeling than anything solid, but I don't believe Prudence would endanger Mom. She might be willing to let us *think* she would, but . . .

"Prudence won't hurt her. Whatever she may think about Katherine, or about me for that matter, she doesn't hold it against Mom. If anything, I think Prudence took Mom out of the picture to keep her safe. I don't know about you, but I'm pretty okay with that, at least until this is all over."

Dad still looks skeptical.

"That doesn't mean I'm not going to call her right now," I say, "because this kind of creeps me out."

I put my plate in the sink and grab my tablet. That reminds me why I brought it downstairs in the first place, so I turn back to Connor. "Do we have anything I could use as a disguise? Not just period costumes but something to make me look different. I can't just go around looking like this on jumps."

"Like what?" Connor asks.

"Like me. Like Prudence. Obviously, when I'm at school being a good, little sheep, it doesn't matter. But when I'm doing things that are potentially truce breaking, it's kind of dumb not to use a little subterfuge. Hair color? Floppy hat? Fake glasses?"

They both nod, but I don't think they get the full picture. Of course, they didn't see the look the woman at the barbecue gave me when I bumped her plate. It was almost like I'd honored her by knocking fruit onto her shoe.

A phone rings, and Dad pulls his cell out of his pocket. "Oh. It's my mom."

For a weird moment, I think he means Evelyn, and then I realize it's Grandma Keller. "Tell her hello for me," I say as he heads into the living room.

I pull up the image search from earlier and slide the tablet over to Connor. "This is what I'm talking about. There are paintings of Prudence going back several hundred years, and they're way too close for comfort. Well, except for the pregnant ones, thank God. What's up with all of those?"

He casts an uncomfortable look toward the living room.

"Really, Connor. I'm not asking about the mechanics. Obviously, Prudence was pregnant at some point, and I've already had the little talk about how that happens. Why is it central to their mythology, or whatever?"

"Well, Saul needed people on his side who could use the key. Both to tweak the timeline and, maybe, from the religious side of things, to be the ones the Cyrists view as eternal and unchanging. With Prudence, he had two options, right? She could go back and convince his former colleagues or their offspring to join the Cyrists, but I don't think Saul had many friends among the other historians. Also, the CHRONOS gene seems to get weaker each generation, at least in my own experience, and the trait isn't always expressed. The other option would be to use Prudence to create his own little cadre of time travelers. And that last option might be easier, since those kids could be born at pretty much any point in time."

My omelet stirs uneasily in my stomach, both at what I'm thinking and at the realization that I've been a bit naive about all of this. Given the pictures, I assumed that Prudence had a child or children, but I hadn't really thought about those pregnancies as being a conscious strategy. And that raises a whole host of other questions.

"You don't really think Saul would . . ." I pause, not wanting to finish the sentence.

"I don't know. He's planning on wiping out half of humanity, so who knows where he draws the line. But I assume that he . . ." He rubs his eyes with the palm of his hand and then looks up and continues in a very matter-of-fact voice, "That he . . . bred her with one or more of the other historians or one of their children or grandchildren. But I don't think we can exclude anything, and I'm not sure that it really matters now."

"Of course, it matters. How can you even say that?" I look back down at one of the images, a painting of Prudence with small children gathered around her feet and one more clearly on the way. Suddenly, it's hard for me to think of the Prudence I met at the Expo. All I can think of is the girl I saw at Norumbega the other day. She'd looked haunted. Maybe even drugged.

Connor looks a little hurt. "That's not what I meant, Kate. Yes, it matters. She's your aunt, Katherine's daughter. In that sense, it definitely matters—"

I cut him off. "Prudence was fourteen when she disappeared. How old was she the first time she was—I can't even believe we're using this word—*bred*? Was it her choice? Did she have any say at all?"

"Whether or not Prudence was a willing participant in all of this doesn't change anything for us. It doesn't change—"

Dad comes back into the kitchen, and Connor stops when he sees Dad's face. We both ask what's wrong at the same time, and Dad kind of sinks down onto the bench at the breakfast nook.

"It's my dad. He . . . he had a stroke."

"Oh my God. Is he going to be okay?"

He shakes his head. "They don't know. He's in intensive care. Mom's a wreck. Listen, Katie . . . I need to . . . I need to go, okay?"

"Of course! I'll pack some things—"

"No," he says. "You should stay."

"But I want to see him!"

"Kate, he's not conscious right now. There's nothing you can do."

"But Grandma is conscious. I don't want her to think I don't—"

"Baby, it's okay. I told her you have school and that someone needs to stay here with Katherine. She understands. I hate leaving you right now, but—"

"No. No, Dad. You need to go."

"It's okay," Connor says. "We'll take care of her, Harry."

Dad's expression is hard to read. It looks for a moment like he's going to snap at Connor, but then he takes a breath and shakes his head. "I should only be gone a few days. I still don't like it. What god-awful timing."

I spend the next hour repeating many of the same things I told Mom the week before she left—*I'll be fine. I'm a big girl now.* I leave out the part about being really busy, because Dad knows exactly how busy I'll be and thinking about what I'll be doing while he's gone won't make either one of us feel any better about him leaving.

∞

Maps of downtown areas don't change much over time. After staring for about half an hour at a grainy, low-resolution 1938 map of Athens, Georgia, we found online, I compared it with Google Maps and found only a few new streets and one or two name changes. Otherwise they were identical, so I'm sticking with the digital version that doesn't give me a headache and does give me useful stuff, like estimated walking times.

Yesterday was divided between language lessons and going over the details for the 1938 recon jump. The plan is to go in and, simply put, observe. I need to get familiar with the city, the era, and the customs. If I'm feeling ambitious, I'll watch the three historians from a distance, but I'm not going to make contact.

I'm in the middle of counting the blocks from the stable point to my destination when there's a tap at my door—and I promptly forget whether I counted seven or eight. I rub my eyes. "Come in?"

"I won't ask if you're busy," Connor says, "because I already know the answer. But I need your CHRONOS gene for a few minutes."

"Too bad I can't rip it out and hand it to you. What do you need me to do?"

He sits on the arm of the couch and leans forward. "I think I've found Wallace Moehler. I'm not sure we want to let Katherine know this yet, but if I'm right, he didn't go to Russia. He went to Copenhagen. And it's 1955, not 1957."

"Okay. That's incredible. How did you manage to track him if she gave us the wrong year and the wrong country? *Sputnik* was in 1957, right?"

"Yes, but I asked Katherine a few . . . clarifying questions, shall we say . . . about Wallace when her medicines started kicking in last night. She mentioned something she hadn't before, something about him attending the International Geophysical Year. IGY was this huge scientific conference held in 1957 and 1958, but the planning began two years earlier. So I started poking around and pulled up this article about how the U.S. and U.S.S.R. were just starting the space race and some Eisenhower administration bigwig announced we'd have a satellite in orbit as part of our participation in IGY. And that tiffs off the Soviets, whose representative at IGY calls—you guessed it—a press conference to say the Soviets will do it first. And theirs will be bigger. The international press sort of rolled its eyes, but the Soviet guy was right."

He tosses me a printout of a photograph. Men in suits, mostly middle-aged, sit in front of a window. A slightly younger guy stands off to the left. The only odd thing about the picture is the curtain, which is white lace and looks out of place for a press conference.

"Which of these guys is Moehler?"

"Funny," he says and then looks like he's considering it. "Hmph. I guess he could be in the photo. Hadn't really thought about that. Katherine's description is average height and weight, thinning hair, glasses, kind of geeky looking."

"So pretty much any one of them. Is there a stable point nearby?"

"There are only two stable points in Copenhagen for the 1950s, so it will be pretty easy to check. The one at Rosenborg Castle is closest to the Russian Embassy, so I'd start there. The newspaper article says the press conference was August 2nd. He might have come in earlier, however, so maybe check August 1st as well."

He hands me my old nemesis, the *Log of Stable Points*, and I groan.

"You'd prefer doing the language lessons?"

"*Nyet*. I'll let you know what I find."

"What were you doing with the maps? Is that something Katherine or I could take over?"

I shake my head. I mean, they could figure out how many blocks I'll be from the stable point, but it's really more about getting a feel for the place before I go, and I'm not sure how to farm that out. "Maybe one of you could make some coffee? The good stuff."

He comes back twenty minutes later with a big mug of coffee, a protein bar, and an oatmeal cream pie. "Brain food or comfort food?"

I snatch the oatmeal pie. "But leave the protein bar. I'll get to it eventually."

"Any luck?" He sits down beside me on the couch and looks over my shoulder at the *Log*, even though I'm pretty sure he's only seeing row after row of black squares.

"Yeah, actually. Maybe too much." I grab the pen and notepad from the coffee table, jot down another entry, and hand it to him. The list now includes six different jump coordinates, and I'm not quite finished. "There was apparently a lot going on that Moehler wanted to see on August 1st. He had several different suits, and he's wearing a mustache one time, but mostly he's just really average looking. Three different versions of him could be standing in a group, and you'd never notice it was the same guy."

I take the list back and tap the third entry, which has a little star next to it. "So far, this is my best guess for which one was his final jump—the one after Saul's attack. Everyone else has been a little off balance when they land from that jump. Katherine said she was knocked over. Evelyn twisted her ankle. When I was researching Port Darwin, Adrienne looked like someone had punched her in the gut. She just sat there in the stable point, stunned, for two or three minutes. But I haven't found anything like that yet."

Connor goes back to the library, and I go back to viewing the stable points. About five minutes later, I find Wallace Moehler's last jump. He arrives in the little nook along the stone walls at the rear of Rosenborg Castle at 5:45 a.m. on August 1st. When Moehler lands, he sways on his feet for a split second and then falls flat on his ass, his legs splayed out in front of him, nearly smacking his head against the wall. He's less than a foot from the stable point, so I mostly see his torso. He has a black briefcase in his lap and the CHRONOS key in his left hand.

Moehler sits there for maybe thirty seconds, probably trying to process what he's just seen at headquarters. Then he tucks the medallion into his jacket pocket, straightens his glasses, and starts to stand. He's about halfway to his feet when he rocks backward again. This time his head does hit the wall, and he slumps against it. I watch Moehler's face in the display for several seconds, wondering what happened. Then I see the small red circle on his forehead and the thin red line spreading downward onto his nose.

$$\infty$$

BOSTON, MASSACHUSETTS
July 31, 1905, 10:25 a.m.

Kiernan transfers the Copenhagen stable point to his key and then hands the *Log* back to me. It's stupid, but I feel better now. Katherine wasn't able to stabilize the display enough to see it, and, of course, Connor couldn't see anything. I knew I hadn't imagined it, but it's nice to know that someone else has seen the shooting, too.

Kiernan's still in his Boudini bathing suit, his hair sticking up in spikes. He drums his fingers along the edge of his CHRONOS key before pulling it up to watch one more time.

Only a few minutes have passed for him since we returned from Norumbega—it was the one time that I knew for certain he'd still be in the room. But he seems a lot drier than he should be, given that he was soaked when I left.

I'm about to ask why when he says, "You're sure no one took the key from Moehler after he was shot?"

"As sure as I can be without watching it straight through. I fast-forwarded in thirty-second increments for the next three hours, until a groundskeeper finds his body and calls the police. Before the groundskeeper arrives, the only things that come into the picture are a bird and a stray piece of paper that blows past. We need to go back through and watch the entire thing to be sure, but—"

"I'll handle it. When we get back from the Athens jump."

"Thanks," I say, and then something about his voice stops me. What exactly is he saying he'll handle? That he'll watch the stable point in real time, no fast-forwarding? Or . . .

"What do you mean you'll handle it?"

He just looks at me.

"No. Absolutely not. Do *not* retrieve that key. There's someone in the garden with a gun, for God's sake."

"C'mon, Kate. I could blink in, grab the key, and be back before anyone has time to aim and fire. For all we know, the KGB saw Moehler hanging around the Russian embassy and decided he was a spy. Even if it's Simon or some other Cyrist in the garden, which, I repeat, we do *not* know, they're not expecting me—"

"Bullshit, Kiernan! We don't know what they're expecting. They're watching us. Not just you, not just here, but me as well, and Prudence apparently doesn't like what she's seeing."

He raises his eyebrows expectantly, and I tell him about Eve's warning to me at the party. "So, unless they have cameras in Katherine's house, which Connor says isn't possible, they've either seen me here in your apartment or when we were walking around Boston."

I take a ragged breath before continuing, the words tumbling out. "Or, yes, even more likely, when we went to Norumbega. And please do not remind me that you tried to cancel that trip. I was wrong, okay? Let's just accept as given that I'm incredibly stupid and this is all my . . ."

Kiernan reaches over and takes my hands in his own, and my sentence trails off in midstream a few words later. It's actually a very clever tactic for shutting me up, since I always use my hands for emphasis when I'm agitated. I'm a little surprised that no one has done it before. Then I look at Kiernan's face, and I'm pretty sure that *he* has done it before. More than once, judging from his expression.

He looks down at my hands and runs his thumb across the Band-Aid on my forefinger. I lost the other bandage somewhere during the day, and he pulls that hand toward him, pressing his lips against the chafed knuckle. When he looks back up at me, his eyes are on the brink of tearing over.

"I don't know what to do, Kate. Before, when things went all to hell and you were upset, I'd take you in my arms and hold you and tell you it would all be fine, all be okay." He laughs—a brief, bitter sound—and shakes his head. "It was a load of crap, and we both knew it, deep down, but somehow it seemed like maybe everything would be okay when I held you."

I look down, focusing resolutely on his hands clasped around mine, warm and strong. I don't dare catch his eye, because there's this rebel voice in my head telling me that it would be really nice, unbelievably nice, to feel like everything will be okay. Even if it was only for a minute. Even if we both knew it was a load of crap.

"I went back, Kate. Back to Norumbega. Not to finish the show—Operation Boudini is on ice for the time being."

An image flashes through my mind: the audience at Norumbega, frozen in place, waiting for Kiernan to return. Or not return. Or is it both at the same time, like that experiment with Schrödinger's cat?

"I went back when the theater was empty," he says, "and I set a stable point in the auditorium, up in the fly space. The area above the proscenium?"

I have no idea what either of those words mean, but I nod so that he'll keep going.

"That way I could see the entire audience. They aren't there every show. Tito was exaggerating. I've been doing this for over two weeks, and they've been there maybe one show out of three. Usually Simon is with her. Sometimes it's June. She's the doctor down at Estero. Once it was another guy—I don't remember his name. Pru just watches. Just stares at the stage when I'm up there."

"That's what she was doing when I saw her. She looked . . . odd."

"I didn't get close enough to see her very clearly, but it's like she's, I don't know, drugged or something. I'm pretty sure she was expecting—she was always wearing one of those dresses that are gathered up high, so it's not noticeable, or at least not as much. I've seen Pru at every age, Kate—well, every age between seventeen and, I don't know, maybe forty. I've seen her both times she was with child, and I've seen her pretty near stark, raving mad. But I've never seen her like that. Like she was a shell, almost, with no one inside at all."

I finally look up at him and nod. That's pretty much what I thought when I saw her at Norumbega, even though it was only a brief glimpse.

"So Prudence had two children?" I ask.

"She had two pregnancies. One was miscarried. And I have no idea how many children. I'm guessing maybe twenty total."

He sees my expression and shakes his head. "After the first two pregnancies, Pru put her foot down. Told Saul she was tired of puking all day, and he agreed but only on the condition that she give up her eggs. There were dozens of Cyrist women more than happy to carry her babies to term. And let's just say Estero had an extremely *modern* infirmary from the very beginning."

"Who was the father?"

Kiernan shrugs. "To be honest, I don't know. It wasn't something Pru ever brought up, and I wasn't stupid enough to ask."

He draws in a deep breath and releases my hands, then reaches up and rubs his temples. His eyes stay locked on my face, and I feel like he's measuring me, deciding whether or not to say what's on his mind. "There were six men at the Farm, the one we were at in Illinois, who had some ability with the key, including me, although I was nowhere near a man at that point and my abilities may have been the weakest of the lot. My da was a lot better with it. And I know for a fact that they tried to convince him to . . . shall we say, donate to the cause?"

"Did he?"

"No. I didn't understand a lot of what was going on back then, but I put the pieces together later. It was one of the things he fought Pru about. Not the main one, but . . . I remember him telling her once that he was doing his damnedest to get his one child out of their clutches so why would he be fool enough to let her take more of them hostage. It didn't make sense then, but looking back . . ."

We sit there in silence. I have other questions, but I don't have the energy, physical or mental, to ask or process the answers.

Kiernan finally pushes himself up and stands. "I need to get out of this suit."

While he's dressing, I remember the second reason I'm here. "I'm thinking it would make more sense if we . . . I mean, if you don't come with me on these other jumps. We don't know what information they have. They might be scouting out the same locations we are."

His shadow pauses momentarily behind the red curtain, and then he resumes dressing. He doesn't respond until he comes out from behind the barrier, and judging from the annoyed look in his eyes, he doesn't like what I've said, but he's having a hard time disagreeing with it.

"Okay," he says, plopping down on the bed next to me. "You're right. We shouldn't be seen together anywhere they might be watching. That doesn't mean I'm letting you go in alone. I'll jump in ahead of you and come back after you've finished. But I'll stay in the background, like I did at Port Darwin."

"But . . . you didn't go to Port Darwin."

"Did you really think I'd let you out onto the beach with that monster prowling about?"

"Monster?" I stare at him blankly for a minute, and then my mouth falls open. "The crocodile? Kiernan, what did you do?"

"What do you think I did? I shot the bloody thing."

"My God, Kiernan, you can't do that! Those animals are endangered—I mean, well, maybe not in 1942, but—"

"Endangered? What on God's green earth could possibly *endanger* that creature? Three bullets to the head and it was still coming at me."

I cover my face with my hands. Is it worth explaining about the endangered species list? Is it even relevant? The turtles those crocs grab from the shoreline are probably even more endangered.

"Never mind. It doesn't matter. What did you do with it?" I ask. "I think I saw where you shot it, but there was just a big red puddle in the sand."

"I didn't do anything with it. Four men came over from that camp up along the ridge—"

"The military post?"

He nods. "I think so, yes. Anyway, they heard the shots and came to see what was up. They fired a few more rounds into the thing for good measure and asked if I wanted it. When I said no, the four of them heaved it onto their shoulders and carted it off the beach. I'm pretty sure they were going to eat it."

Ick. "Really?"

"Seems fair enough to me. It would certainly have eaten them, given the chance."

He slides off the bed and opens the cubbyhole beneath, removing a leather holster and a revolver. Just looking at the thing, cold and black in the palm of his hand, makes me nervous.

"Another crocodile hunt?"

Kiernan looks at me, his eyebrows raised. "Probably not. But there are other sorts of monsters. And a gun won't do me much good if I don't have it on me." He slides the floorboard back into place and straps the holster over his shoulders, then clips the revolver into place. "I'd be happier if you were armed, too, but since I never could get you to carry one in the past . . ."

I bite my lip, hard. "Do you have another gun hidden under the bed?"

"No," he says, his voice both surprised and a little worried. "I can get one, but you'll need to learn to use it. And there's no point, unless you think you actually *would* use it if you had to. Are you sure?"

I'm not at all sure, but I nod anyway. As much as I hate the idea of carrying a weapon, I know it's stupid not to be prepared. Holmes had a gun. Simon has a gun. Whoever shot Moehler most definitely had a gun, and I'm sure he's not the only Cyrist that Saul has armed. And no matter how many hours I spend in the attic, no matter how hard Sensei Barbie's eventual replacement works me, I'll never be able to dodge bullets in midair.

He leans his head back against the bed and stares at the stars on his ceiling for a moment. "I have to clear out of here. So, I'll contact you." He tosses me his key. "Put in a place and time that works for you."

It's a little before one at Katherine's. I put in three—even though Moehler's killing has disrupted the schedule a bit, I have a promise to keep at 2:00 p.m.

"Where will you go?" I ask.

"Jess's, for tonight—or at least I need to check in with him and Amelia before I go. Tomorrow, I'll head south, find a place near Athens. It's always easier if my jumps are just temporal, not to a different physical location as well. Might help to give us a base location for the 1938 jumps, too."

"Okay . . . but don't you need to keep doing the Norumbega shows? Otherwise, they'll know we know—"

"Not if I do the shows at some point. Houdini still has the key, and we still have to get it."

"Could you build up a small buffer of shows now? How many trips do you think you can manage tonight?"

"Two, at most. I've already jumped here and then back to the theater to check on Simon and Pru. But I'd rather keep those as an emergency escape, after what we've just seen. Boudini can wait for now."

I nod and give him a little smile, because I don't want to admit why it bugs me to leave this hanging. It's not because I think it's a risk—I honestly don't know one way or the other. The real reason is that it hurts my brain to think about a theater full of people, just sitting there, suspended in time, while Kiernan is either in or not in that tank on the stage.

Or maybe both at the same time.

∞12∞

I'm at the townhouse and have just finished watering the plants when Trey rings the bell, a few minutes before two. I open the door and laugh at the look of surprise as he takes in the round black glasses and pale blue shirtwaist dress I'm wearing. I've added a few streaks of gray to my hair with a temporary dye Connor picked up at the drugstore. It won't fool anyone if I come under close inspection, but it's better than nothing.

"Your dating-an-older-woman warning from last night came true a lot quicker than I'd imagined." Trey takes my glasses off and looks through the clear plastic lenses, then kisses me before putting them back on my nose.

"Hopefully this will keep anyone from mistaking me for Prudence and falling down to worship at my feet."

"Good. Can't have them stealing my job."

I roll my eyes. "Seriously, Trey, how many hours a day do you spend thinking those up?"

"Is it my fault if you keep feeding me straight lines?"

He follows me into the living room, which is uncharacteristically neat now that Mom and I aren't in here on a regular basis to clutter it up with books, papers, and assorted junk. "You want something to drink? I swiped some sodas from Katherine's fridge.

And some of Dad's energy drinks. Or I can make coffee, but we threw out the milk before Mom left."

"A soda is fine."

Trey is standing in front of the fireplace, looking at the pictures on the mantle, when I come back with the drinks. He's holding a framed photo of me when I was about six. I'm sitting on the front stoop of the apartment we lived in on campus for a few years while Mom was finishing up her degree, and I'm wearing a pair of hot-pink Supergirl roller skates. Both knees are bandaged, but I'm grinning from ear to ear, clearly displaying the gap where my two front teeth are growing in. "Cute," he says. "I'm going to need a copy of that."

"I'll get right on it." I hand him his drink and put the picture back on the mantle. We sit down on the sofa, and he puts one arm around me and then reaches over to pull my legs across his lap. My heart catches in my throat at how easily we fall back into old patterns. How many movies did we watch this way in my room at Katherine's house?

"So, I was supposed to meet you at Katherine's. Why the change of plans?"

I shrug and take a sip of my Red Bull. "I knew Katherine would have a hissy if you came over during a jump. I don't know if it's the tumor or the meds making things worse, but she loses it over the tiniest things now. I didn't want to set her off about something so easily remedied."

"Hey, I'm not complaining. No chaperone, all alone with a beautiful older woman—"

"Who is getting the dye from her hair all over your T-shirt."

"True," he says, and we both try to brush it away, but it just makes a gray streak against the black.

I give him a wicked little smile and tug upward at the hem of his shirt. "I know a very obvious solution to this problem."

He inhales sharply as I press my lips against his collarbone. "Yes, but that solution is likely to create an entirely different problem."

After a long discussion in the car last night, we decided to take things slow and gradually work toward the point we were at last time. While it's a little frustrating for both of us, I know it's the right decision.

A few minutes later, Trey gives me one last kiss, this time on the nose, and says, "You need to get going. Otherwise . . ."

"Yes. I know." I chug down the rest of the energy drink, making a face at the end.

He laughs. "Why drink it if you don't like it?"

"It's bitter, but I need the buzz," I say, crossing over to the mirror to repair the damage to my hair. Trey follows me and reaches around to put the fake glasses back on.

"You look very librarian."

He's right. The blue dress falls just below the knee and is probably the frumpiest-looking thing I've ever worn, but at least it's loose enough that I can fight in it if I have to.

"Personally," he says, "I prefer the red dress from last night, but I'm guessing it might raise some eyebrows in the thirties. And since you're going to be hanging out with this other guy instead of me, I give the librarian costume two big thumbs-up."

There's a smile on his face, but it's not exactly a happy smile. I step toward him, slipping my arms around his neck. "Hey, I'll only be gone for a minute. Promise."

"Yeah, a minute here, but a lot can happen in that minute on the other end."

"Well, if it's any consolation, he'll hate that my hair is up."

"Because of this?" His finger traces the edge of my scar.

"Partly. He feels guilty, although that's beyond stupid. I could have died. But even before the scar, he said I don't look like his Kate when my hair is up."

"Then you should wear it up all the time." He makes a face and shakes his head. "That came out all jealous-boyfriend, didn't it? And while that's kind of true, what I meant to say is hair up, hair down, doesn't matter. You're my Kate, either way."

I offer to set a stable point in the living room, since the current one is in my room and Trey is likely to crack his head on my sloped ceiling. But he wants to see my room anyway, so he follows me up the stairs and stretches out on the twin bed, propping his feet on the headboard.

"I like your room," he says as I sit on the edge of the bed beside him. "The skylight, the glow-in-the-dark stars. They're very you."

I laugh. "Thanks, I think. Charlayne used to say the skylight spooked her. She felt like someone was going to jump through it and land on top of her. But I miss it when I'm not here. It's my built-in night-light."

I remove my CHRONOS key from the little leather pouch. Trey reaches over and touches the medallion, running his fingers over the hourglass in the middle.

"It looks so ordinary. Hard to believe it's going to yank you all the way to Georgia and nearly a century back in time."

First it will be yanking me back to Katherine's so that I can meet up with Kiernan, and then we'll be going to Georgia. But this is confusing enough as it is, so I just smile.

"I think the skeptic needs a demonstration." I lean over and give him a quick goodbye kiss and then set this spot as a local stable point.

Trey, who of course can't see the interface my fingers are touching, gives me a crooked grin. "Are you having fun texting on your imaginary phone?"

I nudge him with my hip. "I'll be right back—one minute."

"Too long."

"I could make it thirty seconds."

He smiles, settling his head into my pillow. "Better."

∞

I'm waiting in the kitchen for Kiernan when Daphne sticks her cold nose into my hand, then runs to the back door, tail swishing. I open the door, and she bounds out over the patio, heading straight for the trees behind the storage shed where the squirrels hang out. I doubt she'd know what to do if she ever caught one, but her endless quest keeps her in shape, despite the fact that everyone in the house is guilty of slipping her too many people-food snacks.

Katherine is there when I turn around, still in the robe and slippers she was wearing when I came running into the library earlier with the news about Moehler. She seems to have a bit more color in her face than she's had in the past week or so, although the dark circles are still under her eyes.

"The past few months have aged both of us, Kate."

I raise my eyebrows in question and then remember the gray streaks in my hair. "Oh, right. Does it look okay?"

She smiles. "You'd never pass inspection with the CHRONOS makeup team, but I think you'll do. Although a hat would make more sense. Did the cloche I ordered ever come in?"

It must be clear from my clueless expression that I have absolutely no idea what a cloche is, because she waves me off. "Never mind. I'll check with Connor. I found it online. A few years out of fashion for 1938, but hey, it's the Depression. People wore whatever they could find."

Katherine pours herself some cranberry juice and sits down in the window seat, pulling her robe tighter around her shoulders. "Care to run the game plan past me?"

I've gone over everything with Connor several times now, but Katherine's involvement has been confined to the role of indirect advisor. Connor discusses things with her and then comes back with suggestions, and we tweak. Most of the time, she stays in her room. I don't know if it's to shield me from her temper or if she's just feeling too weak to deal with social interaction. While it's true that she rubs me the wrong way a lot of the time, I miss talking to her, and I doubt she likes being on the sidelines.

"Sure," I say, sitting down next to her. "But I'll have to make it quick. Kiernan will be here soon."

"You're still planning for him to shadow you instead of working as a team?"

I nod. "It might be an unnecessary precaution, but I'd rather play it safe. Okay—according to the diary, Delia's group is interviewing the owner of the Morton Theater. I'm not going to talk to them, but I'll probably follow them when they leave. The goal is mostly to get a feel for the place. Kiernan will set up some stable points around their hotel, or wherever they're staying, so that he can observe them from the cabin. Hopefully we can figure out a good place and time to approach them."

"You look nervous." Katherine squeezes my hand. "Relax—you'll do fine."

I think I like her new meds. "Any insider tips for Georgia 1938?"

She laughs. "You can never say sir or ma'am too often. And that goes double if it's someone in authority."

"Yes, ma'am," I say, grinning.

"Save it for Georgia." She gives my knee a squeeze and then gets up to let Daphne in. "I'm going to clear out so that you can get going. I'm feeling . . . okay, but my moods are unpredictable, and Kiernan probably already thinks I'm a harpy from hell." I start to protest, but she holds up her hand. "It's okay, Kate, really. I need to get Daphne out before Kiernan pops in anyway, or she'll be nervous all day. Oh, I almost forgot—have you heard from Harry?"

"Yes. He arrived at the hospital a few hours back. Grandpa's still in ICU, but he's stable."

"That's good news. Does Deborah know yet?"

"I sent her a text."

Katherine hesitates and then says, "Connor told me you think Prudence arranged Deborah's trip. And you're not worried?"

"I can't be certain she arranged the trip. And Kiernan said Pru is very erratic, so I could be wrong about Mom being safe. But I don't think she holds any of this against her."

A shadow passes over Katherine's face, and I know I've just reminded her of exactly who Prudence does blame, so I shift focus. "Mom sounds happy. She's leaving next week for the first trip to Bosnia, and she's made friends with a couple of the graduate students who are working with her. And I really do think she may be safer there than she is here."

Katherine gives me a tired smile. "You may be right, but that's a two-edged sword. If Prudence has whisked Deborah thousands of miles away to protect her, that makes me a wee bit concerned about what they might be planning on this side of the Atlantic."

∞

Somewhere in Georgia
Sometime in 1905

I blink into the location Kiernan set and open my eyes to trees—lots and lots of trees. They seem a bit blurry, however, and I realize it's because I'm standing inside a screened porch. I step out into the front yard. It's mostly dirt, probably due to the heavy tree cover, but a few patches of tall, red-tipped grass grow around the house, along with two large bushes. Fragments of white flowers, the edges browned by the summer sun, still cling to the branches.

It's late morning or early afternoon here, wherever here is. Kiernan was super mysterious when he showed up at Katherine's, insisting on transferring the stable point into my key rather than giving me the coordinates. He took one rather dismayed look at the streaks of gray in my hair and said that I needed to bring the dye with me if I really wanted to use it. Happy that Katherine wasn't in the room to remind me when aerosol cans were invented, I stuffed the spray into the bottom of my bag, underneath the cloche hat that Connor finally found under a stack of papers in the library.

The sun is high and bright against a clear sky with only a few feathery wisps of white. One of the trees out front is unusual, with thick, sprawling limbs that hang almost to the ground. A faint breeze ruffles the leaves and the scattered patches of gray moss hanging down from upper branches. I glance back over my shoulder at the little dark green house, with sage-colored trim, and catch a faint whiff of paint. The wire screens are so new that they still reflect the sunlight.

There's a flash of blue on the porch, with a tall shadow behind it, and then Kiernan steps outside to join me.

"What do you think?" he asks.

"About?"

"The house," he says. "It's mine. Do you like it?"

"You bought a house? Where are we?"

"Near Bogart."

I raise an eyebrow. "The guy from *Casablanca*?"

"Who?" he asks, then rolls his eyes. "No, we're in Georgia. About nine miles outside of Athens."

"*When* are we?" I realize now that his hair, which was quite short in Boston, is once again shaggy, hanging slightly in his eyes and brushing against his collar. Which is exactly the way I like it, and I really wish my brain would quit going there. "How long has it been since I left you in Boston? While we're at it, why did you buy a house? For that matter, how did you buy a house?"

He grins. "Again with twenty questions. Let's see. It's the third of October 1905, which makes it nine weeks and one day since I saw you last. How did I buy a house? A strategic investment in a sporting venture."

It takes me a second, and then I say, "You placed a bet."

"Several of them, actually." He parks on the middle step, stretching his long, denim-clad legs out in front of him, and breaks off a few pieces of the tall red grass. "If I suggest a trip to New York City or Philadelphia in the next few years, remind me that it would be a very bad idea. And what was your last question?"

I start to repeat it, and he says, "Oh, yes. Why? Well, I need a place to stay, and we need a base of operations, preferably a bit isolated, near Athens. Two birds, one stone."

"But we need a base of operations in 1938. Not 1905."

Kiernan kicks the edge of the bottom step with the back of his boot. "Built three years before I was born. It is standing *long* after 1938—I checked. I have one hundred and twenty-two acres, a little over seventy-five of that arable land, the rest woods. Closest neighbor is about a mile now, maybe a half mile by 1938."

"And what are you going to do with this place between now and 1938?"

Kiernan shakes his hair out of his eyes, and I get a brief glimpse of a purple bruise a few inches above his brow, with about a half-inch-long cut that looks like it must have been painful a few days ago.

"The farm will be managed by a caretaker named Owens and his family starting in about a week. They'll live in the bigger house on the back forty. They'll also be charged with keeping this"—he nods his head back toward the house—"my so-called hunting cabin, in good repair so that I can visit, although I won't be doing much of that. The business side is run by my attorney in Athens. Given the percentage that sharecroppers make around here, the Owens family is very happy with the financial arrangements. The attorney thinks I'm a damn fool Yankee for being so generous, but he's smart enough not to say what's on his face. Then, in the spring of 1938, my son—a very handsome young man, the spittin' image of his da, I might add—showed up at the attorney's office with the title, saying he'd be living in the cabin for the next few years while he attends the University of Georgia."

I notice his use of the past tense and say, "So you've already done all of that? Even the 1938 visit from your 'son'?"

"Yes. I've been very busy." He bites off the end of one of the grass stalks and offers me a piece. "Sourweed. Tastes kind of lemony. Want some?"

"No, thanks." I join him on the steps. "It sounds like you've got it all figured out."

He moves his eyebrows up and down and then grins. "Now that you mention it, I do believe I have."

"And you really made enough betting on sporting events to buy a farm?"

"Yes, and I guess I should thank you for the idea. The movies with the boy on the flying board? Auto doors that open straight up instead of out?"

I sigh, not bothering to correct him, even though we both know that he's never watched a movie with this version of me. "Given that you nearly talked my ear off about baseball the other day, I'm pretty sure you'd have figured it out without assistance."

He wrinkles his nose. "I don't bet on baseball. I mean, it's okay if other people do, but it just feels . . . wrong for me. Mostly it was title fights, a few football games. Took me about a week, because I couldn't place all the bets in the same town. Altogether I pulled in a little over thirty-eight hundred."

It must be apparent from my expression that I'm trying to calculate the rate of inflation in my head, because he laughs. "No clue how much that is in your money, but I still have twelve hundred in the bank—maybe three years' salary for the average person in 1905. Come on, let me give you the nickel tour."

He stands up and reaches down to help pull me to my feet. His hand is warm, and I feel that same electric tingle run through my body that I always feel when we touch. I let go quickly, pretending to brush something off my dress, and follow him around to the back of the house.

"What happened to your head?" I ask.

He laughs. "Oh, that. Just one of the many perils of home ownership. I banged it up while fixing some things inside the cabin."

We round the corner and enter a backyard that looks considerably different from the front where tall, mossy shade trees dominate the view. Back here, it's mostly grass, with just two trees. One is similar to the trees out front, and the other, judging from the pits that are scattered on the ground, is a peach tree. A small lean-to shack sits to the left. The rear tire of a bicycle, propped against the wall, peeks out from the metal siding that forms the longer wall. Alongside the bicycle is a big tin washtub and some miscellaneous tools. About twenty yards behind the cabin and the shack is a wire fence, and off in the distance, a barn and another building that must be the other house Kiernan mentioned.

There are no cows or horses in sight, although it looks like there are a few chickens wandering around near the barn. "It seems a little bare, Farmer Dunne."

"I've been too busy to play farmer. The livestock will come in around the same time Owens arrives."

He opens the back door to the cabin, although it's a good deal more spacious than the word *cabin* suggests. We enter a large room with hardwood walls and flooring. A multicolored woven rug is in front of the fireplace, and there's a ladder leading to a loft up above. I see a small kitchen near the front of the house and two doors on the right side of the main room. It's maybe twice the size of the cottage Dad and I shared at Briar Hill, when you add in the loft.

"It's really nice, Kiernan. A lot more room than your other place." I'm about to ask why he decided to invest in a house right now, in the middle of everything, but I heed the little voice whispering that I probably don't want to know.

"There's no electric and no cell phone tower. But we do have indoor plumbing. Hot water, too."

"You're kidding? In 1905?"

"Not kidding." He crosses over to one of the doors and opens it to reveal a bathroom, complete with a toilet, sink, and a big white claw-foot tub. There's also a cast-iron contraption, which looks like something from the cover of a steampunk novel, attached to the wall. It's about three feet tall, with one end extending upward through the ceiling and silver pipes coming out the bottom and running underneath the sink and tub. A third pipe winds behind the sink and through a hole in the left wall, so I'm guessing it goes to the kitchen.

"That's the monster that conked me on the head when Charlie and I put it in. Runs on gasoline. You light the pilot and turn on the water. Just don't touch it once it gets going. You can heat up a towel just by hanging it near the thing."

"And you can buy this contraption in Bogart, Georgia?"

"Actually, no. Had to drive to Atlanta for it. I've gained quite the reputation as an odd Yankee as a result. Charlie—the local guy I hired to help me install it—talks nonstop, so I shouldn't be surprised, I guess. They can laugh all they want, though. I'm tired of cold showers where it takes half an hour to get the soap off you. The one at my old place had a line halfway down the hall most days, and when you finally did get in, it was like a squirrel peeing on your head."

"Ick."

"Yes, it was ick." His eyes take on a teasing look, and he adds, "Perhaps I could run you a bath, so you can wash that god-awful paint out of your hair?"

"It's not supposed to be attractive. It's a disguise."

"A travesty's more like it. But I guess it'll have to do for now."

He motions for me to follow him back into the main part of the cabin. "My room's up there," he says, nodding up toward the loft. "This one's yours."

Maybe he notices me tensing up, because he quickly adds, "I mean, it's the guest room. Yours when you need it. I know you've been putting in more hours than there are in the day, so this is another place you can go, if you need to get away. Just don't forget to charge your computer first, and don't count on accessing the internet."

The door swings inward to show a small room with a single window opened halfway. A double bed, covered by a patchwork quilt, takes up most of the room, but there's also a small dresser with a mirror that has those little knobs on the side so that you can adjust the angle. It's very much the image of a turn-of-the-century bedroom, until my eyes drift upward and I see the glow stars.

I laugh, shaking my head, and he says, "I'll take 'em down when I'm not here. But I couldn't leave those behind." He nods toward the bed. "Amelia, Jess's wife, gave me the quilt before I left. Jess said to tell you hello, by the way."

"How is he?"

"He's okay, I guess. I hated to leave him up there with no one else believing him, but . . . I told him I'd pop in when I can."

"It's a lovely room." I give him the best smile I can manage, even though the room and the effort he's put into the entire cabin make me feel a little strange, maybe even a little guilty. I know he doesn't really think I'll be staying here, at least not often, but it's beyond obvious that he wishes I would. He built this place with Other-Kate in mind—a house with as many of the comforts of the twenty-first century as he could possibly offer. Showing it to me is the closest he can get to her being here to see it.

"Your 1905 dress is in the closet there, along with a few other things. I bought two pairs of boy's jeans that should fit you. You might want to slip a pair on before your lessons."

I narrow my eyes. "What lessons?"

He opens one of the top drawers of the dresser and pulls out a gun. It's smaller than the one he showed me before and looks more modern—square, a shorter barrel with engraving, and a pearl handle.

"Unless you've changed your mind?"

I swallow hard and shake my head. "The situation hasn't changed, so I don't have much choice, do I?"

"Not unless you're willing to let me stay by your side all the time. And truthfully, I'd still prefer that you were armed, just in case. But I'm not turning a gun over to you until I'm sure you can use it safely." He sets it down on the edge of the white crocheted doily in the center of the dresser, which somehow makes the gun look even more sinister, and then taps the bottom drawer with his knuckles. "Jeans are in here."

"Why do I need to change? I can shoot a gun in a dress."

"True. But for the other lesson, you're gonna want the jeans. Trust me." He closes the door behind him before I can ask any other questions. And while I'm tempted to open the door and follow him, perhaps it's best to just humor him for now.

The jeans aren't really cut for a girl, so they're a little tight in the hips and a little loose in the waist, but they'll do. The shirt in the closet must be one of Kiernan's, because I have to roll up the sleeves and the hem falls nearly to my knees.

I open the door and then realize that the gun is still on the dresser. Kiernan probably left it there intentionally, so that I'd be forced to pick it up. A logical first step, given that I'll have to touch it in order to learn to shoot.

This would have been much easier before Chicago. I've never liked guns, but having Holmes fire one at me elevated a simple dislike to something closer to an outright phobia. And somehow the modern look of this gun makes it worse. The one Holmes fired at me was a revolver, but like the gun that I saw in Kiernan's apartment, it looked more like a prop—like something you'd use with a Halloween costume. This, on the other hand, looks exactly like something you'd use to kill people.

It's not a snake, Kate. Just pick the damned thing up. It's probably not even loaded.

I wrap my fingers around the gun and lift it, centering its weight in my palm. Then I raise it higher and take practice aim at a leaf on the tree just outside the window.

"Don't pull the trigger, okay? Window glass isn't easy to come by."

It's good that my finger isn't on the trigger, because I jump at the sound of his voice. Suddenly the gun feels a lot heavier. "It's loaded?"

"Of course. What good is an unloaded gun?"

"I wasn't going to pull the trigger," I say, lowering the pistol to hide my shaking hand.

He smiles, but his eyes remain serious. "I'm glad. Because if you'd taken a shot holding it like that, with just one hand, you'd've landed square on your bottom and possibly knocked out a tooth to boot." He holds his hand out. "I can carry it for now, if you want."

"I'm fine." I grip the handle a little tighter and follow him outside.

Kiernan has set up a board between two sawhorses, with eight tin cans in a neat little row. A gun similar to mine is tucked into his belt.

"Where's the other one? The revolver?"

"Gave it back to Jess, just in case. This one's better anyway."

"It looks too modern for 1905."

He holds it up so that I can read the information on the side. *Automatic Colt Calibre 32 Rimless Smokeless.* Then he flips it over. *Browning's Patent. Apr.20.1897 Dec.22.1903.*

"These are both Colt Model 1903. Yours is a little newer than mine. Let me see it."

He points to an engraved number just above the trigger. "Mine is 1903, and it has a four-digit serial number. If you look here, yours has five digits, which means it's newer. They look modern because this model's a classic. Police and military, and quite a few gangsters, will use this model until the 1950s. So you've probably seen it in movies. I bought it because it's easy to conceal and easy to shoot. You remember how Jess's gun had a hammer at the top, right?"

The only hammer I can picture in my mind is used to pound nails. It must show on my face, because he laughs.

"The little thing you pull back with your thumb? That's the hammer. This model Colt has the hammer inside, so you don't have to cock it. The bullets are in a cartridge, making it easier to reload. Eight bullets to a cartridge. Fires a lot faster, too."

"Okay. A nice upgrade." I take the gun back and smile at him. "But I can't believe you bought me a girly gun. A pearl handle?"

"Quite a few gunfighters carried pistols with pearl grips."

"Who?" I ask. "Belle Starr?"

He shakes his head. "Tell you what, I'll demonstrate with mine, and then you can fire yours. We'll see if you still call it a girly gun after you feel its kick."

He takes a step forward, aiming his pistol at the first can. "Fair warning. I'm not exactly a crack shot. I'll be lucky if I hit half of them."

I stick my fingers in my ears the first time, but it's actually not as loud as I'd expected. Kiernan hits five the first time, and we line the cans back up. He manages six the next time around, and then it's my turn.

I'm less nervous now. I think part of it is that we're just aiming at cans, so it seems more like a video game than actually doing anything lethal. But I'm also getting used to the feel of the gun. I hold it out with both hands, like Kiernan did, and start to take aim, but he stops me.

"Okay, this model has less recoil than most guns, but you still have to get used to it. Keep both arms level, and angle your elbows out a bit."

He steps behind me, and I inhale sharply, because I just know he's about to do that thing where the guy comes in close and presses his body against the girl to show her how to hold a weapon. But he doesn't. I exhale, relieved, but now my skin is hyperalert. He repositions my elbows, first the right and then the left, his touch gentle on my bare skin. A shiver runs through me, even though his breath is warm against the side of my face.

"Are you sure you're okay, Katie? You don't have to do this."

I let out a little laugh and shake my head, glad that he's misread my body language. It's not the gun that has me nervous right now. Bowing my elbows slightly, I take aim and fire at the first can.

I miss. By a mile. I'm not sure I'd call the gun's recoil a *kick*, but the abrupt movement still catches me off guard, and I take a few steps backward, directly into Kiernan.

I may have given him a bit too much credit, because he probably knew that would happen. And while his arms are perfectly positioned to help me maintain my physical balance, they aren't exactly helping my emotional balance.

I curse under my breath, partly annoyed at missing the target but mostly annoyed at my response to Kiernan. Why does his touch evoke such a strong, instinctive reaction that I have to fight it back each and every time? I remind myself that Trey's waiting at the townhouse for me to return and make my feet step a few inches away.

"It's not as easy as it looks, is it?"

"Nowhere near as easy," I mutter, biting the side of my lip. "That shot was way off. How far do these bullets go?"

"A good distance, which is why we're firing toward the broad side of the barn. Although you may have missed that too."

"Oh, ha, ha. You're a real laugh riot." I raise the gun again and fire. I miss, but I do hit the board, and all eight cans tumble to the ground as a result.

"I win," I tell him. "The goal was to knock down the cans, right? I knocked down all eight with one bullet. Can't beat that."

"I'm afraid that's not how it works, love."

He sets the last few cans upright and steps away. This time, I hit the second can. I was aiming at the first one, but it's a definite improvement.

A half hour or so later, he's taught me how to reload and where the safety is, and my aim is improving rapidly. I'm routinely hitting six out of eight and finally manage a clean sweep. The trick, at least for me, seems to be holding my breath when I fire and, most importantly, thinking of this as a game. If I remember that it's a real and potentially deadly weapon in my hand, my aim isn't nearly as good.

"My turn," Kiernan says as he steps forward, his mouth pressed in a thin line. He gets seven this time, and then it's back to six again. And the next time, it's still six.

I'm doing a really good job of keeping a straight face, until he looks over at me and raises his eyebrows, at which point the triumphant grin sneaks out of control. "I played a lot of this video game called *Duck Hunt* when I lived in Iowa. So maybe . . ." I shrug.

"Yeah, right. I'm going to put these back in the house," he says, his lower lip out slightly in a mock pout. "You have a moral obligation to help repair my shattered male ego, now that you've totally emasculated me, so you might want to start thinking of how you're going to manage that."

I snort at his retreating, broad-shouldered, totally *un*emasculated back and wonder who slipped him a copy of Freud a decade or two in advance. I'm looking around for a bin or someplace to discard the mangled cans when Kiernan comes up and pulls some sort of hat onto my head.

"What the—"

"Safety precaution." He's wearing one, too—it looks kind of like a leather helmet, with long brown flaps that hang down over his ears.

"You look like Daphne," I say.

"I've had worse insults. But you really should look in the mirror before talking."

"And this is a safety precaution for . . . ?"

He leads me around the corner and into the shed. The rear bicycle wheel I noticed earlier is attached to a bike that looks pretty much like Mom's, which I occasionally ride in DC, except there's a weird cylindrical object attached beneath the crossbar and a few extra parts here and there. There's another bike a few feet away, identical other than the wicker basket strapped to the back fender.

"These are actually football helmets," he says. "There's no such thing as a motorcycle helmet in 1905, but since I suspected you'd never get on one without a helmet . . ."

"Kiernan, those just look like bikes."

"Well, they *are* bikes, for the most part. With a motor added, so you can go faster. I have a car waiting in 1938, but it seemed pointless to try and teach you how to drive here, because autos change a lot between now and then. So I bought these. They'll be fine here in the shed for a couple of years, and—"

I sigh, closing my eyes. The house I kind of understand. But the bikes? Kiernan seems to be building up a fantasy where I stay here in 1905 with him and wander around the countryside, going on rides and having picnics or whatever.

"Kiernan, you need transportation in 1905. I don't. The CHRONOS key takes care of that."

He leans back against the wall and gives me a long look. "I was hoping we could do the fun part first, but you're right. Let's go back inside. You need to see the mess your grandpa left in 1911."

∞13∞

I sit down at the small kitchen table and pull my helmet off. The inside is now a nearly uniform shade of gray. I run my finger across it, and sure enough, it comes away coated with the temporary hair color.

Kiernan climbs down from the loft, a yellow box under one arm. He hands it to me, and I run my fingertip over his wrist, leaving a silvery trail. "Oops," he says, looking back up at me. "Sorry about that."

"Ri-i-ght. I don't believe you for even a second. How badly is it smeared?"

"Um . . . it's bad. Looks like you're wearing a gray helmet."

I narrow my eyes and yank the box toward me before noticing Kiernan's expression. He's looking at it as though it houses something poisonous. I decide to treat it with a bit more caution and lift the lid gingerly.

No snakes or spiders. Aside from the CHRONOS diary at the bottom of the box, it's nothing more than newspaper clippings, maybe a dozen in all, with headlines like "Grisly Scene in Backwoods Church," and "Greene County Deaths Still a Mystery." Most of them are just text, dated late September 1911, but two of the articles near the bottom have photographs.

I begin with those, but after I see the pictures, I wish I'd started with the text-only articles and worked up an immunity. The images are both black and white, and they aren't especially gory. But they are eerie as hell.

"How many dead?" I ask.

"One account said forty-seven; another said forty-eight. There was at least one small kid, so maybe someone just counted the heads in the pews and didn't look in laps. The village is isolated, but they're pretty sure it was the entire population. A few of their people always came into town for supplies once a week, like clockwork. When they didn't show up two weeks in a row, someone went looking."

The pictures are both taken inside a tiny, rustic church with a simple pulpit, adorned only by a cross in the middle. To the right of the pulpit is a woman's body, tall and thin, sitting upright on a bench, her head slumped against the top of the dark wood panel separating the pulpit area from the small choir loft directly behind it. A chest about the size of a coffee table, standing waist high on long, thin legs, sits off to the left, the lid open. Something inside the chest reflects light from the windows, but I can't tell what it is.

My eyes instinctively avoid the foreground of the image, where bodies slump to the side or lean against each other in most of the pews. A child's arm dangles over one side. The bodies seem intact, but the skin looks strange. And they're emaciated, some appearing almost mummified.

"Notice anything odd?" Kiernan asks, crouching down beside me to look over my shoulder. "Other than the fact that they've all died inside the church. And that they all look like the life has been sucked out of them."

"Well, they're mostly women and girls. Two-thirds, at least. Sort of like at Estero."

"That's true," he says. "Based on what I've seen, however, that's true of most cults. I'll pass on speculating as to why they might attract more women than men, since my best guess will likely earn me a kick in the shin."

He gets the kick anyway, just for thinking it. "Funny, coming from the guy who was once a loyal Cyrist—"

"Because his *mother* dragged him along, in case you've forgotten. See anything else unusual? Or at least unusual for Georgia forty-some years after the Civil War?"

I look a bit more closely at the pictures. It's hard to tell, because the photographs are grainy and low resolution. The bodies aren't exactly in tip-top shape, either, but it looks like some of them are white, while others are African American.

"It's a mixed-race congregation. That's not common down here, is it?"

"No," he says. "I thought it was unusual, too, and one good thing about being an eccentric Yankee visitor is that you can ask questions anyone else would know and locals aren't surprised. You might not get a full or truthful answer, but I think I got enough to piece things together. The lady at the store where I buy the local paper, Mrs. Morton, said a lot of the churches did have mixed membership before the Civil War, because the plantations were spread out. Slaves were taught to worship as their masters did, and it was easier if everyone just attended services together. After the war, most religions split off into a colored group and a white group.

"I thought they might be Quaker at first, but the pews are arranged different in a Quaker church, and Mrs. Morton said the Quakers left Georgia long before the war. She figures they were Pentecostal of some sort."

"Okay, this is interesting and all, not to mention really creepy. But why do you think it has anything to do—"

"They died from some sort of bacterial agent, Kate. The best official guess is that it was something in the well and they knew they were dying and gathered in the church to go out together."

"Do they know what type of bacteria?"

"No clue, although I doubt there'd be a very rigorous investigation in rural Georgia in 1911, especially for a group with few ties to the outside world. They assume that it hit fast—there's one grave dug in back of the church but no one in it. So one of the articles is thinking they gathered for the funeral of the first victim and then it hit the rest of them. But there's no coffin, no body laid out at the front, ready for burial, unless it's the old lady slumped off in the corner. The story got a bit of coverage, because it's creepy, but it dropped off the radar pretty fast."

"What bacterial agent would act that quickly?"

"I don't know. I'm guessing it doesn't occur naturally. And . . . I've seen bodies like that before. Around 2070, on my little tour through time with Simon."

I pull a few more articles out of the box. "And you just happened to stumble on this, what—six years into the future? That's . . ."

He glances down at the floor. "No. I was looking. I really didn't have much to go on, just something Simon said one night in New Orleans, back before I met you. He was angry at Saul for chewing him out about something. About ten drinks in, Simon starts ranting about Saul not having room to talk after his screwup at Six Bridges. He got really nervous when I asked him about it later. Of course, he denied ever having said anything about Six Bridges. When he could see I didn't buy it, he told me it happened when Saul was younger and suggested that I shut the hell up if I didn't want my ass kicked. As if he could."

"Why didn't you mention this to me before?"

He rocks his chair onto its back legs. "Because it was a dead end. Kate asked Katherine about it, before, and Katherine said that if it was something that Saul did, it would probably have been in the 1850s, probably in Massachusetts, Illinois, or Ohio. They searched all of those areas and came up with nothing. Katherine even looked in Georgia around the time the FWP was there, because she said Saul was at that site at least once, but she came up blank. And when they expanded the search, they still didn't find anything called Six Bridges, aside from a beer, a movie from the 1950s, and a bike trail somewhere. The problem is only the locals call it Six Bridges, because that's how many bridges you cross to get there. It's not an actual town or anything. And it doesn't even exist in 1938, when Katherine was looking through the Georgia maps. I'd almost forgotten it until Charlie, the chatterbox who helped me put in the water heater, said something about going duck hunting with his brother out on Six Bridges Road."

"So what do you think we should do? We don't know that this was caused by Saul, and if it was, we don't know what he used. I don't think we can just drop in and wait for him to show up. What if it's airborne?"

"True," he says. "But we don't have to watch in person if we go in and set up stable points in advance, like I did when I was looking for Pru and Simon at Norumbega. Six Bridges is maybe an hour from here. We go down there a week or so ahead, set up our 'cameras,' so to speak, and leave. Then I'll watch those points from here in the cabin. If Saul shows up and puts something in the well, then we go in. If this is what he's planning to use for the Culling, we need a sample."

My eyes widen. "There's no way I'm taking something that's potentially that lethal back with me."

"It's not like we really have a choice, Kate. If Saul has an antidote for his Chosen, someone else needs to start working on an antidote as well."

He has a point, but I still don't like it. "You do realize we can't stop this from happening, right? If we change anything at all, it could tip Saul off, and that could have repercussions on the only timeline where we know for certain we're here to stop him. And, yes, I'm well aware that I sound like Katherine, but we both know it's true."

"I know," he says, glancing back down at the photos. "I'd do this on my own, but I'll attract more attention by myself. Like you said, it's mostly women. If we go in together, we're just a couple out for a weekend ride. We can pretend there's a problem with one of the bikes, maybe. Even if we only have time to set up one or two stable points, I can jump back in later, in the middle of the night or something, and add more in the specific spots we need to watch."

I guess he's right. We need to check this out. The only question is whether I should jump back and discuss this with Katherine and Connor. But we're only setting up stable points, so I'm not sure what purpose would be served by an hour-long meeting to hash through these new developments.

I toss Kiernan the leather helmet. "See if you can get that clean while I go wash the rest out of my hair. I take it there's a dress for 1911 in the closet?"

"Yes. But maybe you should learn how to ride the motorcycle first?"

"Kiernan, those things are *not* motorcycles. They're barely even mopeds. I drove a scooter around campus for over a year before we moved from Iowa. I have a license to prove it, so maybe I should be the one teaching you."

∞

GREENE COUNTY, GEORGIA
September 7, 1911, 10:00 a.m.

The farm looks a bit livelier when we step out the back door into 1911. The field behind the house was planted with corn, but I assume it's been harvested already, because it's just dry brown stalks, some of which have already been cut down. The shed has had a recent coat of paint, and maybe a few boards were added—it looks more substantial than the lean-to construction I saw during our target practice. Behind the shed, a row of about a dozen peach trees stretches off in the direction of the farmhouse. I catch a faint whiff of fermenting fruit from the carcasses of overripe peaches scattered in the grass.

As it turns out, I may have overstated the similarities between this bike and the scooter I rode in Iowa. It's about the same height, but it's twice the weight. Still, it only takes ten minutes or so before I'm able to keep up with Kiernan, and he isn't handicapped by an outfit that has to be constantly watched to make sure the fabric doesn't get caught in the spokes or catch fire on the motor, which gets really hot after a few miles.

Rural Georgia roads aren't exactly biker friendly. We draw hoots and hollers from drivers who clearly don't get the concept of sharing the road. I suspect most of the catcalls are due to the fact that I'm a female riding in a split skirt. It looks like a normal long skirt when I'm standing, but now that I'm astride the bike, it's obvious that I—*gasp*—have legs that actually connect some-where in the middle. I saw women riding bikes on the streets in Boston and even back at the World's Fair, so apparently Georgia is a decade or so behind the rest of the country on this issue. It's not like you can ride a bike sidesaddle.

Each time a horn honks, Kiernan looks back like he's going to turn the bike around and go teach someone a lesson.

"Would you just ignore them?" I decide not to point out that it's really all he can do, when they're zipping by at forty-five miles an hour and we're tooling along at twenty-five or even less if we're going uphill.

Idiot drivers aside, the ride was actually kind of pleasant back on the main road—I haven't been out in open air for more than a few minutes at a time for ages, so it's a nice change of pace. Now that we've turned onto Six Bridges Road, I'm wishing this thing had a gel-padded seat like Mom's bike. It's becoming painfully clear that the name *Six Bridges Road* is truth-in-advertising only in the sense that there are Bridges, presumably Six by the time we get there. The Road part is deceptive—it's more of a bumpy, rutted trail through the woods, dotted with the occasional puddle that could double as a kiddie pool.

We've almost reached the final bridge when Kiernan veers off the trail and pushes his bike a few yards into the woods. I follow and watch as he pulls a wrench out of the basket on the back of his bike. He removes both bolts from one of the two brackets that hold the motor in place, then he tosses the wrench and the bolt, along with the corresponding nut, behind a tree and drops the second nut and bolt into his pocket.

"Okay, the wrench I get. But why throw away the other bolt?" I ask.

"They'll definitely have a wrench. But they'll probably have to hunt for a nut and bolt to fit."

"Hey, that's a good idea."

"You sound surprised."

"No," I say as we roll the bikes back onto the road. "It's called a compliment. You're supposed to nod and say thank you."

"Really? I'll keep that in mind for next time."

"That's a bit of an assumption, isn't it? I have to ration these things. If I hand compliments out too freely, they lose their value. And your ego—"

"Which you've bruised beyond belief by outshooting me and then refusing motorcycle lessons."

I fake an annoyed look at his interruption. "As I was saying, your ego doesn't need to be inflated."

But as I say the words, I realize that I don't think they're true. Every now and then I catch him watching me at an unguarded moment, and his eyes are so vulnerable I almost feel like I'm looking at his eight-year-old self. He clearly enjoys the banter back and forth, however, and we seem to drop into that routine naturally. So naturally, in fact, that I can't help but wonder if this is how he was with Other-Kate. Is he thinking the same thing I thought about Trey—that we so easily slipped back into our old (at least for me) and comfortable patterns? Or now that we've been around each other for a while and he knows me better, does he see someone who only looks like the girl he loved?

He laughs. "Ah, but I can always count on you to poke a pin in me if I puff up like a balloon."

And I guess that answers my question.

Like the previous two bridges, bridge number six is just slats of wood with big gaps, through which you can see the murky water below. We roll the bikes onto the slats, and Kiernan says, "If my previous experience with the South holds true, they may offer us food and drink. Since we're only guessing that Saul hasn't been here yet, I'd suggest we avoid anything that might have come in contact with water from their well—so pretty much everything. If they offer, let's turn the hospitality thing around on them. There's a bag of candy at the bottom of the basket. I doubt these kids get sweets very often, and Jess gave me enough to last a year."

"I hope it's not that nasty hoarhound stuff," I say, and his grin reminds me that it's exactly what Other-Kate would have said.

About fifty feet beyond the bridge, the trail curves and the trees thin out to reveal a small cluster of buildings, circled by rings of farmland in varying shades of green and yellow, bordered on all sides by dense woods like the ones behind us. Two boys and an older girl are tossing a ball around in one of the fields ahead, about halfway to the village. It looks like they're playing keep-away with a dog, a short-haired mixed breed of some sort.

"Kids," Kiernan says, his voice flat.

"Yeah."

"They're ghosts, Kate. We have to think of them as ghosts. Nothing we can do to change it, so . . ."

"Okay. Ghosts."

The dog either hears us or catches our scent, because it suddenly whirls around and barrels down the trail toward us, barking loudly.

The girl runs after him. "Bull! You get back here!"

Bull is, fortunately, much smaller than the Cyrist Dobermans. He's at least part Boston terrier, with buggy eyes, a coat that's brindle and white, and a whole lot of attitude. He stops about three yards in front of us, and Kiernan moves his bike ahead of mine, turning the wheel inward as a barrier.

The girl, who upon closer inspection is only a few years younger than I am, comes running up behind him, the two boys on her heels. They're twins, around seven or eight years old, with reddish-blond hair hanging over their eyes, plentiful freckles, and overalls. Both sets of eyes are glued to our bikes.

They're very lively ghosts.

"Bull, I said *no!*" The barking continues until she yells, "Bad dawg!" At that point it's like someone flipped a switch. Bull's bark morphs into a yelp, and he wriggles toward her, leaving a thin, wet trail on the dirt beneath him. I doubt the girl has beaten him, but I suspect someone has, and I'm pretty sure that someone yelled "Bad dawg!" at the same time.

The girl tugs downward on her dress, which is too tight and several inches shorter than the current fashion, and tucks a strand of long white-blond hair behind her ear as her pale blue eyes sweep over us, a bit warily. She takes in my split skirt and the bikes, then lingers for a few extra seconds on Kiernan. Her face turns pink, and her eyes flit back over to me.

"Don't worry. Bull don't bite," the girl says.

As if to prove her wrong, Bull gives us one last halfhearted growl and sinks his teeth into the ball she's holding.

The two boys nod, and one adds, "But he *will* latch onto yer leg if he gets a chance an' sniff in places you prob'ly don' wanna be sniffed."

"He'll pee on yer shoes, too," says the other boy.

"Jackson, you hush your nasty mouth. You, too, Vern. There's ladies present."

Vern, or at least I think he's the one she called Vern, gives her a sassy grin. "I don' see but one *lady*, Martha. You ain't nothin' but a girl."

Martha yanks the ball out of Bull's teeth and flings it at the boy, but he ducks.

"An' you even throw like a girl."

The other boy claps him on the shoulder and says, "Good one, Jack!" Then they both run off toward the village. Bull looks longingly in their direction, but in the end, he decides to stick with Martha.

"Y'all ain't from around here," she says. It's not a question, just a flat statement of fact. "You at the univers'ty up in Athens?"

"Yes, ma'am. I'm Matthew Dunne, and this is my fiancée, Kate Keller. She's a student over at the Lucy Cobb Institute." We had agreed earlier that his foreign-sounding name and my hyphenated surname would only add to our strangeness, but the fiancée bit is improv. He's probably right, since being engaged would make it a bit more acceptable for us to be out alone, without a chaperone, but it still sounds weird.

"Martha Farris." She dips into a faint imitation of a curtsy. "Them boys 're my cousins, Jackson and Vernon. You'll have to excuse 'em, miss, 'cause they ain't got a bit of manners. We try, but it just don't seem to stick."

I respond with a nervous laugh. "That's okay. I've seen worse, believe me."

When she looks back over at Kiernan, he releases the bracket holding the motor and shows her the bolt in his hand. "We were out for a ride, looking for a good picnic spot, but I'm afraid we've had a mishap with one of the bikes. Don't suppose you know anyone who'd have a wrench and maybe an extra bolt?"

"Hold on a minute," Martha says, veering a few feet off the trail to collect the ball. Her face crinkles in disgust when she realizes it's now coated with dirt, held in place by dog spit. She bends down to wipe it off on the grass before sticking it into her pocket.

"Come on. Earl's got a wrench. Don't know about a bolt, but he shoes the horses and fixes the wagon, so if he don't have it, we ain't got one." She walks along the side of the trail next to me, with Bull at her heels, pushing through the tall grass along the edges. "Ain't ever seen a skirt sewed up the middle like that, even up in Greensboro. Are ladies really wearin' those in Athens?"

"Only when they ride bikes," I say. "It makes it a lot easier."

She glances at the bike again and nods. "Guess so. Ain' ever seen a bike with a motor, either. I bet they ain't cheap."

"Cheaper than an automobile," Kiernan says. "And nearly as useful. At least until it rains. Or the motor comes loose."

He flashes his best smile, the one that lights up his eyes and makes him damn near irresistible. Martha's face and neck instantly flush a deep pink. In a town with fewer than fifty people, two-thirds of them female, I'm guessing she doesn't encounter many young men. I bump the wheel of my bike against his to signal that he should rein it in a bit, but that just makes him turn the smile on me, even broader now, because he clearly thinks I'm jealous.

I roll my eyes and look back at the girl. "You have a pretty village here, Martha. What's it called?"

She shrugs, tugging her skirt again. "Some here call it Six Bridges, like the folks in town do. But Sister Elba says we oughta use the proper name, God's Hollow."

Of course that immediately inspires a Harry Potter flashback for me, and I eye the meadow nervously, half expecting to see a large serpentine shadow winding through the tall grass.

"Well, God's Hollow is a much more poetic name," I say.

Martha's expression suggests that she doesn't really agree, but she smiles politely. Then her head snaps up like something's caught her attention. After a second, I hear music—a hymn that seems vaguely familiar. The sound is faint, and the notes waver in an eerie vibrato that's strangely beautiful.

"What is that?" I ask.

She huffs, clearly annoyed, and glances toward the village. "Sister Elba remindin' me about my music lesson."

"But what is the instrument?"

"It's called an armonica. Kinda like a glass harp. Sister Elba's granddaddy passed it down to her and taught her to play. She taught Brother Ellis years ago. But he's even older'n she is, so someone younger's gotta learn it, 'cause he ain't gonna be around forever and she cain't preach and play at the same time. So I got picked."

Her tone makes it clear she doesn't consider that to have been a great favor. "Well, it sounds very pretty," I tell her.

Kiernan adds, "I'll bet you play beautifully."

Martha's blush is back, but she also smiles. "And you'd lose that bet. Jack says it sounds like I'm killin' baby pigs. And he's kinda right. Sister says I just need to practice more."

The music ends just before we enter the village, which consists of maybe a dozen buildings, mostly small, neat houses. It looks deserted.

"Where is everyone?"

Martha nods to the left. Two clusters of people and a few horses are off in the distance, near the trees surrounding the village. "Out in the fields. I'll be out there, too, later on, but I'm helpin' Sister Elba with the little 'uns this mornin'."

The first building on the right seems to be the church—no steeple, but there's a large wooden cross above the double doors in the front.

"Do you think Sister Elba would let me see the glass . . . what did you call it?" I ask as I push my bike over to the side and prop it against a large tree next to the chapel.

"Armonica. You can ask her. I gotta take you to her 'fore we go see Earl, anyways. I 'spect that's where Jack and Vern run off to, lettin' her know we got visitors in from town."

And she's right. The doors of the chapel open a few seconds later, and the boys reappear, each holding the hand of a tall, thin woman in a navy-blue dress, helping her down the steps. It's instantly clear that this is the woman whose body was at the front of the congregation in the photographs. Her iron-gray hair is stretched back into a braid and coiled into a tight knot, her skin the warm light brown of coffee with cream. She seems foreboding at first, due to the ramrod straight posture, but as we draw closer, I see that her smile is open and unguarded.

"Welcome to God's Hollow! Isn't it a glorious day?" Her voice wavers a bit. Unlike the kids, who have a deep southern twang, she has only a slight accent. "I'm Sister Elba Terry, the leader of this small flock."

"I'm Matthew Dunne, Sister Terry, and this is Kate Keller. We're sorry to intrude, but we were out looking for a picnic spot, and I'm afraid we've run into a small problem with one of our motorcycles."

"Just call me Sister Elba, or Sister, like everyone else." She moves a few steps closer, and that's when I realize she's blind or very close to it.

Sister Elba lets the twins guide her until she's right in front of us and then reaches out to run her hands over Kiernan's bike. I'm about to caution her that the motor is hot, but she must feel the heat rising off the engine, because she pauses with her hand about an inch away.

"What a marvelous contraption. How fast can it go?"

"About thirty-five miles per hour, ma'am."

I shoot Kiernan a sideways glance. The only way this bike would go anywhere near that fast is if it were carrying a half-starved kid down the side of a mountain. But apparently Kiernan really wants to believe the pitch the salesman gave him, because he seems totally unaware that he's stretching the truth well beyond the breaking point.

"That's incredible," Sister Elba says, laughing. "Isn't it amazing the things they come up with these days? Twenty years ago, when these eyes were stronger, I'd have asked to take it for a ride."

She turns her head back toward me and says in a crisp voice, "Jackson tells me that you've adopted rational dress."

I'm confused for a minute, until I realize she's talking about the split skirt. "Oh, only when I'm riding the bicycle," I say, but then it occurs to me that she wouldn't be likely to call it *rational* dress if she found it offensive.

She squints down at the skirt, so maybe she can see a tiny bit after all. "Well, I'm glad it's had a revival, and I hope it sticks this time. I wore bloomers for a while myself, back before the War, when I traveled around, speakin' against slavery. But everyone was so busy staring at me that they ignored most of what I was preaching. So I gave it up. As I've told Martha and the younger women in our congregation, the bloomer dress was much more practical for everyday wear. But they think it looks silly. Isn't that right, Martha?"

Martha looks a little uncomfortable, like she doesn't want to lie but also doesn't want to insult my choice of clothing. She finally settles for middle ground. "That pair you showed me did look silly, Sister Elba. But what she's wearin' looks kinda like a real dress most of the time, 'cept when she takes a big step. I might could get used to that."

"Then I'll see if I can find a pattern to give to your aunt for the next time you need a new dress."

Martha's nose wrinkles up a tiny bit. "Yes, ma'am. Thank you."

"My pleasure, Martha. Boys, is Brother Earl in his shop or out in the field?" Sister Elba looks over her shoulder to where she'd left Jackson and Vernon. They're now playing some sort of game on the chapel steps with two younger children who've wandered over. A fifth child, who looks like he's barely out of diapers, is sitting on the grass, holding out his pudgy hands for Bull to lick.

One of the boys yells, "We don' know. We been out in the field with Martha and Bull."

"I'll walk him over, Sister," Martha offers. "The boys won't be able to explain the part they're needin'. And Miss Keller was wonderin' if she could take a look at your armonica."

I fight back a smile, because Kiernan would be perfectly capable of explaining the part we're looking for if the boys walked him to the shop. Martha seems to realize a few seconds too late that she's offered a paper-thin excuse for tagging along with Kiernan. Her face flushes even deeper, and she stares down at her feet.

Sister Elba chuckles softly. "That's fine, Martha, but take the boys with you. If Earl is out in the field, they can run fetch him. Once you find Earl, you come on back here for your lesson." She puts a slight stress on the last word.

"Martha's doin' that sassy thing with her eyes again, Sister Elba."

Martha pulls the ball out of her pocket and hurls it at the boy. This time she doesn't miss, and he lets out a yowl when it connects with his shoulder.

"Martha, was that really necessary? And, Jackson, I don't need eyes to know your cousin would rather be outside on a nice day like this, but we all have responsibilities, don't we? When you and Vernon get back, take the younger kids over to the chicken coop, because I'm pretty sure there's a chore that you haven't finished. And don't let Isaac sit down inside the pen this time."

Vernon groans and does a pretty good imitation of Martha's eye roll before he and his brother take off down the street.

Kiernan reaches over to squeeze my hand. "See you shortly, Kate."

It's the first time that I've really looked at this side of his face when he wasn't wearing the biking helmet. The cut I noticed earlier, just above his eye, seems smaller, and the bruise beneath it, which was bluish purple, has begun to fade. I file this observation away for later, since I can't really ask him about it now.

Sister Elba takes my arm, and we climb the steps to the church, dodging two small girls who are a study in contrasts. One is blond and pale, like Martha and the twins, her legs long and thin with knobby knees. The other girl, who looks slightly younger, is

African American, still bearing the chubby cheeks and build of a toddler. I give them a smile and tug the CHRONOS key out of my blouse so that I'm ready to set a stable point as soon as I have both hands free, saying a silent prayer of thanks that the only people around are either too young to pay attention or too blind to see what I'm doing.

"Are you musical, Kate?" Sister Elba asks when we reach the top of the steps.

"No, unfortunately not. I took piano lessons for a couple of years, and it wasn't for me. But I am a student of history, and Martha tells me the harmonica is quite old."

"It's actually *ar*-monica, without the *h*," she says. "And it's definitely old. If my uncle is to be believed—and I must admit I'm not entirely convinced on that point—this was one of the instruments made by Benjamin Franklin himself."

We walk into the small building I remember from the newspaper clipping, and my breath catches in my throat. I can almost see the bodies in the pews and the officials standing in the aisle.

Sister Elba, who is still holding on to my arm, must feel the change in me, because she asks, "What's the matter, child?"

I scramble for a viable excuse and finally go with something semitruthful. "I was just reminded of my grandfather for a moment."

"I'm guessing he's passed on now?" she says, patting my arm. "Well, he's in a better place. You're just missing him. And that's okay. All part of the natural order. You got an angel watchin' over you every day now."

A shiver runs through me with those last words. Watching over me—quite possibly. Angel, not so much.

The layout of the sanctuary seems to be second nature to her. She works her way to the front of the church, tracing her fingers over the pews on her right. I take the opportunity to pull up the interface on the CHRONOS key and set a stable point just behind the back row and then follow her down the aisle.

The church looks different when I view it from the front—it's not the same angle as the photographs, so I'm not as bothered by afterimages of dead bodies. The room is beautiful in its simplicity, the afternoon sun shining softly on polished wooden benches topped with homemade cushions. It's a far cry from the opulence of the Cyrist temple, but it seems much more likely to me that someone in search of divine guidance might actually find it here.

"You have a beautiful church, Sister Elba." I set another stable point from this angle, then walk across to the other side.

"Oh, the church isn't mine, child. I just have the privilege of teachin' here."

"What denomination is your community?" I ask, partly because I'm interested but also because it gives me a chance to set a few more stable points if I keep her talking.

"Now, that's a very good question. Unfortunately, I don't have an answer. Some of my family were with the Friends Church. You probably know of them as Quakers. But we got all different kinds of believers. I just preach what I know in my heart, and sometimes they agree with me; sometimes they don't. And that's okay. All in the natural order of things that people will worship in their own way. If some of them disagree enough that they can't be happy here, they eventually get tired of grumbling and move on. Like Martha. She's nearly grown, and she'll leave us before long. Nothing here to hold her, so she'll head into the city, and the good Lord willin', she'll find a man of her *own* and stop making eyes at those who are already taken." Sister Elba laughs, shaking her head. "But I hope Martha finds her way back to us eventually, and when she does, she'll know there's a place here for her."

She turns her head toward the spot where I was the last time I spoke and squints, then moves her head around until she finds me again. "Lord above, child, you flit like a butterfly. What's got you on edge?"

"Nothing, really," I say as I set another point, this one looking toward the smaller door on the right side of the church. "I just tend to be a little hyperactive." I'm not sure that *hyperactive* is even a word in 1911, but I guess she'll piece it together.

Her eyes rest on me for a minute longer, unfocused. I get the strangest feeling, like she's seeing straight through to my thoughts.

"But that's not true, is it? Somethin' is definitely weighing you down. You're not worried about your young man out there with our Martha?"

"Oh, no, ma'am. That's . . . not a problem."

"I'm a good listener, if you'd care to unload."

I'm silent, and she chuckles quietly. "Sounds like you're not ready. Well, then come on over here, and let me show you Ben Franklin's invention. It makes mighty pretty music once you teach it who's boss."

She opens the wooden chest, which looked rectangular in the newspaper photo but is actually tapered, with one side nearly twice as wide as the other. The case is over a yard long and maybe half that wide and deep at the larger end. Inside is a glass creation, shaped a bit like an ice-cream cone, broad at one end, then tapering off at the other. As I look more closely, I see that it's actually dozens of crystal bowls nested inside each other and threaded onto a spindle. The bowl rims are painted seven different colors, in sequence. Tucked at the front of the box is a flat dish filled with water.

Sister Elba runs her forefinger lovingly over the ridges of the instrument. "Franklin was from a Quaker family, you know. Supposedly he made this for my great-great-grandmother. One of the bowls cracked off when I brought it down from Canada. Cost me more money than I could spare to move it, and I worried the entire way it would get busted. Another bowl there's got a crack—See it? Right here?—so we'll probably lose that one, too, before long. A shame, but I guess that's okay. All part of the natural order, I suppose. Want to give it a try?"

"Sure." Truthfully, I'd rather just go now that the stable points are set, but since this was my excuse for coming into the chapel, I feel obligated.

"Ever use a sewing machine?"

"No." I've seen Grandma Keller use hers, but since hers is an electric model that plugs into the wall, I don't mention it.

"Well, this pedal down here spins the armonica, like the one on a sewing machine moves the needle. You pump the pedal, then dip your fingers in water and hold them against the edges of the glass while it spins."

"So, the different colors are different notes?"

"That's right. The primary colors give you a C-major chord. Go ahead, give it a try."

I pump the pedal with my right foot and moisten my fingers, then hold them against the red, yellow, and blue bands in the middle. It screeches, and the notes waver in and out.

She smiles. "Keep your fingers steady. Try to use the same pressure on all of them."

As I press a bit harder, the notes blend together. I wouldn't call it music, but it's a bit less painful to the ear. I try a few more notes and see why Martha's frustrated. The piano is easier.

After one particularly screechy note, I laugh and step aside. "It would take a lot of work before I could play anything as pretty as what you were playing earlier."

"It does take time. And that's why, even after three months, I still have to twist Martha's arm to get her in here."

"But . . . Martha said she's learning to play the armonica so that she can eventually take over. And just now . . ."

There's a question in my voice, and Sister Elba smiles. "Why train her if she's leaving? Well, I get to spend time with her in the lessons. I talk to her, try to get her to talk to me, and let her know she's wanted here, even though she'll never stay. I think it's important to know you're wanted, maybe even needed, don't you? Gives you somethin' to hold on to when you're off in a strange place. Kinda like you are now, right, child?"

"Well, not really," I say. "We're both at the university in Athens."

"But you're not from these parts. There's no Georgia in your voice. I traveled around a lot, back before the War, and I'm usually good at accents, but I can't place yours at all. Your young man's is a bit odd, too, and there's definitely some Irish in there. But yours . . . yours is all mixed up."

"My parents live near Washington, DC. They're teachers. I've traveled a good bit." And I probably learned half of my speech patterns from television and movies, but I don't add that.

"Teachers! Well, that must be why I liked you right off. We left Georgia for Canada when I was a little girl. My family stayed up there after the fighting was over, but I came back south to teach with the Freedmen's Bureau. Earl, the one your young man's over talkin' to right now? He's one of the first men I taught to read and write. Of course, the government cut the money for those schools pretty quick. And there was still work to be done, so some of us set up God's Hollow not long after. We had seventy-four people here at one time, but we're growin' old, and most of the kids don't stay, although we do take in strays and orphans from time to time. I expect we'll die off eventually and the trees'll gobble the land up again. And that's okay. All part of the natural order."

A chill runs through me as I wonder how long it will take for the trees to reclaim the village after Saul takes things into his own hands. There's nothing natural about what he's planning, and while Sister Elba might not have many years left, those kids outside have their entire lives before them.

"Well, I'd better go over and join . . . Matthew and the others. Thank you for showing me the armonica, Sister Elba. It's beautiful."

"You are more than welcome."

My hand is on the door when she speaks again.

"And, child?"

"Yes, ma'am?"

"Whatever that problem is that's eatin' at you, well, you seem like a smart enough girl. You'll figure out how to fix it."

"But what if it can't be fixed?" I ask before I even realize I'm going to speak. "Or if I can't fix it without hurting even more people?"

Sister Elba pauses to close the armonica case and then walks toward the steps, stopping a few short feet away from the bench where she will die. "People faced those kinds of decisions every day during the War and after. It's a hard lesson in life, but you have to accept that some things are out of your hands. Otherwise, you'll never know a single minute of peace. You mend what you can, and you let the rest go. You just let it go."

I have to get out of here before I break down and tell her to pack everyone up and head back to Canada. I push through the door, relieved that the kids are no longer on the steps.

I set a stable point on the lawn in front of the church. Another near the side door. I start heading in the direction that Martha took Kiernan, setting two more stable points as I go.

And then I hear laughter off to the right. The twins and two other children are inside a large mesh pen behind the houses, with chickens running around their feet. The youngest is trying his best to pull up the wire so that he can get inside with the others, and Bull is running back and forth in front of the coop, barking at the chickens. They must be used to it, because they ignore him and keep pecking away in the muck.

Beyond the chicken coop, I see the well.

I duck between the two houses and hurry over, setting two stable points facing the stone well and one behind it. Then I move closer and set a final point directly above the opening. Anyone who arrived via this stable point would end up at the bottom of the well, but it's the only way I can be sure we'll see clearly if Saul tampers with their water supply.

"Hey."

I jump, but it's just Jackson. Or Vernon. The other twin is right behind him. They both smell a bit off, probably due to the brown gunk lining the hem of their overalls.

"Whatcha doin'?" one of them asks.

I decide to give them the simple, unvarnished—although admittedly not entire—truth. "I'm looking down into your well."

"Why?" asks the other twin.

"Because I like wells."

The first twin nods sagely. "Yeah, this one's real deep. Were you gonna throw that ol' necklace down to see how long before it goes plunk at the bottom?"

I laugh. "I thought about it. It's pretty ugly, isn't it? But my grandmother gave it to me, so I'd best keep it."

He looks disappointed. "Guess we can just use a rock."

"I actually need to be going. Can one of you tell me where Brother Earl's shop is?"

"It's right next to his house."

"And which one is his house?"

"Last one on the left. Just go down the road, an' you'll see it."

The other boy looks at his brother and then back at me, a grin stretching his freckled face. "Martha keeps looking at him, y'know."

"At Brother Earl?" I ask, teasingly.

"No! At your *boyfriend*." And then they both collapse into giggles.

"Well, then I guess I'd better get over there right away, hadn't I?"

I give them a smile, but it freezes on my face as I'm gut-punched by the reality that they'll both be dead before the month is out. I turn and hurry back toward the road, but tears are blurring my vision, and I run smack into Martha when I round the corner.

"I'm sorry." I duck my head as I go past, but she sees that I'm crying.

"Hey, wait! What Jack and Vern told you—it ain't true."

"It's okay, Martha."

She grabs my arm. "No, really. I don' want you gettin' all mad at . . . him. 'Cause he ain' even looked at me. I swear it."

I bite my lip and try to rein in the tears. "I know, Martha. It's not that, okay? Really. I'm not mad at him. Not mad at you. The music just . . . it made me a little sad, okay? Reminded me of some things I'd rather forget."

She doesn't look convinced, but she nods. "Yeah. Music does that to me, too, sometimes." She shoves a lock of hair back behind her ear, nodding down the road. Kiernan is already coming toward us, pushing the bike. "I gotta get back to Sister Elba, or she's gonna lecture me 'bout responsibility again. Anyway, it was nice meetin' y'all. Hope it's a good picnic."

"Thanks, Martha. Nice meeting you, too."

Martha heads toward the church, stopping just long enough to yell in the direction of the chicken coop. "Jack and Vern, if the two of you have the sense God gave a billy goat, you'll be in the next county by the time I'm done with my lesson."

"Ain't scared of you, Ma-a-r-tha." Followed by giggles.

Ghosts. Just ghosts.

Kiernan can see that I'm upset, and he looks a little unsettled himself. "Were you able to . . . ?" he asks.

I nod. "Maybe ten in all. The church, some outside, and also at the well."

"Good girl," he says, putting his free arm around me and pulling me close. "I say we get the bikes over the bridge, stash 'em back in the woods, and take a shortcut home."

"You'll get no argument here."

We walk quickly past the church, and I grab my bike from its resting spot against the tree. The music of the armonica, discordant and even more eerie under Martha's fingers, drifts through the open windows as we push the bikes back to the road. I pull the handle to start the motor before the wheels even leave the grass, to block the sound. I don't even put my helmet on, just gun the motor and take off down the trail, eager to put as many miles and years as possible between me and God's Hollow.

∞14∞

Trey is on the bed, propped up on his elbow, staring at the stable point when I return to the townhouse, exactly thirty seconds after I left, as promised. I think there was still some part of his brain that didn't fully believe all of this is real, because his eyes are wide, his jaw has dropped about an inch, and he looks a little pale.

I probably look a little pale, too. The six hours we spent in 1938 were anticlimactic after God's Hollow. Kiernan tried to talk me into resting first, but all I could think about was getting the trip over with so that I could get back home. Back *here*. I'm too tired to give the full report Katherine and Connor will expect the moment I arrive. Trey, on the other hand, said he doesn't want the details, and right now that's beyond fine with me.

After a long moment, Trey closes his eyes and shakes his head. Then he reaches out and pulls off the hat and glasses. "You changed your hair."

"Yeah, well, the gray wasn't working for me. I like the hat better."

"So—how long were you gone?"

I give him a tired smile. "Thirty seconds."

He taps me on the head with the hat and then reaches down to pull me up next to him. "That's not what I meant, and you know it. I asked how long were you gone, not how long were you not here."

"That doesn't make any sense at all, you know."

"Kate, none of this makes any sense."

"Fine. I've been gone a little over sixteen hours. I had to make a side trip, and things got crazy."

"Crazy how?"

I am not going to cry. I've done enough of that for one day. So I just bite my lip and look away. The first thing my eyes land on is my ceiling, covered with my own glow-in-the-dark stars. I used to love those things, but now I'm tempted to stand up on the bed and yank every single one of them down.

Trey pulls me in closer, so that my head is on his shoulder, and then tips my chin toward him. "Hey, I was just curious, okay? This isn't an interrogation. You look wiped out. Do you want me to go so that you can get some sleep?"

"No. I mean, yes, I'm tired, and I'll probably be rotten company, but . . . I really don't want to be alone. Would you stay? For a little while? Maybe we could put in a movie."

We go downstairs for drinks, popcorn, and *The Princess Bride* DVD and then take them back upstairs to my room. We put real butter on the popcorn, which usually means I crunch the unpopped kernels and slide my fingers along the bottom to get the last bit of salty, buttery goodness, but I'm too tired to eat more than a few pieces. The last thing I remember is Buttercup climbing into the harness and wincing as Fezzik begins to lug the three of them up the Cliffs of Insanity.

When I open my eyes, the sky framed in the window above me is a dark blue, with a few faint streaks of dusky orange and purple. My head is on Trey's chest, and he's reading my copy of *The Fault in Our Stars*.

I reach over to the nightstand and grab the soda I was drinking before I conked out. I swish it around my mouth a bit to chase away the dragon breath, then roll to my side and snuggle up against Trey.

"Hey, sleepyhead."

"I'm sorry. How long was I—"

He plants a kiss on the top of my head. "About three hours. And no apologies. I've been planning to read this for a while now."

"You could have gone home."

"I know. And I'll definitely have to go in an hour or two, because we have school tomorrow. But right now, I'm hungry."

"Yeah. Me, too." Aside from a handful of popcorn, the last time I ate was about ten hours ago, before we left for 1938—slightly squished cheese sandwiches and fruit from the picnic basket. But then I noticed the bag of candy was still in there, and I was so angry at myself for forgetting to give it to those kids that I lost my appetite.

"So," Trey says, "should we call for pizza or Chinese?"

"Mmmm . . . *moo goo gai pan* and wonton soup. And an egg-roll. From Red Dragon. They're good, and they're like six blocks away, so it's really fast."

An hour later there are empty cartons of comfort food scattered about on the coffee table. We crack the fortune cookies, and Trey learns that a new "wardrope" will bring great joy and change in his life. Mine says that constant grinding can turn an iron "nod" into a needle. Apparently the fortune cookie company needs a better proofreader.

Trey helps me clear off the table, and while I'm rinsing my hands at the sink, he comes up from behind and puts his arms around me. I turn around and give him a long, slow kiss. I could have stayed right there for at least an hour, but he pulls away much sooner than that and leads me back to the couch, where we curl up.

I assume we're going to pick up where we left off at the sink, but he asks, "So, what happened today?"

"I thought you didn't want the details."

"I don't, but part of that whole open-and-honest-communication thing is sharing how you feel. You don't have to give me a play-by-play, but I want to know what made you look so sad. Not just now, but every few minutes since you got back. It's like a cloud passes over your face."

The truth is I'd really rather not talk about this to anyone right now, not even Trey. In some ways, especially not Trey, because I don't like the moral choices I'm having to make. Will he look at me differently when he realizes that my decisions are going to result in a bunch of innocent people dying?

But if I don't talk to him, he'll think I'm hiding things, and that's not good either.

"You know the Culling thing I mentioned?"

"Where your grandfather is planning to take out half the planet?"

"Yep, that's the one. We think Saul did a test run on a little village in Georgia in 1911. Whatever he used, it killed everyone, nearly fifty people in all. The authorities found them sitting in their little church, all very dead, a few weeks after it happened."

"I thought Saul couldn't use the key?"

"He can't. This was when he was younger, back before he destroyed CHRONOS."

"And you know it was Saul?"

"There's some pretty strong circumstantial evidence, but no, we aren't certain yet. That was our first stop today. We set up stable points so Kiernan can monitor various locations around the village. I got to meet a really nice old lady and some kids, who are all going to die in a couple of weeks, along with everyone else in their community. And I could stop it, Trey. I could go back and tell Sister Elba to pack everyone up and leave before Saul comes. I could make her believe me."

"So . . . why don't you?"

"Because he'll find another secluded little town and try again. We're lucky we found this place—it's probably our only chance to find out what he's planning to use for the Culling. I could take extreme measures and shoot him, but that has its own set of complications, since we don't know for certain that Saul is the only CHRONOS member who was in on the sabotage. There's a really good possibility that anything we do will change the timeline that results in me being here to stop the Cyrists. Simply put, I can't do anything that tips him off that someone knows what he's up to. And that makes me feel guilty and angry and . . ." I press my palms against my eyes and then slide them back, tugging at my hair. "Ugh. All of the choices just suck."

"But some suck worse than others, right? There are lesser evils you have to accept to stop a greater evil."

"I guess. But it's a lot harder to be objective when there are faces attached to the people that this so-called lesser evil will kill. And at what point do you pile up so many lesser evils that they aren't lesser anymore?"

Trey is quiet for a minute and then says, "Okay, this may sound a little cheesy, but anytime I face a moral dilemma, Estella recites this serenity poem, prayer, whatever. I don't remember the exact words, but it's something about changing what you can and accepting that you can't change everything. You may need to accept that you can't save everyone and focus on the people you *will* save if you stop Saul."

It's pretty much the same advice that Sister Elba gave as I was leaving the chapel. And it's good advice, I know it is, but . . .

"The big problem here is that there's an *if* in there. *If* we stop Saul. And I don't know for certain that we can do that. Isn't the last part of that serenity prayer about having the wisdom to tell what you can't change from what you can? It's not so simple when everything is all mixed up like this, and there are things that I could, in theory, change, except that it will screw up who knows what else. Including my own existence. Is there a serenity prayer for that?"

∞

After Trey leaves, I consider going upstairs to sleep. But I'm too wound up from talking about it, and I keep running through the same things over and over in my head. Might as well thrash them out with Connor and Katherine. I just hope she's in a reasonable mood, because I suspect she's the only one who will have the answers I need.

They're both on the couch in the living room when I get downstairs. Katherine's showered and changed out of her nightclothes since I spoke with her in the kitchen earlier. I'm hoping that's a positive sign.

"Okay," I say, sitting in the chair opposite them. "The good news is that 1938 went pretty well. I spent a little over five hours hanging around Athens, near the campus and over by the Morton Building, where Delia, Abel, and Grant were working today. I got some awkward looks when I walked into a café on that side of town, because it didn't occur to me that segregation sort of works both ways. I mean, I'm sure they would have let me buy a cup of coffee, but the guy behind the counter looked really nervous when I walked in, probably because I was by myself. I just acted like I was lost and asked for directions to campus. And I saw all three of them—they left the Morton Building together. I walked behind them for a few blocks before they split up over near Broad Street."

Katherine nods and says, "Grant. What did he look like?"

"Average height, muscular build, sandy hair. Young, seemed nervous. Delia was jumping his case about something."

"Grant must have been a first-year. If this was one of his first trips, then he'd have been your age or a year older, at most. Delia was nice enough, but she had a reputation as a tough instructor. She's a bit of a stickler when it comes to rules."

Katherine kind of wrinkles her nose as she says this, and I bite back a chuckle. It's way past ironic to hear her sniping at someone else for enforcing rules. I sneak a glance at Connor and see that he's also trying to hold it together. As soon as we catch each other's expression, we both break into laughter.

"What?" Katherine rolls her eyes when she gets it, and she ends up laughing, too. It's been a while since I heard her laugh. I wish I could just stop the discussion here, on a cheerful note. But they're both looking at me, waiting for me to go on.

Katherine says, "I'm guessing that's not all you wanted to discuss, is it?"

Her arms are pulled into her sides, and she's hunched over slightly, and I wonder for a moment if she's cold. There's something familiar about the position, however. I glance down and realize that I'm sitting the same way, like I'm bracing for a blow.

"Do you remember Saul mentioning a place called Six Bridges? In Georgia?" I ask.

"No. Is it near Athens?"

"About thirty miles away, over toward Greensboro. He might have also referred to it as God's Hollow."

"It's not ringing any bells. Why?"

"Everyone who lived there was killed in September of 1911, about fifty people total. They were found all together, in their church. Kiernan says the bodies look a lot like those he saw after some war in the 2070s, something Simon showed him. Simon also mentioned Six Bridges to Kiernan one night when he was drunk.

Apparently it was something Saul told Simon about a mistake he'd made long ago."

Katherine raises an eyebrow. "Saul admitted to a mistake? Doesn't sound like him."

"I don't know, Katherine. I'm just reporting back what Kiernan told me. Anyway, we took a trip over to—" I stop and hold up a hand, because she's clearly about to interrupt. "We drove over a few weeks before the deaths happened and set up some stable points so that we could observe the village. The authorities think whatever killed them was in the well, so I have a few points set there and several in the church. Kiernan's going to watch those locations. I'll check back with him shortly. Hopefully we'll be able to find out what happened."

"And what do you plan to do if you discover something? You can't stop it—"

"Yes, I know," I snap, then remind myself to breathe deeply and get a grip before I go on. "I know that, Katherine. I've been reminding myself of that fact for the past few hours. If the well was tampered with by Saul, or anyone else with a CHRONOS key, we'll go in afterward and get a sample. Connor, can you see about ordering something we can use to transport a . . . I guess it's called a biohazard? I'm hesitant to bring something like that back with me, but it might not be a bad idea to have someone working on an antidote. If I can't stop Saul, maybe we can at least limit the damage."

It's obvious from both of their faces that they don't disagree with that point, but then Katherine starts in about how it's too dangerous for me to go back to God's Hollow, and Connor asks who we would get to examine the sample. They're both talking over each other, and I sink back into the couch and close my eyes.

Finally, Connor clues in that I've checked out and says, "Okay, this is getting us nowhere. If we determine that it's Saul, we obviously need that sample, so either Kate or Kiernan or both of them will need to go back and retrieve it. It would probably be best to have Kiernan handle it, like you did with Copenhagen. So all we need to do is find someone who has the technical skill to analyze the sample and who doesn't have ties to the Cyrists or the govern—"

"What did you say?"

"We need someone with the technical skills—"

I sit back up and stare at him. "No. Before that. About Copenhagen. And Kiernan."

"Just that you'd probably get him to handle this one, too," he says and then looks down, shaking his head. "On a personal level, I'd prefer that my ancestor didn't have to take that degree of risk, but I know that there's a lot more at stake here than getting my family back. And at least you took precautions. If he hadn't been wearing body armor, one of those bullets might have done permanent damage—"

He stops suddenly, my facial expression finally registering. "Oh. You didn't know."

"I most certainly did not." I yank my CHRONOS key out of the leather pouch and pull up the coordinates Kiernan and I agreed upon before I left his cabin. I'd planned on doing this tomorrow evening, after school, when I was better rested and my head was clear, but he's forced my hand. "We'll have to finish this conversation later."

Katherine reaches over and grabs my wrist, causing the display to waver. "Katherine," I say, "please let go. Kiernan and I need to have a little chat."

She releases her grip, but as I'm pulling up the stable point again, she says. "I was just going to note that Kiernan made the decision we would have made as a group, Kate. Having him retrieve Moehler's key in Copenhagen was the logical decision."

"Yeah, well maybe that's your view, and Connor's, but unless I missed something, Kiernan didn't bother to get input from any of us, did he? This was a . . ." My brain is beyond tired, and I have trouble finding the word for a second. "A rogue operation, Katherine. He didn't have the right to make that decision, to take that kind of risk, on his own."

∞

BOGART, GEORGIA
October 6, 1905, 4:00 p.m.

Kiernan's mouth is set into a thin, firm line, and he's staring at the stable point. It almost feels like he can see me. Judging from the look in his eyes, he knows exactly how pissed I'm going to be. And he doesn't care.

My first thought is to play it cool. He's expecting angry, because his Kate would have been angry. So I'm going to give him calm and collected.

That lasts for maybe two seconds after I jump in. The first thing that I notice is that the left leg of his jeans is unusually tight about six inches above the knee, the fabric straining to accommodate a bandage. At that point, I lose it, spewing forth a string of words that would get me grounded for a week if Mom was in the room.

"Are you finished?" he asks, his voice cool.

"No. I'm pretty sure I'm just getting started."

"Fine. Since I'd much prefer to discuss this with a rational human being, I'll just sit here quietly until your childish tantrum runs its course."

"Childish? How can you call me childish when you're the one who rushes off into danger without discussing this with anyone? You could have been killed, Kiernan!"

He shrugs. "I wasn't. And you'd have faced exactly the same risk if you'd been the one who went in. Give me one good reason why the risk would have been any less if you'd gone in rather than me."

I think for a moment. "I was talking about both of us going in, but actually, yes, it would have been less for me, because I'm a smaller target."

Kiernan rolls his eyes. "I'll grant you that. But if you think me taking a risk was stupid, then both of us taking one would be doubly stupid."

He has a point, even though I'm not inclined to admit it. "You have to agree that the risk to the timeline is greater when you put yourself at risk. I never had kids, Kiernan. Grandkids. *Great*-grandkids? Connor has sacrificed a lot, you know. He realizes getting his family back may not happen, but you getting killed would wipe out all hope. And we'd also have to keep back one of the CHRONOS keys to avoid having him pop out of existence, right?"

"Connor was quite happy to get Moehler's key. Don't put this off on him. This is about you not getting to call the shots."

It's nice to have him misread me for once, to have him assume that this is some sort of weird control issue. Because it isn't. Truthfully, I'm not entirely sure why I reacted so strongly. We're both taking risks—and so are Connor, Katherine, even Dad. Maybe even Trey and his family. It probably would have been riskier if we'd both gone, and I'm pretty sure he could have convinced me of that point if he'd tried, as much as it would have worried me.

"I don't want to call the shots, Kiernan. I—"

His right eyebrow is raised, like he's waiting for me to finish, and I remember the cut on his forehead. It's entirely healed now. There's a very thin, faint pink line where the cut was, but the bruise has faded to the point that it's indistinguishable from the other skin on his tanned face.

I've been the first one to jump almost every time we've traveled together. With very few exceptions, Kiernan has followed behind me on each jump. And unless he's the world's fastest healer, he's sometimes following several days later.

"How many days since I was here last, Kiernan? When you taught me to shoot the gun? You told me to come back in three days, right?"

He nods, reluctantly.

"And that's what I did, but it's been more like a week for you, hasn't it? And when we jumped to 1911, before we rode the bikes over to God's Hollow, you had to wait a few days, didn't you? That cut on your head was pretty fresh when I first arrived, and I noticed when we were talking to Martha and Sister Elba that it had faded. So, I'm thinking you weren't able to follow me immediately. Am I right?"

I wait for him to respond, but he just looks at me, so I go on. "How far out of your own timeline are you right now? Do you even know?"

His mouth twists. "Of course, I *know*, Kate. I'm not a bloody idiot. I'm eleven days and seventeen hours off my normal timeline right now. And, yes, there have been a couple of instances where I've had trouble with the key. I told you it's not easy for me. I'm doing the best I can."

"Yes, but you're doing things you don't have to do! What if you'd gotten to Copenhagen and couldn't manage to get back immediately? You could have been killed."

His eyes drift away from my face, and there's an odd downward twitch to his mouth. He pushes his chair back and gets up.

"That's it, isn't it? That's why you were shot. You couldn't steady the interface the first time."

Kiernan doesn't answer. He just turns toward the door and walks out, limping. He bangs both the cabin door and the porch door on his way out. Pretty sad for someone who seems to think he's being the adult here.

I follow him outside to a sprawling oak tree at the edge of the woods. He's leaning against a limb that swoops out almost parallel to the ground. I walk over and pull myself up onto the bough, a foot or so away from where Kiernan is standing.

We stay like that for a minute or so, just looking out at the woods, saying nothing. I swing my feet slowly beneath the branch, taking deep breaths, trying to rein my temper back in. After my outburst, I suspect Kiernan is reassessing his comment about me being a calmer version of his Kate, but if he was this big of an idiot around her, it wasn't just Katherine who kept her angry.

"How bad is it?" I ask.

"I can do an average of two round trips a day, more or less, depending on how far in time and distance."

"Not that. I meant the bullet wound."

He shrugs dismissively. "Flesh wound on the outer thigh. If it had been two inches to the left, it wouldn't even have grazed me. Looks more like a gash or a burn than a bullet wound, really. Missed the family jewels, so Connor is theoretically safe. Although I have no idea who the woman is in that picture he showed me. Or even where that farm might be."

"Connor showed you the two different family pictures?"

"After I asked, yeah. I do like the look of the farm family a lot better than the one where I'm toting around a Book of Cyrus. But judging from the age of the kids in that one, I should have started on that family a few years back." He slides over a little closer to where I'm sitting on the branch. "And it's hard to get enthused about starting a family with someone I've never met when . . ." His voice trails off when I close my eyes. The words hang in the air, unspoken but unmistakable.

After a few awkward seconds, he shifts the subject a bit. "I did use that Kevlar stuff, you know. You can check up in the loft if you'd like—I haven't had a chance to take it back yet. Even managed to mostly hide a helmet under one of those stupid-looking fur hats. I wasn't hotdogging."

"I didn't say you were, Kiernan. I just wish you'd be honest with me!"

He looks over at me, his eyes doubtful, and holds my gaze for a long moment. "You're sure that's what you want?"

"Yes."

The word is barely out before his mouth is on mine. He slips one arm beneath my legs, lifting me off the branch, while the other curves around my back, pressing my body against his. Kiernan groans softly and shifts the pressure away from his injured leg when my weight is added to his, but he doesn't let me go. He just leans his shoulders against the limb and pulls me tighter, the kiss deepening.

The rational voice inside my brain clears its throat and whispers Trey's name. Brain and body are clearly not speaking the same language, however. My hands, instead of pushing away, clutch tighter for just a second—one grips the collar of his shirt, and the other holds the back of his neck, my fingers laced through his hair.

And then the rational voice realizes that polite insistence simply isn't going to cut it and screams loudly enough that my body has no choice but to listen.

Kiernan senses the change in me and breaks off the kiss. I start to turn away, but he doesn't release me. His hand slides up to the back of my head, and he turns my face around to his so that I have no choice but to look him in the eyes.

"*That* was me being honest, Kate. That is what I want to do every second I'm near you." His voice softens, and he leans forward, pressing his lips against my neck. "And that was you being honest, too, before you decided to put your mask back on."

I start to speak, but he shakes his head. "I'm not saying you don't care about Trey. I *know* you do. You might even be in love with him, although I don't like thinking about that possibility. All I'm saying is you have feelings for me, too. And don't give me any crap about my inflated ego. I've seen you in love with me before, and I still see something of that in your eyes. I've tried to tell myself it's just wishful thinking, but it's not. If you want to keep pretending, I won't stop you, but please don't lecture me about honesty unless you're willing to stop lying to me and to yourself."

Kiernan slides me down to the ground, and I take several steps away. It's not that I don't trust him. I'm pretty sure he's made his point. But I've put mind and soul under far too much stress for one day, and I'd rather keep a little distance between us.

Because I know that he's right. I care for him more than I should, more than I want to, and way more than is fair to Trey. That's the not-so-simple truth, and I've known it since we kissed on the Wooded Island, even if I didn't want to admit it.

"While we're being honest, love," he says, "this leg is bloody killing me. Can we finish this conversation inside?"

I nod and follow him back into the cabin. Kiernan hobbles over to the couch and sits at one end, propping his leg on a large ottoman. He has on his get-back-to-business face, and I'm not even slightly inclined to argue. I sit down on the far end of the couch and turn to face him, trying to get my brain back into some semblance of order.

Kiernan tugs a folded sheet of paper out of his pocket, wincing slightly when he moves the injured leg. "This is a list of the coordinates you should watch—times I've located so far where Saul shows up. I still need to finish watching inside the church itself, but, yeah, it's him. I watched the location above the well first, and he clearly drops a vial of something into the water. It was night, and I couldn't see much, other than the fact that he was wearing gloves and some sort of mask over his nose and mouth. He looks a little younger than he did at the Expo, but that could just be because he's clean shaven and in normal clothes rather than the rich-bloke costume he wore at the Fair. He talks to Martha in front of the chapel for a long time. She had that same look as when she was staring at me. They seriously need to introduce that kid to some boys closer to her own age."

A shadow passes over his face, and I'm pretty sure he's just remembered that no one will be introducing Martha to anybody. "And Saul—I mean, I can't hear what he says, but his expression. God, it made me want to jump in and knock his stupid head off, because he's . . . what? . . . thirty? She can't be more than thirteen."

She's probably closer to fifteen, but the point is still more than valid.

He pulls in a deep breath and says, "I'm sorry, Kate. Okay? Not for kissing you. I'm not one bit sorry about that, though I'll try not to do it again without your permission. I'll *try*." He gives me a fleeting smile and then goes on. "What I meant is I'm sorry we didn't discuss Copenhagen first. I was just so damned angry at you—"

"Why? What did I do that you're pissed at me?"

He starts to speak, then stops, leaning back against the sofa and rubbing his temples for a few seconds before he continues. "Maybe it's not fair. But you left here the other day with hardly a word about what happened at Six Bridges. You insisted that we immediately go to 1938, and then once we were finished, you rushed off. Like the situation was entirely my fault, like you blamed me for bringing it to your attention."

"Kiernan, no. I was tired and upset. I wanted to go home. As a matter of fact, I'm still tired and upset. That was only a few hours ago for me. I was reporting back to Connor and Katherine when they mentioned Copenhagen and said you'd been shot. That you were lucky you weren't killed. I was *worried* about you, okay? And pissed that you didn't tell me what you were doing, that you could have been killed and it would have been my fault."

His eyebrows go up. "Why would it be your fault? You don't control my decisions, Kate. I should have discussed it with you, but I'd have retrieved Moehler's key from Copenhagen whether it got the Cyrist Fighters' stamp of approval or not."

"Yes, but you wouldn't even be involved with this if I hadn't taken you back to Estero and . . ."

My voice trails off, but it's out, and I suspect he caught it, too. I never took him to Estero. That was Other-Kate. When did I start thinking of the things she did as my responsibility?

He watches my face for a minute. I assume he's going to gloat, having so often pointed out that I am she and she is me. But his eyes are sad, and when he finally speaks, his voice is low, barely a whisper.

"Do you think so little of me, Kate?"

Okay. What did I miss? I just shake my head, confused.

"Do you think I'd have just stood by and watched Saul wipe out countless innocents? Or, hell, countless people? I don't care if they're innocent or not. Do you think it doesn't twist my gut to walk among those people at Six Bridges and know they're all going to die at Saul's hand? That I could physically stop it, but . . ." He shakes his head. "Or maybe you just think I'm so bloody stupid I'd never have caught on and would've followed Cyrist orders to kill—"

"Stop it! You know I don't think any of that."

"Then why say that me getting hurt is your fault, Kate? I'd have been fighting them with or without you. It was just a matter of time."

We're both silent for a minute, and then he sighs. "I know this isn't fair to you, but you're the only person I can talk to about any of this. You have your dad, Connor, and Katherine, who all know what's goin' on, right? And most likely Trey as well, 'cause I'd bet the farm—now that I have one to bet—that he's where you headed when you left here in such a rush."

The answer is on my face, so I don't say anything. And I'm just thinking he doesn't have the right to guilt-trip me about this when he says, "I'm not out to make you feel bad. You were upset, and it's only natural you'd seek out comfort. It's just . . ."

"You needed comfort, too."

"Yeah. I'm not asking you to hold my hand and tuck me into bed at night, not that I'll argue if you find yourself so inclined. But we're partners until this is over, and I'd like to think that you at least consider me a friend—oh, Kate, don't cry, okay? You look like a shamed pup, and I never want to make you feel that way. If you cry, I'll end up crying, too."

I wipe the tears away with the back of my hand and try to hold them in, because they're just making him feel worse. "I'm sorry. I've been acting like a spoiled child. You have every right to be angry."

"I'm not angry at you. Yeah, I was, but mostly at this whole situation that has you turning to someone else instead of me."

I bite my lip to keep it from quivering, but another couple of tears sneak out of the corners of my eyes. Kiernan tries to move toward my end of the couch but grimaces when he moves his leg and mutters a few muted curses.

"God, would you just come here, Kate? I'll behave, I promise. It wrecks me to see you cry and not be able to hold you. Or if you can't do that, go to him and let him hold you. I'm making a bloody mess of everything."

He looks so miserable. I can't tell him no. I'm not even sure I want to.

I slide to his end of the couch and curl up next to him. We hold each other, and I cry—tears for the things we can't change, or won't change, but most of all, for things lost. And I fall asleep in his arms when we're both cried out.

It's dark in the cabin when I open my eyes, so I've no idea how long we slept. But it was deep and dreamless, and I don't get much of that these days. I move away carefully, so that he doesn't awaken, and then look around for a pencil and paper so that I can leave him a note.

Kiernan ~ I'll be back tomorrow morning at eight. Please wait until I'm here to finish watching the points at Six Bridges. You shouldn't have to do this alone. ~Kate

I underline the word *wait* three times, then give him a soft kiss on the cheek and tuck the note into the crease of his arm. And then I pull out the medallion and jump back to Trey.

Is that wrong?

Maybe.

I don't really know anymore. All I know is that I have to stay true to the letter of the promise I made Trey, because I seem to be ripping its spirit to shreds.

∞15∞

The front porch of Katherine's house is one place I'm reasonably sure Trey will be, since he's picking me up for school at seven fifteen. My other option is to go back to the townhouse yesterday, but that carries a risk of bumping into my earlier self. While I could also run into myself here, this is my later self, and she will know I'm sitting out here on the porch swing at this moment. So if I'm dumb enough to look outside before Trey rings the doorbell, I deserve whatever headache may follow.

Trey comes through the gate a few minutes early, wearing the khaki pants and white button-down shirt that is the Briar Hill warm-weather uniform for guys. It's what he wore when he'd stop by to see me after school in the last timeline. He's a little less crumpled now than he usually was by day's end, but this is his everyday look, the one I remember best, and my breath catches in my throat.

He smiles when he sees me on the swing, but it's a confused smile. He's expecting me to be in my school uniform, ready to go, and I'm in jeans and a T-shirt, both wrinkled. My face is probably still puffy from crying, and my hair is wild.

"I know what you're about to say," I begin, "and unless I oversleep the alarm, I'm already in my school clothes. Probably in the kitchen, finishing breakfast. I'll go back and get a good night's sleep before you ring the doorbell. I just needed to see you now."

He sits down next to me on the swing and pulls me toward him. "I know. I felt the same way after last night, but since I'm not blessed with a CHRONOS key—"

"Cursed."

He nods. "Yeah, that's probably more accurate."

The swing rocks us back and forth, and he just stares out at the road for several seconds, silent. I'm about to ask what's on his mind when he says, "I thought about what you said. And you're right, okay?"

"About?"

Trey gives me an odd look and then laughs. "About *us*?"

I'm not quite sure which thing about us he's referring to, but he keeps going.

"And I know it's a school night, but with your schedule right now, it could be weeks before you make it through five days of school, right?"

He's definitely right. I'm going back to Kiernan's as soon as we finish classes today. It's not fair to make him watch the stable points at God's Hollow on his own. I can't even imagine being in that cabin alone, watching those people die.

"So, I'm thinking . . . maybe dinner tonight? I'll get reservations someplace nice, so we can make it special."

I'm a bit torn. I'll probably be lousy company, given all that's going on, but I did promise to try to give him equal time.

"I think that'll be okay," I say. "But pick me up at the townhouse."

"Got it. Six o'clock?"

I nod, and then a big yawn hits me.

He kisses me on the forehead. "You need sleep. We have a big day and a big night ahead. Sweet dreams."

I almost say "you, too," until I realize that would be silly, so I just give him a sleepy smile and pull out the CHRONOS key. "Give me a couple of minutes, then ring the bell."

I'd rather jump straight to my room, but I set the coordinates for the foyer, a minute after I jumped away yesterday afternoon, so that I can update Katherine and Connor.

They're still on the couch, with their backs to the foyer. Katherine is grumbling about something, so I clear my throat to announce my presence.

"Kiernan's okay," I say.

Connor huffs. "As I said just before you took off."

"You said it could have been a lot worse. Not the same thing. Anyway, the massacre at God's Hollow, Six Bridges, whatever you want to call it, is definitely Saul's work. I'm going back tomorrow after school to get more details. Right now, I'm going to sleep."

When I get to my room, I call Dad to check on Grandpa, but I get his voice mail again. It feels like he's been gone a week, so it's a bit of a jolt to look at the time and see that it's not even nine yet, which means he's only been gone about eight hours. There's also a message from Mom, but I'm too exhausted to chat.

I drink some water, run the toothbrush across my teeth a few times, and then collapse into bed, hoping to get a solid ten hours or so of nightmare-free sleep. But the fire dream sneaks up on me a little before daybreak. My subconscious clearly doesn't go in for subtlety, because this time, in addition to all of the strangers, Kiernan and Trey are among those I "save" by tossing them out the window onto the sidewalk below, where they shatter to tiny bits. There's no way to sleep after that. On the bright side, I have time to exercise before school.

After working out and showering, I eat my protein bar on the patio with Daphne, mostly so I won't be tempted to peek at the front porch, where Trey will arrive in about two minutes. I don't hear his car when it pulls up, but Daphne does. She gives a few barks and runs to the patio door before I call her back over. I think she can hear us talking out front as well, because she keeps giving me these pitiful looks, like she can't understand why I'm here, but my voice is out there. And, more importantly, why I'm keeping her from her job as household greeter.

I'm at the door when Trey rings the bell a few minutes later, and I let Daphne out onto the porch, so she can get her barking, tail wagging, and sniffing out of the way. Then I reach up to give Trey a kiss.

He glances back over his shoulder at the swing, which hasn't quite stopped moving, before he steps inside. "You know, this would be a lot easier to get used to if you had to go back to your TARDIS or whatever before you disappeared."

"I'm sorry. I'm really not trying to mess with your head. It's just that I'm having to find creative ways to keep my promise."

"You still look tired," he says, slipping an arm around my waist.

"Dreams." I grab my backpack from the closet. "You look kind of wiped, too."

"Yeah, well, I had a lot on my mind. But none of that today, right? First day of school! Aren't you excited?"

He's giving me a look that suggests he's the polar opposite of excited, and I laugh.

"I know. I usually like school, but it's hard to get enthused. I mean, I like that I'll have classes with you. And Charlayne will be there—that's a plus . . . I think. But so will Eve and her groupies, and there'll be a bunch of new Cyrist teachers. I kind of feel like we're walking into a snake pit."

"Thanks, Kate. Way to make the new guy even more nervous."

"Oh, give me a break," I say, closing the door behind us. "I've never seen you in any social situation where you seemed even the slightest bit nervous."

We arrive at Briar Hill with only a few minutes to spare. I point Trey toward his homeroom, which is, unfortunately, not the same as mine. He gives my hand a brief squeeze before he walks off. It's a very clandestine squeeze, since we're both pretty sure that the PDA rules are about to undergo a drastic overhaul.

I slide into my seat just as the first bell rings and glance around. The first thing I notice is Charlayne, two seats behind me. She gives me a little finger wave when I catch her eye and then turns back to say something to a guy seated on her right. The second thing I notice is that all of the new girls, most of whom I assume are from Carrington Day, and maybe a quarter of the girls I recognize from my classes last year at Briar Hill, are in a different style of uniform. The blue-and-gold plaid skirt that hits about an inch above the knee has been replaced with a longer beige skirt that's only a few inches shorter than the one I've been wearing in 1905.

Apparently some of us missed a memo.

Two teachers—one I vaguely remember seeing in the halls last year and the other a short, middle-aged guy I've never seen before—are passing out folders of some sort. The new teacher slides one of the folders onto my desk, and I note the lotus tattoo on his hand. I hadn't really looked at the tattoo on any of the male Cyrists, and I'm surprised to see that it's blue, instead of the pink they use on the girls. I have to choke back a laugh, but it's only partially successful, and I pretend I'm coughing to cover. The folder must be something that was used last year, because there's a Carrington Day logo—a Spartan helmet with a Cyrist symbol on the side.

Eve and one of the three girls Charlayne tagged as an "Evelette" stroll into class just as the final bell sounds. Seats are assigned, so

Eve is near the front. Her friend must be closer to the end of the alphabet, because she gives Eve a little pout and starts toward the back of the classroom. She's only taken a few steps when she spots me and then hurries back to whisper something in Eve's ear. Eve wrinkles her nose in distaste and flashes me an annoyed look, then whispers something back to the other girl, and they both laugh.

The Smart Board blinks to life for the morning announcements, and the Briar Hill mascot, a falcon that looks like the artist played too much *Angry Birds*, appears in his usual spot at the middle of the opening screen. Instead of his normal deep blue feathers and gold beak, however, he's an odd plum shade. A collective groan goes up, not just from the Briar Hill crew but from everyone, followed by assorted grumbles.

The Briar Hill teacher finally says, "Enough. You'll have time to voice your opinions later. And the answer to any questions you have is in the folder."

The Pledge is apparently not recited at Carrington Day, because they sit silent and stiff at their desks while the rest of us stand. After we're done, it's our turn to sit uncomfortably as they all rise to face the Cyrist symbol on the screen and recite the Creed. When they reach the part where they say, "Enemies of The Way will face our Wrath and Judgment," Eve shoots me a look. She's clearly trying to get under my skin, and it would almost be funny if it wasn't also kind of sick. With everything that's on the line right now, everything the Cyrists are planning, Eve is still interested in stupid schoolgirl games.

I wait until Eve and her friend push through the door and then stuff the magical answers-to-everything folder into my bag.

Charlayne is standing next to my desk when I look up. "Well, that was enlightening," she says. "Did you hear what Bensen, the guy sitting next to me, called the new bird mascot? The Purple Pigeon. I think that has a certain ring to it."

"Or maybe they should switch things up," I say. "We could paste the blue-and-gold plaid from the Briar Hill uniforms on the Carrington Day mascot, and he'd be the Tartan Spartan."

We merge into the flow in the hallway. Everyone seems much taller now that the middle school crowd has been shipped over to Carrington.

"That's even better," she says. "And maybe the Tartan Spartan could carry the Purple Pigeon around on his shoulder. This could be good. Too bad no one will listen to us."

"Yeah. Although to be honest, I'm not really into the whole school-spirit thing."

"I can see why, with a bird for a mascot." She turns to the side so that I can see the emblem stitched to her backpack—a guy with a purple helmet and cape that hangs slightly open to reveal his well-muscled arms and torso. "But I liked our Spartan. He's ho—" She stops, takes a deep breath, and rephrases. "He's . . . historical."

I laugh. Non-Cyrist Charlayne is still in there. Most definitely.

"Yeah," I say. "Historical is nice. And he's also wicked hot."

Charlayne rolls her eyes, but the sides of her mouth twitch, and it takes several seconds for her to tamp down the grin that's trying to sneak out.

"If you say so," she says primly. "I hadn't really noticed."

∞

I glance around the cafeteria for Trey, but I can't find him. I only need to watch one side of the room, however, because an invisible line runs through the center, separating the Cyrists from the more familiar Briar Hill faces. The one positive thing I can say about the merger is that it seems to have at least partially erased the social cliques that divided us. There's a sense of solidarity, and several students I'm pretty sure didn't know I existed last year gave me friendly smiles in the hallway. They probably don't have a clue who I am, and probably don't care, but the shorter plaid skirt tags me as one of *us*, not one of *them*.

I finally locate Trey at the other entrance to the cafeteria and give him a wave. We merge into the line and pick out a few of the less icky options. Apparently the cluster of kids directly in front of us is used to a better assortment, because they whine and complain all the way to the cashier. And, yes, Briar Hill's lunches do kind of suck. If not for the salad bar and yogurt, I'd definitely pack a lunch from home. But their tone still gets under my skin, and I suspect the same is true for the servers, because one of them plops a scoop of mashed potatoes onto a Cyrist guy's plate hard enough for it to splatter onto his shirt. And she doesn't look the least bit sorry.

We've just found an empty table, close to the virtual Berlin Wall, when Charlayne and the guy from homeroom, the one she called Bensen, drop their backpacks into the other two chairs.

Charlayne scans our food. "You're the only person I know who's survived a Briar Hill lunch. Can I assume the chicken sandwiches and fries are edible?"

"The fries aren't bad, but Trey's gambling with that sandwich. The salad bar is good. Real bacon, not the fake stuff, assuming it's not already gone."

As I suspected, bacon is a major selling point for Charlayne. She smiles and tugs at the guy's arm. "Come on, Ben."

I'm returning her smile when it occurs to me that something is wrong with this picture. It was natural for Charlayne to walk with me to history, since we're in the same class. But then she walked with me to second period, and gym isn't exactly on the way to the Arts Annex. She was also near my locker between third and fourth period, and now she and Ben are the sole Cyrists sitting in the Land of the Unwashed Heathen.

The smile freezes on my face. Charlayne is spying on me.

"The sandwich isn't half bad if you add ketchup," Trey says, and then notices my expression. "What's wrong?"

"Charlayne. I'm pretty sure she's been told to sit here. Look around. Are there any other Cyrists on this side of the cafeteria?"

He smiles sadly. "I thought you'd already figured that out. I mean, it's a little too convenient, don't you think? Your best friend from before plays for the other team, but she wants to be your BFF again."

Now I feel stupid, because, of course, he's right. Just because my conversation with Charlayne felt natural, just because she seems like the old Charlayne, doesn't mean she is. I felt a connection, but I was probably the only one who felt it. Wanting something doesn't make it real.

Trey dips one of the fries in ketchup and waves it in front of me. I shake my head, and he shrugs, popping it into his mouth instead. "So, do we tell them to go back to their own side or play along?"

"Play along. I'd much rather sit here with just you, but I can't let Eve or Prudence or whoever the hell is behind this know that I finally . . . *finally* . . . caught on. Playing dumb shouldn't be too tough—it seems to be a natural talent."

Trey fakes an offended look. "Excuse me?"

"Not you. I've seen you undercover. You're like James Bond. I'm the gullible one. Mom says I'm too trusting, just like Dad. Apparently she's right."

"Maybe. But do you want to go through life assuming the worst about everyone you meet? One of my favorite things about you is the fact that you have the personality of a golden retriever."

I narrow my eyes. "I'm neither blond nor fluffy."

"And you don't have doggy breath, either. I said *personality*. You're kind. Loyal. You give people a chance. Do you want to be the type of person who'd automatically assume Charlayne was bad, before the evidence was in?"

"Well, no." Even now that I'm pretty sure what she's up to, I don't like thinking of Charlayne that way. I push my salad around on my plate, stab a few veggies, and then put the fork back down. "I actually don't believe Charlayne's bad. I mean, not really bad. She could have reasons we don't . . ."

I stop, because Trey is grinning. "I rest my case. We need to find a good golden retriever nickname for you." I kick his foot under the table, and he laughs. Then his eyes take on a different sort of light as he rubs his calf gently against mine and says in a soft voice, "I'm looking forward to tonight. Maybe you could bring that thing you were wearing?"

I raise an eyebrow. "The librarian outfit?"

Trey rolls his eyes. "Yeah, right. You know exa—" He snaps his mouth shut as Charlayne and Ben come up from behind, sliding their plates onto the table.

"Only bacon crumbs," Charlayne grumbles. "And the lady snapped at me when I pulled the container out of the bar and dumped the rest on my plate. What was I supposed to do?"

Bensen, who hasn't spoken until now, says, "I think she's just grumpy. She's the one who splashed gravy on my brownie. And it's not even next to the potatoes."

I suspect they're talking about the same cafeteria lady I saw earlier, and I'm torn. Part of me is thinking it's not cool to be prejudiced against all Cyrists just because some are jerks, and the other part is sizing her up as a potential ally against the Dark Side. Although she's older than Katherine and seriously out of shape, so I'm not sure how much help she'd be.

We talk about classes for a few minutes, although most of the conversation is carried by Charlayne. When there's a lull, Trey jumps in with a question.

"Aren't you afraid you'll get shunned, sitting on this side of the Great Divide?"

Ben smiles, a fleeting upward twitch of his lips that I'd have missed if I'd blinked at that moment. "I'm on scholarship," he says. "Partly need based, which makes me a charity case, which means I'm shunned by definition. But I don't know what Charlayne did to piss them off."

Charlayne gives him a dirty look. "No one is pissed at me, Ben. This isn't kindergarten. I can sit wherever I want."

"But you have a tattoo," I say, looking over at Bensen's hand. "So I thought . . ."

He shrugs, tossing a bit of dark hair out his eyes. "Mom wanted me to go to Carrington Day. Charlayne's mom told her I could probably get a scholarship if I'd agree to the . . . conditions. So I ran the odds. The average male of Indian descent loses his virginity around nineteen. Additional factors: I'm fat, short, and my favorite book is *Lord of the Rings*. Put those together, and it's virtually certain that I'll be a virgin at twenty with or without this tattoo, so I might as well reap some sort of benefit from it. And I've heard the tattoo will make me forbidden fruit for nonbelievers."

Ben's eyebrows flick upward a fraction of an inch.

"Shut *up*, Ben," Charlayne hisses. "I thought you were supposed to be smart. Do you believe every locker-room fantasy you hear?"

"Only the ones your brothers tell me." He does the little lip-twitch grin again. This guy has clearly mastered the art of understated facial expressions.

"How long have you two known each other?" Trey asks.

It's the same thing I was thinking. They snipe at each other like siblings.

"Too long," Charlayne replies. "His mother was our nanny. She still helps out from time to time, when my parents have to travel or something. *She's* nice. It's not her fault Ben's a jerk."

"There's a picture of us in the tub together when we were two. It's as close as I'm likely to get to a naked female for quite some time, so I carry it in my wallet. Would you like to see?"

Charlayne jabs him with her elbow. "I've half a mind to report you to the temple, you little twerp."

A tiny shake of his head and a miniscule smile. "Rah. Ool."

I glance over at Trey, and he seems as confused as I am. And then something about Charlayne's expression makes me realize that Ben is teasing her about a guy. Someone named Raoul.

I manage to keep from laughing, but it's a close call. If I had any doubts at all whether the real Charlayne was still inside this crispy Cyrist shell, they're gone now. And even though I know the primary reason she's here is so she can report back to her Cyrist overlords, knowing that she's still Charlayne gives me hope.

The first day of senior year ends without casualties, aside from a bruised elbow I pick up when some guy with an uncanny resemblance to Gaston from *Beauty and the Beast* shoves me against the lockers. The shove may have been an accident, but since the big lunk was with Eve in the cafeteria a few minutes earlier, I think it was accidentally on purpose.

Trey and I are both a little preoccupied on the drive home. I'm thinking about the fact that I'll be in Georgia in half an hour, watching for evidence of my grandfather's crimes, and that sort of winds my stomach into a knot. I'm not sure what's up with Trey— maybe he's still annoyed at the Gaston guy. He drops me off at the house with a quick kiss and a promise that he'll see me at six.

I grab a bag of chips and a soda from the kitchen, because there are no nacho-cheese Doritos or diet sodas in 1905.

"Are you running away, dear?"

Katherine is standing in the doorway, with one of the CHRONOS diaries in her hand. She's wearing her robe and looks like she hasn't been awake for long.

"No. Just taking a few supplies with me." She opens her mouth, and I can tell there's a lecture coming about carrying out-of-timeline items, so I quickly add, "Kiernan's cabin is in the middle of woods, Katherine, and I swear to God, I'll bring back every single wrapper, okay?"

She gives me a resigned look but doesn't say anything.

"Did you just wake up?" I ask.

Katherine nods and then crosses over to grab the kettle from the stove. "These new medications tend to make me sleepy in fits and spurts during the day. Then I'm awake half the night. How was school?"

I groan and shake my head. "We now get the Cyrist Creed along with the Pledge of Allegiance and Cyrist teachers along with our regular teachers. No holding hands in the hallway and a new dress code. My outfit for the Expo showed more skin. We have until next Monday to comply, but I'm not ordering it. If this isn't over before then, you and Dad can homeschool me. It's bad enough to be stuck in a uniform, but the boys' uniform doesn't change at all. What's with the Cyrist focus on female chastity? I mean, according to Adrienne, Saul wasn't exactly a prude." In fact, Adrienne told me pretty much the opposite, noting that Saul tried to sleep with almost every female at CHRONOS, but Katherine's expression suggests I might want to skip the specifics.

"No," she says, "but he wouldn't be the first to decide that rules of behavior should be stricter once they no longer affect him personally. We have plenty of that type in public office today. If I had to guess, I'd say it's the result of co-opting so many different religions. Like any partnership, each group has to compromise a few things when they merge."

The image of our new Purple Pigeon mascot pops into my head, which makes me think of homeroom and the Cyrist teacher who handed out the folder. "I didn't realize until today that the Cyrist men have a blue lotus tattoo, instead of pink. How cliché."

Katherine chuckles silently. "That's been true since the Cyrists started the whole tattoo thing back in the 1600s. Saul was not a gender historian, so he obviously assumed that was the natural order of things—pink for girls, blue for boys—since there are still remnants of that in the future. But it's a much more recent custom. In the timeline before Saul inserted his Cyrists, pink wasn't associated with girls until the 1940s. I don't know why they even use the tattoos for males. The whole chastity thing for them is sort of wink-wink, anyway—a token nod to gender equality."

She sits down next to me and dips her tea bag up and down in the water, a reflective look on her face. "But . . . I don't think the choice of values the Cyrists adopted was entirely coincidental. Looking back, Saul was always a bit . . . misogynistic. He'd make comments about the good old days when men were men and women knew their place. About how it was natural for the stronger to rule. He didn't care for my counterargument that there are different kinds of strength, that in a civilized world, upper-body strength isn't all that relevant. We'd always pretend it was a joke, but even then I knew there was a bit of truth under the banter."

"So . . . how would Saul have felt about having to rely on Prudence to set up Cyrist International? About sharing power?"

"He would hate it. And he'd fight it, especially if he thought Prudence was developing a following. Saul never cared for anything that took the focus away from him."

"And Prudence does precisely that. She's the human 'face' of the Cyrists. When I was at the temple in the other timeline, Charlayne said that few people had seen Saul but many had seen Prudence—and she always looks the same, eternal. That makes sense, because only those with the CHRONOS gene can go forward to see Saul, but Prudence sometimes appears in front of entire congregations.

So it makes sense that Saul would push all of this weaker-vessel crap—he wants them to see her as his subordinate."

Katherine shakes her head. "I just wish I could talk with Prudence. That she'd speak to me. I find it hard to believe she's willing to help Saul in this Culling thing. Prudence could be a difficult child, but she and Deborah were both very compassionate. They'd pull the last coin out of their pockets if they saw a beggar on the streets. Prudence once saved her allowance for an entire year to give to this international children's group that came to their school. I can't fathom how she could change so much."

"Well, Kiernan did say she was different when she was younger, before her mind became all muddled. Apparently, Saul has a very convincing . . . I guess you'd call it a demo reel for future events. Kiernan said Simon took him around to select locations—wars, famines, environmental devastation—and he said those sights made it easy to believe that the future needed changing. Maybe Saul showed the same things to Prudence when she found him?"

"Maybe. There are certainly plenty of examples to choose from, both in this century and the next. But things *do* get better. Most of the environmental problems have been addressed. Famine isn't a problem in my time—truthfully, it wouldn't be a problem now if we had the political will to address it. Political conflicts still happen, but they're rarely armed conflicts. Those are on the decline now, compared to the rest of history, although people don't seem to believe it. The 2300s are not utopian, but . . . they're a vast improvement over the present. I think you'd agree if you could see it."

"So why aren't there any stable points after . . . 2150, I think it is?"

"Well, for one thing, we have solid documentary evidence of most events we'd want to view after that point. But I think the more important reason is that's when the mechanism we use for time travel was invented. The cutoff prevented us from going back and tweaking things that affected our personal lives and from going back and uninventing CHRONOS, I guess."

I snort. "Uninventing CHRONOS sounds pretty good to me right now. What I don't get, if things are really okay like you're saying, is why Saul and these Objectivists wanted change."

"You'll always have discontents in any system, Kate. Some people feel they're being oppressed or held back, even if they have everything they need or everything that a reasonable person could want. Some people always want more."

She takes a sip of her tea. "Everyone knew that the Objectivists argued that CHRONOS technology wasn't being used to its full potential, but it seemed like . . . I don't know, an academic exercise, maybe? An ongoing esoteric debate. Only a handful of the DC-area Objectivists had any connection to CHRONOS. I attended a few functions with Saul but stopped going, because I didn't like the way he acted around them. He seemed like a different person, especially when Campbell, the group's leader, was around. Campbell was a nasty man, but to his credit, he opposed Saul's ideas on using religion as a tool for shaping history."

"He didn't think it would work?"

"I don't know whether he thought it would work or not, but he thought it was a bad idea. He once poked fun at Saul and said that increasing the role of religion in society would make things worse, not better. Saul said that depended on the religion, and they went back and forth. Like everyone else, I tuned it out, assuming it was a pointless, ongoing argument between two—what's the word they're using these days? Frenemies? I never thought . . ."

Her voice is small and sad. And as I watch her staring into her cup of tea, I realize she looks old. Old and weak and very ill. I've never known Katherine when she wasn't terminally ill, but despite that, she's always seemed strong to me. Forceful. That's certainly how Mom thinks of her—a force of nature you encounter at your peril.

The woman I met at the Expo also seemed strong. She was good at her job, poised, and self-assured. But somewhere in that mix was the fragile, insecure young woman I saw in her diaries, a girl so in love that she ignored the signs that the man was a psychopath. And now she blames herself for not knowing, not realizing, not having the strength to ask the hard questions about Saul before it was too late.

Just like I'm going to blame myself if I can't set things right before she dies.

I sigh, slip my backpack over one shoulder, and grab the unopened chips and soda. Might as well get on with it.

"I'm going to go up to change clothes and then check in with Kiernan. I'll be back soon."

"Kate?" she says softly as I'm turning to leave.

"Yes?"

"I know you know this, but I have to remind you anyway. You can't stop this thing in Six Bridges. I'm sure you want to. And I understand, but . . ."

I lean over and give her a hug. "It's okay, Katherine. I know."

∞16∞

Even before I jump in, I can tell that Kiernan ignored my request to wait. It's something about the set of his jaw as he sits there at the kitchen table. He isn't staring at the stable point, all combative like he was last time. He's just looking down at the floor, tapping his right foot in a nervous jitter against the chair leg.

His eyes flick over to my feet when I arrive, but he doesn't look up.

"Why didn't you wait?" I ask.

"I was bored."

Yeah, right.

The box that holds the newspaper clippings from God's Hollow is on the other side of the table. One of the articles is outside the box, a few inches from his arm. It's one with a photograph, so I avoid looking at it as I pull one of the other chairs around so that I'm facing Kiernan.

"You know this isn't fair, don't you?" I ask in a quiet voice. "You can't complain about me not treating you like a partner unless you're willing to do the same."

Kiernan's laugh is short and bitter. "Kate, you don't want to see what I saw."

"You can't protect me from everything."

He looks up, his eyes imploring. "Trust me, please?"

When he can tell that it's not working, he sighs and hobbles over to the couch. He's dragging the injured leg even more than he was yesterday.

"Saul tested whatever it was he put in their well. He also tested the antidote. Both passed with flying colors. Then he went back to whenever. Leave it at that, okay?"

"Maybe I would. But there's something you're not telling me."

He leans his head back against the top of the sofa and lets out an exasperated huff, avoiding my eyes.

"I can see it in your face, Kiernan. Either give me the coordinates I need to watch or make yourself comfortable for the next day or two while I go through every single one of them. Because I will."

"Fine, Kate. Have it your way. Bring me your damn key."

I sit down next to him and tug the medallion out of my T-shirt. It would be easier to hand it to him, lanyard and all, but there's nothing like Connor's contraption to make this cabin a safe house, and I'm not inclined to put too much space between me and the medallion.

Kiernan copies one item from his key to mine and hands it back to me. "That's the only one you need to watch. Martha's not among the bodies in the church."

"You're sure?"

He nods, but his expression keeps me from even starting to hope that this means Martha escaped. "As best I can tell, Saul locked her up someplace, probably in a cellar, during the two days when people were sick and dying. I'm guessing he used her as the test case for the antidote, but there's no way to tell for sure."

I take a deep breath, then slide over to the center of the couch and bring up the coordinates he gave me. It's the chapel, Friday, September 15, 1911, at 2:54 p.m. The static image I see initially is from the stable point I set at the back of the church, where the view mimics the newspaper photographs. The bodies are all in the same position, but from what I can tell, the mummified look is only apparent on some of them, and it's partially due to some sort of rash or discoloration. Others look like they're just taking a nap, although their eyes are sunken and the skin seems almost deflated, probably due to dehydration.

One small arm hangs over the side of the left-hand pew, two rows from the back. Unlike in the black-and-white newspaper photos, I can now see that the head resting on that arm is reddish-blond. Another flash of the exact same color is just barely visible a few feet to the left, one twin slumped against the other.

At the front of the church, Sister Elba is on the small bench, facing the congregation. Even in death, her posture is exemplary—she's sitting upright, arms crossed in her lap, her head tilted back toward the ceiling.

I watch for about thirty seconds, but the image stays the same. I'm about to check and see if something is frozen when I remember the image isn't changing because everyone is dead and corpses generally do not move.

A few seconds later, the door on the right side of the chapel bangs open and the afternoon sunlight floods in, framing the dark outline of a man standing in the doorway. As the man advances a few steps into the chapel, the door slowly swings shut behind him.

When my eyes adjust to the change in lighting, I realize there are actually two people. Martha is directly in front of Saul, pulled close against his chest, facing the bodies in the pews. He seems to be lifting her up so that only her toes touch the floor. I can't tell whether it's because he dragged her through the door or because he's worried she'll faint. Maybe both. She's in the same dress as before, but it's now caked with dirt, and her hair is mussed. Her mouth hangs open as she stares at the bodies, and then she brings her hands up to her face and begins to scream.

For once, I'm very glad CHRONOS didn't add audio. This is horrid enough as a silent movie.

It's the first time I've seen Saul without the odd facial hair from the 1800s. I now see why Katherine—and apparently others—thought he was handsome. His dark hair contrasts with his pale skin and sharp, almost chiseled features. And dressed in jeans and a plain white shirt instead of an ancient suit, his thin but muscular body is evident.

The creepiest thing is that Saul is smiling, even as Martha screams and pulls at her hair. It's not one of those grins that you see when the villain comes on-screen, with manic eyes and an evil bwah-hah-hah laugh. His expression is one of . . . bliss, I guess. His face is tilted upward, like he's basking in the warmth of the sun on a beautiful day in the park. One sleeve of his shirt is partially ripped away, and it flaps to the side as he drags Martha toward the pulpit. Two long stripes that look like fingernail scratches are visible on the exposed skin of his shoulder.

He drops Martha behind the pulpit, which partially obscures my view. She rolls to her side, covering her head with her arms. Saul just stands there, looking around at all of the dead bodies, smiling his horrible, peaceful smile, and a shudder runs through me. It's not just the idea anyone could wear that expression when faced with the sight before him but also the knowledge that this inhuman creature formed one-quarter of my DNA. I want to dig inside my body and claw out every speck of me that is Saul.

Any doubts about whether I can kill him are gone. If I could reach into the display, I would kill him this very second.

Saul closes his eyes for a moment, still smiling, and pulls in several long, deep breaths. Then he crosses to where Martha is curled up. He yanks one of her arms to the side, forcing her to face him. Her mouth is open, so I think she's still screaming. And although a moment ago I would have sworn that he couldn't possibly disgust me more, my hatred surges when he leans down and begins to kiss the side of her face, working his way down her neck.

Then he does something I can't see, but whatever it is, it breaks through Martha's shock, and she begins to fight him. His hands clamp down harder on her arms to hold her still, but he persists with kissing her shoulder as she struggles to break away.

After a second, Martha relaxes and just lies there, perfectly still. Saul leans back a bit and smiles at her. Then he goes flying several feet to the right as she plants both of her feet into his stomach. His head bumps against Sister Elba's legs, and her body slides to the left.

Martha crawls for a few seconds and then manages to get her feet under her and starts to run. Now Saul is up, and he follows, still slightly hunched over. As he starts after her, his foot catches on one of the legs of the chest holding the armonica, and it crashes to the ground. The lid pops open, and pieces fly off the spindle, shattered bits of glass tumbling onto the floor and under the front pews. One of the smaller bowls bounces down the two steps, miraculously still intact. It rolls under the corner of a pew and then several feet down the center aisle before it flips onto its bottom and spins slowly to a halt in front of the stable point.

In her panic, Martha runs toward the far left side of the chapel, where there is, unfortunately, no door. He's too close behind, so she sprints down the outer aisle, hoping to reach the front before he does. Saul takes the center-aisle shortcut and comes barreling toward the stable point. The last thing I see is the white of his shirt, and then they're both past my field of vision, and it's just the dead bodies, the chapel, and a small mound of crushed glass in the aisle where the armonica bowl had been.

"Is that it?" I ask Kiernan, my voice shaking.

"She runs past the stable point you set in front of the church. Saul is right on her heels."

"Maybe she got away—"

"No."

"You can't know that for certain!"

"Yes, I can." He leans over and wipes a tear from my cheek. I didn't even know I was crying. He gets up from the couch and limps over to grab the box and the article from the table.

"I could have gotten that, you know. All you had to do was ask me."

"Leg gets stiff if I stay in one place too long." He sits next to me and removes the top of the box, pushing the CHRONOS diary up on its spine so that he can dig through the articles beneath it. Then he pulls out the article with the photograph taken from almost the same angle as the stable point I was just watching.

Even before I look down at the picture, I realize something is very wrong. When I was inside the chapel with Sister Elba, the view was so similar to the photo I'm holding that it gave me a touch of déjà vu. When I first pulled up the stable point, before Saul and Martha arrived, I had the same thought.

But the chapel I was watching just now was in disarray. A broken armonica case, shattered glass everywhere . . . In this photograph, the armonica case is still standing, its contents unbroken.

Kiernan places the second image in my lap, the one that had been outside the box on the table. In this version, the armonica is again in pieces on the floor. "The CHRONOS field from the diary shielded the one that you're holding. I went back and picked up another copy the day the story broke in the local paper. If you read the text, you'll see there's another change."

He taps the third paragraph down, and I read:

A shallow grave was found at the rear of the church, containing the body of a young woman who had been strangled, her body showing evidence of other assault.

The murdered girl appears to have died several days earlier. As no report of an attack was made to county law enforcement, she is assumed to have been assaulted and killed by a resident of the Six Bridges community.

The bodies found inside the church are assumed unrelated. Authorities stress that there is no evidence that the illness is in any way contagious.

"Martha." I just sit there for a moment, staring at the two articles side by side, unsure what this means.

"She wasn't supposed to die, Kate. Martha escaping was the mistake that Saul told Simon about. She has to be. It's the only way this makes sense."

I shake my head, still not sure what could have changed her fate. "Do you think we did something when we were there? Something that—"

"No," he says. "I think it's what we didn't do. What *I* didn't do."

"So . . . you think we're supposed to save her."

He shrugs. "I don't know what you're supposed to do, Kate. I think the safest thing for you to do would be to stay here. But, yeah, I'm going."

I lean back and rub my eyes, trying to think. What sort of ripple effects could this produce? Did knowing he made a mistake change Saul's actions in any way? And if so, how did it change them?

"If you go, I go. We clearly have to set this straight. But we can't kill him, Kiernan. As much as I really, really want to right now, and as hard as it's going to be not to when I see him, we can't. And he can't know how she gets away."

"I know," he snaps. "I don't need a lecture."

"I wasn't lecturing you. You don't have to be a jerk about it."

He's silent for a good five seconds. "I'm sorry. It's just that I've been sitting here for the past four hours, going over this, examining it from every angle and watching that sick—"

"And that's why I asked you to wait until I was here!"

"What did you expect me to do, Kate? Just sit here in this cabin, thinking of you back there with him?"

I clench my teeth to avoid saying anything I'll regret, because this is really beginning to piss me off. "You can't keep turning this back around on me. I've been honest with you about Trey."

"And I've been honest with you!" He bangs his hand on the table so hard that the cigar box jumps. "I didn't promise to wait. You just assumed, once again, that I would follow your stupid directions."

"Stupid? I'll tell you what's stupid. Stupid is—" I'm up out of the chair, in his face, before I realize what he's doing. "Ha. Good try, Kiernan. Make me mad, and maybe I'll storm off. That way you can claim I left you no choice but to do this on your own."

A long silence follows, so I'm pretty sure I nailed it. He finally says in a softer voice, "I *know* I can't kill him, Kate. I do intend to hurt him, however. And I'll take great pleasure in it."

"I get that. But, Kiernan?" I try to think of a way to word it diplomatically but then decide to just be blunt. "You couldn't hurt anyone right now. You can barely walk. Are you sure it's not infected?"

"I'm sure. I have antibiotics."

I glance down at his leg. The jeans seem even tighter around his leg than they were yesterday. Either he's replaced the bandage with a bulkier one or the leg is swollen, and from the way he's walking, I'd bet it's the latter.

"If you don't believe me, you're welcome to take a look."

"I'll pass," I say coolly. "But even if it's not infected, you need time to heal. Do you have food in the house?"

"Campbell's Soup. Crackers. Pickled eggs. Maybe some canned beans."

"Bleh. What do you want?"

He raises his eyebrows. "I wouldn't say no to a pizza."

∞

I've discovered two things that make me a little sad about eventually having to give up the CHRONOS key. The first is that I can get pizza almost instantly. You place the order, set a stable point at the front door, jump forward thirty minutes, and scan in sixty-second increments until the delivery guy shows up. One minute and twenty-four seconds from the time I picked up the telephone.

The second is that you can go back five hours, plug in your iPad, and then jump forward to find it fully charged. Same goes for downloading movies.

Of course, none of that outweighs the negatives, but it's nice to find a silver lining.

Katherine would give me all kinds of grief about bringing Kiernan the iPad. But he's by himself in the middle of nowhere. And if anyone does show up at the cabin, he's smart enough to shove the thing under the sofa cushions. I pop back in twice daily to bring supplies and recharge the tablet. In this fashion, six days pass for Kiernan in a little over an hour for me. He makes his way through five books and half the movies I own. I can tell he's still sore, and I argue that we should wait a few more days, but he's losing patience.

I make two final jumps before we go. First, it's back to the town-house to drop off all forbidden technology and a trash bag filled with various takeout containers. Then I set the key for my room at Katherine's at 1:00 p.m. this coming Wednesday so that I can pick up the biohazard equipment that Connor express ordered. It's by my desk as promised—a small, clear kit with biohazard transport bags, several pairs of latex gloves, an oversized glass dropper, along with two shiny white suits and bizarre-looking face masks.

I hold them up for Kiernan's inspection when I jump back to the cabin. "Our chemistry set has arrived."

He snorts but doesn't look up from the sketch he's making. "Fortunately, neither of us will be doing any experiments. I collect the sample, you take it back to Connor. Any ideas what to do with it after that?"

"Connor bought a tiny fridge to go inside Katherine's safe. He'll store the sample there until we can locate someone trustworthy to examine it."

Kiernan slides the paper he was drawing on across the table to me. "Take a look at this."

It's a detailed map of God's Hollow, with the church, the well, and the chicken coop. Smaller squares line both sides of the road that runs through the center of the village. Two of these, the squares that are three and four doors down from the church on the opposite side, are marked with an *X*.

Kiernan taps the page near the two buildings that are marked. "Saul goes between those two houses, stays about two minutes, and then comes back that same way when he brings Martha to the church. That's the only time I see any activity between the two of them, other than the one I mentioned before, when Saul is woo-ing her."

That seems like an odd choice of words, but I guess *hitting on her* might not be in Kiernan's vocabulary, so I just nod.

"They get about ten yards down the street, toward the church, and she sees something off to the side of the road that frightens her. I'm thinking maybe it was the dog's body. It looks like she's screaming, 'Bull.' Anyway, after that point he has to basically drag her. She's fighting him hard . . . rips his sleeve and scratches him up."

"Go, Martha."

Kiernan points at the house on the far side of the two marked with an X and says, "I watched from each of the points you set and never saw Saul take her inside either of those houses. Given the mud on her dress and legs, I'm guessing he had her in a root cellar or something. We should go in at night and set up a stable point between these houses. That way we can see exactly where Saul takes Martha and get her out ahead of time. Before Saul comes back to get her."

"And what do we tell her, Kiernan?"

"To get the hell out of there, what else? We can show her where the motorbikes are hidden."

"I think she'd run, but I'm also sure she'd come back. She's restless, but it's her home. And if she comes back quickly, I think there's a good chance she'd contact the authorities. Based on what we know, she didn't do that, right? They just put two and two together on their own when no one from the village showed up to do the weekly shopping."

"So what's your plan?"

"We hide in the chapel. That's the only way to be sure that we change this but nothing else. Martha will see there's nothing to come back to, Kiernan. She'll know she has to leave, find someplace to start over. When she breaks into a run, we stop him from following her."

He shakes his head. "You really want the kid to see everyone she loves dead in that church?"

"No," I say. "It's going to haunt her for the rest of her life. But don't you think she has the right to know? Once she sees what he's done, she's going to want Saul to pay, and I'll do my best to convince her that we'll make him pay."

"And you think she'll be quiet? That she won't talk about two people who appear out of nowhere and save her while the rest of her village dies?"

"We'll just have to convince her that talking would be a very bad idea."

∞

GOD'S HOLLOW, GEORGIA
September 15, 1911, 2:42 p.m.

We look like aliens, covered from head to toe in the biohazard suits. Even though the masks are supposed to block most odors, the place reeks of vomit and human waste.

I watched the scene three times through the key, trying to build up my resistance. I don't look at the faces, just keep my eyes on the ground. If I think of these bodies as people, I'm going to lose it, so I push emotion aside.

Pipe wrench in hand, Kiernan walks past the bench where Sister Elba rests and climbs over the wooden divider that separates the choir from the platform holding the pulpit and the armonica. He presses his back against the wall, partially shielded by the red curtain hanging from above.

I take up position on the other side of the pulpit. The curtain won't hide me, since the door where Saul will enter is directly opposite, so I crouch down behind the choir bench and pull the Colt out of my pocket. This was one debate that Kiernan won, and although it makes me nervous to carry it around, he's right. I can't actually shoot Saul, but a few shots could provide a useful distraction if a whack across the head doesn't slow him down.

I take some deep breaths as we wait, trying to calm down. Then a scream cuts through the silence. After watching everything transpire through the CHRONOS key, I'd forgotten we'll have audio this time.

As the sound moves closer, I make out a few words. She's screaming about the dog, just as Kiernan suspected.

"Bull! That's Bull! Let me go!"

There's a scuffle outside the door, and Saul, whose voice I'd imagined as deeper, says, "Oh, no, you don't. Come on, Martha."

The door swings inward, and their heads, which are all I can see from this position, are silhouetted against bright sky. "Why are you fighting me? I'm just taking you to Sister Elba and the others, as I promised."

He kicks the door, and it closes behind them. The smell must hit Martha first, because she coughs and turns her head away. When her eyes adjust to the dimly lit church, her mouth falls open, and her eyes glaze over. There's no sound for several seconds—I don't think she's even breathing. Then she makes a keening sound, soft at first, and then it builds as she brings her hands to her face and begins to scream.

Saul spins her around, I guess to be sure that she gets the full picture. "See, Martha? Just like I told you. They're all here, waiting."

The platform shakes as he drags her up the two short steps. I lean back slightly to be sure Saul can't see me when he turns and dumps her behind the pulpit. I can't see her from this angle, but I can hear her, and the image I saw earlier of Martha's arms clutched around her head, rocking back and forth, is seared into my memory.

Saul turns back toward the pews, that sick, blissful smile on his face. How can he stand to take such deep breaths when the smell is nearly overpowering even behind a mask?

He looks around at his creation for a moment and then crosses over to Martha, kneeling down beside her. I can't see either of them now, but Saul is shushing her softly, like you would a crying toddler. My heart races, and I wait for my cue—the moment when Martha kicks him backward and takes off.

But that never happens. Kiernan jumps up about thirty seconds ahead of schedule, hops over the railing, and whacks Saul on the back of the head with the wrench. I wait for Martha to start running, but she doesn't. She's frozen, staring at Kiernan in the white suit and mask. I climb over and grab her arm, but she yanks away from me, and the sobs turn into shrieks again.

Kiernan lets out a huff that's audible through the mask. He reaches down and tugs Saul off Martha, then scoops her up into his arms like a baby and takes off down the center aisle. I hear a low moan from Saul's direction as I'm about to start off after them, and I see he's now up on his knees.

I pull back my foot and give my grandfather a solid kick to the kidneys. He lets out a very satisfying *oof* and slumps back to the floor as I run for the front entrance.

Kiernan is just ahead, still carrying Martha. Although he seemed okay when we jumped in, his limp is back, probably because the leg is used to carrying Kiernan's weight, not an additional hundred pounds. The fact that Martha is fighting him clearly isn't helping his progress, so I catch up with them quickly, just a few yards beyond the tree where I parked my bike on our first trip to God's Hollow.

"Why didn't you wait?" I say, yanking off my mask.

Kiernan pulls up his mask as well, his face conflicted. "Sorry, but you weren't standing where I was, Kate. I could see . . . I wasn't gonna let him touch her like that."

Martha stops trying to get away when she hears him speak, and then she looks over at me. "You're . . . before. Y'all were here . . . before." Her eyes are still wide, but a bit of reason seems to be coming back into them.

"Yes," I say. "Martha, we need to get you out of here, before Saul comes to. Can you walk on your own? Maybe even run a little?"

She nods, and Kiernan slides her to the ground.

"Maybe we should all leave?"

Kiernan shakes his head. "No. We need the sample. And I don't want to come back." He pats his pocket. "I've got my pistol. I'll keep an eye on the church. If I see him, I'll jump straight to the rendezvous point. You just get Martha there."

I tiptoe up to kiss him on the cheek. "Be careful."

"I'm always careful." He tips the mask back down, then hands me the pipe wrench and hurries around the back of the church toward the well.

I grab Martha's arm. "Come on, sweetie. We need to hurry."

"Where's he going?"

"He needs to get a sample of . . . the poison. We need to find out what Saul used—"

Her lower lip begins to quiver, so I just tug her arm again. "Let's just go, okay? He'll be right behind us."

We run down the path toward the bridge and have just passed the point where Martha and the twins were playing catch when she stops suddenly. "Miss Kate, what about the other fella?"

My heart stops in midjog, and the wrench falls to the ground. "What other fellow?"

"The one he's travelin' with. Said his name was Grant."

Oh my God. I glance back over my shoulder at the village and then toss the mask to her. "Get across the bridge, Martha. Wait in the woods on the other side, okay? Hurry!"

I take off at top speed for the village, but I've barely started when the front door of the church opens. I dive into the tall grass on the side of the road and peer through the weeds as Saul staggers out, his hand pressed to the back of his head. He looks to the right first, and I guess he sees Kiernan, because he doesn't even bother to look my way. He shambles off toward the well, and as soon as he rounds the corner of the church, I pull my gun out and fire a warning shot into the air, just in case Kiernan doesn't see him coming.

Then I run, scanning the village ahead for any sort of movement. About the time I veer over to cut through the field, there's a gunshot. It doesn't sound like the Colts we've been firing, so it must be Saul. Or maybe Grant. I pull to a halt at the corner of the chapel, peeking around the edge before I approach.

Saul leans against the side of the chicken coop, one hand against the back of his head. The chickens are all silent, red and white piles in the deep brown muck, most of them only a few feet from the water trough.

At first, I don't see any sign of Kiernan. Then I notice the blue glow of his CHRONOS key behind the well.

And so does Saul.

He hurries toward the well, his gun raised, as I dart around the corner of the church, ducking behind the chicken coop for cover. I point my gun at Saul's back, hoping Kiernan will disappear before I have to shoot.

Saul swings out to the left a few steps, pivoting the gun toward the well. The glow is still there, which means Kiernan is still there, and I have maybe a second left before Saul reaches him.

I lift the gun, aim, and fire.

The shot echoes strangely. Small fragments fly into the air as a bullet hits the upper edge of the well. Then I see Saul on his knees, clutching his right arm, his gun a few feet away.

It wasn't my bullet that hit the well. That was the second shot, from Saul's gun.

And the blue glow is gone.

I crouch behind the chicken coop and tug my key out. My hands are shaking as I pull up the coordinates for the spot across the bridge where we stashed the bikes. I set the time back four minutes, hoping Martha and Kiernan will both be there when I open my eyes.

They aren't, but I hear feet crossing the bridge. A shot rings out in the distance as I step out to look down the road—I think it's the warning shot I fired. Then I hear a noise behind me, and Kiernan's arms encircle me. He squeezes me to his chest, pressing his lips against my hair.

"Where is Martha?" I ask.

"She's coming—"

Just then Martha bursts through the underbrush and sees us. She gasps and takes a step backward too quickly, landing on her bottom.

She looks back toward the village. "How did you . . ."

I kneel down beside her. "Martha, we'll explain soon, but two quick questions, okay?"

She closes her mouth and nods.

"How did . . . those men get here? Did they drive?"

"Men?" Kiernan asks.

"Later." I look back at Martha, eyebrows raised. "They had a car?"

"An old red truck. Told Sister they was studyin' for the ministry up in Athens and wondered—"

I shake my head. "Later, okay? Where's the truck?"

"Down by Earl's place." She turns her head back toward town as two shots fire in rapid succession, but she continues. "That's where they was sleepin' before . . ."

Kiernan and I both yank out our keys.

"I'm going," I say. "You can't risk another jump."

"I know that. But I'm the one who set the stable point outside of Earl's shop. It's not on your key." He transfers the coordinates to my medallion, and then I blink back to six minutes ago, when all four of us were in the church.

I don't see the truck at first, but then I spot it across the road. A collection of tools hangs on the shop walls. I scan quickly for something that will pierce tires, settling on a large pair of shears. I dart across the road and plunge the shears hard into one of the rear tires. Moving to the front of the truck, I raise my arm to puncture a second tire but then realize it's unlikely Saul will have two spares. I need to slow him down, but he still has to get back to his stable point to return home. So I drop the shears and jump back to Kiernan and Martha.

She looks like she's going to throw up.

"Let her touch the medallion," I say.

"Why?"

"I have no idea why, but it seems to help."

He still looks skeptical but grabs her hand and presses it to the CHRONOS key.

"I've probably only bought us a few minutes. We need to get her out of here."

Kiernan glances at Martha, whose color does seem to be improving a bit from the greenish shade she was a moment before. "Martha," he says. "Have you ever ridden a bicycle?"

She shakes her head. "I can ride a horse. But I'm guessing they're all dead now, like Bull."

He looks back at me. "You said men. Who's with him?"

"She said Grant. I never saw him. Martha, when did you last see the other man?"

"I ain't seen him since Saul shut me in the cellar."

"How long were you there?" Kiernan asks.

"I don't know. I was down there with Bull part of yesterday and all night. He brought us some bread and water this mornin', and then Bull started gettin' sick, so Saul let him out, but he made me stay down there till he come and got me. I still didn' see the other guy. Maybe he got sick, too."

Kiernan turns to me. "How much time do you think you bought us?"

"Twenty minutes if he stops to change the tire. If he even knows how to change a tire. He'll probably just drive on the rims. So maybe a five-minute head start?"

"I guess she could ride with me," Kiernan says, but I can tell from his voice that he doubts the bike will carry both of them.

"I think you could outrun a truck with a flat tire on this thing if it was just carrying one person, but . . ."

"Yeah," he says, and grabs both bikes, walking them farther into the woods. "We can't outrun him."

I reach down for Martha's hand. "Come on, okay? I'll explain things as we go."

I take one of the bikes from Kiernan, and we follow his lead until he stops at the bank of the creek. As we walk, I try to think up something we can tell Martha that won't result in her being locked away in an asylum if she, at some point, needs to talk about the past few days. So far, I've drawn a blank.

The creek winds through dense woods, so you can't see the bridge from here. But a truck limping on its rims isn't exactly silent. A clanking, thumping noise comes from that direction just as Kiernan props our motorbikes against a tree.

I crouch down beside the creek and bring up our stable point near the road. As I predicted, Saul didn't bother changing the tire, at least not yet. The truck limps down the road. Grant is in the truck and appears either dead or comatose, because he doesn't stir at all, despite the fact that his head bumps the passenger-side window every few seconds.

Once they pass, I scan the road for the next twenty minutes, skipping forward in ten-second increments. There's no indication that Saul turns back. That doesn't mean he isn't parked a mile or so up the road, changing the tire.

When I look up from the medallion, Martha is watching me, her head cocked to one side.

"You prayin'?"

"Umm . . . sort of."

"Is that some kinda rosary? Miz Carey's sister, when she was visitin', she had a rosary. But hers had beads."

"It's not a rosary," Kiernan says. "Listen, Martha, we need to explain some things."

"That's okay. I figured it out when Miss Kate disappeared back there. Did Sister Elba know?"

"Did she know what?" I ask.

"That y'all were angels?" Judging from her expression, if she were born a century later, she'd have added the word *duh*. "I'm guessin' she didn't, just like she didn't know what *he* was either. I loved her an' all, but Sister trusted almost ever'body. Maybe if she'd'a been a little more suspicious . . ."

"Maybe," I say. "But that would have made her a very different person. And Martha, it wouldn't have mattered. She couldn't have stopped Saul."

"So this is one of those things that was . . ." She pauses, like she's trying to remember the word. "Predestined? Like my mama and daddy dyin' so young?"

I glance up at Kiernan, and he just gives me a shrug. It seems wrong to let her think we're some sort of divine messengers, but it's a lot easier than explaining. And here in 1911, saying she's seen angels is less likely to get her locked in a padded room than the truth, if she ever decides to tell anyone.

"There are some things we can't change," I tell her, thinking of Sister Elba's last words to me. "We just have to find a way to go on when those things happen, so we're ready to change the things we can later on down the line."

"Why me?" she asks, her voice suddenly angry. "Why'd you save *me*? I was darn close to not believin' at all, and that church was full of folks who praised God all day long. Even Jack and Vern . . ."

Her body starts shaking, and the tears that have been near the surface spill over her cheeks. I wrap my arms around her and hold her as she cries, because it's all I can do. Because I don't have the answers she needs. Kiernan just watches us, and I can tell he's feeling the same helplessness that I do.

Her tears eventually stop, and Martha pulls away, then leans back toward me, her fingertips brushing my face.

"I didn't know angels cried."

Part of me screams out that she deserves the truth, and Kiernan must be watching, because he steps in just before I break.

"Sometimes angels do cry," he says. "We don't get to make the decisions, you know. Just doin' what we're told. And as for why we saved you, you just need to believe that there was a reason, okay? You may not see it yet, but maybe you'll do great things—or maybe it's your son or your granddaughter or great-great-great-granddaughter."

She laughs a little at that, but it's a worried laugh. "I don't even know where I'm gonna go or what I'm gonna do. I got the clothes on my back, and—"

"If you were meant to get out of God's Hollow alive," he says, "I don't think you're meant to die of starvation on the streets. I'll help you. I know a family that I'm pretty sure I can convince to take you in for a few years, until you're ready to be off on your own. But listen, this whole angel thing—it needs to be our secret, okay?"

Martha nods solemnly. "Y'all don' need to worry about that. Ain't no one gonna believe me anyhow."

∞17∞

There are only two bikes, so I say goodbye to Martha and jump directly to Katherine's library, where Connor is waiting, as scheduled. He holds open the door to the safe, and I place the kit containing the sample from the well inside. Then I jump to my room and shed the suit, the mask, and everything I was wearing underneath, stuffing it all into a large black trash bag. While I'm sure that this protocol wouldn't pass muster with the CDC, it's the best we can do for now.

I stay in the shower much longer than usual, scrubbing every inch of my body until my skin is pink and my scalp is sore. I still can't say I feel completely clean, but that's probably because the shower can't wash away the images in my head.

Connor and Katherine are waiting when I get downstairs. The briefing goes about as well as I'd expected. I considered lying about Martha but ended up being honest. Katherine finds a dozen reasons why we should have done things differently and engages in a lengthy rant about all the things I may have changed by injuring Saul. I'm too numb to argue, and after a few minutes, Connor cajoles her into going back to her room.

I grab my phone from the charger on the counter and check my messages. There's a call from Mom, which I expected, given that it was my first day back at school. A text from Charlayne came in twenty minutes ago, and that's something I definitely wasn't expecting. We exchanged numbers after English class, in case we had homework questions or whatever, but I'm surprised to get a message so soon. More evidence that I'm being played, no doubt. Still, I click to open it.

Ur profile is lame.

At first, I have no idea what she's talking about. Then I remember Trey shared some photos on Facebook and I set up an account to access them. I didn't even post a profile picture, so it's just that blank girl head where my face would be.

I text back: *Don't do FB much. You?*

There's a pause, and then she responds: *Can't have FB account. Mom said yes. Dad said no. As usual. I'm on WayBook. So-called Cyrist equiv.*

After a few seconds, she adds: *Do you have page numbers for Miller txt?*

I respond that I'll check when I get up to my room. And then I call Dad.

I'm so glad that he picks up, because he's the only person I want to talk to right now.

"You okay?" he asks. "Because you don't sound okay."

"I've been better." I spend the next few minutes filling him in about the past two days, and I end up in tears.

"Your grandpa is stable now, Kate. Maybe I should come home."

"Dad, no. It's okay."

There's a long silence, and then he says, "I'm still trying to get past the idea of you with a gun. Where did you . . ."

"Kiernan. Once my hand stopped shaking, I discovered that I'm actually a decent shot."

"Apparently, since you put a hole in Saul's arm rather than his head. I know it's probably not much consolation, Kate, but at least you were able to save one person. That's something for the positive column, right?"

Connor walks in, and I glance over at him as I say, "I'm glad to see someone agrees with me on that point."

"Katherine and Connor are angry?"

"Katherine is. Not sure about Connor."

Connor looks at me with his eyebrows raised when he hears his name.

"Listen, Dad—I'm okay. Talking helped. Stay with Grandma Keller. She needs you more than I do right now. I love you—and I'll call you back later, okay?"

"What are you not sure about Connor?" Connor asks.

"If you're angry that we saved Martha."

He's silent for a moment and then says, "No, I'm not angry. I hope Kiernan was right, and based on what you told me about the photographs, his conclusion makes more sense than anything else I can think of. And . . . uh . . . I'm not sure Katherine would want me to tell you this, but she got this sudden change of expression when we got back to her room, like she'd had some sort of epiphany. She asked me to grab her personal diary. All she would say is that maybe Saul getting shot wasn't something new—that he came back injured one time."

"That's right. But . . . she said it was a burn of some sort. He wouldn't go to—" I break off when I see Katherine in the doorway.

"To CHRONOS Med," she finishes, giving Connor a slightly perturbed look before turning her eyes back to me. "I'm sorry I lost my temper, Kate. While I can't be sure, based on what I recorded that day, this would explain why Saul was reluctant to let anyone see that injury. I suspect he knew CHRONOS Med could tell the difference between a bullet graze and a burn."

∞

Trey is disappointed that the restaurant isn't the rooftop place he saw on the website—apparently that's the bar, and it's only for ages twenty-one and up. The maître d' told him we're welcome to go up and check out the view before we leave, and he seated us at a table overlooking the White House with the Washington Monument in the background.

Since Trey is usually much more at home in places like this than I am, it's strange to see him fidget, tugging at the sleeve of his blazer. He's been nervous since he picked me up at the townhouse.

After we give the waiter our order, I reach across the table and squeeze Trey's hand. "What's wrong?"

"Nothing. I'm . . . just . . ." He smiles. "Did I tell you that you look beautiful tonight?"

I nod. "Twice, actually. Once when I answered the door and once after I ran back upstairs and changed into this."

This is a red-and-black brocade dress I swiped from Mom's closet when I saw Trey in a gray blazer over black pants and a black shirt. I also grabbed her new heels from the closet, where she tossed them after our dinner with Katherine this past spring, and have now discovered exactly why she left them behind when she packed for Italy.

"You didn't answer my question. What's wrong?"

"No," he says, looking down at his water goblet. "I guess I didn't. I just wanted everything to be perfect, and when I made the reservations, the person on the phone said . . ." He looks up and laughs when he sees my expression. "And I think I'm obsessing a bit. Sorry."

"It's okay." I lean forward and kiss his knuckles. "You need a character flaw of some sort. Otherwise, you make me seem like a total wreck. But this really is absolutely perfect, so maybe you should cut yourself just a teensy bit of slack?"

The waiter arrives with our drinks and a bread basket that smells heavenly.

"So," Trey says, "how was your day at the office, dear?"

"Probably not something you want to discuss over dinner." The closest people are three tables over, but I lower my voice anyway. "I'll just give you the thirty-second version—Kiernan was shot, but he's okay now. We went to Six Bridges and got the sample, which we're holding in a locked fridge until we can track down someone . . . let's just say sympathetic to the cause . . . who is also qualified to analyze it. On the bright side, we were able to save one girl. On the not-so-bright side, we learned that Saul wasn't the only historian there. Another guy was with him. The same trainee that is with Abel and Delia in Athens 1938. We're getting ready for that jump now."

"Okay, can we back up to the part where Kiernan was shot?"

"I wasn't with him. Kiernan kind of went rogue and fetched the key from the guy who was killed in Copenhagen, Moehler. I told you about Moehler, right?"

Trey nods.

"Anyway, he says he wore protective gear, but a bullet caught him in the leg."

"Who shot him? Do you think it was this trainee you saw?"

"No. CHRONOS had very specific fields of study, and Katherine's pretty sure Grant wasn't a Europeanist. He was almost certainly specializing in American history, so I can't imagine any reason they would have approved a jump to Copenhagen. Probably not for Saul, either, so I think we can safely say it's not one of the original historians. Whoever killed Moehler, probably the same person who shot Kiernan, is one of the second-generation travelers, like me, Prudence, Simon, Conwell—I guess Eve is a possibility, too, although I have a tough time imagining her with a gun."

Of course, I have a tough time imagining *me* wielding a gun, and yet there's one with my fingerprints on the trigger back in 1911.

I take a sip of my water and then go on. "Or it could be someone else entirely. Kiernan says there are maybe a half dozen others. Hell, for all I know, it could've been Houdini."

The waiter slides the salads in front of us, grinds a bit of pepper and Parmesan on top, and then vanishes. We're too busy eating for the next few minutes to really talk, and it's probably just as well, because I can tell that Trey still has questions, and I think the odds are good that they're questions for which I have no answers.

My phone buzzes inside my purse. I give Trey an apologetic smile. "Sorry. I'd like to turn it off, but with Katherine and with Dad in Delaware . . ."

"It's okay," he says as I glance down at the display,

"And it's Charlayne." I shake my head. "I'll answer her later. I'm guessing she's come up with another bogus question about homework."

"How long are you going to be able to keep up the pretense before you snap and slug her?"

I shrug. "I'd like to think she has a good reason for agreeing to do this, but who knows? Maybe she just wants to suck up to Eve."

When the waiter asks about dessert, Trey tells him we have other plans, and a short elevator ride later, we're on the balcony of the top floor. Trey wraps his arms around me from behind, and I find that there is a benefit to these wretched heels after all—I'm now the perfect height to lean my head back against his shoulder. We just stand there, looking out at the sunset, and it's nice to have a moment, even a short one, where everything is peaceful, quiet, and perfect.

Then he says, "You do know that I love you, don't you?"

My heart catches in my throat, because it's not like the last time he said it for the first time. I hear doubt in his voice, like this is something he thinks he should say but he's not really sure. And he probably thinks he should say it because I said it to him, weeks ago, which makes it overdue in his book, even though it's not. Maybe that's why he's been so nervous, so on edge tonight.

"Trey, you don't have to—"

He steps around to face me. "No, Kate. I want to. I mean, I'm not saying we're going to last forever. I don't think I could know that even if the timeline wasn't at risk of shifting and yanking you away at any given moment—I'm eighteen, you're seventeen. I'm not sure forever talk even makes sense at our age. But right now, you are everything to me. I want to spend every second with you, and when I can't be with you, I'm thinking about how much I want to be with you. You were right, Kate. *This* is right."

Trey bends down to kiss me, and the kiss almost convinces me. Almost. I finally push away the annoying little voice in my head telling me that this feels a little forced, that maybe things are a little too perfect. I can't keep comparing everything to last time.

We break the kiss a few minutes later. Trey tugs at my arm, pulling me toward the door that leads back inside. "So. Have we had enough sunset?"

I give him a little nod, and he says, "Okay then. Let's go."

"Dessert?" I ask.

He laughs and pulls me up against him. "Yes, definitely dessert."

The restaurant is on the second floor, but as we head back down, the elevator opens on the fifth floor. Trey steps out, so I follow. He turns at the first corridor, pulls a digital key card from his pocket, and slips it into the slot above the handle.

"It's not a suite, but at least we have a nice view of the city."

Okay, I guess I'm slow, because I don't catch on until I see the king-sized bed in the middle of the small room. There's a tray of chocolate-dipped strawberries on the table next to the window, and the room is decked out in shades of gold and cream, much like the dining room. And did I mention the king-sized bed?

Dear God.

"Trey? Why are we here? I thought . . ."

He puts his arms around me. "Because as much as I like your room at the townhouse, like I said before, this should be special. Perfect." His eyes are growing a bit wary, probably because I'm not really responding as he'd expected. And as much as I'd like to be able to just accept this, something seems very, very wrong. You don't go from hands above the equator to this in a single day.

"Trey . . ."

His lips silence me for a moment, and then he says, "Hmmm?"

"I thought we were going to take things slow?"

"Well, yeah, but then last night—"

"We were still taking things slow."

His arms fall down to his sides, and he looks at me in disbelief. "What happened . . . well, nearly happened . . . in my room last night wasn't taking it slow."

I back away and sink into one of the chairs by the window, my hands over my face. "Can you please tell me exactly what happened in your room? Because I kind of don't remember any of that."

He's silent for so long that I think I'm going to have to repeat the question, and then he sits on the edge of the bed and says in a soft voice, "You've got to be kidding me. Are you saying that wasn't you? Or that it's you two weeks from now, when you've decided taking it slow was a bad idea?"

I can tell he's angry, and I can't blame him. "I don't know, Trey. That's why I need to you tell me what happened."

"I was almost asleep. And then you showed up. Wearing this white lace thing . . . remember, I asked if you'd bring it or wear it or whatever?"

"I thought . . . you were joking."

"Yeah. The librarian outfit. I thought *you* were joking."

"So what did . . . this person say? What convinced you it was me?"

"You didn't say much of anything. It was more the appearing out of nowhere, holding that stupid key, and the crawling into my bed. I practically had to—"

I can't read his expression when he finally looks over at me. It's some weird mix of embarrassment, annoyance, and confusion. "Damn it, Kate. You're really saying that wasn't you? It was Prudence—is that what you're saying?"

"I don't know, Trey! All I know is that I've never been in your room. I don't have a stable point set anywhere near your house. I can't entirely discount the possibility that it was me, at some later point, but if so, I would remember this night. And believe me, I would have done everything possible to avoid . . . this."

I glance around at the room again. I have no idea how, or how much, he paid for this evening. And now, if and when we finally make it to our first time, this colossal fiasco will be in the back of our minds.

"Could you start back at the beginning again?" I say, trying to keep my voice level.

"My room around eleven. Me, nearly asleep. You, or someone who looks exactly like you in the moonlight, crawls onto my bed and starts . . ." He tilts his head back and stares up at the ceiling. "Holy crap, Kate, I do not believe this."

We're getting nowhere with his narration, so I shift to questions. Specifically, the main question that's on my mind.

"Did we . . . I mean did you and this other person *do* anything?"

"No, but only because I was pretty insistent that I didn't want your first time to be in a twin bed, under a shelf with my soccer trophies, two rooms down from where my dad was sleeping."

"Do you think she was . . . our age? Or maybe older?"

"I don't know, Kate. It was dark. I didn't get a close look at your face. But you didn't feel old."

I wince and realize I really don't want him to clarify what he meant by that.

"Did you kiss her?" Maybe Trey wouldn't even know it wasn't me if he kissed Prudence, but I don't want to believe that.

"No. She kind of left in a hurry."

I'm glad beyond belief to hear him finally say *she* instead of *you*.

"How do you think she got in?" Trey asks. "We have a security system, and Estella is really careful about who she lets in the house."

I move over to the edge of the bed and sit next to him. "It's an old house. Did your grandparents have a security system? Or what about whoever owned the house before them? Prudence could have set the point in 1900, for all we know, as long as she knew which room you'd be in now."

"Fine then, why? Why would she do that?"

Trey looks at me, and for a second, I imagine a bullet hole on his forehead, exactly where it was on Moehler's.

My heart stops, and I squeeze my eyes shut. When I open them, the hole isn't there.

But that doesn't change the fact that it could be.

"She's sending me a message. That they're watching. That they can get to the people I love."

That the truce is off.

For a fleeting moment, I consider jumping back a few days. I could show up at Trey's house, unannounced, and get him to take me upstairs. I'd set my own stable point, and then when Prudence showed up . . . I probably wouldn't actually kill her, but the thought is tempting.

Of course, that would pull Trey into this even further. It would put him and his family at greater risk.

And that's not happening.

Katherine was right. Dear God, I hate saying this; I really, really do, but I should never have pulled Trey into this. The smart move would be to jump back and yank that manila envelope out of my hands before I ever hand it to Trey. Reverse the past few months and keep him safely, blissfully unaware that I even exist. But that would result in so many dueling memories that it's not a viable choice.

"I'm sorry, Trey. I'll pay you back for everything." I glance around the room. "This must have cost you a fortune."

"So I spent my birthday money for once. Big deal. I'm not upset about the money, Kate." He leans forward and kisses me very gently. "Hey, I'm okay with taking it slow. Let's just rent a movie. Eat the strawberries. I meant what I said. On the roof. I love you."

"I love you, too."

I do. And while I think I really was ready for this step with the other Trey, in the other timeline, we're not there yet. I can tell he *wants* to be in love with me. He may even be part of the way there.

But even if he'd said it with every bit as much conviction as last time, it wouldn't matter.

Because I'm not the same either. Maybe it's because I know Trey is not totally in love with me, or maybe it's because I have these niggling, little doubts where Kiernan is concerned. Either way, I'll never be able to take this step with Trey until I sort all of those things out.

And above all else, I won't let Trey be used as a pawn in Prudence's games.

"I'm sorry I pulled you into all of this, Trey."

He reaches for my hand when he sees that I'm holding the CHRONOS key, but I move away.

"Hold on, Kate. Let's talk this—"

"No. Maybe your dad was right about you finishing school down in Peru. I'll find you when this is over. I promise. Once we have all the keys, once I know that Saul and Prudence can't hurt you. Can't hurt anyone. When this is *completely* over, one way or the other. I will find you, I will kiss you, and I will do whatever it takes to make this up to you."

I don't stop to kiss him goodbye. I don't even look at him, because I'm afraid I'll lose my nerve. I lock in the stable point for my room and blink, seconds before the tears that would have made it impossible to focus flood my eyes.

As much as I want it to be true, I'm not an ordinary girl with an ordinary life, ordinary friends, and an ordinary relationship with an extraordinarily wonderful guy.

And unless I stop pretending, I'll never get the chance to be one.

∞

I indulge in a brief pity party when I get back to my room, the first stage of which consists of a ten-minute cry in the shower. The second stage is a talk with Mom, even though I have to jump back a few hours to synch things up with Italy time. If there's a teeny, tiny silver lining to this evening, it's that I have something I can actually talk to her about, as long as I avoid the details and stick to the basic fact that Trey and I are no longer together. And even though I can tell she's sad for me, and maybe a little worried, I'm glad I called. I needed my mom, and I think she needed to feel needed.

There are two text messages from Trey, but I don't read them. I can't. Not until the 1938 jump is behind me.

No pity party is complete without ice cream, so the third and final stage is the pint of Ben & Jerry's I saw in the freezer this morning. It's missing when I get down to the kitchen, however, and I'm pretty sure Katherine didn't eat it. Since I'm positive I need it more than Connor does, I jump back to earlier in the day, snag it, and pop back to the present. If he ends up with memories of both eating and not eating my Cherry Garcia, so be it.

Connor comes in when I'm down to the last few bites. He casts a brief, confused glance at the freezer, then looks up at the clock, back at the ice cream, and then at my face, which I'm pretty sure is still puffy from crying. "Do you want to talk?"

"I don't want to talk about the me-and-Trey part. But is Katherine busy? This affects everyone."

The house no longer feels private. Everything I told Trey about how Prudence could have placed a stable point in his room is, as far as I know, also true for this house. Who owned it before Katherine? How long was it on the market, sitting empty and waiting for someone to stroll in and set up stable points or even listening devices?

Ten minutes later, Katherine and Connor are up to speed. I edit the story a bit, because I'm not sure how they'll react to Trey booking a hotel room. Both of them look around the room nervously at least once while I'm talking, so they're probably thinking the same thing about the house not feeling private.

"I had the place thoroughly checked for listening devices when we moved in," Connor says. "We have two security systems, put in by two different companies, and they both ran a magnetic scan before I started moving in our equipment. I don't see how anyone could have planted a device since then, unless it came in with a pizza box, in which case it would have gone out again a few hours later. But there's no way I can check for whether someone set a stable point locally on their specific key before we moved in. So, yeah, it's possible."

Katherine says, "If they've been watching us, they know we've collected four additional keys. Prudence would have known for a while that you weren't keeping your side of the bargain. So why wait until now to react?"

"Maybe the keys at Athens are the only ones they need," Connor suggests.

"Could be," I say. "But does anyone else get the feeling we're being played?"

∞18∞

BOGART, GEORGIA
October 8, 1905, 9:00 a.m.

I'm not surprised to see Kiernan near the table in his cabin, since he knows I'll be arriving at nine and that's where he usually greets me. I'm a little surprised to see that he's had a haircut and his skin is about three shades darker than usual.

What surprises me to the point that I nearly blink myself into the cabin on accident, however, is seeing him with his arm around a woman about twenty years his senior.

A woman who can only be my aunt Prudence.

I watch for several minutes, barely breathing.

They aren't alone. A blond woman, who is probably in her fifties, stands near Prudence. I don't think I've seen her before, although she reminds me a bit of Katherine around the eyes. The guy just to Kiernan's left is in his twenties or early thirties, and I get the feeling that I *have* seen him before, but it could just be that he looks a little like Simon. He's better looking, though, thinner, maybe fifteen years older.

Both of them seem eager to leave.

Prudence is doing most of the talking, but without audio, I can't tell what she's saying. Apparently something she said was funny, because Kiernan laughs. Afterward, he leans in and kisses her.

It's not a long kiss, but it's certainly not platonic, and a flood of different emotions rushes through me. Mostly betrayal, some confusion, and a hefty dose of anger, but I'd be lying if I didn't admit there's a tiny bit of jealousy in the mix.

I lose the stable point and decide it might be a good idea to wait a moment before pulling it back up. I need to think.

Kiernan knew I was coming in at nine, and it didn't look like he was trying to rush them off. It's impossible to be late when you arrive via CHRONOS key, so he knew exactly when I'd arrive.

I toss the key on the bed and consider whether to talk this through with Katherine and Connor. That would mean a half hour, at least, of debate over whether Kiernan has been working with Prudence from the start. Connor or Katherine or both will say they suspected it all along.

And in the end, it will come down to the exact same thing. I'll have to go in and piece this together on my own. If it turns out to be a trap and I don't come back, neither of them will be able to do a damn thing to help me.

The only one who can help me is Kiernan. And he just freaking *kissed* Prudence. Not young Pru, either, but the one he claims is borderline insane.

Kiernan kissed her when he knew I'd be looking.

He wants me to know they were there, so I don't think this is a trap.

And if Prudence does decide to show up and confront me, I'm kind of okay with that, too. We have a few things to settle.

I pick up the key, lock in 9 a.m., and watch the whole thing again.

The kiss was apparently a goodbye kiss, because Kiernan's guests, including Prudence, blink out a moment later. At 9:04 a.m., he glances around the room for a second and then stares directly at the stable point where I always enter, the spot he knows I'll be watching. His expression gradually grows impatient. Finally, after about three minutes, he throws up his hands and walks out of the cabin.

I give it another thirty seconds and then blink in. The cabin is chilly, so I toss the last log onto the fire and kneel on the floor, jabbing at the embers with the poker to get it going. It sputters and then flares up a bit when the front door swings open, creating a brief gust.

Kiernan comes in, carrying an armload of wood. He deposits it in the bin next to the fireplace before setting another log on top of the one I added. His limp, which was still visible when I left him with Martha, is now completely gone.

I want to ask him about Martha, but I don't know who's watching or maybe even listening. So I just stand there, waiting for him to speak first.

"What, no good morning?" He gives me a quick kiss on the lips. I stiffen automatically, but he whispers, "Play along, Kate."

"Good morning. You just . . . caught me by surprise." I give him a stiff smile and pull away, walking toward the room where my things are stored. "I need to get dressed for Athens."

"Don't you want to look at my notes first?"

"After I'm dressed."

I realize as I close the door that Kiernan was probably trying to tell me something. But it would look suspicious to change my mind now, so I just tug off my jeans and T-shirt. The 1938 outfit is hanging in the closet, where I left it last time. There's a sweater I don't recognize, but I'm glad to see it, because it's October here and this cabin is a bit drafty.

As I remove the dress from the hanger, it dips to one side, and I realize there's something heavy in the pocket. It's the pistol. I start to pull it out, but then I remember Kiernan cautioning me when we were training to always put the pistol on a flat surface. He said the safety on this model isn't foolproof and it's been known to go off accidentally when dropped. If Kiernan has hidden it in my pocket despite that warning, I probably need to keep it out of sight.

I step into the dress, a simple blue shirtwaist, and pull on the sweater, which is long enough to cover the pocket holding the gun. I stuff my phone in the only safe location I've found on these trips—my bra. Not comfortable, but unlikely to fall out. My glasses and the cloche hat are still in the dresser. The disguise is pointless now, but Prudence doesn't know that I know, so I tuck my hair under the hat and push the stupid glasses onto my nose before joining Kiernan. He's seated at the table, still in the same jeans and flannel shirt, reminding me, once again, that male time travelers have it really, really easy.

He pushes a sheet of paper across the table. "These are some notes I took while observing the stable points at the boarding-house where Delia is staying."

It's just a few bullet points, most of which look like city and street names. Watkinsville is circled. The others are crossed out, but there are two that he's both circled and crossed out.

"I've narrowed down where they're going," he says, his voice oddly formal. "Thought it might be one of these other spots, but I'm pretty sure it's Watkinsville or just to the south." He taps the word *Watkinsville* on the paper and then slides his finger down to where the word *G's Hollow* is circled and then crossed through. Just below that is *Colt Springs Rd.*, with the entire thing crossed out and just the word *Colt* circled.

"So, we go to Watkinsville," I say. "Any clue where in Watkinsville?"

"No, but it's a small town, and I know the road they're taking and what they're driving. We'll wait till they're near town, then pull out and follow them. Should be a snap. Like I said before, we were just spinning our wheels trying to get the keys in Athens."

He stresses the last sentence very distinctly and looks straight at me as he says it.

I give him a confused smile and say, "Okay," even though I don't recall him ever saying anything of the sort. I get the message on the paper—Pru doesn't know about the events at God's Hollow or about the gun. But I'm not sure what he means by the comment about Athens.

"Okay, then let's go," I say, and start toward the door.

"Uh, Kate?" He's looking at me, eyebrows raised, his expression slightly worried. "The truck is in 1938."

"Right." I give him a fake silly me smile and pull out my CHRONOS key. "You first."

∞

BOGART, GEORGIA
August 11, 1938, 10:00 a.m.

The cabin is warm, and I smell coffee. I glance around and see that everything is pretty much the same, aside from a new lamp in the living room. The kitchen table is empty, except for a newspaper with the headline "FDR to Speak at UGA Commencement" and a thermos with the words *Icy-Hot* on the side.

Kiernan taps the newspaper with his index finger. "Delia's group will head out of Athens around ten thirty, during Roosevelt's speech. FDR's car goes through Watkinsville on the way to the next speech, over in Barnesville. I'm thinking their goal is to see how the locals react. FDR's car may even stop there briefly—I don't know."

He holds the thermos out to me. "We may have to wait awhile. I didn't jump ahead to check the exact times."

"No problem. I'm sure you've been much too busy with other things."

I tried to keep the sarcasm to a minimum in that comment, but I must have failed, because Kiernan rolls his eyes.

"There's no milk. Is that okay?"

I nod. Hopefully Kiernan's coffee is better than his great-grandson's.

He opens the back door, and I follow him out into the yard. The place is clearly a working farm now—several cows graze near the barn, and a tractor sits among the brown remnants in the cornfield. The paint on the shed has faded. An older man in a white shirt and overalls is perched on a small ladder beneath one of the peach trees, which have grown considerably since 1911.

Two dogs, a collie and some sort of mixed breed, rest in the sun a few feet away. When the door closes behind us, they begin barking. The man looks over and waves one arm as he climbs down from the ladder.

Kiernan groans. "I was hoping we could avoid Bill. If he asks, you're at the university. I just drove you out here to see the cabin before we go back into town to hear FDR."

We walk toward the shed where the man is now waiting, a canvas bag, half full of peaches, slung over his shoulder. He pulls off his cap and stuffs it into his pocket. "Boy, you sure do look like yore daddy. I know I tell you that most ever' time I see you, but it's like the good Lord made a carbon copy when he made you." His eyes slide over to me. "And who is this purty young lady?"

"This is Kate Keller, Mr. Owens. She's in one of my classes, and I brought her out to look at the farm before we head over to hear Roosevelt's speech."

Owens looks surprised and starts to say something. Then he changes his mind, giving Kiernan a smile and a wink before glancing back over at me.

"It's a right pleasure to meet you, Miss Keller. I'll let you young people get on with your day, but here—" He reaches into the canvas bag and pulls out two peaches, handing them to Kiernan. "Y'all need to take some of these peaches. We had a bumper crop this year, more'n Alice knows what to do with. I'll have her bring by a few jars she put up, now that you'll be around a bit more often, with the school year startin'. Maybe some of her pickles and plum jam, too."

"I would certainly appreciate that, Mr. Owens, if it's no trouble."

"No trouble. No trouble at all." Owens reaches into the bag and pulls out two more peaches. "Here's a few for you to take back to your dorm, young lady. Y'all have a good time, an' give ol' FDR my regards."

"Would those be your good regards or the other variety?" Kiernan asks.

Owens throws his head back and laughs. "You know which ones."

Kiernan shakes his head as he opens the door to the truck, a black flatbed. "I totally forgot the truck's been here all morning. He knows I didn't drive you out here to look at the cabin."

"Then why—"

"That's what the wink was about. He's assuming you were there all night. I just hope he doesn't chatter to Mrs. Owens, or I'll have a stack of church pamphlets about the dangers of sex before marriage on my porch, along with the pickles and jam. And she'll probably drop a well-intentioned, motherly note up to Boston to let my father know his boy is misbehaving."

"And you'll write back later, thanking her for letting you know."

He grins. "Precisely."

The truck is already uncomfortably warm, so I tug off the sweater and crank down the window as Kiernan starts the engine.

He shoots a nervous glance in my direction once the truck is on the bumpy trail leading out to the road. "So . . . no twenty questions about Pru?"

I glance around. "Is it safe? I wasn't entirely sure if someone could set a stable point in a car."

He snorts. "If they did, it's still back in the shed."

"What about listening devices?"

"Not unless they did it in the past hour or so, and I think Owens would have told me if anyone was poking around my truck. Truthfully, I don't think there's a device in the cabin, either. But there are definitely stable points, and I wouldn't put it past Leo to read lips."

I'm quiet for a minute, because I have absolutely no idea where to start. I open the thermos and take a swig of the coffee, which is so hot it scalds my tongue but otherwise not bad.

"First," I say, "please tell me Martha is okay."

"Martha is fine. I put a few hundred dollars in a savings account for her and told Bill to give it to her when she came of age or got married. Meanwhile, Martha stayed with them. Mrs. Owens has four boys and was happy to take her in. She was less happy to take the two motorbikes, but her menfolk insisted."

"And you think these Owens people will be good to her?"

"I know they *were* good to her. She married a guy from Atlanta, but he died in World War I. Martha and her little boy came back to the farm for another year or two after that. I saw pictures—he was a cute little tyke. Then she married again and moved over near Bishop, close enough she can drop by and visit every few weeks."

"How did you explain—"

"I kept her here at the cabin until the police found the scene at Six Bridges and removed the bodies. Then I arranged to be at the local store at the same time she showed up asking what happened to everyone in her village. She's a good little actress and played her part just fine—after that, I made the arrangements with Mr. and Mrs. Owens."

"And Prudence knows nothing about it?"

"To the best of my knowledge, no. She had no reason to watch the cabin in 1911, because I never told her we were there in 1911. And you know how long it takes to watch stable points. I'm pretty sure she's got other—"

"Why don't you explain why in hell you're telling Prudence anything?"

"Well, I'd planned to start with that. You're the one who wanted to know about Martha first. And stop looking at me like I'm some sort of bloody traitor, because I'm not."

I don't say anything. We reach the end of the dirt trail, and Kiernan makes a left onto a two-lane road before glancing back over at me. "It didn't make sense, okay? This has gone much too easy."

"You take a bullet in the leg and you say it's been easy?"

"That wasn't Pru. That was probably Simon. Or someone else Saul sent out."

"Which makes zero difference. Despite their internal squabbles, they're on the same side, right? It doesn't matter which ones you're talking to and which ones you aren't if they're working toward the same thing."

"Maybe. But it might matter that they want the same thing for different reasons."

"No," I say. "Not when the thing they both want is to wipe out a huge chunk of the world's population."

"Okay, you're right. But . . . Pru's reasons might make it possible to negotiate with her. To change her mind. But, Saul . . ." He shakes his head and reaches over for the thermos, then hands it back after he takes a swig. I wouldn't have thought twice about drinking after Kiernan before this morning, but after seeing him kiss Prudence, the coffee doesn't seem nearly as appealing.

"You know I was with Prudence and Simon for a few weeks after my Kate disappeared, right?"

"Yes. You said you convinced Pru that you didn't remember your Kate and that you couldn't really use the CHRONOS key. You said she decided to leave you alone."

"Well, it may not have been that simple. I just couldn't shake the feeling that we were being played, Kate."

It's really strange hearing him say that, having just said the exact same thing to Connor and Katherine.

"So," he continues, "after we finished at Six Bridges and I got Martha settled, I decided to go back to Estero 2038 and see if I could get some answers. Chopped off my hair again, wore the same clothes. I jumped in maybe ten seconds after I left Pru last time. I asked her exactly why we broke things off. She gave me the same story she did before, which is total bullshit, but this time I pretended to believe it. And we patched things up."

Kiernan grabs the thermos and takes another swig. He looks uncomfortable enough that I have absolutely no doubt what he means by *patched things up*.

"With Older Pru?"

"Yeah."

I'm silent, and after a moment he continues, his voice a little exasperated. "It's not like I wanted to, Kate. But it's the only way she'd trust me. Anyway, I hung around at Estero for about two weeks—long enough to find out that Saul, Simon, and about half of the inner circle have moved into the big house near the regional temple in Miami. No surprise, since Saul has been spending most of his time there anyway. And I sneaked in a few jumps up to Boston for shows at Norumbega. Simon is still there, pretty much every day, with . . . her."

"Young Pru."

"Yeah," he says, his voice strained.

"And Older Pru doesn't know what's up with that?"

"Older Pru sometimes doesn't know what she had for breakfast."

That cranks the *eww* factor up even more, but I keep quiet.

"Anyway," he says, "about a week in, Pru's talking to Philippa one morning and makes a joke about you getting the keys from Timothy and Evelyn in Dallas. Pru says maybe she needs to slap baby's hand for breaking the rules, but it's clear she doesn't care one bit about those keys. Her only concern seemed to be that you'd start poking around in what they're doing in 2038. So . . . I offered to babysit."

"You what?"

"I told her I'd keep you out of the way, since you seemed sort of taken with me."

I really do want to hit him, but he's driving. I grit my teeth and say, "So she went for it?"

"No. Not at first. So I shrugged like it didn't matter and went back to reading my book and sunning by the pool. Later she said she should put some surveillance on Katherine's house, and I told her I was bored. At least she could let me take care of that minor task."

"You hired someone to spy on us?"

"Sort of." He glances uneasily at my clenched fists and then goes on. "That blue van you've seen out front—"

"Connor says that belongs to the neighbor."

"It does, sort of. I went back a few years and had someone at the local temple buy the house next door when it was up for sale. The guy I hired stays there. He uses the van to get a visual confirmation when anyone is coming and going. And he was told to report back to me if his audio equipment picked up anything about the specific locations where I knew we'd already been. The first report I handed over to Pru said you were planning the trip to Australia and had also worked your way through a few of the stable points at Estero between 2028 and 2030."

"But I haven't . . . I didn't even know there were—"

"Yeah, I know all that, and you know all that, but you're missing the point. Me saying you were poking around in the future is what made Pru reconsider—she decided me keeping you busy wasn't such a bad idea after all. And that's why she's left us alone."

"Left us alone? She's threatened me twice, Kiernan. She left the message with Eve and . . . she broke into Trey's house."

He looks a bit surprised at the last part but says, "Has she hurt anyone? Like I said before, Pru's not playing with a full deck, and I expect she can't resist getting in a few blows. But if things go as planned today, we'll have all of the keys. Well, except for Houdini's, but I'm still working on that."

I'm starting to wonder whether Kiernan is the one not playing with a full deck.

"What difference does it make?" I scream. "You've already said Prudence isn't interested in any of those keys! The question is why? Are they replicating CHRONOS keys somehow? You said they had at least six . . ."

"Yeah. But I'm thinking now that I was right the first time—it's more like twelve, maybe thirteen."

I stare at him, dumbfounded.

"Think it through, Kate—there's only one possible answer. There were thirty-six historians, but only twenty-four in the field, including Saul. They're not worried about the ones you've been looking for, because they have the other twelve."

"But . . . how? The system doesn't allow jumps past 2100-something—whenever it was that the equipment was invented. There aren't any stable points after that."

"I think maybe there's one," he says. "CHRONOS headquarters at the time the teams were supposed to return. It's what all of us see at first, before we figure out how to use the keys. Do you remember? At the beginning, it's all black, with bits of static. I think maybe that's what's left of CHRONOS. It may be a very *unstable* stable point, but I think it's there, and I think it's where Pru landed when she accidentally used the key."

The black void Katherine talked about. I only saw it briefly that first time I held the key, but then Katherine was a little surprised at how quickly I was able to lock on to images. After only a second, I saw the wheat field and Kiernan, then white buildings near the water. After that, there was darkness. Someone crying. And then I was back in the wheat field again. But none of those were really like viewing a stable point for me. All of my other senses were active, too, which never happens when I pull up locations on the key now.

"Why go to the trouble of grabbing keys scattered about time and space when they had twelve all waiting in one spot?" he continues. "Prudence never came out and said directly that's what happened, but she did say that neither she nor Saul is particularly worried that one little girl can use the equipment, especially when that girl is barking up the wrong tree."

I clutch my head, which is pounding mercilessly, as I try to separate the threads of everything Kiernan has just said. It's a tangled mess, but I find one semicoherent thought sticking out at the edge and follow it. "Okay, so why didn't you go back and tell me I was barking up the wrong damn tree?"

"Two reasons—no, wait, three. First, that would have resulted in a lot of screwy memories for both of us. Second, this kept my cover, which could help us later on, because all of the times I was with you, in Boston, at Katherine's house, in Georgia, were no longer a problem once Prudence said I should keep you busy."

"But, Prudence just recently told you to do that, after you'd already . . ."

"But she didn't *know* that, did she? You can't think about this linear—"

"Yes, I know! I know. Just tell me the third reason. And find me some ibuprofen."

"I can't help you there, love. Gave the last I had to Jess. But the third reason is that the keys we've collected are only irrelevant if Prudence and Saul think we're not going after the ones they stole from CHRONOS after the explosion. If we prevent them from getting those keys in 2305, which is precisely what I plan to do, then you'd better believe they'll come looking for the ones we've been collecting."

∞

Kiernan executes an impressive multipoint turn on a narrow trail lined with densely packed pine trees, so that we're now pointed out toward the road we were just driving on, in perfect position to pull out once we see their car pass by. I've been silent for the last few minutes, and he keeps shooting nervous glances my way. I can't shake the feeling that he hasn't told me everything, but it could be because my head is still throbbing from trying to sort out everything he has told me already.

"You're certain Prudence trusts you?"

"Kate, I'm not kidding when I say she's crazy. If she doubted me in the slightest, I would—at a bare minimum—have claw marks up and down my face. More likely, I'd be dead. You saw Philippa and Leo back at the cabin, right? They're with her most of the time. Leo's pretty good at talking her down. Not as good as Simon was and not nearly as good as I am, but he helps. And Philippa has a syringe ready if that doesn't work."

"And those people, Leo and Philippa, they trust you, too?"

"I doubt it," he says. "But it's more because they don't like me hanging around Pru than that they're worried about me going to the other side. I'm not even sure they know about me and . . . Kate."

I grab at another thread from the tangle in my mind. "Why does Leo look like Simon?"

He shrugs. "Same mother. The gene pool is pretty shallow at Estero. If you ever want a family reunion, we can just stop by the Cyrist Farm after, say, 2030, and I'll introduce you to the entire gang."

"No thanks. By same mom, you mean Pru, right?"

He nods.

"So, Simon is my cousin?" I wouldn't have thought that our encounter on the day Katherine disappeared could be any more repulsive, but this ratchets it up a level.

"Yeah. And so's Leo and Philippa. Eve—I guess she's sort of a half cousin. Of the ones who can use the key, there are only three I know who aren't descended from Pru—me, Patrick Conwell, and one other woman named Edna. The Patterson woman, the one who's president in your time, that's Edna's great-granddaughter."

"Can Patterson use the key?"

"No. But she's inner circle because of the family connections."

I finish off the last of the coffee. "Okay. Let's put aside family ties and personal relationships for the time being, although it might help if you draw me up a family tree when we get back. I need you to give me the bigger picture. You say Saul and Prudence are at odds. I get the sense that part of it is that he just doesn't like the idea of her having a bigger following among the Cyrists than he does, right?"

"Yeah. That's part of it." He leans forward a bit as a car passes by on the road in front of us, then relaxes again.

"But not all of it, right?"

"No. It's more of a . . . schism. Sort of a civil war. Saul's trying to keep a lot of very different groups together, Kate. He pulled in smaller faiths and movements that already existed, the Koreshans and a bunch of others. Then you have those who are only around because the *Book of Prophesy* gives pretty solid stock tips to the faithful. Others came on board because the religion seemed woman friendly, though they tended to start questioning that when they saw Prudence treated more as Brother Cyrus's assistant than as a prophet in her own right. And finally, you've got Cyrists who joined up because they're worried about the damage being done to the earth by overpopulation, global warming, corporate farming, you name it. They find it a wee bit puzzling when church doctrine claims the End is coming to protect the earth but still encourages those who follow The Way to invest in the companies doing the damage."

"I'm guessing those last two clusters are more attracted to Prudence's side?"

"Yeah," he says. "At least that's true for those who realize that there *are* factions. Most of the local temples just focus on what seems important to their people and skip the other stuff. Sometimes you'll have two in the same town who can't agree on a bloody thing, but both call themselves Cyrists."

"So, like most religions? Okay then, let's get back to the big-picture questions. Why build the Cyrists? Why go to all this trouble in the first place? If Saul just likes killing people, if all he's after is death on a massive scale, wouldn't he simply replicate this toxin and release it?"

A blue sedan drives past, and Kiernan waits a second and then pulls out onto the road behind it. After we've settled in about a quarter mile behind the car, he answers my question. "I don't know, but when I was down in New Orleans with Simon? When he was drunk and running his mouth about Six Bridges? He said Saul started all of this because he has a wager with this guy Campbell at his club."

"What? A *wager*? You mean he's doing all of this because he made a bet?"

He shrugs. "Yeah, that's pretty much the sum of it."

"That's crazy."

He looks at me out of the corner of his eye. "And this surprises you? You saw him in the chapel, same as I did."

I just sit there for a few minutes, pondering the fact that one-quarter of my genetic makeup is seriously screwed up. "And you think Prudence inherited his crazy?"

"I'm not sure I'd go that far, although the jury is still out on Simon, since he seems to think the whole wager thing is funny. Pru's has come on gradually, and it's pretty clear, at least to me, that it's due to too many jumps and too many memories that clash. It's like she sometimes can't tell what's real anymore. Pru—I think she sees the Culling more like collateral damage. Saul sees it as his bloody masterpiece."

"Did Prudence send my mom to Italy?"

"What?"

I realize I've never mentioned that theory to him and explain my reasoning.

"I don't know," he says. "But she's never spoken against her sister. I don't think your mom is in any danger, at least not from Pru."

That's pretty much what I thought, but it's a relief to hear it confirmed by someone who has shared more than a few dozen words with her. That thought, however, reminds me exactly how much he's been sharing with Prudence, something that bothers me on many different levels. His reasons for getting into Pru's good graces make sense on the surface, but I can't help but feel that there's something he's not telling me.

The truck is cooling off now that we're moving, and the breeze feels nice on my face. We pass a cemetery named Mars Hill, and after that the woods we're driving through begin to thin out a bit, with a few farms scattered here and there.

About a mile later, we approach an intersection. The road ahead is lined with cars and tractors and even a few horses, some of which are attached to carriages. The blue car pulls onto the shoulder, and Kiernan parks just behind. Delia and Grant, both seated in the back, step out and cross over to the left side of the road, where a group of maybe fifty are gathered.

"Do you want to get out or wait here and follow them someplace less crowded?" Kiernan asks.

"Out," I say. "I want to see FDR. But let's keep our distance from Delia's group." There are too many people around to risk talking to them here, but I want another chance to observe them before we approach. Also, the temperature seems to have gone up by several degrees since we left the cabin, and the truck is stifling hot—it has to be cooler out there than it is in here.

Kiernan starts to get out, but I grab his sleeve. "How much do you think Grant knows about Saul and Six Bridges? I mean, he looked unconscious when Saul drove past the stable point, but . . ."

"No idea. When I asked Martha, she said he kept to himself and was kind of Saul's shadow. Which makes sense if Saul was his trainer. Katherine doesn't remember anything about him?"

"Only that he was probably first-year CHRONOS. She didn't have a lot of interaction with trainees."

"Well," Kiernan says, "the only way it matters is if he was in on Six Bridges. And I really doubt that, if Saul saw fit to knock him out."

Abel, who has been waiting in the driver's seat, gets out of his car just as I'm about to open my door, so we wait a minute longer, watching as he strolls over to a group on the right side of the intersection. He's a large man, tall and muscular. I hadn't realized exactly how big he was when I saw him in Athens, but I think he may have been trying to make himself less conspicuous. No one is paying attention now, and he walks with a more confident gait. He leans back against one of the trees and pulls a pack of cigarettes from his pocket, offering a smoke to the two men standing next to him. One of them takes him up on it, and they start a conversation.

I look at Abel under the trees and then at the opposite side of the street, where the summer sun is blazing down on the spectators. "The pictures I've seen always show the whites getting the better accommodations in the segregated South. And yet Abel gets the shade?"

"Athens is to the north. The folks on the white side of the street will see FDR first."

It will be a few seconds' advantage at most, so personally, I'd rather be in the group with the shade. And I'd also rather leave the sweater in the truck, but since it helps to hide the gun I'm carrying, I guess I'll have to roast.

Given the physical road separating the two groups, the racial divide was immediately apparent. But as we get closer, I see there's also something of a gender divide. A few younger couples are together, but otherwise, the men are off a few yards to the north, with the women closer to the fence. Kids are scattered all over, younger ones near where the women are talking and older ones chasing each other around or climbing on the fence that keeps the cows from wandering onto the highway. And it actually *is* a highway—according to the sign, which looks pretty new, it's U.S. Highway 129. It's nothing like the six- or eight-lane roads around DC that I'm used to, but it's wider and in better condition than the narrow road we drove in on.

Kiernan and I stand by the fence, near the other couples. Grant is with the men by the road. He looks out of place, and I remember one of the first things Katherine told me about CHRONOS historians—they all loved their jobs because they were naturally good at them, better than they'd be at anything else. Maybe Grant would have reached that point eventually, but right now, he looks like he'd rather be anywhere but here.

Delia, on the other hand, seems totally at ease. When I first saw her in Athens, I couldn't help but think that her looks would be a liability in her line of work. Long dark hair, flawless skin, hourglass figure—she tends to draw most eyes toward her, male or female, and I think that would make it tough to blend in with a crowd. She walks toward the cluster of women, stopping near a young mother with a fussy toddler propped on her hip and a girl, my age or maybe a bit younger, who holds a small infant against her shoulder. The toddler is wriggling and whining nonstop, clearly intent on getting his mom's attention.

Delia crouches down a bit, her red skirt brushing against the grass. Once she's at the same level as the grumpy boy, she makes a silly face, crossing her eyes and using her fingers to stretch out her lips, which are outlined in a red as vivid as the skirt. The kid looks suspicious at first, but he stops screaming and tries to make the face back at her. Delia counters with an even sillier face, and he giggles, reaching out to tug at her scarf.

The sudden change in temperament finally causes the mom to look at the kid, and she exchanges a smile with Delia. A few seconds later, Delia's chatting with the women like they're old friends. She hands the kid the scarf from around her neck, and he seems content, at least for the moment, to wave it back and forth. I'm not close enough to catch what they're saying, but the women seem to be telling her about their children, because the toddler's mom points at a group of kids a few feet away from where Kiernan and I are standing.

Grant is watching Delia, too, clearly envious of how easy she makes it seem. When he catches me looking at him, he squares his shoulders, walks over to two of the men, and says something. One of the guys, who looks a few years older than Grant, glances at his watch, so I guess he's telling Grant the time. After that, Grant just hangs out on the periphery, listening but not joining in.

Every minute or so, a car approaches from the north and the conversation halts momentarily, picking back up as soon as everyone sees it's a truck or some other vehicle that's clearly not presidential.

"Do you know if he even stops?" I ask Kiernan in a low voice.

He shrugs and leans back against the fence post. "He's been known to in the past, and it's an election year. Not a presidential election, but FDR is headed to a speech right now where he's going to ask people to vote against their incumbent senator in the primary, a fellow Democrat Roosevelt thinks is too conservative. So I think he'll stop, if only for a few seconds. The real question is how close he stops to the intersection."

I raise an eyebrow, and he nods toward the group of white men. "Democrats in Georgia have a whites-only primary. Almost all registered voters are Democrats, so the primary is the real election—whoever wins there will win overall. I doubt any of the blacks will successfully cast a ballot. Roosevelt probably wishes that wasn't the case, because he's more popular with them than with the white guys."

I glance over at the other side of the street. A few other men and one woman are chatting with Abel. Looking around, I realize that she is the only woman on that side of the street, and there are no children running around beneath the trees. I can't help but wonder whether simply showing up at a gathering like this is an act of rebellion and maybe considered a bit dangerous for women and children of color.

"You said white guys. But these women can vote, right? For nearly two decades now."

"They can vote," he says, "but most of them will vote as their men say. Owens makes out a list for his wife to take to the polls to be sure she doesn't kill his vote."

I wrinkle my nose, not entirely happy with Kiernan's choice for Martha's foster dad. "How does he know Mrs. Owens doesn't go into the ballot box and vote *against* everyone on that list?"

Kiernan laughs. "She might. That's probably why some men go into the ballot box with their wives."

"Is that even legal?"

"Don't know," he says, shrugging. "But it doesn't matter whether it's legal if no one challen—"

Kiernan stops and looks toward the highway. A large black convertible is slowing down. Even though I know this is a very different situation, I can't help but feel a shiver of dread, thinking about my recent jump to Dallas—another convertible, another president.

FDR is seated in the back. He waves to the group of men as the car passes, and the driver keeps rolling about ten yards, pulling to a halt in front of the women.

Kiernan chuckles softly. "Nicely played. Both sides of the street can hear him, and he looks like he's being a gentleman by stopping near the women."

The men drift closer to the car. One of them, a young guy with a suit jacket slung over his arm, moves a little faster than the others, trying to get in close so that he can snap some pictures. Grant follows, staying a few steps behind the guy with the camera. Delia has shifted a little closer to the car as well. The group that Abel was talking to remains on the other side of the street, but they've walked out of the trees, standing at the edge of the intersection to get a better view.

Roosevelt isn't wearing the trademark glasses I'm used to seeing in pictures, but the same wide smile is on his face. He tips his hat to the ladies, nods to both groups of men, and then begins speaking in the booming voice I remember from the "Day of Infamy" speech in history class, without the crackly static.

"Friends, my driver tells me we're a bit behind schedule, as we're due in Barnesville at two o'clock, but I just wanted to stop and share a bit of good news. Most of you know I've considered Georgia my second home for some time now, but today I can finally tell you that I am officially a Georgia Bulldog."

During the last sentence, he grabs a different hat, a mortarboard, from the seat next to him and slaps it on his head, waving a rolled piece of paper in the air. There are a few polite chuckles and some scattered applause.

Once the applause ends, he takes the hat off and continues in a more serious tone. "I'd also be remiss in an election year if I did not remind all of you that even though our nation has come a long way in the past few years, much remains to be done. You have a perfect right to choose any candidate you wish, but because Georgia has been good enough to call me her adopted son and because for many years I have regarded Georgia as my 'other state,' I feel no hesitation in telling you what I would do if I could vote in the senatorial primary next month. I hope you'll join me in supporting United States Attorney Lawrence Camp."

There's some scattered grumbling, and several men start asking questions, but Roosevelt waves them away. "Senator George is a good friend of mine, but there are issues on which we disagree. I did not come to this lightly. I'll discuss it in more detail at Barnesville, and I'm sure it will be in your papers. All I ask is that you consider my recommendation and keep the welfare of the nation in the forefront as you decide. And now, we must go, or we'll keep the good people in Barnesville waiting. I hope to see you all again soon!"

With that, the convertible pulls away and continues down the highway.

I expect the women near us to start gathering up the kids for a quick departure, given that the day is hot and it's lunchtime. But Roosevelt apparently dropped something of a bombshell, because the chatter closer to the road is getting heated. The women are quiet and seem a little on edge.

All I pick up are snippets—one guy says FDR is a "damn fool Yankee," and someone else says, "He don't know doodley-squat about Georgia."

The man with the camera says something I can't hear to the guy next to him, the beefy middle-aged guy who just made the "doodley-squat" comment. Doodley-Squat takes offense and jabs a forefinger into Camera Guy's shoulder. Camera Guy shoves him back, a lot harder than I would have guessed, given his slight build, and Doodley-Squat stumbles a few feet backward into Grant and another younger guy. The shoulder of the road is a bit higher than the ground where the rest of us stand, and both Doodley-Squat and Grant lose their balance, crashing into several of the women, including the one holding the fussy toddler.

None of the women are hurt, but the toddler starts crying again.

Delia tries to help Grant up, but before he can grab her hand, she's shoved to the side by Doodley-Squat, who, for no apparent reason, seems to have decided Grant was to blame for his fall. Or maybe he's just lashing out at the nearest unfamiliar face. He grabs Grant by the collar and jerks him to his feet.

Grant's eyes widen, and the blood drains from his face until it's only a shade darker than the white of his shirt.

"Boy, you need to watch where you're goin', don'tcha?"

Grant opens his mouth, but nothing comes out.

The girl holding the baby—which is, amazingly, still asleep—says, "We're okay, Daddy. He didn't mean no harm."

That remark earns the girl a foul look. She bites her lip and takes a few steps back toward the fence, hugging the baby closer to her chest.

Several of the men move closer, joking and elbowing each other, which makes me suspect that Doodley-Squat's short temper is a local source of amusement. Camera Guy says, "Put him down, Willis. Ain't his fault you can't walk and chew gum at the same time. You're the one who pushed him into them girls in the first place, so maybe you oughta do the apologizing."

"You might wanna stay out of this, Phillips, unless you'd like to eat that camera of yours. I don't know why this little shit tripped me . . ."

One of the other men clears his throat. "Watch the language, Willis."

I expect this Willis guy to let go of Grant and turn on the other guy, but he just twists Grant's collar a little harder. I don't think Grant is actually choking, but his face begins to go from pale to pink, and he claws at Willis's hand.

"Mr. Willis," Delia says, "he didn't mean any harm. We're just passing through and heard the president might stop here. If you'll just let him go, I'm certain he'd be happy to apologize to your daughter and these other ladies."

Grant is trying to nod, but Willis's hammy fist is in the way, so the best he can manage is to bump his chin against it a couple of times.

Willis looks over at Delia, and a slow smile spreads over his face, as though he's noticing her for the first time. His eyes travel from head to toe, lingering at strategic points along the way. Delia blushes, and I can see her jaw twitch slightly before she pastes on a nervous smile and steps forward.

She stops in midstride as Willis's smile disappears and he grabs the front of Grant's shirt with his other hand. "I don't know who you people think you are, but—"

Camera Guy—Phillips, I guess—grabs Willis's right arm, the one twisting Grant's collar, and at about the same time, Grant pulls his foot back and kicks Willis in the knee. Willis drops Grant and pulls back his left arm, probably intending to punch Phillips and then finish dealing with Grant.

I don't think Willis intended for his elbow to connect with Delia's nose. I'm not sure he cared one way or the other that it did, but I'm pretty sure it wasn't planned. Willis even looks a little surprised at the crunch when his elbow hits her face, slowing down his punch long enough for Phillips to duck out of the way.

Delia's hands fly to her face. I think she would have dropped to the ground, but Abel is behind her. He grabs her under the elbows and steadies her, and then he takes a step toward Willis. I didn't see Abel approaching, but the look on his face is pretty much the polar opposite of the downcast eyes and shy demeanor he wore in Athens.

Abel's jaw is clenched, his body a tightly wrapped coil, but his voice is polite, almost deferential. "I think you owe Miss Delia an apology, sir."

Willis stares at him and then spits on the ground about an inch from Abel's foot. "And I don't give a damn what you think, nigger."

Panic flashes into Delia's eyes, and she pulls her hands away from her nose so that she can grab Abel's arm. Unfortunately, there's blood on her hands, and I don't know if it's the offensive word that makes him take that first menacing step toward Willis or the sight of his wife's face, the lower half covered in blood, her nose smashed and bent to the side at an odd angle.

Abel doesn't throw the first punch, but he definitely throws the second one. And I think he may have thrown the third one, too.

∞19∞

Willis is down, and for a moment, I think he's out. Then he stumbles to his feet, just as a second guy jumps in to take a swing at Abel. I start to run forward, but Kiernan grabs my arm, pulling me back.

"Kate, no. You really think we can take all of them?"

"No, but I don't think *all* of them are going to join in. They were laughing at that Willis guy—"

"Until Abel punched back, yeah."

I scan the crowd and see that he's right. Their expressions have changed. No one is laughing anymore. They look angry, for the most part. I'd like to believe they're all angry at Willis for smashing Delia's nose, and some of them may be. I think Phillips, the guy with the camera, and a few of the other men fall into that group, and maybe half of the women.

But most of the women aren't staying. The mother with the fussy toddler grabs two of the older kids by the fence. She hands the little one to the oldest and says, "Y'all take Timmy and get in the car. I'll be there in a minute." The girl nods. The boy looks like he wants to argue, but he snaps his mouth shut when he catches his mom's expression.

The other side of the street is now empty, with the exception of the sole woman in the group and the man who took the cigarette from Abel. They're still watching, but they're standing inside the doors of their car, ready to make a quick departure if necessary.

Two guys grab Abel's arms. They're having a tough time holding him, until a third guy grabs his shirt collar and yanks it backward. Delia and Grant try to pull them off Abel.

"Get your hands off of him!" Delia shrieks. "Abel!"

Then Grant takes a punch to the chest, stumbling backward.

Kiernan curses softly, shaking his head like he knows he's going to regret his next move. "Get Delia to the car. I'm going to see if I can help Abel."

I take off, running around the edge of the spectators, and grab Grant's arm.

"I'm with CHRONOS. Let's get Delia to the car."

He just stares at me for a second, his jaw hanging.

"Now!" I say, holding up the medallion and tugging the leather cover down a fraction of an inch so that he can see the glow.

That snaps him into action. Grant turns out to be quite impressive when he has direct orders to follow. He runs forward and spins Delia around, then bends down so that his head is almost level with her waist, flinging her over his shoulder in one swift motion. Delia doesn't go peacefully, but he has a solid grip on her legs.

I run alongside, glancing back over my shoulder at the crowd once we reach the road. Things don't look like they're settling down. If anything, they're getting worse.

"Can you get Delia to the car and keep her there?"

"Yeah," Grant says, although he looks a little doubtful.

"Okay. I'll be back."

Delia claws at me and misses as I run past. She's still screaming for them to let Abel go, her screams interspersed with a rather impressive string of profanity aimed at Grant and me for pulling her away.

I catch a brief glimpse of Kiernan at the far side of the crowd as I get closer. From the way his head whips backward, I think he's just taken a punch.

I can't see Abel, so I push between two broad-shouldered guys to get in closer. That's when Willis, who has apparently realized he can't beat Abel in a fair fight, pulls a knife.

There's a collective whoosh of breath from the crowd, and most of them take a step back. Willis charges at Abel, knife raised. Abel dodges to the left, then swipes his right leg outward, causing Willis to stumble. Before Willis can regain his balance, Abel crashes into him. They both land on the ground, wrestling for the knife. Abel finally latches onto Willis's forearm, pushing the hand holding the knife out to one side.

Willis's hand is mere inches from my foot, so I stomp his fingers as hard as I can. He lets out a roar, but before I can see whether he dropped the knife, there's a chuckle from one of the men behind me and someone yanks me backward, out of the circle.

I hear the dull thud of fists pounding and then the sharp crack of a gunshot.

"All right, that's it. It's over." The voice comes from the other side of the circle, near the back.

Someone else on that side says, "Mitchell, you ain't wearin' no uniform, and this ain't no traffic offense, so why don't you go on home?"

A few people laugh, and then there's another shot, and one of the men who was next to Phillips earlier pushes forward. His face is thin, with deep-set eyes that scan the crowd. "Don't nobody in the middle move. The rest of you, get on back."

A few of the men trade glances, like they're debating whether to obey. Finally, one guy steps back, and the rest of them follow, several of them grumbling as they go.

Kiernan's arm is paused in midpunch. Blood pours from a cut on his cheek. His knuckles are smeared with even more blood, but from the looks of the guy in front of him, some of that isn't Kiernan's.

Mitchell, the man with the gun, nods at two guys on the periphery. "Carlton, Briggs—y'all grab the Negro and put him in the back of my truck. There's some rope back there. Tie his hands and feet." They step forward and take Abel, who is barely conscious, from the guys who were holding him down so that Willis could punch him.

"Willis, you gonna go peacefully down to the jail, or you gonna fight me? 'Cause we can do this either way. Entirely up to you."

Willis is bent over, clutching his right thigh. His pants leg is drenched in blood, and the knife, bloodied as well, is in the dirt at his feet. He spits on the ground, and there's blood in that, too. "If you mean do I want to press charges, then the answer is hell, yes. But it'd be a whole lot easier if you'd just go on home, Mitchell, or write some traffic tickets or whatever it is you're s'posed to do and let us handle this matter."

"Well, that ain't happenin'," Mitchell says amiably. "Come on, Willis. You know as well as I do that the sheriff ain't gonna let you string that boy up, 'specially when you started the whole thing *and* pulled the knife."

Willis and several others protest that point, but Mitchell holds up his hand. "Save it for Judge Cramer." He nods toward the guys who were holding Abel's arms during the fight. "I ain't got room for all of you in my truck, so I'm gonna hold the two of you responsible for seein' to it that your uncle is at the jailhouse by the time I get there. And y'all don't go wanderin' off, 'cause we're gonna need statements from both of you, too."

Willis leans against one of the younger guys, muttering something about jurisdiction as they go off toward the cars. Mitchell watches them for a couple of seconds and then turns and motions toward Kiernan. "What's your name, son?"

Kiernan looks over at me and then back at Mitchell. "Dunne, sir. Kiernan Dunne."

"You two boys go get in my truck. Jody, you get up front. Dunne, you're in the back. I'll be there in a minute." He turns back to the people milling around. "The rest of y'all, go home. I know who was here, and I'll pass that along to the sheriff. If he needs information from any of you, he'll be in touch."

Jody starts off toward the cars. Kiernan stops and hands me the truck key, then pulls me close so that he can stick his pistol into the pocket of my skirt.

"Go to the cabin, and get some cash—under my mattress, up in the loft. You may need to bail me out. Maybe both of us. I'd rather not use my key unless I have to, and this will give me a chance to talk to Abel. You work on Delia and Grant." He leans down and kisses me on the cheek.

"Boy?" Mitchell is staring at him. "This ain't the time."

"Sorry, sir. She's with me. I had to give her the keys to my truck. Didn't want her stranded out here alone."

Mitchell glances at me, and there's a touch of sympathy in his blue eyes. "Can you drive, miss? If not, I can give you a lift into town. You'd have to sit next to Jody, but . . ."

My first thought is that I'd much rather ride in the back with Kiernan and Abel than up front with the jerk who hit him, but I shake my head. "I think I can handle it, sir."

I'm actually pretty positive that I *can't* handle it, given that I've never driven a car, let alone anything with a clutch, but Kiernan's right—I need to talk to Delia and Grant.

Mitchell looks around, scanning the area on both sides of the street. Everyone else is near their vehicles, about half of which have already pulled away. He rubs the bridge of his nose and huffs out a long breath.

"Dear Lord, what a mess," Mitchell says, more to himself than to me. He starts off toward his truck and then turns back. "You friends with the woman that fool Willis injured?"

I decide to go with the truth. "I know her, but not very well."

"I'm guessing that other fella took her into Athens to get her nose looked at. If you see 'em, tell her that they're gonna need to come back into Watkinsville and give a statement. Otherwise things could go a lot worse for her driver. Your young man should be out by nightfall, or tomorrow at the latest, dependin' on how annoyed the judge is at havin' to deal with all this. He got family around here? Anyone who can vouch for him aside from you?"

"His family is up in Boston, but his dad owns a farm over near Bogart. He has some friends over there."

"Well, all I can say is you both shoulda kept out of it. Yeah, I saw you stomp Willis's hand, but I'm gonna do you a favor and forget it. There's a fine line between brave and stupid, young lady. It ain't ever a good idea to get in the middle of these things."

I don't say anything, but I guess he can tell from my expression that I don't agree, and to his credit, he looks a little embarrassed. "I didn't say what Willis did was right. Not by a long shot. He's about as big an idiot as they come, and ever'body in town knows it. I'm just sayin' that it don't pay to interfere, especially when you ain't from around here."

I give him a curt nod but don't respond.

"Tell your friend to come on down to the jailhouse if you see her, okay?"

"Yes, sir."

When I turn back toward the road, Delia's car is no longer there, and I have no idea where they've gone. I climb into the cab of Kiernan's truck and lean my head back against the seat, taking a few deep breaths to settle my nerves. After about a minute, Mitchell pulls up beside me.

"You okay?" he asks, leaning across the guy he called Jody, who I'm delighted to see has a busted lip and rapidly swelling eye.

"Yes, sir," I respond. "Just need a minute to catch my breath."

He nods and drives away, pausing at the intersection as a couple of cars pass. Abel is sitting up now, propped against the corner of the truck bed. Kiernan waves as they pass, glancing at the spot where Abel and Delia's car had been. I just shrug, and then the truck turns right and disappears down the highway.

I wait until the last car pulls away, because I don't want an audience when I try to start this thing. I really wish I'd paid closer attention to what Kiernan was doing when he was driving. I stick the key into the ignition, scooching forward on the seat to reach the pedals, which are odd-looking round things rather than the type I'm used to seeing.

Nothing happens the first time I turn the key. I think it's because the seat is too far back and I can't push down hard enough, so I crouch down to search for the lever to adjust the seat.

"You'll need to use the clutch, love."

I jump at the voice, my head banging against the steering column.

"Holy crap, Kiernan. Could you give me a little warning next time?"

He's standing outside the truck in a clean shirt. His face has been washed, and the cut on his face is bandaged. He looks angry.

"Give me my gun back."

"Why? When . . . are you coming from?"

"Because I need it, and tonight around ten."

I hand him the gun. "Do I want to know why you need it?"

"Probably not." He sighs, and some of the anger seems to evaporate. "I don't want to screw things up worse than they already are by making you second-guess yourself. Just go with your instincts." He shoves the gun into his pocket. "And Kate?"

"Yes?"

"This other thing—with Pru. It's business." He reaches inside and tilts my chin toward him so that I can't look away. "Unpleasant business, but I'd do it again, even knowing the mistrust in your eyes. Just know that I have only ever loved one girl, and that girl is you. Past, present, future, this timeline or some other—still you."

And then he kisses me.

I don't kiss him back. Part of me wants to, but my rational side has a secret weapon now. All it has to do is toss up the visual of him with Prudence.

But I still can't quite bring myself to push him away.

"You said you weren't going to do that again without permission," I say when he pulls back.

"No. I said I'd *try*." Something apparently catches his eye at that point, because he grabs his CHRONOS key and blinks out.

Seconds later, Grant pulls up next to me in the blue car. I suspect he saw Kiernan, but it's hard to read his expression with his right eye swollen half-shut. I don't see Delia, so she must be lying down in the back.

That assumption is shattered as soon as Grant shuts off the engine and I hear the thumping inside the trunk.

Grant is still sitting behind the wheel when I tap on his window.

He rolls it down and I ask, "Why on earth did you put her in the trunk?"

"I didn't want to, but it's the only way I could keep her from running back over there. Abel is—"

"Her husband. Yes."

He looks across the street to where the cars were earlier. "Where is he?"

"Abel was arrested. So was the guy with me. Help me get Delia out of the trunk."

His expression borders on horror.

"Well, you knew you'd have to let her out eventually when you put her in there, didn't you?"

"Yes. But there weren't any alternatives. And she has a temper." His hand goes up to his swollen eye, so I'm guessing that's Delia's handiwork rather than something won in the fight.

We walk around to the rear of the car, and I knock on the trunk. "Delia? My name is Kate. You know my grandmother, Katherine Shaw. Grant is going to open the trunk now, and he's really very sorry for putting you in there. We're all on the same side, so no hitting anybody, okay? We need to focus on how to get Abel and Kiernan out of jail."

Grant eases the trunk open, and Delia props herself up, glaring first at me and then at him. Her face is a wreck, and her nose is very clearly broken. The skin on the bridge is split open, and the entire center of her face is beginning to discolor. Her sleeveless white blouse is now nearly as red as her skirt, and her face and arms are streaked with blood and tears.

"I don't know you," she says as she drags her feet over the edge of the trunk, one shoe missing. Her voice sounds like she has a really bad cold, which is hardly a surprise given the extent of the damage. "Where's Abel?"

"Abel and my friend Kiernan are on their way to the county jail. One of the guys here seems to have been a police officer of some sort. And like I said, you knew my grandmother at CHRONOS. Katherine Shaw?"

I pull out my phone.

"Looks like there've been some changes at CHRONOS," Delia says, her voice flat. "A lot of changes, if they're letting you carry that on a jump."

"I'm not exactly CHRONOS."

I click to play the recording of Katherine. It's a slight variation on the one I played for Timothy and Evelyn, the one I played for Adrienne at Port Darwin, and the one I would have played for Moehler if he hadn't been shot.

I watch Grant when Katherine reaches the part about Saul. His eyebrows go up a bit, and then a look of resignation settles on his face.

Katherine tossed in a comment about a training mission she was on with Delia and something about Abel and a sandwich. It doesn't make sense to me, but Delia's mouth twitches the slightest bit when Katherine says it. It's more of an about-to-cry twitch than an about-to-smile twitch, but I can tell Delia believes that it's really Katherine. Whether she believes what Katherine told her is another question.

"Well, that's interesting," Delia says. She reaches back into the corner, fishes out her other shoe, tugs it on, and starts climbing out of the trunk. Grant tries to help her, but she pushes him away. That's a mistake, because she's obviously light-headed. Grant props her back up when she stumbles, and she rewards him with a foul look before staggering over to the driver's side.

Grant says, "Maybe you should let me drive?"

Delia stands there for a minute and then says, "Have it your way." She works her way around to the passenger side, holding on to the front of the car as she goes.

I slide into the backseat. Delia mutters something about not inviting me, but I think Grant is relieved to have me along.

"Until we get Abel and Kiernan out, we need to stick together," I say, deciding to omit the part about me being unable to drive the truck.

She doesn't respond, just leans her head back against the seat as Grant starts the car. "Take a right at the intersection."

"We should find you a doctor first," Grant says. "You're still bleeding—"

"If Abel's in police custody, that's where we're going. This can wait."

"Delia," I say softly, "you're speaking as Abel's *wife*. But they assume you're his employer, and I'm pretty sure our chances of getting him out of this are much better if they keep on thinking he's your driver. That might be more believable if you get your face taken care of and change into fresh clothes before we talk to the judge or sheriff or whoever's in charge."

I can tell Delia really, really wants to disagree with me, but she knows I'm right. She slumps down in the seat, and Grant takes the left turn toward Athens.

"There's a hospital near the boardinghouse," he says. "On Milledge, I think—St. Mary's or something like that."

"Fine," Delia says. "But go to the stable point first. I want to try to pull up HQ. No offense, Kate—oh, hell, I don't care whether you take offense or not. I'm not buying your story, and I'd much prefer having CHRONOS Med patch up my face than some nun with a needle. And when they're done, Angelo can help me figure out a way to get my crew home safely."

I start to tell her that Angelo is dead—Katherine seems to have forgotten to mention that part this time around. But I decide that can wait. Delia is having a bad enough day, and the fact that her boss is dead in 2305 is truly a moot point when she's stuck here in 1938.

∞

Grant sinks down next to me on the wooden bench, which looks like a repurposed church pew. He's holding the compress that the nurse gave him against his swollen eye with one hand and a small paper cup of water in the other. The room is empty, aside from an elderly man slumped in a chair at the far end of the narrow waiting area, who's snoring loudly. I can understand why he's asleep. The heat makes you want to close your eyes and melt. The only thing the fan in the window seems to be accomplishing is sucking in more hot, humid air.

I waited in the car, on Delia's orders, while she and Grant tried their keys at a stable point located inside this odd, octagonal-shaped brick chapel next to a women's dormitory. They were gone maybe five minutes, and when they returned to the car, it was as if they'd switched roles. Grant led Delia back and helped her into the passenger seat. Neither said a word on the short drive to the hospital.

Delia found her voice as soon as we arrived at the hospital, however. The nurse, a very patient woman, who identified herself as Sister Sara, practically had to drag her into the examination room. Delia kept glancing back over her shoulder at us, all the way down the hall.

"Is Delia always this afraid of doctors?" I ask Grant, mostly to have something to say. The only thing he has uttered since leaving the stable point was a short, not-very-convincing promise to Delia that everything would be okay.

"I don't think she considers them doctors," he says. "Would you trust medical personnel from a few hundred years ago? Back when they still used leeches? I mean, they seem nice, and I'm sure they wouldn't hurt her intentionally, but . . ." He shrugs. "Now that

Delia's not here, you want to tell me why that other guy was with you when we pulled up?"

So he *had* seen Kiernan jump away. "Kiernan had to get something he'd left with me. He was jumping back from later today—tonight, actually."

"Did he say where Abel was?"

"No. He was kind of cryptic."

He opens his mouth to say something else, but I interrupt him. "You trained with Saul, right?"

"Yeah," he says, his hazel eyes growing wary. "Only once, two jumps before this one. No offense, since he's your grandfather and all, but he's a total ass."

"No offense taken. Did you come to that conclusion before or after hearing my grandmother in the video?"

"Before." He gives me a worried look. "You swear you're not with CHRONOS?"

Something in his tone of voice makes me smile. I was predisposed to dislike him, but he seems like a decent guy. "Cross my heart, hope to die. Pinky-swear, if you'd like."

"I'm not familiar with that last one, but I'll take your word. Let's just say Saul screwed me over on the training jump."

"What did he do?"

He gives me a long look again, like he's trying to decide whether to trust me, and then sighs. "Our jump was to Atlanta—September 1911. Some religious conference. I'm not a religious historian. I do nineteenth- and twentieth-century legal history. There was this string of murders in Atlanta—some two dozen black women were murdered in the last half of 1911. The papers dubbed the killer the Atlanta Ripper, and the cases were never solved. I wondered if they tried very hard, given the state of race relations at the time, so Angelo decides I should tag along with Saul and see if I could get an answer to that research question."

Grant drinks the last bit from the cup and then crushes it. "Apparently, he didn't ask Saul's opinion on the matter, because Saul was completely whizzed off to be stuck with a trainee. We get there, and Saul attends maybe one session at the conference, then says he's got a side trip planned. Claims a lot of the historians do it and tells me to hang out in Atlanta until he gets back. But I said no way. It was only my second jump, and I wasn't supposed to be left on my own for more than an hour, tops. So he says fine, I can come with—he's studying some small cult about two hours from Atlanta. It may even have been in this direction. I'm thinking a few counties over?"

"So . . . what happened?"

"We get there, and it's not much at all. An old lady runs the place, sort of like a collective farm. She was super friendly, offered to let us stay overnight, since it was late when we arrived." He shakes his head. "You ask me, it was all about some girl. She was half his age, too. Pretty enough, but . . . I'd even have considered her too young. Maybe Saul just gets off on breaking rules."

"That's a pretty safe bet."

"Anyway," Grant continues, "I got horribly sick that night. Saul says I was drunk, but I only had one glass of this homemade wine the old guy we were staying with gave us. He gave some to the girl, too, so I don't think it was very strong. Hell, I didn't even finish the glass—it was too sweet for me. Next thing I remember, it's the next day, and we're in the truck, halfway back to Atlanta. Saul tells me if I breathe a word to Angelo about the side trip, he'll say I took off and he found me trashed in a bar. But if I play along, he'll tell them I got food poisoning and that's why I came back with almost nothing for my research."

He tosses the cup into a wicker basket next to the bench. "CHRONOS Med checked me out pretty thoroughly when we got back, however, since Saul said I'd been sick. They never actually questioned the food-poisoning story, but I don't think they bought it. Or maybe I'm just a crappy liar. Anyway, the next jump, I'm scheduled with Delia, the most by-the-book trainer of the bunch. They must have told her something about the Atlanta jump, because she lectured me for a good hour before we left—said I was to watch and observe, and limit my interactions as much as possible without looking out of place. And what happens? Just by standing there, I manage to whizz off the biggest jerk in the crowd and get Abel arrested."

"Well, you can hardly be blamed for that."

"I should have punched the idiot myself. I really, really wanted to. But I held back, because I kept hearing Delia harping on about staying in the background. I already had one black mark on my record from the jump with Saul. I didn't want to add another."

A woman walks in, one child in front of her and two others trailing behind. The child in front is cradling her arm and looks a bit woozy. The woman leads her over to the reception desk and shoos the other kids to the waiting area, where they take the bench opposite us.

I slide over a little closer to Grant so that there's less likelihood of anyone overhearing us. "If you'd hit Willis, you'd be the one in jail."

"Yes, and that would be a billion times better. Like I said, I study legal systems. White man hits white man in 1938 Georgia, and even if he's a stranger, there's a decent chance that they'll listen to the outsider, especially if there are witnesses who back him. So I think your friend will be okay. Black man hits a white man, however—hits three, maybe four of them in this case—and reason flies out the window. And that Willis guy was getting his ass kicked before the others jumped in, so he's going to be in a vindictive mood."

One of the two kids, a girl of about nine, is watching us, possibly because we're spattered with blood. I tug at Grant's sleeve, nodding toward the door. The heat isn't much worse outside, and there's less chance of being overheard.

I tell the receptionist we'll be outside, and we walk out onto the porch of the hospital. The place looks more like someone's house than a medical center. There's a large shade tree on the lawn, and we sit down beneath it.

"We'll get Abel out," I say.

"I hope you're right. But even if we do, being stuck in 1938 isn't exactly good news for an interracial couple. And here's the irony—Abel's five or six shades darker than his parents. Delia's several shades lighter than hers. Why? CHRONOS doesn't need multiracial historians—they'd have a tough time blending in any time before the twenty-first century. So they tweak appearance as well when your parents sign you up. I don't look much like my family, either."

"So—they do that to all the historians?"

"Yeah," he says. "Hair color, eye color, skin tone—mostly stuff like that."

I'm silent for a moment, preoccupied with wondering what I'd look like if all four of my grandparents hadn't been genetically altered.

"Not that being stranded here is good news for me, either," Grant says. "On top of everything else, there's a draft coming up in a few years. I can't believe I could end up as a soldier, for God's sake. In an actual *war*—how ironic is that? This is just wrong on so many levels."

"I'm not sure my era is a lot safer right now—it's just that no one realizes they're in danger."

"And this danger in your time is from *Saul*?" Grant asks, with an incredulous look. "From these Cyrists he's created? I know he's a jerk, but . . ."

He's not convinced, and I don't blame him. And just as he did a few minutes ago with me, I stare into his eyes, trying to determine whether I can trust him. It's probably not a great method even when both eyes are readable, and one of his is now swollen almost completely shut.

He could be lying. He could be in on it with Saul.

I don't get that sense, however. I've seen a homicidal maniac quite recently—two, if you count Holmes along with Saul. Three, if you count Prudence, although Kiernan seems convinced that she views the Culling more as collateral damage. Grant *could* be that type, I guess—a true believer so intent on some cause that he sees human casualties as a necessary evil—but that seems hard to believe. He looks like an average guy who just got some really bad news—and who got the crap beaten out of him as well.

"What can you tell me about your time, Grant?" I can see that he's taken aback by what seems like an abrupt change of topic, so I add, "I'm not asking for spoilers, although I'm not sure they can really be considered spoilers when I'll be dead long before then. I'm just trying to get a sense of what Saul's people want to change. Are there trees in your time? Animals? Do you have to live under a bubble in order to breathe?"

He looks at me like I'm crazy. "No, to the last one. Yes, to the first two, although . . . it's nothing like what you have around here. We have parks in our urban areas, trees on most of the large housing centers. Wildlife refuges scattered around the world, and controlled numbers of most of the species that were endangered—they've even restored many that went extinct. At least, the ones that weren't dangerous."

"Do people still have political rights—like free speech, free religion, democratic government?"

"Yes, yes, and yes—although there are limits."

"What sort of limits?"

"Well, pretty much the same as here. No yelling fire in a crowded movie house. And even after we get past this racial nonsense, the U.S. isn't really a true democracy—you have representatives, right? So do most countries in my time."

"But are most people happy with the system? I'm trying to get a handle on why Saul and this club of his would be so dissatisfied with their situation that they'd be willing to wipe out half of humanity to change it."

"What club?"

"They called themselves the Objectivists. Apparently spinning off from some group from my era."

He laughs. "Those guys? They're . . . they're like a debate group or something."

"Katherine seemed to think the leader, somebody named Campbell, influenced Saul. That maybe he was in on the plan."

"Maybe, but I can't see it. All I ever heard Saul and Campbell do was argue. I went a few times—CHRONOS historians have an open invitation, because we can fill in some of the blanks about history. When I was there, they spent most of their time talking about alternate history." His voice takes on a pompous tone. "But what if the Revolutionary War had ended differently? If slavery hadn't been abolished or if the Progressive Era never happened? If this president or that one had lived or had died? If 2092 turned out differently?"

There's that date again. "So . . . what happens in 2092?"

Grant thinks for a moment and then shakes his head. "You'd be pretty old, but you could live that long, so I'm thinking that's a spoiler."

I narrow my eyes, but he's probably right. "Fine. Have it your way. So you're saying you'd go back there if you could? To your time?"

He looks at me like it's a really stupid question. "Yes."

"What if you'd been stranded in some time and place other than 1938 Georgia?"

"I'd still pick 2305. I have a life there. Someone who's expecting me to return." He glances over at the hospital. "Staying here isn't what I signed up for. It's an interesting time to study, but . . . I can't live here."

Grant could still be lying, but if so, he's really good at it. I think back to my conversation with Trey in the cafeteria. Maybe it's my golden-retriever personality coming to the forefront again, but Trey was right—I don't want to be the kind of person who believes the worst of everyone. It's bad enough to know that there's one individual out there who thought nothing of killing an entire village of innocent people to test out a theory, who even reveled in their deaths. The evidence, at least what I have at hand, doesn't point toward Grant being another one.

"If you have doubts about the Cyrists," I say, "whether they exist, their numbers, or whatever—the university is less than a mile away. Find the library, check a few history texts. Or go back inside and ask the receptionist for a phone book. There's a tiny Cyrist temple in Darwin, Australia, in 1942, so I'm guessing there's one or two around here as well.

"But," I continue, "if you're wondering about Saul, you've been around him more than I have. And even if you can't remember it, you were with him when he did a . . . test run. At the village—Six Bridges, God's Hollow—not sure what Saul would have called it. All but one of those people are dead, Grant. If the university has local newspaper archives, you can find proof of that. The date they died will synch up with when you were there with Saul."

He looks stunned. "How?"

"Something in the well. We're pretty sure he tested the antidote on the girl who survived. He would have killed her, too, but . . ." I hesitate. "Let's just say she got lucky."

"Martha, right? The blond girl?"

"Yes."

"She burned him, didn't she?"

The question catches me off guard at first, until I remember that Grant would have seen the wound on Saul's arm on their trip back.

"Something like that."

"He killed them all?" Grant asks. "Even the kids?"

"Yeah. Some of the articles had pictures." And, yes, I could show him with the CHRONOS key, but he'd also get a glimpse of me and Kiernan in biohazard gear, in addition to Saul, Martha, and the bodies in the chapel. If he finds out the role we played, it's going to lead to a lot of questions I don't have time to answer.

I stand and brush off my skirt. "I have to make a quick jump, okay? We need bail money, and I need clothes that aren't blood splattered. I'll wait here for Delia when I get back, if you want to go change or grab some lunch."

"No lunch," he says. "I've lost my appetite."

∞

BOGART, GEORGIA
August 11, 1938, 1:20 p.m.

I feel like I'm being watched.

I know it's my imagination. The odds of anyone viewing this stable point at this exact moment are slim to none. But I keep picturing Prudence and her followers—or keepers or whatever they are—here in Kiernan's kitchen earlier in the day. Well, earlier in the day for me. As far as I know, she hasn't actually been here since 1905, but it's still unnerving.

Someone else has been in the cabin since we left, however. A basket of peaches, cucumbers, tomatoes, and other vegetables is in the middle of the table, along with a half dozen Mason jars and a note from Mrs. Owens telling Kiernan to please let her know if he runs out of anything, because she has more than she knows what to do with. At least there are no religious tracts, so perhaps Owens decided to keep our presumed romantic adventures to himself.

I climb up the ladder and sit on the floor next to Kiernan's bed, which probably hasn't been slept in since 1905. It's not that the room is dusty—Mrs. Owens must come in to clean when he's away—but more that it just doesn't feel lived in.

I dig around under the mattress for several minutes before I locate the large manila envelope wedged between the mattress and the bedsprings in the upper rear corner. It's constructed of heavier paper and has one of those odd figure-eight string ties on the back, but it still reminds me of the envelope I left with Trey that held our collected memories from the other timeline.

It's mostly money inside, about $300 in ones, tens, and fives. There are also three pencil drawings that tumble out with the bills. The artist is no Da Vinci—I'm sure if we saw these hanging in a gallery, Sara would note that the perspective and proportions are off. Still, the work is very good for an amateur, and there's no mistaking the girl in each of these drawings, even in black and white. One of them was folded at some point, and there's a pattern of weathered creases on the page. That one is clearly of me, *this* me, sitting on a grassy bank, my feet in the water, with the towering buildings of the Expo in the background.

The other two drawings are my face, my body, but unless he's imagined the settings, they're all of Other-Kate. They could also be of Prudence, but I don't think so. The first drawing shows her in a boat that's slightly larger than the canoes we saw at Norumbega. There's a palm tree in the background, and I'm pretty sure the dress she's wearing is the one that I saw hanging from the bedpost when I watched the video she made at Estero.

The scene in the final drawing is more familiar. It's Kiernan's room back in Boston. The girl in the picture is curled on her side, asleep, her hair fanned out against the sheets. One arm is under the pillow, and the other rests on top, in an arc above her head, her hand near her face.

If you watch me sleeping on any given night, this is probably what you'd see. What you wouldn't see is the ring she's wearing.

Just a simple band. Ring finger, left hand.

∞20∞

Delia waits in a chair in the hallway, a large white bandage over the center of her face. Her blouse is still spattered, but the blood has dried, and they've washed her up a bit, so she looks less like a victim from a slasher film than when we brought her in.

Grant and I follow the nurse over to the reception desk. She leans toward us, her eyes troubled.

"Miss Morrell insists on being released, but the doctor thinks we should keep her overnight. We're concerned she may have a concussion. Did she fall as well?"

"No. Just the one blow to the face," Grant says, and then looks like he's remembered something. "But she may have bumped her head getting into the car. She was . . . upset."

The nurse jots something down on the clipboard. "We only found a small bump, but some of the things she's been saying are . . . odd. Does she have a history of psychiatric problems?"

Grant and I exchange a look.

"Not that I know of," I say. "I think all of this has just been a bit of a shock for her."

The nurse's expression is far from convinced, making me wonder exactly what Delia said back there. "I see. Does she have family in the area?"

She has a husband in a nearby jail. It won't help to note that, however, so I just shake my head.

She responds with a tsking sound and then shoots an uneasy look at Grant before glancing back at me. "And you say they *caught* the person who did this?"

We both catch her implication, and Grant's mouth tightens. I'm pretty sure he's about to explain, in no uncertain terms, that he's not the one who messed up Delia's face, so I jump in before he can begin.

"Yes, Sister. They have him in custody over in Oconee County."

Another shake of her head and another tsk. "Well then, I guess there's nothing to be done but to release her into your care."

To be honest, I kind of like the idea of Delia staying here overnight, sedated. I'm not sure how emotionally stable she is—not that I blame her, given everything that's happened. But my long-term goal is getting her to give up her CHRONOS key, which means getting her trust, and that's far less likely to happen if she thinks I had anything to do with keeping her here.

The nurse hands me a sheet of paper and says, "She needs to keep still and avoid activity. Even talking is ill-advised, otherwise those stitches may not hold. We gave her laudanum for the pain, and I'll send a few doses home with her. Just keep a careful eye on her. The doctor wants to see her again in a few days, after the swelling goes down, because we're pretty sure that nose needs to be reset."

Grant pays the bill, which I'm stunned to see is less than I've paid for a T-shirt—a cheap T-shirt—and then we walk Delia out to the car. I'm not sure what laudanum is, but it seems to have taken the edge off Delia's panic. Grant helps her into the backseat, and I sit up front with him, something I suspect she'd have balked at before her brief stay at St. Mary's. She leans her cheek against the seat, the purplish-black circles under her eyes vivid next to the white bandage.

As he pulls away from the curb, Grant whispers, "Do you think she's going to be able to talk to a judge or whatever in this condition?"

"*She* is awake," Delia says, "and would appreciate being included in the conversation."

"Sorry, Delia." Grant shoots me a look, because even though her brain seems engaged, the words are slurred.

I shrug, and he continues. "While you were seeing the doctor, I drove to the university library and did a little research on these Cyrists. Kate's story checks out, at least concerning their existence and early history. There were some images of paintings that show this Cyrus, and he looks a lot like Saul to me."

Before Delia was released, Grant told me that he also pulled up information on Six Bridges, but he doesn't mention that. And that's fine with me, since it would raise issues I don't think we need to get into right now.

"I also bought this." Grant reaches into his pocket, pulls out a small copy of the *Book of Cyrus*, and tosses it onto the backseat.

Delia looks at the cover for a few seconds, then drops it back on the seat, closing her eyes again. "Did you read it?"

"The entire thing? No. I thumbed through it. It's boring. Repetitive. Some parts are a bit creepy, if you ask me."

Their boardinghouse is about ten blocks from the hospital. I help Delia inside and up the stairs so that she can change, while Grant stays downstairs to fend off questions from the landlady.

Several minutes pass, and I'm still waiting, so I tap on her door. No response. I knock again and then check the handle. It's not locked, so I ease it open.

"Delia? Are you okay?"

She's sitting sideways across the narrow bed, eyes closed, her back propped against the wall. "I'd have to say no. Why are you here?"

"Grant and I were worried that—"

"No," she says, opening her eyes to look directly at me. "Why are you *here*?"

"Like Katherine said in the video, I need to collect your CHRONOS keys so that Saul's people—"

"So why don't you pull out that gun and take it?"

I take a deep breath, annoyed both that she spotted the gun and that she keeps interrupting me. And then she interrupts me again, before I can even start to answer.

"We were unarmed," she says, once again closing her eyes. "You could have snatched the keys the minute we arrived. We might have fought you, but you'd have won, given the gun and the element of surprise. So why'd you wait?"

I sit down in the wicker chair across from the bed and consider my answer. At this point, I don't see what harm can come from leveling with her. "We tried that once, in a different timeline. Snatching your keys. There were . . . repercussions."

"For you or for us?"

"Both. Shortly after, someone snatched *my* key. Apparently Katherine's as well. Then Saul's people made some rather major shifts to the timeline."

"But you're still here."

"It was a different version of me, if that makes any sense. Different Katherine as well. But I have the diary the other Kate kept. I know some of what happened to you and Abel in that timeline. And what happens in this one, if we don't find a way to prevent it."

"So? I'm supposed to avoid talking, remember? Stop making me ask questions."

"Oh. Okay. Sorry. You end up teaching at a school up in New England." I glance down at my hands, dreading my next words. But there's no way to sugarcoat this, so I just spill it. "Abel doesn't make it out of Georgia. I don't have the details, but he's killed sometime within the next day or so."

Delia doesn't react. Either she was expecting this, which could well be the case, given the events earlier today, or that laudanum stuff is very potent. "Grant?"

"No clue. Katherine couldn't find any record of him, and you either didn't know or wouldn't tell her when she tracked you down in the 1970s."

"The same thing happened to Abel in both timelines?"

I nod. "To the best of my knowledge, yes. Except we're going to change it this time around."

"How?"

"That's the part we haven't figured out yet, since it kind of depends on how and when he's killed. The first step is getting you to Watkinsville so we can see what the charges are and whether they're going to set bail for Abel and Kiernan. They think Abel is your driver, so maybe they'll release him into your custody if you say you'll leave the state. I mean, he was trying to protect you."

"Have you run that little plan by Grant?" she says disdainfully.

"He's not optimistic."

"Smart boy."

"I'm not optimistic either, but the first steps are still going to be the same, right? We need to get back to Oconee County and see what we're up against."

∞

WATKINSVILLE, GEORGIA
August 11, 1938, 4:32 p.m.

"You could drive around a few minutes, and we'd find it, Grant," Delia says. "It's not like this is New York or Atlanta or even Athens."

"Or just stop, and I'll go in instead," I say. "My face hasn't been punched, so I'm less likely to attract attention."

Delia slumps down in the seat, shaking her head. "Right. A stranger asking where the jail is located in a tiny little burg like this won't attract any attention at all."

"We need gas anyway," Grant says.

That ends the argument. It's very likely that this Buick will be used as a getaway car in the next twenty-four hours, and a nearly empty tank would be a definite liability.

"If that's the case, no one needs to get out," Delia says.

That doesn't make sense to me until Grant pulls into the tiny station on Main Street and a young man leaning against the wall hurries over to the driver's side. "Fill 'er up?"

"Yes, please."

Despite the fact that it's late afternoon, it's still horribly hot in the car, even with the windows open. A thermostat near the store's door displays two bathing beauties seated on the Coca-Cola logo—one from 1886 and the other from 1936. According to the mercury, it's ninety-one degrees. In the shade.

And I'm thirsty.

As soon as I open the door of the small store, three sets of eyes latch onto me. Two sets belong to the middle-aged man and woman behind the counter, neither of whom I've ever seen. Another man, slightly younger, is perched on top of a large red cooler at the back of the store. He was in the crowd earlier today, but I can't remember which group he was in—the one trying to beat Abel to a pulp or the one doing nothing to stop it.

When I start moving in his direction, he hops up, walking toward the window, probably to get a better view of Delia and Grant. I take three sodas from the cooler and grab three Moon Pies and a bag of chips from a nearby shelf.

"Forty-two cents. You payin' for the gasoline, too?" the woman asks.

"Yes, ma'am."

"Gonna have to wait a minute then, 'cause Dale ain't done fillin' your tank. There's a bottle opener on the edge of the counter for the Co-Colas."

I nod and pop off the caps before asking, "Could you tell me how to get to the jail?"

The younger guy has resumed his post on the cooler and says, "You drove in from Athens, right? Go back the way you come in, and take a left on Third, a few blocks down. Corner of Third and Water Street. Which fella you hopin' to spring?"

"Both." Even though I try to keep my voice neutral, it comes out sounding a bit defiant.

He grins, but it doesn't feel friendly. More like he's poking fun at me.

"Only reason I'm asking is 'cause one's already out. You can prob'ly find him over at the Eagle. Don't know if he's stayin' there or just gettin' a bite to eat, but Mitchell and some other guy walked him over maybe fifteen, twenty minutes ago."

"Thank you," I say.

He doesn't respond. The woman at the register says, "Three dollars gas, so that'll be three forty-two."

I hand her a five, and she counts back the change. "And a dollar fifty-eight makes five." Then she pushes the paper bag toward me and adds in a low voice, "Y'all might want to finish your business in town in the next coupla hours, hon."

"Frieda." It's the other man, who's been so silent up to this point that I'd almost forgotten about him. There's a note of warning in his voice, and his wife's eyes narrow slightly, but she doesn't say anything more.

I give her a quick nod of thanks, grab my purchases, and leave.

"The jail is a few blocks back, on Third Street," I tell Delia and Grant as I climb into the car. "We drove right past it. But Kiernan's already out. The guy inside said he was at the Eagle—sounds like it might be a hotel. He said across the street, but maybe he meant across from the jail. We should stop there first, in case he knows what's going on with Abel."

Grant takes his soda and gulps most of it down before starting the car. I glance back at Delia and see that drinking from a bottle is going to be a challenge for her. "Should I go back in and see if they have a straw?"

"I'll manage."

I take a sip of the Coke as Grant takes a left back onto Main. "If either of you are hungry, there's food in the bag."

I see the sign for the Eagle Tavern and Boardinghouse on the right about thirty seconds later. It's an old building, and it looks kind of misshapen, as though sections have been added on over the years.

Kiernan is halfway to the door when I step inside, so he must have been watching for us. The right side of his face is swollen, both along the lower jaw and around the cut on his cheek, but someone must have found him a shirt. He pulls me into a hug and then leads me to a table with three coffee cups and three mostly empty plates in the center.

The place is small, and while it isn't exactly packed, it looks like it's doing unusually good business for a late Thursday afternoon.

About half of the tables are full, and all of the stools at the bar are taken. Most of the occupants keep sneaking looks in our direction.

"What's going on?" I ask.

"I'm charged with disorderly conduct. The judge will rule tomorrow, but Mr. Peele, that's the attorney I told you about, who handles stuff for the farm? Anyway, he has me out for now, but I can't leave the county."

"So why did you need me to go and get the money?" Thinking about getting the money brings his drawings to mind, and my face flushes. Did he even remember those drawings were in the envelope? Or maybe he wanted me to see them.

"I didn't think about calling Peele until I reached the jail. And we'll need the money anyway."

"We got their stuff from the boardinghouse and also stopped by the bank to get their new papers and stuff from the safety-deposit box, in case they need to make a quick getaway. So Delia has some money now, too, if you need more for bail."

He winces. "It's not going to be that simple, I'm afraid. That's what we were talking about here." He nods over at the empty plates on my side of the table. "Peele's willing to represent Abel, if need be, although he's not exactly enthusiastic about it. Might have to reassess my choice of attorney at some point. I barely got to talk to Abel in the truck—just long enough for us to plan a cover story. They tossed him into a cell upstairs as soon as we got to the jail. The judge hasn't set bail for him, last I heard. And even if we could get him out on bail, I'm not sure it's a good idea."

"Why not?"

"Did you see the crowd across from the jail?"

"No. We haven't been there yet. We were on our way, but the guy at the Texaco station said you were here, so . . ."

He pulls my chair over a little closer to his so that I can see out the window. Across Main Street, a block down on the right side of

Third, about a dozen people are gathered. Maybe a dozen more are hanging out in front of the courthouse directly opposite the Eagle.

"Willis was bailed out just before I was," Kiernan says. "The guys over by the jail are a bunch of his buddies. Willis is claiming the knife was Abel's and that Abel tried to kill him. His nephews are backing him up, and so is that fool Jody I was fighting. Mitchell says maybe a dozen others say they saw it, too—although half of them weren't even there. Mitchell and that guy with the camera— can't remember his name—they're telling the truth. Some others, too, but I'm not sure it's going to make a difference."

"But . . . Mitchell's, like . . . a deputy or something, right?"

"Not exactly. Georgia State Patrol. They've only been around about a year, and there's still a bit of friction between him and the county officers. Some residents think Mitchell and the state shouldn't be poking around in local affairs. And the camera guy—"

"Phillips."

"Yeah, that's right. He works for the Athens paper. Still lives here, his dad's the town dentist, but Mitchell says the general consensus is that Phillips thinks his"—he gives a wry grin and clears his throat—"his feces . . . have no odor. Not exactly how Mitchell put it, but you get the point. His word won't count for much."

"So what's the charge?"

"Hasn't been decided yet. Willis is arguing attempted murder."

"And you think the judge will listen?"

He shakes his head. "I don't know. All I know is that Mitchell is convinced Abel is safer in jail than he'd be if we try to move him. And he may be right."

"Then what should we do?"

"Delia needs to give her statement. So do you and Grant. On Mitchell's advice, I booked two rooms here—one for me and Grant and one for you and Delia—so bring your things in and leave them upstairs." He casts a meaningful glance down toward my pocket, where the Colt is hiding.

Yeah. Probably not a good idea to take that into the jail.

He glances around and lowers his voice even further. "I told Abel we'd get him out, one way or the other. But Delia needs to tread very carefully. I don't know what she said. Maybe nothing. But certain *rumors* are going around about the nature of her relationship with Abel."

∞

The man behind the desk—Deputy R. Beebe, according to his badge—is young and thin, with a splotchy complexion. The sweat stains under the arms of his uniform spread out like tree rings, so I'm guessing he's had a long, hot day. He looks nervous, like he's wishing this was all over. I know I am.

Delia gave her statement first, and she's waiting outside with Grant now, in the chair I occupied for the half hour she was in here with Beebe. Grant and I didn't talk much, since there was an officer watching us from the desk in the corner. There were no magazines or newspapers. I have a sneaky feeling they do that on purpose. It felt a lot like when I was a kid and my mom would send me to the time-out chair with no book or music, just the command to sit there and think about what I'd done.

I give Deputy Beebe the cover story the four of us rehearsed in the car. Kiernan and Abel decided on the way to the jail that they'd need to drop the Federal Writers' Project cover story Delia's group had been using, because it would be easy to check that with a few phone calls. The new story is that Kiernan and I know Grant, Delia, and Abel because we're members of the same church up in Boston. Delia is writing a book, so her group has been doing research in Athens for several months. Kiernan is registered to attend the university in the fall—and he actually *is* registered, if they bother to check. I'm Kiernan's fiancée, and I'm in Georgia to visit the university, since I'm considering enrolling, too. Kiernan and I decided to drive over this morning to see if we could catch a glimpse of the president here, since it was too crowded in Athens. The CHRONOS keys we're wearing are religious medals of St. Eligius, patron saint of clock makers—a standard CHRONOS cover story and subtle in-joke, because Eligius foresaw the time of his own death.

I happily walk over to Beebe's desk when he asks to see the medallion, taking the opportunity to set a local stable point before sticking it back in the pouch. He looks at me like I'm crazy as I run my fingers in the air above the key, shaking his head at what must look like a weird religious ritual. I've set two other points in the front office and one in the restroom, which sits at the back of the building near the stairwell going up to the cell block. Kiernan managed to set one in the corridor between the cells and one in the stairwell going down to the front office. Whether they'll be of any use remains to be seen.

After I finish with the cover story and my version of the fight, Beebe starts asking questions, most of them multiple times, in slightly different ways. This is the third time he's asked about Willis's hand.

"No, sir." It feels weird to call someone this young *sir*, but Beebe seems like the type who enjoys being in authority, so I follow Katherine's advice. "As I said before, I didn't stomp anybody. It's possible someone shoved me onto his hand. All I remember is some man picking me up and yanking me backward. I was standing near where Delia—Miss Morrell, that is—had just been assaulted, and everything was kind of crazy."

"From what I've been told, what happened to Miss Morrell was an accident, not an assault."

I shrug my shoulders and frame an answer that avoids an out-right lie. "I can't know what that man's *intent* was. All I know is that I saw him hit her very hard with his elbow. He knew he hit her, and he didn't even stop to see if she was okay. Most people would apologize or at least check on the person they'd hit if it was an acci-dent, especially if it was a lady. Wouldn't you agree, sir?"

He doesn't answer the question, just kind of grunts, but I can tell from his expression that he does agree, even if he isn't inclined to admit it. "Were you watching when the Negro pulled the knife?"

He says it as *niggra*, a slight step above the slur that Willis used but still bad enough to bug the hell out of me.

"No, sir," I say through gritted teeth. "No one else was watch-ing either, because that never happened. I was, however, watching when Mr. Willis—"

"Mr. Felton," he snaps. "Willis is his first name."

"Fine. I was watching when Mr. *Felton* pulled the knife out of his pocket."

"Which pocket?"

He didn't ask that the first time, so I have to stop and think for a minute. "His right pocket. He pulled it out, kind of flicked it open, and then he lunged at Mr. Waters."

"And you're sure of that?"

"Absolutely positive."

"Was this before or after Miss Morrell was injured?"

I sigh, because this is getting really tedious. I suspect it's stan-dard procedure to ask the same things over and over, but I wish he'd wrap it up. "After. As I said before, at least twice. The fight broke out when Mr. Waters suggested Mr. Felton should apolo-gize. Then Mr. Felton stopped picking on Grant—Mr. Oakley—and started in on Mr. Waters."

"And exactly why are you in Georgia, Miss Keller?"

As I repeat that information for the second time, it occurs to me that there is at least one advantage to life in the 1930s. In my own time, a quick online check of any part of this cover story would expose us as frauds in five minutes flat.

"Is Mr. Waters also a member of this church?"

"Yes."

The deputy's nostrils pinch in a tiny bit at that, and I have to remind myself to keep my expression neutral.

"What is the nature of his relationship with Miss Morrell?"

"Are you asking about Mr. Oakley or Mr. Waters?"

"I was referring to Mr. Waters," he says, "but you can answer for both."

"Mr. Waters and Mr. Oakley are her colleagues. They are also members of our church. I believe Mr. Oakley is her cousin as well."

"And there is no . . . romantic . . . involvement between Miss Morrell and either of them?"

I take a deep breath, reminding myself that the goal is to get everyone out of here alive, not to school this guy on his racist attitudes. Then I paste what I hope is an offended expression on my face. "Well, I would certainly hope not! Like I said, I think Grant is her cousin. And Mr. Waters, well . . . why would you even suggest something like that? Did you ask *her* that question? No wonder she looked so—"

"I think that's all we need, Miss Keller." He shuffles the papers in front of him. "You're staying at the Eagle until the arraignment?"

"Since we've been told not to leave the area, yes."

"Then we'll be in touch if we need any more information. Could you send in . . ." He glances down at the paper in front of him and flips back to my statement. "Mr. Oakley."

I give him a curt nod and go back to where Delia and Grant are seated.

"You're next," I tell Grant. "Have fun."

"Yeah," he says, glancing around the office. "You, too."

Delia's eyes aren't as glazed as they were earlier, but the circles below seem darker. She washed up at the hotel, but sitting next to her, I see that her hair is still matted together in spots from the blood. And I suspect the laudanum is wearing off. Her shoulders are stiff, and she's shaking slightly, like she has chills or maybe she's on the verge of losing it.

"Are you okay?"

"They won't let me see him," she says in a whisper almost too soft to hear, her jaw clenched, her lips barely moving. A single tear sneaks out and is instantly soaked up by the gauze bandage across her face. "I *need* to see him."

I reach over and squeeze her hand. "We'll get him out, Delia."

∞

It's after six when Grant comes out, his hands curled into tight fists by his side. "He says we can go."

I tug at Delia's sleeve, and we follow him outside onto the small porch attached to the building. Kiernan is parked in front, the rear passenger door lined up with the base of the porch steps. There's no question why he decided we needed chauffeur service, even with the Eagle barely a block away. The crowd across the street is twice the size it was when we entered, and the window on the driver's side is smeared with mud and other substances that I can't—and probably don't want to—identify.

As we're getting in, an egg splats against the back of the car. A few younger guys step out in front, and Kiernan guns the engine threateningly. Others are moving toward us, and then everyone stops, looking past us toward the jail.

"Y'all quit causin' trouble. I don't wanna have to write you up."

It's the first time I've seen Beebe standing, and my eyes slide down to the belt around his waist—a gun on his right and a key ring clipped to a loop on his left.

A gangly-looking guy, who seems to be the ringleader, says, "What I don't understand is why you ain't out here with us, Rudy." Beebe's face turns red, and everyone starts laughing. Then the one who spoke to him spits on the windshield of the Buick and struts back across the street.

I scan the faces in the crowd as Kiernan drives away. It's mostly men, although I see a few younger women sitting in the back of a pickup truck. Some older kids, too—a few of them look like they're no more than nine or ten.

We're almost to the intersection when a bright flash of blue light pulls my eye toward one of the cars near the back of the crowd. It's gone as quickly as it appeared. Two patrol cars are parked on that side of the road, a few yards beyond the crowd. It was probably just a reflection, but for a moment, it looked like a CHRONOS key. I turn back to see if I can get another look through the rear window, but it's nearly as gunked up as the sides.

"Did you see a flash of light over there?" I ask Kiernan.

"What kind of light?"

"Blue." I glance pointedly at his chest.

"You're sure?"

"No," I admit. "Not even slightly. It was probably a reflection from outside . . . maybe even from inside."

There are, after all, four CHRONOS keys in the car, and even if they're tucked inside clothing, they still cast a bit of light.

"Never mind. I probably imagined it."

He reaches over and squeezes my hand, then turns the car into the lot behind the Eagle. The tavern is busy, with about a dozen cars in the parking lot already.

"I'm going to pull up to the back door," Kiernan says. "You three get out, and I'll park."

"Let Delia and Grant out. It's mostly men, and they're less likely to cause trouble if I'm with you."

Kiernan glances skeptically at Delia's face in the rearview mirror.

"Yeah," I say, "but Willis didn't plan that. I doubt he regrets it, but it wasn't planned. If you're alone or with Grant and someone picks a fight, it's your word against theirs. If it's you and me, more people will believe they started it. Although, the mood I'm in right now, if one of them even looks at me wrong, he's going down."

A tiny smile lifts one corner of his mouth. "Then I guess it's you and me, love."

He seems to think I'm joking, but I'm not. I don't know if it was being at the jail or the creepy sensation of everyone watching us when we walked out or maybe that probably-imaginary flash of blue, but the whole thing has me on edge.

Just as Grant opens the back door, a dark gray car marked *Georgia State Patrol* pulls up.

Mitchell rolls down his window, glancing down at the crud on the side of the Buick. "Looks like y'all encountered some mud puddles. And a henhouse. Maybe an outhouse, too."

"Not by choice," Kiernan says.

"Yeah, I seen 'em over by the jail. Mostly kids who are bored—not much to do around here—but there are a few troublemakers in the bunch, too. Anyway, I just drove by Mars Hill Road, and I see your truck's still there. Not a good idea to leave it aside the road like that. Why don't you walk Miss Keller inside, and then I'll drive you out to get it?"

Mitchell must catch my expression, because he shakes his head and laughs. "Or Miss Keller is welcome to ride with us, if she'd prefer. Go ahead and park. If you're worried about the folks under the trees over there, they ain't gonna be a problem. They're just watchers. If they were the rowdy type, they'd be over with the boys who used your car for target practice."

Grant gives me a nod and takes Delia inside. Kiernan parks the car, and then we both get into the back of Mitchell's sedan.

"I hope they weren't too rough on you and your friends over at the jail, Miss Keller. Was it the sheriff or Rudy Beebe givin' you the third degree?"

"You can call me Kate," I say. "It was Beebe. He wasn't too rough on me. Haven't had much chance to talk to Grant and Delia, but I think they got the worse end of the deal."

"Yeah, I figured it was Beebe. Sheriff Parks had his appendix out on Monday, so I doubt he'll be in unless things get crazy." Mitchell fishes a cigarette out of his pocket. "I don't know if your fiancé mentioned it, we've got a bit of a balancin' act goin' on here. There's not much love lost between me and Sheriff Parks, or the judge for that matter, but neither of 'em want to see your Negro friend wrongfully prosecuted. Less sure about Beebe, but . . . he'll do what his boss tells him. The bigger issue is that the sheriff and judge don't want to lose the next election. And Willis is Judge Cramer's second cousin on his mama's side. Even though Cramer knows Willis is a lyin' fool, he's probably gonna pretend to believe him. My guess is he calls it aggravated assault and your friend'll be out in a year or so."

I stare at him in the rearview mirror. "A year or so? For something he didn't do?"

"That's the best I think you can hope for, yes. Less than that and I think we could have some trouble. The whole reason you got that crowd across the street right now is that they're worried Cramer's gonna be too soft—and some of them are going to say anything short of attempted murder is too soft."

"But why? It was self-defense! Anyone who was there knows that knife belonged to Willis."

"Yeah, but your friend hit Willis, so most of them are willing to overlook that. Add to that the fact that he ain't from here. That's a negative in your column as well, young man. And even though I was born and raised about fifteen miles from here, the fact that I'm now driving a Georgia State Patrol car means I'm at least halfway to outsider in the eyes of a lot of these folks. We're lucky they even listened to me today—"

"Willis hit him first," Kiernan says. "All he did was say Delia was owed an apology."

"I already told you it wasn't what he said. It was the way he said it." He exhales just as I inhale, and I'm behind him, so I pull in a lungful of foul-smelling smoke. "The Morrell woman didn't help matters, screaming out his name like she did as y'all were draggin' her away. Now we got rumors goin' round that this Waters guy is doin' more than just drivin' her car . . . and that's illegal in the state of Georgia. It don't take much to get somethin' started around here, and men have been lynched for a whole lot less. Nine men were dragged out of that very same jail a little over thirty years ago, tied to a fence, and shot by a firing squad of about a hundred, mostly because they decided the jail was too full."

"So what makes you think Abel's safer in there?" I ask. "Sounds like it didn't work so well for those nine men."

Mitchell's mouth tightens. "Miss Keller, every decent man and woman in this town would like to avoid a repeat of that night, and most of the people here are good people. But then you got maybe fifty, sixty damn fools out there right now who want to drag him out and lynch him just for the hell of it. Half of 'em probably ain't even from this county, and most of those who are know full well the man ain't guilty of any crime greater than bein' an uppity Negro. As the story of what happened today makes the rounds, it'll get worse—that mob across from the jail will be double by midnight, and most of 'em will be drunk. I'm just hopin' Cramer's smart enough to keep his mouth shut about which way he's leanin' on sentencing until tomorrow."

"So Abel doesn't even get a trial? It's up to this judge?" I ask.

Mitchell shakes his head, and from the look on his face, he must think I've asked a really dumb question. He takes another draw on the cigarette and says, "If you think a jury trial would make things better for your friend, you don't understand the situation at all."

He takes the left onto Mars Hill and does a U-turn in the middle of the road, pulling up behind Kiernan's truck.

"I'm gonna follow you back to the Eagle. I think you're both smart enough to know you need to stay inside until tomorrow. The food at the Eagle ain't the best, but it will keep you alive."

Kiernan nods and says, "Thanks for the ride, Mr. Mitchell."

"The ride wasn't nothin'," Mitchell says. "What you need to thank me for is the advice. I know y'all don't like what I've been sayin'. I don't blame you. And again, I ain't sayin' it's right. I'm just tellin' you how it is, so you can prepare yourselves and your friends, especially if he really is her man and not just her driver. There ain't no happy endin' where Abel Waters gets back in that car tomorrow and drives off into the sunset."

∞21∞

The Eagle's boardinghouse is small, just four stale-smelling rooms that share a single bath in the hallway. The four of us are huddled in Grant and Kiernan's room, because it has a window that faces the street. Our view is obstructed, however—partly by the trees outside and partly by the cars along the street, so we're mostly watching what's happening through the CHRONOS keys.

Delia's eyes have barely moved since we transferred the stable points from the jail to her key so that she could see Abel's cell. Kiernan is monitoring two of the stable points he set facing the crowd outside the jail. I split my viewing time between the other exterior point and one aimed at the corridor between the cells and the door into the cell block. Grant moves back and forth between the point in Beebe's office, where the deputy has been catching a nap at his desk for the past twenty minutes, and the one I set near the front desk. He's looking for a block of at least three minutes where the front desk is unmanned and Beebe is snoozing, but no luck so far.

Kiernan and I have pretty much concluded that the only way to get Abel out is through the bathroom window downstairs. We'll have to get the keys, get him out of the cell and downstairs, and all of that's going to need to happen at a time when the front desk is empty. There are only two bright spots—the office is under-manned, with the sheriff recuperating, and Abel was the last person left in the cells after Kiernan was released. The fewer people in that building when we go in, the better.

I finally convinced Delia to eat half of a Moon Pie and take another dose of the laudanum around eight. I'm very glad I did, because a half hour later, Beebe strolled past the cell carrying Abel's dinner— an unwrapped sandwich, which he tossed through the bars and onto the floor. Abel just gave the sandwich an idle glance and left it there. Delia, however, started cursing and was ready to storm across the street and rip Beebe's head off. If the laudanum hadn't already started kicking in, we'd have had to physically restrain her.

Sounds from the street drift in through the open window. The low hum of crowd chatter blends with the occasional addition of a racial slur, drunken laughter, or a war whoop. It seems to have gotten louder in the past hour, although Kiernan thinks that may be due to more alcohol rather than more people. Mitchell's estimate of the mob across from the jail is about right—maybe sixty in all, although it seems like maybe it's thinned out a little in the past half hour. There are maybe fifty more hanging around on this side of Main Street and in front of the courthouse, but they aren't causing trouble. Most of them seem more worried than entertained. The ones across from the jail, however—the ones Kiernan and I are watching through the keys—are obviously ready to rumble.

When I see the blue flash again, it lasts maybe a second before something moves in front of it, blocking my view. About ten seconds later, I see it again. I note the time and rewind thirty seconds so that Kiernan can watch as well.

He views it twice before saying, "Yeah, I see a blue light."

I tense up, and then what he's said sinks in. If the light was from a CHRONOS key, Kiernan would see it as green, not blue. "Not green?"

"Nope." He yawns and stretches. "Keep an eye on both of those points outside the jail for a few minutes, okay? I'm going down to the kitchen to see if they'll make us up a few sandwiches and maybe grab some sodas or a pitcher of water. It could be a long night."

"I'll come with you," Grant says just as I'm opening my mouth to say the same thing. "I need to stretch my legs."

Kiernan shrugs and looks at me. "You and Delia okay here on your own?"

I nod, grudgingly, and Delia mumbles, "We're fine."

They've been gone maybe ten minutes when I see the blue flash again.

I move over to the other twin bed, where Delia's sitting, propped up against the wall, still keeping vigil over Abel. "Delia, can you take a look at this? Look for a brief flash of light."

She pulls her eyes away from her own key and stares at mine. "Hmph," she says a few seconds later. "Somebody has a CHRONOS key."

Okay. It's still *possible* that Kiernan isn't lying to me. "What color are the keys for you, Delia?"

"Lilac."

The door opens, and Grant walks in, carrying a paper bag and a pitcher of water. I look behind him for Kiernan, but he's alone.

"Where's Kiernan?"

He looks confused. "Maybe the bathroom?"

I push past him and run down the hall to the bathroom. I knock. No answer. I bang on the door again and then try the handle. It's unlocked. It's also empty.

I head back to the room. "I can't find him, Grant. Did he come up the stairs with you?"

Grant is next to the window, looking out at the front lawn. "No. He handed me the bag of sandwiches at the foot of the stairs and said he'd be up in a minute. I didn't think . . ." He shrugs. "Should we—"

Whatever he planned to say is interrupted as a large brick sails past his head, landing about a foot in front of me. It's carrying a note held in place by a rubber band.

Grant bends down and pulls the note out.

"What does it say?"

He holds it up so that I can see—*nigger lovers go home*, scrawled in big letters—then crumples it and tosses it on the floor.

After closing the window—something that seems a little counterproductive when they're throwing bricks—he sits down next to Delia and pulls up the jailhouse on his key. "Something's happening. I can't tell what they're saying, but they arrested three people."

"What time?" I ask.

"Umm . . . 9:34."

"Have they taken them upstairs yet?"

"No," he says. "They're sitting in the chairs where we were."

Well, that's a small break. Abel is currently the only one in the cell block. Things are going to be a lot more complicated if it gets crowded in there.

Bam. Bam-bam-bam.

I jump, and so does Grant. Delia, still in her own little laudanum-laced universe, keeps her eyes on the key. The nurse said one to two teaspoons, but I'm starting to think maybe giving her the maximum dose was a bad idea.

Glancing through the peephole, I see the owner of the Eagle, wearing a stained apron and an angry, frightened expression. She steps in and runs her eyes around the room, pausing on Delia and then traveling down to the brick in front of my feet, which she snatches from the floor.

"Lights out," she says, reaching up to yank the long string hanging down from the single dim bulb above our heads. Then she reopens the window.

"If y'all ain't ready to sleep, stay in the other room you rented. I ain't havin' them damn fools bust out my windows 'cause you can't resist peekin' outside."

I'm about to argue, but Grant says, "Yes, ma'am. We understand. But—before you leave, what happened? The crowd outside seems to be getting louder and," he says, glancing down at the brick in her hand, "less law-abiding."

Her eyes narrow, like she's deciding whether to tell us, and then she says, "Cramer's gonna charge your niggra friend with aggravated assault. Willis Felton's buddies think he's bein' let off too easy."

She leaves, slamming the door behind her. Grant glances at Delia and then says to me, "That's good news, right? Earlier they were talking attempted murder."

"Maybe," I say, remembering Mitchell's comment from earlier. "But the fact that the crowd got wind of it tonight, when they're angry and half-drunk, is definitely *not* good news."

As if to emphasize my point, two pickups drive into view, with six or seven men in the back of each truck. A few of them are in white hoods, and all of them have their faces covered in some fashion. And they're all carrying rifles.

"Delia," I say, grabbing her elbow. "Come on. We need to move."

Grant follows, his eyes glued to his CHRONOS key. Once Delia's inside the other room, he pulls me aside and says in a low voice, "They're inside the jail. Beebe's going to hand him over. If you've got any ideas about how to fix this, now's the time."

I'd really hoped I'd have a partner for this, but I seem to be on my own. *Damn it, Kiernan.*

I run to the window overlooking the parking area out back. There are two or three people standing around, but almost everyone seems to have moved closer to the front so that they can see what's happening. The Buick is right where we left it, and Kiernan's truck is missing.

"Do you have the key to the Buick?"

Grant nods, pulling it out of his pocket.

"Okay, I think you can get to the car. Pull it up to the back door. When I see you in position, I'll head downstairs with Delia."

"What about Kiernan?" he asks.

"His truck is gone. Wherever he went, he's on his own. We're going to have our hands full getting Abel."

As soon as Grant leaves, I pull the gun out from under the mattress where Delia is sitting. She gives me a mildly concerned glance as I carry it over to the window, and then she goes back to the key.

I open the window and wait for Grant, my eyes lingering on the spot where Kiernan's truck should be. I don't know why he lied, and I'm furious that I have cause to doubt him right now, when so much is at stake. He's definitely hiding something. I don't know what, and I don't know why. But the bottom line is no matter which Cyrist is hanging out across the street, I don't believe Kiernan would be a willing party to anything that would put Abel's life at risk. Or that would put any of our lives at risk. He probably thinks he's keeping me safe, which has me angry in an entirely different way.

Grant reaches the car without interference. One guy looks his way, but that's it, and I'm really glad, because I didn't want to waste ammo and draw attention by firing a warning shot.

I grab Delia's arm. "We need to go. Now!"

The biggest challenge is getting Delia to look away from the key long enough to walk down the stairs. We finally reach the bottom, and I half drag her past the kitchen, toward the back door where the car is waiting.

The first thing I notice is that someone cleaned the Buick. It's not a very thorough cleaning, and there are still smears here and there, but someone at least tried to rinse the crud away. I don't have time to wonder about that right now, however.

I push Delia into the backseat, and she immediately starts pulling up the stable point in the cell again.

"Okay, Grant—I need you to loop around the block and come in behind the courthouse. I'll either be there or in the block of trees behind the jail with Abel."

"How?" Grant asks at the same moment that Delia starts screaming Abel's name, panic in her voice.

"Go!" I yell, glad that at least I don't have to try and answer that question.

Because the truth is, I have no earthly idea.

∞

At 9:26 p.m., I jump in at the point I set in Beebe's office. The patrolman at the desk, whose name tag reads *L. Spencer*, stepped outside a little over three minutes ago. He'll be at the front door for two more minutes, then he'll come back inside, make a quick phone call, and wake Deputy Beebe.

The deputy sounds like he's pretty well out. He's snoring softly, facedown on the desk, his head resting on top of his folded arms.

I see the keys as soon as I move to the other side of the desk, but the ring is unfortunately wedged between his body and his leg. I try inching the keys very slowly toward me, but Beebe startles, his left hand flying out and knocking a paper cup half-full of coffee onto the floor.

I'd hoped to do this the easy way, but if Beebe makes too much noise, the other guy, Spencer, is going to hear us. I curve my right arm under Beebe's neck, lining up the inside of my elbow with his Adam's apple and grabbing my left bicep. Then I place my left forearm behind his head and push downward, squeezing his neck between my bicep and forearm. The move is called *hadaka-jime*, and every other time I've done it, my opponent has tapped for me to release the hold within a couple of seconds. It feels wrong to keep holding. But I do, for a full five seconds after I feel Beebe relax.

The bad thing about this hold is that he'll wake up almost as quickly as he went under, so there's no time to waste. With any luck, by the time he comes to, I'll have his keys back in place.

I set a local point behind his desk and bring up the cell-block corridor, rolling the time back to 9:24. I spent a half hour planning this out in my room back at the townhouse before jumping into Beebe's office. There are no perfect options. If I wait until 9:55, when Grant and Delia are in the car and headed this way, the mob will be storming the jail, and judging from Delia's scream as they pulled away, I think they might already have Abel.

There are two downsides to rolling the time back. The first is that Delia and Abel will have a few dueling memories. One set of memories is going to recall Abel stretched out on his bunk, staring at the ceiling for the next half hour, and another is—hopefully—going to remember him leaving with me at 9:24.

The bigger issue is that we're going to have to find someplace to hide for half an hour until our ride gets here. Spencer can see the stairs from his desk, and this is the only time that he's away from the desk long enough for us to possibly get down the stairs and into the bathroom at the back of the main floor.

I don't know if Abel is asleep when I pop into the corridor, but his eyes are closed. I tap the key ring gently against the door as I unlock it. When he finally glances over, I press my finger to my lips.

"I take it you're Kate," he whispers as he steps out of the cell. "I was kind of hoping for a CHRONOS extraction team."

"Well, that's not an option anymore." He's in better shape than I thought he'd be, considering the beating he took, but I can tell from the way he moves that his body is feeling every step.

"Is Delia okay?"

Her nose will need to be reset, she has two massive shiners, she's stoned on laudanum and terrified out of her mind about Abel, but I give him the short version.

"She's fine. Follow me."

I unlock the cell-block door, and we move into the stairwell.

After I relock the door, I say, "Wait here. If I put these keys back, it may buy us a few extra minutes."

I pull up the stable point at Beebe's desk and blink back in. He's still slumped forward, head on the desk. Attaching the key ring to his belt takes less than a second, but before I can get to my feet, I feel the chair move backward, and he starts to lift his head.

Is it harmful to put someone in a second *hadaka-jime* when they're still coming out of the first? I don't know, but I can't see any alternative.

I yank his neck into the hold again and wait, counting off the seconds. Spencer is back in the front office, making his phone call, which means he'll come through the door in less than a minute. Beebe finally goes limp—only a matter of seconds, but it felt like forever. I hastily arrange his arms and head back on the desk and blink out with a few seconds to spare.

Back to the stairwell at 9:25.

Abel whispers, "What's the plan?"

"You and I get out of the building through the bathroom and find a spot to hide for the next twenty-five minutes. Grant will pick us up."

He gives me an incredulous look. "Where's that guy from the truck? Kiernan?"

"No clue. The two officers outside will both be in the front office at 9:34, bringing in three guys they've arrested. Maybe two minutes after that, two trucks roll in with guys in masks. I think every eye is likely to be on those trucks and the front door of the jail, and that's our best time to make a run for it. The bathroom window is on the back side of the building, between here and the courthouse. We go out the window and—"

"This is the best plan Delia could come up with? I think I'd have a better chance waiting to see what the judge says in the morning."

"No, Abel. You wouldn't. You haven't seen the crowd out there, but I'm pretty sure you can hear them, right? About a dozen of them are going to storm the jail with guns a few minutes before ten. Still want to take your chances?"

He shakes his head. "Sorry. You're right. I'm just . . . it's been a rough day."

"I know I'm not the rescue team you'd like between you and a lynch mob. But right now, I'm all you've got, so we need to go."

We have about three minutes before Spencer makes his phone call and then wakes Beebe. The front desk is still empty when we reach the bottom of the stairs. We move quickly into the tiny bathroom, which reeks of pee and bleach, and Abel locks the door behind us. Glancing out the window, I see, straight in front of us, a wide-open space with absolutely no cover. The earth is turned up, like it's a construction site, and I'm guessing it's for the new courthouse Kiernan mentioned.

Looking to the right, across Water Street, there are three empty cars, and two boys in their early teens are leaning against the hood of the car closest to the corner. The boys move toward the front as soon as they hear someone's being arrested—or at least one of them does, because I saw his face when previewing the scene earlier.

Behind the cars are woods—a nice, thick tree cover running alongside the road. We can hide in the trees and gradually work our way toward the corner where Grant and Delia will arrive.

"Take off your shirt," I tell Abel.

He looks surprised, but then glances down and nods. His white shirt is torn and covered with blood, and it would both stand out in the dark and scream Escaped Convict. We look for a place to stash the shirt and my white hat, finally just shoving them behind the toilet.

Abel moves over to look out the window, and the frame suddenly seems tiny next to his broad shoulders.

"Do you think you'll fit?" I whisper.

Abel looks at it for a minute. "Probably . . ."

I tug on the bottom, hoping to inch it up gradually so that the kids outside don't notice. It doesn't move. I yank a little harder, but the window doesn't budge. "I think it's painted shut."

Abel tries, too, and I wince when the wood creaks.

I glance around the bathroom for a tool of some sort, but the only options are a plunger and a bar of soap. I finally pull out my CHRONOS medallion and dig the thin edge into the line of paint attaching the window to the windowsill, crossing my fingers that it's not painted shut on the other side as well, because I think someone's going to notice if we end up having to smash the damn thing.

Or maybe not. The noise from outside is steadily rising. Several men are yelling, and I hear a gunshot in the distance.

Spencer's at the front desk now, talking on the phone, no more than twenty feet away. Abel starts to lift the window again, but I put a hand on his arm. "Wait until you hear him yell 'Beebe'—maybe thirty seconds."

We wait.

I never liked this part of hide-and-seek as a kid. My pulse pounds in my ears, and every sound seems ten times as loud.

I keep my eyes on the window, watching for movement. The two kids finally take off around the side of the building just before I hear Spencer.

"Hey, Beebe!" A distant knock. "Beebe? You awake?"

Abel gives the window a yank. Nothing happens on the first try, but on the second there's a loud creak and it slides to the top.

I step on the edge of the toilet and hoist myself up and out. Dropping about four feet to the ground, I take the gun from my pocket. Abel squeezes through the window, working his feet through first and then one shoulder at a time. I crouch down to peek around the corner. The small stretch of lawn behind the jail is now empty, and there's nothing but the cars between us and the trees across the street.

I'm just about to signal that we should run for it when headlights turn onto Water Street from my left. I motion for Abel to hit the ground and drop to the grass, tucking my bare arms under my body and squeezing my eyes to tiny slits, praying that the driver looks straight ahead at the road. If not, I'm going to have to jump back, tell myself this won't work, and try something else—and I really don't want to do that.

The vehicle slows as it reaches the corner, moving past us, and I let out the breath I've been holding. Then it reverses, the wheels rolling back into my field of vision as it parks on the side of the road. I tug out my medallion, getting ready to jump back, but I risk one glance upward at the car.

Georgia State Patrol.

Mitchell looks straight at me, shaking his head the way he did earlier when he said, "Lord, what a mess." Then he gets out and slams the door. The two teenagers who were hanging out near the cars dart back around the corner and across the street, followed by two others who look about the same age, and they all take cover behind one of the cars.

Mitchell doesn't look our way again, just yells across the street, "Get home, Harlan! Does your daddy know you're here?" as he rounds the corner toward the front of the jail.

Harlan and his buddies don't go home, however. They just squat down next to the parked cars, blocking our route to the trees.

But Mitchell's car is still running.

I shove the idea away, but it comes right back. It may be our only shot.

"Abel," I say, "I'm going to cover you. On three, open the door and slide behind the wheel. I'll be right behind."

"Are you insane? You want me to steal a *cop* car?"

"It's that or stay here. Go, damn it!"

Abel runs forward, hunched over. I have a horrible moment when I'm certain that the passenger door will be locked, but it opens.

I dash after him, slamming the door just as Abel accelerates. He spins the wheel sharply, turning the car in the opposite direction. The rear fishtails slightly, and then we're off.

The four kids run out into the street, pointing and yelling. One of them follows us for about half a block, then stops, doubled over. I'm pretty sure he's laughing.

"Where am I going? And maybe you should be driving," he adds. "Georgia didn't hire black officers in 1938."

"And you think they hired *female* officers?"

The only place I can think of to go is Kiernan's cabin. I'd probably be able to backtrack and find it, but we'd have to turn left on Main Street and drive past the Eagle and the jail, and that's not an option right now. "Take a right. We'll have to find another way around."

Abel turns right at Main, speeding away from the crowd. The gas station we stopped at earlier, now closed for the night, flies past the window. I shove the gun back in my pocket and open the glove compartment.

"What are you doing?" Abel asks.

"Looking for a map."

"You mean you don't know where we're going?" He's shouting, and while I get his frustration, it would be nice if he could scrounge up just a tiny bit of gratitude. "Any time you're on a mission, every step needs to be planned—"

"This isn't a CHRONOS mission, Abel. In real life, sometimes you have to improvise."

"Stealing a cop car when you don't even know where we're going isn't what I'd call improvising."

"I was supposed to have a driver," I say, trying to keep my voice level. "Kiernan is the one who knows his way around here. Just get us out of town, and pull off on a side road. As long as I have the key, I can jump back and get directions."

"How are we supposed to get up with Delia?"

"Again, I have the key. I just can't use it until we find a place to stop, okay? It's kind of hard to set a stable point to get back to here when we're going sixty miles an hour."

There's no map in the glove compartment. When I look up, however, I notice headlights flashing in the rearview mirror. I turn to get a better view, and the lights flash again, twice. Then the driver leaves the lights off long enough for me to see a black truck filled with the bright blue light from a CHRONOS key.

"Pull over as soon as you find somewhere you can hide the car," I say. "It's Kiernan."

About a quarter of a mile up, a dirt path shoots off behind an old shed. Kiernan idles at the intersection while we park, and then I run over, sliding into the seat next to him.

"I don't know whether to hit you or hug you. Where the hell did you go?"

"I could ask the same thing," he says. "I got back to the hotel, and you'd disappeared. You should have waited. I wasn't even gone half an hour."

Abel gets in the truck, and Kiernan takes off again.

"Didn't see any alternatives. Things were kind of heating up across the street," I say.

"So? We were jumping *back* to fix the problem, Kate. Waiting wouldn't have changed a thing. Ten more minutes—"

"So then why didn't you jump back and lend a hand once you realized what I was doing?"

"Because I saw that you and Abel made it out the window. I was coming around to pick you up in the truck, and then you zipped by. If you'd waited, maybe we could have avoided stealing a police car!"

"We didn't steal it. We borrowed it."

I also think there's a decent chance that we borrowed it with permission, because I know Mitchell saw us. But I don't want to get into that with Kiernan right now. I want to know why he lied.

"And maybe I'd have waited if you'd told me the truth about there being a CHRONOS key in the middle of the crowd across from the jail. Given that you lied to me, I didn't know for certain you were even coming back."

He turns and stares at me, his eyes wounded. "Of course, I was com—"

"Eyes on the damn road!" Abel interjects. "Where are you taking me?"

Kiernan looks back at the road, the muscle in his jaw twitching. "It's about five miles up. You'll be safe there."

I thought the cabin was a bit farther away, but I also thought it was in the other direction. The road is winding, so maybe we're taking a different route.

Abel says, "What about Delia?"

"She'll meet us there. I caught them before they went to the jail. That's when they told me where Kate was." He shakes his head. "And then I had to jump back and get my gun. I thought it was in your room."

I glare at him. "*My* gun was in my room. Yours wasn't, because *you took it from me* this afternoon."

"Because I couldn't find it in your—"

"Could we stop with the time travel conundrums?" Abel says. "I have questions. First, why are rank amateurs rescuing us instead of a trained extraction team? And second—"

I pull my phone out of my pocket and start the video I played for Delia and Grant earlier in the day. Abel's face falls when Katherine introduces herself.

Kiernan keeps glancing over at me, but I don't look back. I'm hoping he gave written directions to Grant, because I'm thoroughly lost. He's taken three turns so far, and we've passed about a dozen farms—all dark, so either they're early-to-bed types or else they drove into town for the excitement.

Abel clicks to replay the video, and just as it starts up the second time, Kiernan turns the truck onto a narrow side road. About a hundred feet in, we come to a metal gate. A large lock connects the two ends of a chain looped between the fence and the gate.

"This doesn't look like the road to your cabin," I say.

Kiernan doesn't answer, just gets out and pulls a key from his pocket.

"Is this another of the properties you purchased with your sports investments?" I ask when he gets back into the truck.

"Not exactly."

I look at him questioningly, but he seems to be giving me the silent treatment.

He gets out again and locks the gate behind him, then pulls out the CHRONOS medallion, probably setting a stable point. Katherine's voice drones in the video as we keep driving, first through trees and then through an open field with a farmhouse in the distance.

As we get closer, I see several rooms are faintly lit by a yellow glow. Probably lantern light—I doubt electricity has made it this far out of town.

"Abel?" Kiernan says as he stops the truck outside the house.

Abel turns off the video and looks up. His eyes are filled with the same dull shock I've seen each time the historians start to realize they won't be going home. "Yes?"

Kiernan nods toward the house. "The lady may have some odd comments about me and Kate . . . and maybe angels. Just roll with it, okay?"

"Martha?" My heart sinks. "Do we really have to get her involved?"

"I thought of going to the cabin, but the lawyer listed my address when he bailed me out."

"This will mean she's housing fugitives. She has kids, right?"

The door to the house opens, and a light-haired woman about my mom's age steps out onto the front porch. She's smiling, but she looks nervous.

"Her kids are all grown and gone, Kate. Martha understands the risk. So does her husband. We won't be here long. Just until things quiet down—maybe get some rest and a bite to eat. Take some time to map out a plan."

Abel drops my phone in my lap and opens the door. "What a novel idea. A *plan*." He slams the door behind him.

"You know, other than being twice her size, a different race, a different gender, and maybe thirty years younger, Abel reminds me an awful lot of Katherine."

That gets a half chuckle from Kiernan, and he says, "Kate, I'm sorry about—"

"Let's talk about it inside. Someone needs to introdu—" But when I glance outside the truck, I see that Martha has taken over. She's taken Abel by the arm and is leading him up to the porch, where a guy who must be her husband is now waiting.

"What did you tell her about all of this?" I ask.

"I just said it was her chance to play angel."

∞

Abel and Kiernan are still in the kitchen with Martha's husband, Joe. If he has any reservations about Martha taking in fugitives, you'd never know it—we were welcomed warmly, and he's done his best to make all three of us comfortable. I've just finished eggs, bacon, and biscuits. Kiernan and Abel are still eating. It's a relief to discover that Abel is a little less combative with food in his stomach.

I've moved to the sofa in the living room so that I can watch the front gate through the key. Grant and Delia should arrive any minute now, and I'll need to jump over and unlock it. What I'd really like is to stretch out on this sofa and sleep for a week. The last sleep I had was the four-hour nap I squeezed in before my dinner with Trey. The last time I got a full eight hours was before we rescued Martha from God's Hollow.

A few minutes later, Martha comes in with my coffee cup, which she's refilled.

"Wow. You must be psychic."

"No." She smiles as she hands me the cup and then sits on the couch next to me. "I just saw you yawnin' when I looked in here a little while ago. You know, you're welcome to do whatever it is you're doin' with that thing in the kitchen with the rest of us. I told Joe it was like prayer beads. He ain't ever met but two Catholics in his life, so he might stare a little, but I hate for you to be off all by your lonesome."

"Thanks, Martha, but I think the other car is going to show up pretty soon, and I'm going to have to disappear for a few seconds. That might make Joe do a little more than stare."

She laughs and tucks a stray piece of hair, as much gray as blond now, back behind her ear. "It might at that. I told him a little about what happened, but I ain't ever mentioned the disappearin' part. He already thinks I'm a little crazy."

"It's really good of you to do this, Martha. Both of you."

"Not at all," she says. "Joe and I both have people in our lives who are gone now, people who treated us kindly and taught us right from wrong. I can't pay Sister Elba back for takin' me and my cousins in, but it's like this book I read a few years back, written by a lady down in Augusta—she says you're s'posed to pay it forward. Sister Elba would have taken these people in, so now I'm doin' it for her."

"And Kiernan told you about Grant?"

"The guy that was at God's Hollow? It's okay. I know he wasn't part of it. He was tricked by that devil, same as me and all those who died."

Martha leans over and puts her hand on my knee. It's a very maternal gesture, and something about it reminds me how much time has passed for her, even more than the lines on her face. "And

I know he wasn't a *real* devil, just like you ain't a real angel. I figured that out while I was stayin' with the Owenses. I don't know what that circle thing is, but it keeps you the same age or maybe lets you move around time, like in that Mark Twain book. That's why you look just the same. Except I didn't know about the hair, 'cause it was all tucked under your hat before. You should wear it down more often."

"I tell her that all the time," Kiernan says from the doorway. I'm not sure how long he's been standing there.

Abel is behind him, wearing a bathrobe of some sort over his pants, because there were no shirts that would fit him. He looks at Martha and says, "If it isn't any trouble, ma'am, I'd like to take you up on the offer of a hot bath before Delia arrives. Maybe it won't frighten her quite as much if I get a bit more of the blood off of me."

Martha helps him upstairs, and I turn to Kiernan. "I'm more worried about how Abel is going to react when he sees Delia's face. They should be here soon, right?"

"Yeah. I'd guess in the next five or ten minutes." He sits down next to me. "Kate, it was Simon across the street, okay? I figured as much, but I had to check it out. You getting involved would've made things twice as difficult. But I shouldn't have lied to you. It just complicated matters."

"What happened? Why does he think you're here?"

He shrugs. "I told him the truth, sort of. That I'm keeping an eye on you for Prudence. Keeping you from poking around in their business in the future."

"Do you think he knows you're helping, not just watching?"

"I don't know. Probably not, since he said I'm backing a losing horse when it comes to Pru. Said not to let loyalty to her make me stupid."

"But—why is he here? I thought they didn't need the keys."

Kiernan leans back, rubbing his temples. "I don't know that for certain, Kate. Maybe with the split between Saul and Pru, they want a few more on hand. But I think it's simpler than that. Simon, he's like . . . I don't know. My Kate called him an adrenaline junkie. Simon tends to think of time as his own private amusement park. Who needs your video games or movies when you can jump in and out of the real thing? He nearly got both of us killed in Cincinnati back in 1884. And a few days before I found you on the Metro, he blinked out in the middle of a raid on a speakeasy, in full view of the police. When I saw him tonight, he said I should stick around—" He leans forward, lowering his voice. "That things were about to get good. He's here because he wants to see a lynching."

∞22∞

"You two barely manage to get me out of jail, and you wonder why I don't believe you can take down an organization with millions of members? Some of whom can time travel?"

"Please keep it down," I warn him. Again.

Martha and Joe went up to bed an hour ago, right after Kiernan and I got back from abandoning the Buick on a back road about five miles away. We'd planned to do the same with Kiernan's truck, but it took him three tries to jump back to Martha's yard after the Buick, so I think he's tapped out with the key for a while. His truck is hidden in the barn, and the plan is for Delia, Abel, and Grant to lie low here for a few days, until the fuss dies down, and then head north in the truck.

On that much, it seems, we all agree. But none of them have agreed to hand over their keys.

"Yes," I say. "I know the odds are stacked against our side. But what should we do? Quit? If we can't bring the Cyrists down, they win."

I decide not to add that I still have some niggling doubts about Kiernan's commitment to our side. Keeping secrets, lying, and disappearing when needed aren't traits you generally want in a partner, especially when the stakes are high. But if he's not on our side, then Abel's assessment is even more dead-on.

Delia is curled up on the couch next to Abel. "What about other allies, then? People in power who oppose the Cyrists? Who don't trust them?"

"In power? Maybe. But, at least in my time, they have trouble staying in power if they're open with those views. Cyrists have friends in high places," I say, borrowing a line from Trey's dad. "I've met very few people who'll openly say they're against them."

"Without allies, you're going to fail," Delia says. "So you might want to start looking."

We've told the three of them everything we know in the past hour, even Kiernan's theory about Pru getting the other twelve keys in 2305. Personally, I'm not convinced on that front. Katherine tried to blink into that black void over and over after Prudence disappeared. Abel also dismissed the idea, saying he tried to do the same thing when they locked him in the cell. But I suppose it's possible there was a fail-safe that didn't work on Prudence, since her genetic code wasn't locked into the system. Or maybe, as Kiernan noted earlier, it's just a very unstable stable point.

Grant has barely spoken. When they came in, he sank down into the same chair he's in now, on the other side of the room, and started looking at something in his diary. Maybe he's gone back into trainee mode, since Delia seems closer to her usual self now that Abel is here and they're clearly back in charge. Delia finally asked him to take over what I was doing—monitoring the stable points at the gate and the jail—so I could join in their discussion about the Cyrists. He seemed glad to have something to do at first, but I think he's discovered it's a pretty boring chore. The crowd outside the jail gradually thinned out a little after eleven, and aside from the one car that drove past shortly after I let the Buick through the front gate and another that passed by around midnight, the road has been quiet.

"What about the internal division you mentioned before?" Abel asks. "Between Saul and Katherine's daughter. What you really need is a fifth column. Maybe that group—"

"I'm working on that," Kiernan says. "But both sides . . . agree on certain points, like the need for the Culling. Different reasons, maybe—but same result. Neither like the future they think we're headed toward, and they're willing to take drastic steps to prevent it, so I'm not sure that's going to work."

Delia sniffs. "I can sympathize a bit after today. I've met several people I'd happily 'cull,' given the chance."

"Yes," I say, "but the crowd outside that jail isn't the type Saul would remove."

Kiernan and Abel are discussing Cyrist motives when Grant gets up and goes into the kitchen. He's sitting at the table with the medallion active and doesn't notice when I walk in. At first, I think he's still watching the gate, because the display is dark. But as I get closer, I see it's the black hole that's probably CHRONOS headquarters.

Grant blinks very purposively, twice, but each time he opens his eyes, he's still in the chair.

"I don't think it will work, Grant."

"It *might*."

"But it looks like . . . nothingness. You can't even set a time. What if you blink and arrive in the middle of the explosion?"

"I don't think I would. But even if I did, it's better than staying here."

I'm pretty sure this isn't about his new identity—he has credentials to get him into law school, and that shouldn't be too awful for a legal historian. It must be about the girl waiting back in 2305. I want to tell him he'll meet someone else, he'll be able to start over, and things won't seem so bad in a few years. But the advice rings a little hollow for me right now, and judging from Grant's expression, he's not to the point where he'd listen anyway.

"Where did you leave off with watching the gate?" I ask. "I'll take over."

He gives me an odd look. "I stopped when I came in here."

"No, what *time* were you watching? Like I said when you started, I'd watched both stable points until 12:45, jumping ahead a minute or so at a time."

"I just . . . I was watching the current time. The lot outside the jail is pretty empty, and—"

I sigh. "The point was to build up a buffer, so we'd have some advance notice."

"I'm sorry," he says, tilting his head back and staring at the ceiling. "I didn't hear that part. I'm not used to using the key that way."

His jaw is clenched, and I can tell he's trying really hard to hold it together.

"Are you okay?"

"Not really," he says. "But there's nothing you can do to make it better."

I pour the last of the coffee into my cup and leave Grant to himself, taking up the armchair he vacated. The point outside the jail is fairly empty between 12:46 a.m. and 12:56 a.m. Everyone has left, except for one man in a police car, talking to someone standing outside.

I'm about to check on the gate when I see Delia standing next to me. "I thought Grant was handling that?"

"It's okay," I say. "He seems a bit upset about the new reality. There's a girl back—"

"No." She shakes her head, giving me a sad smile. "*Not* a girl. Which is the problem. I think Abel and I will find somewhere we'll be okay, even in this era. By the time we have grandkids, it won't be too strange that Grandpa's black and Grandma's white. But even if Grant finds somebody else to love, marriage and family are no longer in his future. That may take a while to accept."

Delia goes into the kitchen. Hopefully, she'll be better at consoling Grant. I'm really glad I resisted giving that chin-up-you'll-find-someone-new speech.

I keep an ear on Kiernan and Abel's discussion about Cyrist organizational structure as I watch the front gate through the key. All clear until 1:00 a.m. Back to the jail—clear to 1:15 a.m. Back to the gate.

I'm thinking I may need more coffee when I skip from 1:05 a.m. to 1:06 a.m. and see two sets of headlights at the gate. Suddenly, I'm wide-awake. I skip to 1:09 a.m., and there are a couple of cars across the street and two very familiar trucks. The men aren't wearing their masks now, and I spot Willis, along with his two nephews and several others from the fight. At 1:10 a.m., one of them has an ax and is chopping through the boards in the fence near the gate.

"We're going to have company in about twenty minutes."

I run upstairs to let Martha know. She must not have been sleeping, because she's at the door in her dressing gown as soon as I knock. Joe takes a bit longer, and once we all get downstairs, I realize that's because he stopped to grab a couple of shotguns. He hands one to Kiernan and props the other one up beside the china cabinet.

"The root cellar will hold all of you," Martha says. "I'd go down and get you settled in myself, but I don't like cellars much since . . . not since I was girl."

Joe gives her shoulders a brief squeeze and says, "I'll get them settled. Y'all grab your stuff. We got water and blankets down there in case we have to go down for a tornado or what have ya, but there ain't no outhouse, so y'all might want to take care of that before we go."

A few minutes later, Kiernan and I are outside, waiting for the others.

"How do you think they found us?" I ask.

"I don't know. Maybe the car you saw was following them and they went back to get reinforcements? Did they see you unlock the gate?"

"I don't think so, but I can't be sure. Whoever it was, they were well behind the Buick."

I walk around and set a few stable points so that we'll be able to see what's going on while we're below ground.

Delia steps onto the porch. "Is Grant out here?"

I shake my head. "Last I saw him was in the kitchen."

"Can you look around out here?" she asks, darting back into the house.

Four minutes later, we still haven't found him, and I watch through my key as the first truck drives through the gap in the fence.

"Gotta get y'all underground," Joe says. He unlocks the padlock and swings the cellar door open. "You'll hear a loud bell clangin' soon as those trucks arrive. That'll be Martha. My brother lives the next farm over, and he's got a telephone. If Billy hears that bell five times, he'll call the sheriff and get over here with his gun."

We all thank him for his help, and I add, "Please be careful."

"No need to worry about us. We'll be fine. And if I find that other boy, I'll do my best to keep him safe." Once we're down the ladder, he says, "Y'all might want to get settled before I close this lid. It's gonna be mighty dark down there."

Light isn't a problem, actually. Even if one of us was afraid of the dark, we have four bright blue CHRONOS keys in a hole that's maybe seven feet across.

It's more the size of the cellar that bothers me. There are shelves on one side, and the whole thing reminds me of the linen closet at Holmes's hotel in Chicago. I shiver, partly from that memory and partly because it's chilly down here.

I transfer the local stable points I set outside the farmhouse to everyone's keys as the trucks roll into the yard. The two cars hang back about fifty feet down the road. One of them seems pretty full. Several people get out, some of them climbing up on the hood.

"I can't believe Grant took off like that," Delia says. She's sitting in front of Abel, wrapped in a blanket. Abel's arms are around her, and Joe's second shotgun is near his feet.

"I don't blame Grant for running," Abel says. "We aren't exactly in an optimal situation. This hole is crowded enough with the four of us, and he's probably safer on his own. He's got a new ID. He's got cash for a fresh start. He'll be okay."

"I hope you're right," she says.

When I look back at my key, one of the men is shouting something. They're all dressed similarly, mostly in jeans and plain shirts, but I'm positive the shouter is Willis, judging from his build and the fact that he's moving with a slight limp. I can hear noise from outside, but it's too muffled to pick out words.

We do hear the bell, however, at 1:13 a.m. Martha rings it five times, waits a few seconds, and repeats the signal. Two of the men behind Willis look around nervously and get down from the truck bed, moving around the corner of the house.

"Do you think the sheriff will even come?" Delia asks.

It's not clear who she's asking, but Abel finally says, "Yes. Otherwise there's trouble on all fronts. Some will complain because he allowed a mob to get the upper hand. Others will complain because a dangerous criminal escaped. And they've got grand-theft auto against me now as well."

He shoots an annoyed glance at me, and I'm a little surprised when Delia speaks in my defense. "If she hadn't gotten you out of there, those crazies would have you already, Abel. You're wearing a key, so I think you know that as well as I do. I remember watching them drag you out of that cell. Grant and I were useless, and Kiernan wasn't around—she did the best she could. Thank you, Kate."

Tears spring to my eyes, maybe because I've been feeling a little underappreciated, but also because Delia's thanks now seem misplaced. The "crazies" are mere yards away, and they could drag Abel out again—although with three guns down here, they're going to find it a little more difficult.

"I never said I wasn't grateful," Abel says. "It's just the planning could have been—"

"Shut up, Abel." Delia's words are harsh, but her tone is affectionate, and Abel shakes his head and then kind of chuckles, hugging her to him.

Kiernan has been very quiet, his eyes glued to one of the stable points. When I lean back to see which one he's watching, he quickly shifts to a different view.

So I start jumping between them, trying to see what caught his attention. I watch Willis yelling from two different angles, with others in the trucks joining in occasionally.

Then I shift to look at the cars and find what caught Kiernan's attention. I almost missed the blip of blue light inside the second car, probably because the entire cellar is flooded with the same shade.

"Simon's out there," I whisper. "Why didn't you tell me?"

He catches the suspicion in my voice and hisses back, "I just realized it myself!"

Of course, when you're crammed in a cellar, shoulder to shoulder, whispers aren't really private.

Delia says, "That's the one with Saul, right? His lieutenant."

Thug is more like it, but I nod.

"Why's he here?" Abel asks. "Does he know we're CHRONOS?"

"Yes," Kiernan says, "and I suspect he's here because he's as bloody twisted as his grandda. He wants to be here when you hang or they shoot you or whatever the hell they're planning."

I don't know why I have a hard time believing that's Simon's only reason. He was perfectly willing to put me in the path of a serial killer in 1893. And while the vast majority of people in this county are at home, minding their own business, and wouldn't hear about a lynching until it was long over, I suspect half of the people on Martha's front lawn are there for the same reason Kiernan thinks Simon is hanging around. They wouldn't kill Abel themselves, but they're happy, maybe even a little eager, to watch someone else do it.

I shift from the cars to watching the front porch. Joe is pointing the shotgun at Willis, and I can read his lips perfectly. "Get off my property." There are a few more words, and then Joe's expression shifts from determined to terrified. Delia and Abel gasp at the same moment that Joe lowers the gun.

I know what's happened before I switch to the other view. They have Martha. I shift my eyes over to Kiernan's key and watch as Simon walks toward the trucks. Kiernan blinks twice before I can say, "No, Kiernan. You can't go in there."

I'm pretty certain he can't jump in anywhere, but he keeps trying, his expression furious.

A truck is coming in from the other side of the farm, driving fast across the lawn. A middle-aged man in overalls gets out of the truck, his gun raised, then sees Martha. One of the masked men has an arm around her waist and the muzzle of his pistol wedged under her jaw.

Kiernan might not be able to jump out, but I can. I shove the gun into my pocket, freeing up both hands so that I can set the cellar and current time as a stable point. As I'm finishing, someone bangs on the cellar door.

"It's Simon," Kiernan says. "He just walked around the side of the house."

Kiernan's right. I pull up the stable point outside the cellar and see the back of Simon's head. I can also see the wheels of a car driving up directly behind him.

Then Simon starts talking, his voice muted a bit by the wooden door. "I'm sure you've got guns down there, just like we do up here. Don't start shooting yet. I'm here to negotiate. I know Abel and Delia are down there, and it's mostly you I'm talking to. I'm sure Kate has been painting a dreadful picture of the Cyrists, but she's been . . . I guess you'd say brainwashed . . . by her grandmother. The only reason she's here is that Prudence is protecting her, although I don't know how much longer their little agreement can hold."

Kiernan tenses up beside me, and then he yells, "Get to the bloody point, Simon!"

"Kiernan! I thought you might be down there, buddy. My *point* is that there's a way for Abel and Delia to get out of this safely, if they listen to reason. You, too. Kiernan. My earlier offer still stands, if you're tired of babysitting for Pru."

Kiernan curses under his breath, and Simon goes on, "Abel, there are Cyrist communities, even in 1938, where it will not matter one tiny bit that your wife is white. Where the two of you can make a difference, rather than being second-class citizens for the next four decades."

Abel is still pointing the gun upward toward the door, but I can see his face. Simon has his attention. He's listening. He's thinking about it.

"He's lying," I hiss. When Abel doesn't look at me, and I grab Delia's arm. "You heard Kiernan, Delia. The only reason Simon's here—"

I don't get anything else out, because Kiernan's hand is over my mouth. "Kate," he whispers, "you need to get out of here, love."

Simon keeps talking, elaborating on this bright, shiny Cyrist future he can offer them, as I struggle against Kiernan.

Delia looks over at me, an apology in her eyes. Then she yells up at Simon, "What about the woman those men are holding? If we leave with you, do they let her go?"

"Sorry, Delia. That's an entirely separate situation, a mistake that should have been corrected long ago."

"Then no deal!" Delia says.

"She speaking for you, too, Abel?"

"Absolutely," Abel fires back. "No deal unless you guarantee her safety along with ours. I have no ties to Katherine, and I wouldn't be in this damned hole right now if her granddaughter hadn't screwed things up. But Martha put her neck on the line for us, and I don't betray friends."

Abel doesn't even glance my way, so I don't know how much of what he's saying is truth and how much is negotiation.

"That part's out of my control, Abel—"

"Bullshit!" Kiernan says. "What are you now, Simon? Just Saul's errand boy? Since when do you check every decision with him? You can do whatever you want. Let her and Joe get into the truck with his brother, and all three of us leave with you. Saul will never know the bloody difference, unless you're dumb enough to tell him."

"What about Kate?" Simon says.

"Kate blinked out the second she heard your voice. Don't know where she's going, but I should probably tell you she has a gun."

"Oh wow I'm so scared," he says in a flat voice. "Seriously, Kiernan, what makes you think I'm in control of those idiots out front? All I did was tell them where you were. Otherwise, this is their little party, and I doubt they'll let her go unless Abel gives himself up in her place. He's the only reason most of them are here."

"Yeah, right, Simon. How much did you pay that guy to grab Martha? You already admitted as much. Slip him another twenty—"

"You're missing the point, Kier." Simon starts rattling on about how it's easy to start a mob but not so easy to stop it. Abel and Delia are arguing back and forth with him, but I can no longer follow the conversation, because Kiernan is talking into my ear.

"Save Martha, Kate. You know where she'll be. Get her and Joe to his brother's farm. *Then go back home.*"

He pulls his hand away from my mouth, slowly. I turn to face him, but I guess he can tell I'm still not convinced.

"I can do more on Saul's side than I can on Pru's. Trust me, and just go. Please."

"I could trust you more if you'd tell me everything, Kiernan. What are you hiding?"

"When I can tell you, I will. When I know for certain. I promise—"

"On her wedding band."

He inhales sharply, and I add, "I don't care whether you drew that ring onto her finger from memory or from your imagination. Promise me on that, and I'll believe you."

He grabs my left hand and presses his lips to the ring finger. "I promise, Kate. Just go."

I pull up the stable point on the far side of the house, the one Kiernan and I set before hiding the cars. Right now, at 1:19 a.m., the only thing I can see at that point is the side of an Oconee County sheriff's vehicle, so I guess that answers Delia's question. I don't know how the police may affect the negotiations with Simon, so I show it to Kiernan. Then I roll the time back to 1:09 a.m., just as Joe locks us into the cellar, and blink out.

I didn't realize how much we'd been able to hear in that cellar. It was hard to make out anything clearly, but there was a steady hum of noise from the cars above and from all of the shouting. Now, the farm is eerily quiet.

I run around to the back of the house and see Martha's silhouette through the window. I tap quickly on the door and then open it. She gasps. "Holy moly, Kate, you scared me! I thought Joe—" Then she glances down at the key around my neck and says, "Oh. That thing again."

"Get Joe. The two of you need to go to his brother's house."

"I don't think he'll come, Kate. Joe ain't the type to just leave those people undefended, or the farm undefended, for that matter. Me neither. We can't just up and leave when   "

"Martha, this is the only way everyone gets out alive." I try to keep the doubt out of my voice, because I don't trust Simon, not at all. "Can you drive?"

"What? Yes, but—"

"I'll convince Joe. You get the truck." I reach in my pocket for the keys to Kiernan's truck, but she's already heading for their own truck, parked next to the barn.

"Do you have your keys?"

"In the truck!" she yells back, like it's the most obvious thing in the world, and I can't help but think that car theft must be really, really easy in 1938.

Joe is confused when he sees me, but he must have already accepted that something out of the ordinary is going on, because he never questioned how I knew that the mob would be coming through his gate in twenty minutes. All it takes to get him to leave is telling him that one of those men will soon have a gun to Martha's head.

They're gone less than a minute when the first truck rolls into the front yard. The headlights shine through the curtains, and the driver revs the motor. I hear someone, Willis I presume, stomping up the front steps, and then he bangs on the door hard enough to rattle the windows.

I can't just accept that Simon will keep his word, but there's no reason I have to watch events play out from here. I'll have a much safer, much clearer view from my bedroom.

∞

My phone buzzes in my pocket as soon as I blink into the room, but I ignore it and drop to the floor in front of my bed, clutching my key so tightly that the edge cuts into my palm. I'm suddenly queasy, and my head is spinning. It's almost like the sensation when there's a time shift, but it passes after a moment. Probably stress, lack of sleep, and too much caffeine.

When I've recovered enough to bring up the stable point at the cellar, I see three men with Simon, their guns drawn. One of them is Willis, and one is the guy who was holding the gun on Martha. A large black car is behind them, and someone I don't recognize is at the wheel.

The one good thing about being the person who actually changes an event is that you walk away without the confusion, as long as you don't run into your other self along the way. I remember that guy holding a gun to Martha. I also remember Martha driving away in the truck with Joe. Both things happened, but it doesn't feel like they happened at the same time, because for me, they didn't.

That's not the case for Delia, Abel, and Kiernan. They all look disoriented as they climb up from the cellar. So does Simon, but I count that in the good-news column.

Kiernan is the first up, and he still has the Colt drawn. Abel comes up the ladder behind him, and one of the men steps forward to grab Abel. Kiernan shouts at him and raises the gun, moving it back and forth between the men until Abel and Delia are both in the car. Simon seems to be yelling at Kiernan, something I can't make out, because all I can see is the back of his head now. Kiernan glares back and says something that includes "bloody hell" and a few other obscenities.

They argue back and forth briefly, then Kiernan shakes his head in disgust and gets into the car. What puzzles me most is Simon's expression when he turns back toward the stable point. He still looks a little annoyed, but he also looks relieved. It's the one time I've seen his face when he wasn't sneering or glaring, and it's disconcerting, because that expression doesn't click with my mental picture of him.

Then Simon reaches into his pocket and pulls out a roll of bills. He peels off a few and hands them to the gunmen, then draws back his arm like he's throwing a baseball. Something goes flying toward the front of the house. At first I think it's a grenade of some sort, because the hired guns start running. But they run in the direction Simon threw it, so that can't be right.

It was the roll of money. Simon stands there for about a minute, watching, the usual sneer back on his face. Then he gets into the passenger seat, and the car drives off.

I switch to a stable point out front and watch as a fight breaks out between the man who reached the money roll first and the others, who've clearly decided he needs to share. I skip forward in thirty-second increments until they leave, making sure no one decides to burn down the house and that Martha and Joe are no longer in danger. I have a feeling I'm going to be doing that a lot, even after tonight is over, because I see no reason for Simon not to come back and finish the job. The yard finally clears out about five minutes later. Joe and his brother drive over to check the place out around 1:30 a.m. and talk to a Georgia state trooper, who I'm very relieved to see has located his car.

When I'm reasonably sure all is as it should be, I roll the time back and watch the stable point at the gate until the black car filled with bright blue light takes a left and zooms off into the night.

Then I tuck the CHRONOS key back into its pouch and stare at the carpet, trying to figure out how I'm going to explain to Connor and Katherine why I let Delia Morrell and Abel Waters, not to mention Kiernan, get into Simon's car with their keys and drive away.

My phone buzzes again, and I pick it up, partly because I want to see if there's news from Dad about Grandpa Keller, but also because I really want to delay the conversation with Katherine and Connor, if only for a few minutes. Dad's message is confusing. Grandpa is out of the ICU, but Dad says he's talked to Mom and wants to know what is going on. He says he's worried and asks me to call as soon as possible. I sigh, realizing I didn't call to tell him about my disastrous dinner with Trey. I must have been even more of a wreck than I thought for Mom to call Dad all the way from Italy.

The next two texts are from Trey. The first is a totally unnecessary apology for reserving the hotel. The second, sent about a half hour later, is another apology, along with a request to call him so that we can talk all of this through.

There are also two texts from Charlayne. I have to look away from the phone for a moment, because a bit of dizziness hits me, but it passes quickly. I click first on the text that came in while Trey and I were at dinner, which I'm pretty sure is another homework question. But there's no mention of assignments, just a cryptic message:

Dinner is trap. You were set up. Eve is ROFL, but not really funny IMO.

It was nice of her to try and warn me, assuming this was sincere and not another plank in the ongoing campaign to instill Charlayne as my BFF.

The weird thing is that her second message has the same time stamp. I start to click "Delete," thinking it's a duplicate, but then I open it.

Welcome to the Fifth Column!!

I stare at the phone, trying to remember where I've heard those words recently. My brain is too tired to pull it up, so I move to the voice messages. There are three—two from Trey and one from Mom. But the one from Mom came in three days ago, and I don't remember missing a call. I click to start the message, and after a moment her voice comes on. She's giddy beyond anything I've ever heard, ten times as excited as she was about the research grant.

"Kate, sweetie, I have the most wonderful, incredible news. Call me the second you get this. Unless it's after—argh! I can't think clearly enough to figure out the time zones. Or just talk to your grandmother. Or your dad. I'm calling them right now. I love you! I'll talk to you soon!"

For some reason her excitement has the opposite effect on me. I'm terrified, and Charlayne's text—*Welcome to the Fifth Column!!*—flashes into my mind again. I toss the phone onto my bed and run to the door.

"Katherine! Connor!"

The lights are on in the library, and I start running in that direction. Then a motion from downstairs catches my eye, and I turn toward the staircase instead.

"Kate!" It's Trey. He's sitting on the couch, petting Daphne. I'm so surprised to see him that I miss a step and have to grab the rail to keep from stumbling.

"Why are you here? You can't *be* here, Trey. Something is going on—something with Mom, I think."

Katherine and Connor must have been in the library, because they're hurrying down the other stairway. They look worried, and I feel a cold fist tighten around my insides.

"Mom called. Something happened. What happened?"

"Kate, it's going to be okay," Katherine says, but I'm pretty sure she's been crying.

Trey puts his arm around my shoulders and starts leading me to the couch, but I stop him. "You didn't answer me. Why are you here, Trey?"

The truth is that I'm happy beyond belief to see him. I want him to put his arms around me and make me forget the rest of the world exists, because I don't think I want to hear what Katherine is about to tell me. But I'm also certain that no matter what has happened, Trey is in danger if he's near me.

"Trey is here because he brought us some information," Connor says. "He knows someone who may be able to help us with the antidote."

"And I asked him to stay," Katherine says, "because we've had some news."

It hits me with absolute certainty, and my knees buckle. Trey gets me to the couch, and I lean into him, breathing him in. Without that, without the solid reality of him next to me, I don't think I'd have found the strength to say it.

"She's dead, isn't she?"

"No!" Katherine says. "She's not dead. It's just that . . . she's found Prudence. Or I guess I should say Prudence has found her. Deborah called me a few days ago, and she was ecstatic."

I'm too stunned to speak. I don't know what this means, but it can't be good.

"Deborah believes it was a chance meeting. Prudence gave her some story about having amnesia for the past thirty years, totally unbelievable. Straight out of a soap opera, but Deborah bought it."

Connor makes a wry face. "Because the time travel version would have been *so* much more believable."

"You know what I mean, Connor."

I finally find my voice. "How? I just talked to her tonight, before I left, and she didn't . . . and I was *here* a few days ago . . . and . . ."

Of course, I know the answer before Katherine even starts. "Something changed, dear. A number of things, actually, although the call from Deborah is the only thing that triggered a direct duplicate memory for me. Are the keys still in your room?"

It takes a moment to realize what she's asking. The thing I was so nervous about telling them seems almost insignificant now. "I didn't get them. Any of them. Simon—"

Connor and Katherine exchange a glance, clearly confused.

"We just assumed," Connor says, "given all of the changes that have popped up in the current timeline. And what Trey told us as well."

I turn to look at Trey, and he shrugs. "It isn't much really. It's just—please don't get angry, Kate—after you left, I just couldn't . . . I couldn't let you walk away like that. Dad means well. I know he's trying to protect me, and I know you are, too, but I was wrong to promise him I'd stay out of this. If everything you've told me is true—and I know it is—then nobody with an ounce of decency can stay out of this."

He takes a deep breath and says, "I called Tilson, okay? I didn't give him specifics on what you needed or why, but as soon as I mentioned your name, he hung up. A half hour later, a taxi pulled up outside the house. It was Tilson, and we had a long talk. Outside—I'm a little spooked about saying anything inside the house right now. Anyway, Tilson is part of a large anti-Cyrist alliance. Scientists, lawyers, political leaders—it's apparently been around since the early 1940s, but they're really secretive. Some of them are even Cyrists, working on the inside. He said whatever you need, they'll help."

A large network. Allies.

Exactly what Delia said we'd need if we're ever going to have a chance against the Cyrists.

And that's when the dots start to form a coherent pattern.

The Fifth Column. Those were Abel's words. A group fighting from the inside.

I didn't even realize I'd spoken the words aloud, but Katherine gives me a strange look, and Connor pulls something out of his pocket. It's a small envelope with my name on it.

"This came about an hour ago," he says. "It was attached to a floral arrangement, but who delivers flowers at nine o'clock at night? I was pretty sure it was bugged, so I dumped the flowers into the trash. But I kept the card, because of the name—and just in case you knew what it meant."

I take it from him. It's just seven typed words and a signature:

> *Kate~The Fifth Column welcomes you home.*
> *Julia Morrell Waters*

Acknowledgments

Let me start out with the question I'm often asked—*how much of that historical stuff is real?* A full answer would require another twenty pages, so I'm just going to list a few examples. If there are others you're wondering about, I'd be happy to answer your questions on my blog.

The Koreshan Unity was founded in Chicago by Cyrus Reed Teed sometime in the early 1890s and relocated to Estero, Florida, around 1898, where they lived until the 1960s. The group believed, among other things, that the Earth was hollow and that celibacy would result in eternal life. When Cyrus Teed died, they placed him in a bathtub and waited for him to awaken, agreeing to bury him only when the county health inspector insisted.

Norumbega Park opened in 1897, and the Great Steel Theater (later called the Totem Pole Ballroom) hosted thousands of vaudeville performers and headliners, like Frank Sinatra, until it closed in 1963.

In 1905, an escape artist billed himself as Boudini, hoping that Harry Houdini would get angry enough to challenge him to a public contest. The publicity scheme worked, but Houdini won the challenge—and some say Houdini was behind it from the start.

Oconee County, Georgia, was the site of a mass lynching in June 1905, when nine inmates were dragged from the jail and shot by a firing squad of masked men.

An unknown murderer, dubbed the Atlanta Ripper by the press, killed over two dozen African American women in 1911.

One event, however, is still murky. Dozens of ghost towns exist throughout the South, including one near Hiltonia, Georgia, that the locals called Six Bridges. The place is still listed as an unpopulated historical location on some maps. Legend holds that the residents of Six Bridges were all found dead in the pews of their small church. I was never able to discover whether this tale is based on an actual event or is simply a ghost story designed to keep curious kids from poking around in the woods. The most likely answer to the mystery of Six Bridges, as with any ghost town, is that the residents just moved away. Since the story is probably more fiction than fact, I exercised a great deal of creative license with Six Bridges, moving the village a few hundred miles north of its actual location so that it would better fit my story line. If any readers have more information on what *really* happened at Six Bridges, however, the history geek in me is dying to know.

This book could never have been written without my dear friend and unpaid research assistant, Google, who tirelessly helped every day—finding online archives and newspapers, providing me with detailed maps and images of various locations, and tracking down reliable and accurate answers to the thousands of questions that arise when one writes about historical events. His willingness to work at any hour of the day or night is deeply appreciated, and I'm willing to forgive the many times he pointed me toward Yahoo Answers or convinced me to click on an article that had absolutely nothing to do with the topic at hand.

Thank you to the family, friends, fans, and fellow writers who have cheered me along over the past year and who help me stay sane when the inevitable bouts of writer's block come along. Extra thanks go to those in my Facebook and Twitter networks who aren't shy about telling me to get off social media and back to writing. Big hugs to Gareth and Ariana for shamelessly plugging my books, and to Eleanor for periodic reminders that all work and no play make Rysa go crazy.

Readers who are also reviewers and book bloggers have the gratitude of every writer. Your reviews help to connect our books with the right readers. The time you spend jotting down your thoughts about the books you like (and even those you don't!) is invaluable to other readers, so I'd like to thank the thousands of you who have taken the time to tell others about *The CHRONOS Files*.

I owe a huge debt of gratitude to Jenny MacRunnel, Jen Wesner, Karen Benson, Karen Stansbury, Kristi Clowers, Joy Joo, Pete, Ian, Ryan, Donna, Richard, and Persons-I've-Probably-Forgotten, who bravely volunteered (or, in the case of family members, were conscripted) to beta read *Time's Edge*. Your comments and suggestions were a tremendous help, and I truly appreciate the time you took to read and critique the book, even in its rough and unkempt early form.

Special thanks go to my phenomenal publishing team at Skyscape, especially Courtney Miller, Erick Pullen, and Timoney Korbar, who have gone above and beyond time and time again. Without my wonderfully patient developmental editor, Marianna Baer, this book would have been a very different creature—thanks for putting up with me! Katherine Adams and Carrie Wicks helped patch up my typos, and Katherine tried to discourage my deep and quite possibly irrational love of italics. To Kate Rudd, many thanks for lending my characters your incredibly talented voice. Finally, kudos to Scott Barrie for creating another eye-catching cover.

And again, I close with thanks to my home team here at Casa del Chaos. You've tolerated my anxious moments and assorted insane writer behavior with few complaints and haven't even griped (much) about too many nights with takeout for dinner. I love you bunches.

About the Author

JEFF KOLBFLEISCH

RYSA WALKER is the author of runaway hit *Timebound*, winner of the grand prize in the 2013 Amazon Breakthrough Novel Award contest, and *Time's Echo*, the linked novella.

Walker grew up on a cattle ranch in the South, where her entertainment options included talking to cows and reading books. On the rare occasion that she gained control of the television, she watched *Star Trek* and imagined living in the future, on distant planets, or at least in a town big enough to have a stoplight.

She now lives in North Carolina, where she shares an office with her husband and their golden retriever, Lucy. She still doesn't get control of the TV very often, thanks to two sports-obsessed kids.